"An electrifying read, building from shock to shock.
I haven't read anything so terrifying since *Red Dragon*."
—STEPHEN KING

"Smart plotting. Nary a false note. Suspense that never stops.
If you like Michael Connelly's novels, you will gobble up
Jonathan Moore's."
—JAMES PATTERSON

"Patient, stylish, and incredibly suspenseful."
—LEE CHILD

"A magnificent, thoroughly unnerving psychological thriller
written in a lush, intoxicating style. I dare you to look away."
—JUSTIN CRONIN

"Moore channels the moody intensity of Raymond Chandler."
—*WASHINGTON POST*

"It's *Miami Vice* meets *The Matrix,* and George Orwell
is hosting the party."
—*PITTSBURGH POST-GAZETTE*

"Outstanding . . . Like *Blade Runner* as if it were
written by Charles de Lint or Neil Gaiman."
—*PUBLISHERS WEEKLY*, STARRED REVIEW

"Moody and macabre with an Edgar Allan Poe feel."
—*KIRKUS REVIEWS*, STARRED REVIEW

BLOOD RELATIONS

Also by Jonathan Moore

The Night Market
The Dark Room
The Poison Artist
Close Reach
Redheads

BLOOD RELATIONS

JONATHAN MOORE

A Mariner Original
Mariner Books
Houghton Mifflin Harcourt
BOSTON   NEW YORK
2019

For information about permission to reproduce selections from this book,
write to trade.permissions@hmhco.com or to Permissions,
Houghton Mifflin Harcourt Publishing Company,
3 Park Avenue, 19th Floor, New York, New York 10016.

hmhco.com

Library of Congress Cataloging-in-Publication Data
Names: Moore, Jonathan, 1977- author.
Title: Blood relations / Jonathan Moore.
Description: Boston ; New York : Mariner Books, 2019. |
"A Mariner original."
Identifiers: LCCN 2018033134 (print) | LCCN 2018035448 (ebook) |
ISBN 9781328990211 (ebook) | ISBN 9781328987815 (trade paper)
Subjects: | BISAC: FICTION / Technological. | GSAFD: Mystery Fiction.
Classification: LCC PS3613.O56275 (ebook) |
LCC PS3613.O56275 B58 2019 (print) | DDC 813/.6—dc23
LC record available at https://lccn.loc.gov/2018033134

Printed in the United States of America
DOC 10 9 8 7 6 5 4 3 2 1

For my daughter, Sally Mahina Moore Wang

BLOOD RELATIONS

1

THE FIRST TIME I saw Claire Gravesend she was already dead. She hadn't been that way long. She was lying in front of the Refugio Apartments on Turk Street, still warm, still with color on her cheeks. I put two fingers on the left side of her throat and confirmed what was already obvious. I didn't consider calling 911. The last thing I wanted to do right then was talk to the police. And anyway, it was too late to do her any good.

Even as I watched, the rain was pooling over her open eyes. If there was any part of her that could still see, she was looking up from beneath an ocean. The surface was too far away to reach. She'd taken her last breath and now she was sinking, bringing with her everything she'd ever known.

Claire Gravesend.

Of course, I didn't know her name yet. I didn't know what she would do to my life. It could have been a passing encounter. An unfortunate sight on a Tenderloin street that was already inclined toward misfortune. But instead I took out my camera, and ultimately that was what drew me into it. I only saw her in the flesh for a few minutes, and after that it was just photographs. Pieces of her life, hints. The traces were scattered like shards of broken glass.

In retrospect, I shouldn't have been surprised when

that encounter wasn't the end of it. Once you brush against someone like Claire Gravesend, you're marked. Either you begin to turn the wheels, or the gears move on their own. And when the axles start to spin, the motion is self-perpetuating. An eternal cycle, always renewing.

What I can't shake is that image of eternity. Or it could be fate I'm talking about — the idea that your name and the course of your life were set down in stone before the Big Bang's first spark. That you could live forever and not escape the path that had been laid out for you.

But that's only because of what happened later.

2

LET ME BACK UP and explain a few things.

For five weeks that spring, I had been living in the Westchester, a last-stop hotel in the Tenderloin's rotten heart. I'm not wealthy, but I do better than skid row. It was business that brought me there. I was on a job, and so for the entire month of May I'd been living between a semiretired prostitute and an unrepentant needle user. We shared the bathroom down the hall. The building had thin walls, and so we also shared every possible sound. Outwardly, we had some things in common. We all had our reasons to avoid the desk clerk. We wasted no money on laundry. The nightshift man at the nearest liquor store could have picked any of us out from a line-up. But unlike me, my neighbors probably hadn't pried up their floorboards to plant microphones and pinhole cameras on the ceilings of the tenants who lived beneath them. They didn't spend their nights following whispered conversations, writing coded names in a notebook. My neighbors were more honest than that.

In the Westchester, the elevator is out of service and the shaft is full of trash: syringes and liquor bottles, adult diapers and cardboard boxes from Meals on Wheels. The stairs are dark, but they work. They lead down to a wrought-iron gate, which opens to Turk Street. In the mornings, before sunrise, I'd take the stairs and push through the gate, and wander around a few blocks to see if I was being followed. When I was sure that I was alone — and you might be surprised how very alone you can be in the Tenderloin, just before dawn — I'd walk toward the Civic Center. I have a two-room office over there, close to the courthouses. Courthouses draw the kinds of people who need what I sell.

But for five weeks, I'd only had one client. I was running the clock twenty-four hours a day. I'd get to the office early and sort through the mail. I'd check my messages and pay whatever bills needed to be paid. I had to keep up with my life, such as it was. I'd call the man who received my invoices and signed my checks. And then I'd slink back to my listening post in the Westchester before first light.

That's what I was heading to do on the first Tuesday in June when I pushed out of the gate and checked the cars parked on Turk. I was most concerned about windowless vans. They're the easiest to picture: JOE'S PLUMBING stenciled on the doors; a half dozen FBI and DEA agents hiding inside, crouched around video monitors and talking into radios. But if they were there, I didn't see them. I did a loop around the block, and when I was satisfied that all was clear, I turned west, toward Van Ness and my office.

I was halfway into my walk when I saw the car. It was parked on the sidewalk across the street, directly in front of the Refugio Apartments. Not just any car, but a Rolls Royce Wraith. It had recently undergone a transformation from brand new to totally destroyed. I assumed it was an accident and crossed the street to get a better look. Professional curiosity. I was one step removed from the ambulance-chasing business. But drawing closer, I realized my initial impression wasn't quite right. The car hadn't been hit from the front, or from either side.

The car's chrome grille and smoke-gray hood were immaculate. Its roof was caved in as far down as its gold-plated door handles. Lying inside the crumpled indentation was a perfect blonde. She wore a black cocktail dress, sheer and shimmery in the streetlights. I couldn't see any blood except on her left foot, where it had run down the back of her calf and onto her heel. Her hands were folded across her chest, and her eyes were closed. Her hair was spread in a fan across the Wraith's roof. She had an evening bag looped around her right wrist. One foot was bare — maybe she'd lost a shoe on impact. Her toenails were painted white, like the inside of a shell.

I looked around. Across the street, on a bed of flattened boxes, lay a man. He wore a full-body black snowsuit, and he was either asleep or unconscious. He was either asleep or unconscious a lot. Five weeks on Turk Street, and I could smell Snowsuit Man from two blocks away if the wind was right. If the sound of the woman hitting the car had woken him up, it hadn't disturbed him so much that he stayed awake. And he and I were the only people around, at least at street level. There was no way to account for whoever might be watching from a dark window, and I didn't even try.

I stepped closer. The woman wasn't breathing. I reached out, carefully, and put my fingers beneath her chin. I pressed gently against her throat, searching for her carotid. She was warm, but there was no pulse. I looked up and down the sidewalk again, then back at the Refugio.

Fourteen stories. Hundred-year-old brickwork forming arches and columns on the lower two floors. There were no open windows above the car, but there were ledges. She could have inched onto one and then shut the window. Or she could have gone off the roof. But none of that explained her — her patent leather evening bag, her diaphanous dress, and the insanely expensive car she'd crushed when she landed. None of that made sense on Turk Street, in front of the Refugio. Fourteen floors of bedbugs, and false fire alarms. Police cars skidding up in the middle of the night to break up domestics or serve no-knock warrants. It was better than the Westchester, but not by much.

I backed away and crouched on the sidewalk. Smashed windshield glass crunched underfoot, and I thought better of kneeling. I set down my backpack and opened it. When I left the Westchester, I didn't like to leave anything in plain view. The pinpoint cameras and microphones were hidden, and some of the recording equipment could fit under the floorboards. But I never left my laptop in the room, and I never left my camera. I took out the Nikon now and set it up for a night portrait, no flash.

I heard a siren, but in the Tenderloin that could mean anything.

I stood up and snapped five shots of the suicide blonde on her Wraith deathbed. Then I backed up ten paces to get her with the apartment, and the street. You could say my job is taking photographs. Most of the time, no one sees my work except my clients. But if the opportunity presents itself, I'm not above selling a picture to the *Chronicle,* or any other paying outlet. After the divorce, and especially since coming back here, I've been living between the lines. I take what I can get. When it comes to pictures, I get a lot, because I'm often in the right place.

I saw the man when I lowered the camera. He'd been coming along the sidewalk, rolling a black cart lashed with silver boxes. But he'd come to a full stop, and was staring at the car in openmouthed shock. I couldn't tell whether he could see the girl or not. It took him a while to even notice me, and then he sized me up, looking from me to my camera to the crushed car.

"Who the hell are you?"

"Nobody," I said. "A guy taking a walk. Who are you?"

He didn't answer, but stepped closer. Glass crunched under his running shoes. He was wearing canvas pants and a flannel shirt. A pocket-laden vest over that. His ball cap bore the name of a production company I'd never heard of. For a moment, I thought I'd stumbled onto a movie set. But there were no lights, and no white trailers. No sawhorses blocking off the street parking. And the dead woman was no stage prop.

"What happened?" the man asked when he finally found enough breath to speak.

"Like this when I got here," I said. "Is this your car?"

He shook his head.

"I'm fucked. I'm so completely fucked."

He pulled out his cell phone and began scrolling through its screen. Maybe deciding who to call first.

"Was she with you?" I asked.

"She?"

I tilted my head toward the car, and the man crept closer. He saw her and turned away quickly.

"Oh god."

"You don't know her?"

"I've never seen her before."

I stepped sideways to frame the shot, and when I had the production company guy lined up with the girl and the car behind him, I raised the camera and took his picture.

"Hey!" he said, turning to me. "What the hell?"

"For the papers."

I started down Turk. He didn't call after me, and he didn't follow. At the end of the next block I came on a parked panel truck. The production company's name was painted on the side. There was a college-aged kid in the cargo area, using a flashlight to sort through boxes of video gear. If it was just the two of them, and the loaned-out Wraith, they ran a lean operation. I stepped off the curb and put my hand on the back of the truck.

"Good morning," I said, and the kid finally looked up. "What's with the car?"

"Photo shoot," he said. "Magazine ad."

He turned back to sorting his gear. He'd set aside six white umbrellas and was now probably digging for tripods and remote flash boxes. Just going about his job as though nothing was inherently weird about using Section 8 housing to sell a half-million-dollar car. For all I knew, they were going to drag Snowsuit Man over and use him as a prop.

"You might want to lock this up and go check on your boss," I said. "He's got a problem."

"He's— What?"

"And bring your cell phone, so you can call 911."

That got him looking up again. I shot his picture, using a flash this time so I could get his face inside the dark truck. Then, for good measure, I got the truck's license plate before continuing on.

The door to my office was up a set of stairs between the entrances to a Vet Center and a credit union. I had a little sign hanging down from the portico.

LELAND CROWE AGENCY
PRIVATE INVESTIGATIONS

I climbed the stairs and unlocked the door, using my foot to sweep aside the previous day's mail. I went through the reception room—empty, because I had no receptionist—and into my office. I slotted my camera's memory card into my desktop computer and spent ten minutes sorting and editing my photographs. My client could wait for a moment.

The suicide blonde was beautiful, and so were my shots.

The car's roof had caught her and folded partway around her, holding her arms and legs in place. Because she wasn't sprawled on the pavement, she didn't look like a corpse. She was utterly composed. A woman asleep on a bed of steel. I had a range of exposures and angles—shots that caught the blood on her foot and the shattered glass and the curves beneath her dress that might play well in a tabloid if she turned out to be famous, and shots that captured the scene but blurred out the blood, for the family papers.

I got on the phone and started calling photo editors I'd worked with. I wasn't desperate for cash just then. With my summer assignment in the Westchester Hotel, I was as flush as I'd ever been. But just one lean, hungry winter will develop lifelong habits. You don't pass an opportunity; you don't leave any food on the table.

So I called the editors, starting with the ones who had the most cash, and I haggled.

3

AN HOUR LATER, I had signed, scanned and emailed a boilerplate contract. My photograph would be online by nine, and on grocery store racks in three days. I'd get a thousand dollars from *Just Now!* magazine, with a 200 percent kicker if the woman turned out to be a "Person of Consequence" — a carefully defined term on page three that had probably been drafted by a lawyer on Wilshire Boulevard who didn't find that task any stranger than selling a Rolls Royce by parking it on skid row. I could pretend to sneer all I wanted, but I'd cash the check when it came.

With that done, I picked up the phone again and called Jim Gardner, the attorney who'd bought all my time this summer. He answered on the first ring, already at his desk at six fifty in the morning. Of course he was. He'd just started a trial, and the prosecution's star witness was about to take the stand.

"Good morning," I said, jumping in to cut off his routine greeting. "Just in time. I have something."

There was a beat of silence. He was likely considering how he wanted to sound if the FBI had a tap on his line. Which wasn't an entirely remote possibility. Not if the government had any idea what Jim had been paying me to do this summer.

"Are you on the clock, Mr. Crowe?"

When he was in trial mode, Jim Gardner's most mundane questions began to sound leather-bound and consequential. He'd given his opening statement yesterday, so he was in full swing. And he knew he might be playing to a larger audience.

"Yes, counselor," I said. "This call is privileged and confidential."

"Not enough for me. You've had coffee?"

At the Westchester, there was a guy on the third floor who sold crack cocaine out of his room. He bagged it in condoms cadged from the API Wellness Center on Polk Street. That was as close as my hotel got to coffee.

"The concierge recommended I look elsewhere this morning."

I hung up. I didn't need to ask where we were meeting. The place was pre-set.

"Last night we had an in-chamber conference," Jim was saying. "It didn't go the way I'd hoped."

We were sitting on either side of the manager's desk inside an abandoned auto body shop. Cobwebbed glass walls looked out on an oil-stained concrete floor. The only illumination came from a skylight. A pigeon was walking back and forth up there. *Tap tap tap, tap tap tap.*

Jim had a key to this place because someone in his firm had handled the foreclosure. We met here often enough that I had a key too.

"Nammar's calling DeCanza first thing this morning," Jim said. "He's a good prosecutor, so I thought he'd go all day with him. But he's going to finish at three."

"You'll recess after that?"

Jim swept his hand through his hair. He had gray hair that curled as it grew out. With his deep drawl, his broad shoulders, and his heavy college ring, people probably mistook him for a football coach.

"The judge wants to stick to her schedule. Or she just wants to stick it to me. I don't have a good enough read on her to know which it is. But either way, after Nammar's direct, I have to start my cross. No recess. So I hope you have something."

By stopping at three, Nammar was forcing Jim to split his cross-examination across two days. The jury would hear two hours at the end of the day. Then they'd go home and forget it, and Jim would spend the night wondering whether he needed to hit those points again or call it a loss and move on. I had a solution for that problem.

"Nammar paid a visit last night," I said. "Agent White tagged along. They stayed with DeCanza three and a half hours, coaching him. Threatening him. I've got audio and video—"

"I can't have that. I don't want it. Delete it."

"Okay."

"But tell me all about it, by all means."

"DeCanza's going to bury Lorca."

"Who's Lorca?" Jim asked. "I don't know anyone named Lorca."

"If you say so."

There was no point arguing with him. Jim had picked this abandoned office because it wasn't wired and the feds didn't know about it. But there were lines he wouldn't cross. His client had a story, and Jim's job was to sell it. Anywhere and everywhere.

"Tell me about DeCanza," he said.

"He was high up. Second in command, basically. Lorca—your guy—wasn't just a voice on the phone, or a rumor. He was a face in the room. They worked side by side. So he knows everything. Which you already knew."

I walked Jim through the main points. DeCanza had started the way they all had. A mule, moving packages north across the border. After three trips without getting busted,

12

they trusted him to carry cash. But he was a reader, and a thinker. When the DEA starting using listening stations and ground-penetrating radar to find the border tunnels, De-Canza hired men out of Baja boatyards and set up shop in the desert. Their first submarine was forty-six feet long and sank in the Sea of Cortez. Their second was ninety feet long and made three trips before its crew scuttled it in view of a Coast Guard cutter. But by then, DeCanza and Lorca had suborned so many customs agents, they didn't need submarines. They could load their products onto commercial airliners and fly them straight into New York. They had replaced cash with cryptocurrency, which could be moved invisibly.

If he'd been in an American corporation instead of an international cartel, DeCanza would have an impressive title. Chief Financial Officer, Vice President of Operations — something like that. But the cartel didn't bother with formal titles. Except the one he had now, a title no one wanted: *rat*.

Without DeCanza, the government's case was entirely circumstantial. It could all be explained away. Jim's client was a San Francisco businessman. The name Lorca wasn't written on his California driver's license. It wasn't written anywhere. Which meant that if DeCanza vanished, so did the government's shot at a conviction. People who rubbed Lorca the wrong way had a history of disappearing. This summer, I had been playing a dangerous game. I'd tracked down a turncoat rat and put eyes and ears in his room. If Lorca had known about the Westchester, the prosecution would be short a star witness. I wasn't looking to become an accessory to murder. So to protect myself, and Jim, I'd only told him what he could afford to know.

"It's a nice roadmap," Jim said. "But you're not lifting my spirits. What do you really have?"

I'd gotten it a week ago. I'd held it back, but I'd always meant to tell him at the right time.

"You wouldn't have wanted it too soon," I told him. "So I kept it, and saved you an ethical dilemma."

"I can sort those out on my own."

"Not your call when I'm involved," I said. "Which means before I give this to you, you've got to agree on how you'll use it."

"Agree how?"

"Either you put it in today's cross, or you forget I told you. If it's not today, it never gets used. Use it right now — no warning, no heads-up to your client — and it'll give you a shot. If he doesn't know until the government hears it, there won't be any more blood on your hands tomorrow than there is right now."

"Deal."

Of course Jim would agree, even if he didn't know what I was talking about. He needed what I had. And he probably understood that I was offering leverage. He didn't need to be a genius to guess the form it took. There was one currency that traded above all others on the leverage market. Innocent lives. Women were gold, and children were diamonds.

"They've got DeCanza living like a prisoner," I said. "He's their witness, but that doesn't mean they like him."

"Nothing new there."

"He hasn't seen the sky since mid-May. He's in a Tenderloin shithole. Calling it a safe house is a stretch. They bring him his meals twice a day. They check on him every two hours, plus he's wearing a GPS tracker on his ankle. But they'll take it off when he comes to court today — and if you ask, he'll deny it existed. They'll give him immunity, but it's contingent on a conviction. Which means they really have him by the balls — if he testifies the way they want, but your guy walks, there's no deal."

Jim was tapping two fingers on the banged-up desktop.

"I can get into that," he said. "Even if he denies it, claims

14

they're putting him up at the Holiday Inn, it'll chip away at his credibility. But you've got more."

Of course I had more. I'd be embarrassed to send Jim my invoices if I couldn't give him more than that.

"He's been begging for a phone," I said. "For a month, every day, he asks for one."

"What's he want it for?"

"He won't tell them. But he told me, because he talks to himself," I said. "He wants to talk to his wife."

"She's supposed to be dead."

I made Jim wait a bit. I blew on my coffee and sipped it. I checked my phone.

"You're talking about the thing in Mexico City," I said. "The apartment house that blew up."

"Two snitches saw her on the balcony."

"She was on the seventh floor, and they were a couple blocks away. Did you hear about a DNA test?"

Jim stared at me, processing that.

"Does Nammar know?" he finally asked.

"Not a clue."

His fingers stopped tapping.

"How do you know all this?"

"I gave DeCanza what he wanted," I said. "I gave him a phone."

It had been a relatively straightforward operation. Easy, and yet the dirtiest thing I'd ever done.

DeCanza had regular visits from half a dozen FBI agents and three assistant United States attorneys, including Nammar. He'd asked each of his visitors for a phone, and had always been rebuffed. But if one of them broke rank and gave him a phone in secret, there were enough people in and out the door for anonymity and deniability. So I waited until he'd walked down the hall for the toilet, and then I went downstairs, picked his lock with a bump key and a screwdriver, and left a cell phone on his bed.

Back upstairs, I took off my latex gloves and watched from the camera hidden in DeCanza's ceiling. His quarters were as tiny as mine; when he returned from the toilet, it took him all of three seconds to notice the phone. He looked around the room and went to the window. He stood perfectly still for a full minute, his head down. Then he put the phone under his mattress.

Three days later, he still hadn't used it. So I waited until he went for his shower, and I bumped his lock again and left him a fifth of whiskey. Back upstairs, in crisp black-and-white, I watched him find the bottle and inspect the seal. He didn't flush it or hide it, or pace the room in consternation. He cracked it open, took a single sniff, and then started drinking.

Two hours later, he lifted the mattress and pulled out the phone. I watched him turn it in his hands. I watched him switch it on. He stared at it for a long time. And then, from memory, he dialed a number.

Of course it was a trap.

The phone was one half of a pair I'd bought in Chinatown. Over drinks at a booth in the San Lung Lounge, I'd paid a freelance hacker to sync them. He was finished with the job before he was finished with his Mai Tai. I handed him an envelope of twenty-dollar bills, and that was it.

So when DeCanza dialed his wife, I watched and listened in real time.

He should have known better. No long-term survivor of the Witness Protection Program would ever lay hands on a smartphone. He wasn't cut out for this. I was just saving him time and protracted misery.

"I ran the number and did some digging," I told Jim. "He called a landline outside of Eagle Pass, Texas. A five-thousand-acre ranch, deeded to a Cayman Islands partnership. The partners are all foreign LLCs with stupid names and mail drop agents—you can guess who really owns them. The title is free and clear, so it was a cash sale. Five years ago, when DeCanza was riding high."

I slid a copy of the title report across the desk.

"And the woman who picked up the phone?" Jim asked.

"Maria Lucinda DeCanza," I said. "She's living there with their nineteen-month-old son."

"He's alive too?"

"I could hear him in the background."

Jim Gardner stared at the title report. He picked it up and paged through it, and then he put it in his briefcase. He wasn't a good man, or he wouldn't have been doing what he was doing. And I must not have been an angel either, or I wouldn't have trusted him to do the right thing with the information I'd just given him.

"Come by if you want to watch the cross," Jim said.

He took his briefcase and left the derelict shop. Five minutes later, I followed him out.

I went back to the Westchester. My work there was done, and if things blew up in the cross-examination that afternoon, Nammar and the FBI might start wondering who had been watching DeCanza, and how. So I wanted to empty out my room. Pull all the surveillance equipment, wipe the surfaces clean of prints, and leave the place looking the way it ought to—empty liquor bottles, crushed beer cans, and takeout wrappers piled like a snowdrift in the corners and under the bed. I had a backpack full of garbage, ready to go.

I passed the Refugio on my way. I counted ten black-and-white squad cars, two unmarked Fords that were surely detectives from homicide detail, and an idling ambulance. A van from the medical examiner's office was pulling away from the curb. The suicide blonde was bagged and tagged, but the Wraith was still on the sidewalk. Someone had put traffic cones around it, and stretched yellow police tape from cone to cone. I raised my camera and watched through the lens, shutter clicking. A man pushed through the Refugio's front door. Slim build, dark hair, and a suit that was shiny with wear. A homicide inspector. He pushed through the knot of officers, and then he was looking at me. I lowered the camera and kept walking.

4

AT TEN IN the morning, I went home for the first time in five weeks. I walked from the Tenderloin to Union Square, trading flophouses and liquor stores for luxury goods and wine bars, and then I followed Grant Avenue into Chinatown. Home was a one-bedroom walk-up on the third floor above a seafood restaurant. I turned off the alarm with the fob on my keychain and went inside. Even this home — my new beginning — was tainted with the past. It was all part of a continuum. There were no clean lines and no clear demarcations.

Six years ago, when my marriage exploded, I'd been thrown clear, carrying nothing but my clothes, three broken fingers, and a letter from the California Bar Association confirming my disbarment. It could have been a lot worse. I'd walked up to an associate justice of the California Supreme Court and knocked out most of his teeth. As I was sitting in the back of a police cruiser an hour afterward, jail time and significant restitution seemed inevitable. But both Juliette's father and her future husband found it expedient to keep me quiet. So instead of doing time and going bankrupt, I actually made money. Fifty grand per tooth. The same day the divorce judge posted her decree on the court's electronic docket, I got a cashier's check drawn from my former father-in-law's account. Juliette's childhood chauffer delivered it to me in the lobby of the Oakland Marriott and stood there stiff and humorless as I used his back to sign the receipt. Maybe it wasn't clear to anyone standing in the Marriott, but the residents at the Westchester Hotel would have recognized that check for what it was. Hush money.

It had been an easy bargain to strike. Juliette's new husband needed to keep credibility with California's voters; to that end, his ex-wife probably got even more than I did. And as for me, I'd rather have had the money than the right to talk about Juliette. I didn't even want to think about her. The cash helped. I started with a two-month haze of bar tabs in La Paz, Mexico. I remember lying on my back and watching the shadows cast by a wooden fan on my room's ceiling. I drank mezcal until I couldn't feel anything, until, finally, I felt just fine. I sobered up at a motel in the desert, and headed north again.

There was plenty of money left. I didn't have a job, so I couldn't get a mortgage, but nobody could stop me from buying a place outright, in cash. I had five windows looking down on Grant. My view was partially blocked by the neon sign that announced the South Seas Golden King Seafood Restaurant. It blinked all night, its tubing gold and red.

南
海
金
王
海鮮餐廳

I could hear those characters buzzing in my dreams. When I closed my eyes anywhere but home, the silence would startle me awake again.

There was nothing else to do, so I ran a bath. I had to let five weeks of rusty water clear through the pipes before I could put the rubber stopper in the tub. The fridge was empty except for condiments and a single bottle of Tsingtao. I opened that, and settled into the tub. In the Westchester, I'd never admitted to myself that I was scared. But now, at home, I allowed that much. I'd broken the law before, usually for Jim Gardner. But I'd never wandered so far off the reservation. I'd never done anything to cross the FBI or a federal prosecutor, and I'd never tricked a government witness into betraying his wife's hiding place. I could have kept that last bit to myself, to protect a woman whose only mistake, as far as I knew, was marrying the wrong man. That would have been the right thing to do, and Jim would have paid my invoices when they came due. But I'd told him. I hadn't even debated with myself about whether I ought to.

It hadn't occurred to me until just then that a person could be honest and immoral at the same time. Now I wasn't so sure those attributes were mutually exclusive. And it wasn't at all clear to me anymore which way the scale would swing if I put my character onto the balance.

When the water got cold, I toweled off, turned on the lights, and shaved at the sink. I looked like myself again, but I felt the same way I had when I'd woken up that morning as I set out for my last pre-dawn walk from the Westchester. That got me thinking about the suicide blonde, the rainwater pooling in her eyes, beading her hair.

She came and went from my mind until quarter after three, when I watched Jim Gardner start his cross. Then I had more immediate concerns, problems of my own making.

I had gotten there too early.

Courtroom Five, on the seventeenth floor of the Phillip Burton Building, was silent as I stepped into it. I was expecting a packed seating area, and I wasn't disappointed. The trial was a headliner. The bodies were piled almost as high as the money, and the only politicians not pointing fingers were mysteriously out of town. I recognized a reporter from KTVU, and the crime beat writer from the *Chronicle*. Mixed into the crowd were the usual courthouse regulars. Law students, retirees with nothing better to do. Under-employed attorneys hoping for a scrap. There were also six men sitting side by side in the front row, behind Nammar's table. I couldn't see their faces, but I'd been looking at the backs of their heads all spring. They were DeCanza's FBI minders.

One of them, Agent White, turned around. I hadn't made any sound coming in, but he must have felt the draft. His eyes met mine and locked there. Behind him, on the other side of the rail, Nammar was standing at the lectern between the two tables. DeCanza was on the witness stand to the judge's right. Jim was sitting to his client's left, resting his chin on his hand.

"And the man you knew as Lorca, the one we've been talking about all day—is he here in the courtroom?" Nammar asked.

"Yes, sir."

"Can you point him out to the jury, please?"

Agent White finally turned back around. He wouldn't want to miss this part. They'd been coaching their witness all spring for this moment.

"Right there," DeCanza pointed. "In the black suit. That's Lorca."

"You're certain?"

"Absolutely. I saw him every day for fifteen years. He was at my wedding. I was right there with him when his kid died."

"Is it easy for you, pointing him out?"

"You mean, do I like it?"

"Do you like it?"

"It makes me feel like a rat."

"Are you scared of him?"

I expected Jim to object, but he didn't even look up.

"He's not a nice man, if that's what you mean. You cross him and he doesn't take it well."

"So you're being brave, to sit up there and talk."

"Or maybe I just want to die. I know what he does."

"To guys like you who tell the truth?"

"Guys like me. Yeah."

Nammar had been facing the jury as he asked his questions, but now he turned to the judge.

"Nothing further, Your Honor," he said. "I pass the witness."

Judge Linda Kim turned to Jim and looked across the top of her black-rimmed glasses at him.

"Counselor?"

"Thank you, Your Honor," he said.

He rose and clasped his hands behind his back, straightening his arms to stretch his shoulders. Everything with Jim was a signal to the jury. I could guess what this was supposed to convey: he'd been bored, sitting there for five hours, listening to DeCanza tell lies. Lies that would be as easy to swat down as slow-moving flies. He wasn't concerned about a thing, except that this might delay his dinner.

He went to the lectern. He hadn't brought any papers with him.

"Good afternoon, sir."

Jim Gardner had come to San Francisco after law school. Before that, he'd been somewhere deep in the backwoods of Mississippi. When he was sixteen, his baritone drawl had landed him a job recording radio spots for businesses across the region. Car dealerships and bowling alleys in Tupelo. A strip joint all the way down in Slidell. It was his voice that had gotten him out of Mississippi. Three words into his cross, and he had the jurors leaning closer for more.

"Do you know who I am?"

"Lorca's attorney."

"I represent Mr. Alba," Jim said, indicating his client. "But he doesn't know anyone named Lorca."

"Objection," Nammar said. "If he wants to testify to that, let him put Lorca on the stand."

"Mr. Gardner," Judge Kim said. "Ask your first question and let's move on."

"Thank you, Your Honor. And if I may respond to Mr. Nammar — I have Lorca on the stand. Right now."

"Objection!"

Nammar had jumped to his feet.

"You opened the door and walked into that one," Judge Kim said. Then she turned to Jim. "Ask your first question."

Jim nodded. He turned to the jury.

"Your name is Albert DeCanza. Yes or no."

"Yes."

"Have you ever had an alias?"

"My friends call me Al."

Jim laughed along with the jury. Then he came around and stood in front of the lectern. That wasn't the norm in federal court, but the judge didn't stop him, and Nammar didn't object.

"Isn't it correct that you're the beneficial owner of all of the stock in the Aguila Holding Corporation?"

The levity on DeCanza's face lasted another second. Maybe two. He'd heard the question, but it was taking him a moment to process it. When he did, his face went flat. Ten seconds passed. An eternity in a trial court. Still he didn't answer.

"Should I repeat the question?" Jim asked.

"I've never heard of that company."

"Let me get this straight," Jim said. "You've never heard of the Aguila Holding Corporation? I'm talking about a Bahamas company, which registered as a foreign entity in Texas five years, three months, and two days ago. You've never heard of it?"

DeCanza could only shake his head.

"You have to answer out loud," Jim said. "Our court reporter, this lovely lady down in front of you, she gets heartburn if she can't hear you."

"I've never heard of it," DeCanza said. He was looking at the glass of water in front of him. He took his hands off the witness desk and folded them out of sight.

"Where were you on March twenty-third, 2014?"

"I don't know."

"Strange. You've had an excellent memory for the last five hours," Jim said. "Let me ask you this — what's the nearest airport to Eagle Pass, Texas?"

"I don't know," DeCanza said. He glanced at Nammar, but Nammar was swiveled around, whispering over the rail with two of the FBI agents in the front row.

"You don't know," Jim said. "Okay, let's try this: Who are the directors of the Ranch Four Corporation? If it refreshes your recollection, it was established in the Cayman Islands. Registered as a foreign entity in Texas. On March twenty-third, 2014."

Now Nammar stood up.

"Your Honor," he said. "May we approach?"

"I have a question pending," Jim said. "And I'd like it answered."

The judge looked from Jim to Nammar. Then at DeCanza, whose forehead was now glazed with a thin film of sweat.

"Answer the question."

DeCanza looked up at her. He shook his head, his eyes glassy and wide.

"What was — I mean —" He pointed down at the court reporter. "Can she read it back?"

Without waiting for the judge to respond, the reporter read Jim's last question. Jim was leaning against the front of the lectern. Nammar was back in his chair, in a whispered conversation with the FBI agents.

DeCanza was still shaking his head.

"I don't know," he said. "I've never heard of that company. So I don't know the directors."

"Then let me ask you—"

Nammar stood, and cut Jim off.

"Your Honor—may we approach now?"

"Fine."

The judge reached past her gavel and hit a switch. White noise came out of speakers in the ceiling above the jury box and the public gallery. When Jim and Nammar approached for their bench conference, it was impossible to hear what they were saying. But it was easy to imagine. Nammar wanted to know: *Where the hell is he going with this?* And Jim was saying: *I don't have to give him a map. It's his damn witness. If he doesn't know where I'm going, that's his fault.* The exchange went back and forth for a minute. DeCanza, alone and forgotten on the witness stand, looked like he wanted to run for the nearest window and dive through it. Never mind that we were on the seventeenth floor.

When the judge killed the white noise and the attorneys walked back, I couldn't tell how she'd ruled. Both attorneys wore blank faces. Jim took his spot in front of the lectern. Nammar sat down and turned to the more junior AUSA on his left.

"Mr. DeCanza," Jim said. "Does your ranch outside of Eagle Pass have an airstrip?"

Nammar was on his feet immediately.

"Objection!" And then, in a quieter voice, he added, "Lacks foundation. And counsel said he was going to be asking about foreign corporations."

"And their holdings," Jim said. "I definitely said holdings."

"The witness will answer the question."

"An airstrip? I don't even know about the ranch."

"No ranch in Eagle Pass?"

"No."

Jim walked back to his table and picked up a thin folder. He carried it back to the lectern and opened it. He took his time. The point was to let the jury wonder what damning documents he was about to unleash. And, maybe more important, to let DeCanza twist on the blade.

"You're telling me you don't know a thing about a ranch — a five-thousand-two-hundred-and-forty-six-acre ranch — outside of Eagle Pass, Texas?"

Here, Jim turned to his folder and scanned the first page with his fingertip.

"Three habitable structures, an airstrip, and a hangar, all of which last changed hands on March twenty-third, 2014?"

DeCanza had been looking at Nammar. But Nammar was either talking to his co-counsel or whispering with the FBI agents behind him. He wasn't watching his witness flounder. So DeCanza turned to his only other possible lifeline. Jim's client. From behind, I couldn't tell if I saw a reaction from the man. Maybe there was a nod. Maybe it was just my imagination.

"I — just don't — I mean —"

Jim took three steps forward.

"Let's circle back," he said. "When we got started a couple of minutes ago, I asked you about aliases. Have you ever gone by an alias, sir?"

DeCanza looked at his wrists. They were pale; he'd spent a lot of time indoors just recently. He was going to be spending a lot more.

"Yes."

"You've had an alias?"

"Yes."

Jim took another step forward.

"What alias, sir?"

DeCanza glanced at the defense table again, and then focused on his water glass. If his testimony on direct examination had gone anything like the statements he'd given at the Westchester Hotel, then he would have spent a considerable portion of the morning telling the jury how Lorca dealt with his enemies. Lorca's methods of communication were baroque. He started with power tools and duct tape and graduated to bags of scorpions and a good-sized footlocker. But all his messages ended the same way: with a dismembered corpse burning in an oil drum, some low-level guy stirring the flames and adding fuel until there was nothing left. DeCanza knew, because he'd been involved at every level of the process.

Now, in real time, I could see DeCanza thinking. Nammar didn't know his wife and son were alive. No one was protecting them. He could stick to his story, and then it would be a race to Eagle Pass. Lorca's men against the feds. Jim, with his genial southern manner, was offering DeCanza a simple choice. DeCanza could kneel down and put his head on the block, right now, and spare his wife and child. Or he could hold to the truth and take his chances.

His life for theirs.

"What alias did you use, sir?" Jim repeated.

"Lorca."

"Can you say that again?" Jim said. "You were so quiet, I'm not sure our lovely court reporter could hear you."

DeCanza wouldn't look up. He didn't want to see Nammar, and he didn't want anyone to see him looking at the defense table.

"Lorca," he said, a little bit louder this time.

I heard DeCanza's last answer as I was walking out. From behind me, Jim was talking again. I pulled the courtroom door open. Cold air flooded in from the hallway.

"Why don't we hit rewind?" Jim was saying. "Let's go back to a few minutes ago, when you pointed to my client —"

As I was stepping out, I looked back. Agent White had turned around again. White buzz cut, whiskey-punched nose. Sharp, black eyes. He watched me until the door closed.

5

ON THE GROUND FLOOR, at the security stand, I handed the guard my claim ticket and waited for him to return my phone. I was expecting White to come out of the elevators at any moment, calling after me; I didn't feel safe until I'd gotten out of the federal building.

The government had spent two years and millions of dollars preparing its case. Jim Gardner had eviscerated it in less than ten minutes. It wasn't even a quarter past three. I hurried away from the front entrance. There were SUVs from Homeland Security parked to the left, so I went to the right. Someone was going to pay for what had just happened. They were going to dump everything they could on DeCanza, but there'd be plenty left over for someone else. Someone like me, for example.

I crossed Larkin and stepped into Harry Harrington's Pub. I paused just inside and scanned the place. Twenty people, including the two bartenders. The customers were an evenly split mix of dedicated boozehounds who might as well have had reserved stools, and government workers who'd left work a couple hours early on a Friday. The seven television screens were showing baseball and cricket. I took a seat at the end of the bar, farthest from the door. As soon as I got the chance, I ordered a Wild Turkey, neat.

I didn't think about anything until I ordered the second

glass. For my stay in the Westchester, I'd looked the part. I stopped shaving, and rarely showered. I never did laundry. In thirty-five days, I wore two sweatshirts, and always the same pair of jeans. By the time I was done with it, my thrift store coat might have come from a grave robbing.

I took a drink of my bourbon. Glass in hand, I brushed my knuckles along my cheek. It was still smooth from shaving this morning. I could see myself in the mirror behind the liquor bottles. In my ironed shirt and dry-cleaned suit, I looked like a lawyer. The real kind, who could show up in court and represent a client without getting arrested. Jim should never have invited me to his cross-examination.

Maybe I was just being paranoid. I'd been careful in the Westchester, had taken precautions beyond my appearance. Agent White had turned around and stared at me, but that could mean anything. It didn't mean he'd connected me to DeCanza's implosion.

When the bartender came past, I ordered another Wild Turkey. He poured it for me, but first he gave me a glass of ice water. Meaning it was time to slow down or move on. I finished them both and walked out.

I crossed Van Ness, went into the bookstore there, and found a copy of the *Chronicle* abandoned on a table in the coffee shop. It didn't have anything about the blonde I'd photographed, which wasn't surprising. She'd probably hit the Wraith about the same time the paper was coming off the press. There was a snippet on the Lorca trial, but I didn't read it. No journalist could have foreseen the turn the trial had just taken.

I left the bookstore and kept walking west. I hadn't gotten any real exercise since mid-May. I didn't mind that it was raining. When Jim paid his last invoice, I could have my suit dry-cleaned again. I could throw it away and buy all the new suits I wanted. It didn't matter. I kept walking, looking for green spaces. I went through Alamo Square, and then followed the footpaths along the Panhandle and into Golden Gate Park. It was June, so it would stay light past eight thirty. But it was gray light. Fog light.

DeCanza probably wasn't going to spend the night in the Westchester. If Nammar and White cared about this case or their careers they'd tie him to a chair in a concrete room and take turns on him with a baseball bat. *What the fuck just happened, Al? What's Gardner got on you?* But that wasn't how Nammar operated. I only knew one person who did things like that, and he was the man who ultimately paid my bills.

The rain falling into the eucalyptus trees made a hushing sound. I decided to walk all the way to Ocean Beach, and then take a cab home. After that, I wasn't sure. Maybe La Paz again, or somewhere even farther. Thailand or Vietnam. But when I got to the beach and sat down, my phone vibrated. I pulled it out and looked at the incoming text, from Jim Gardner.

Meet me at your office. Now.

"Lee," he said. "That took forever."

He'd climbed the steps from the street to my locked door, and he was waiting there in the shadows.

When he'd been my boss, I'd called him Mr. Garland, and I was Mr. Crowe. I wasn't used to hearing him say my first name, even though my short term of employment with him had ended six years ago. When I'd returned from La Paz, I'd sat in my new apartment for two months. Finally, I decided I needed something to do. Between my old job and my summers working for a defense lawyer, I could cobble together enough investigative hours to meet the requirements for a PI license. So I took the test, and passed. I had a card printed, and then I went and found Jim. He'd been my main source of work for the first couple of years, but as time went on, I'd found other avenues. Now things were going well enough that I needed an office of my own.

"This is how you show up at the office?" he asked, looking at my soaked suit.

"Only when there's a client waiting."

I took off my jacket and twisted it to wring water onto the floor. We shook hands, and then he took a step back.

"You smell like bourbon, Lee."

"It's my office," I said. "My time."

I took the key ring from my pocket and opened the door. Jim went in and I followed him. He sat in one of the two chairs across from my desk, and took a handkerchief from the breast pocket of his wool suit to dab the rain from his face.

"Nice place," he said.

I doubted he thought so. He had a corner office on a high floor at One Market Street, overlooking the Ferry Building and the bay. He got to his desk while it was still dark and watched the sun come up over the Oakland hills. He had two hundred attorneys working on three all-marble floors. Twenty-four hours a day, money poured into the till. I'd never had any doubts about how I'd gotten my foot through the door. He'd done his research, and let me know it. I was a certified nobody, from a long line of them. So it wasn't my name or my draw that he wanted. He'd wanted Juliette's father as a client. It had been a great strategy until my divorce and disbarment made me useless. To save face, he very publicly cast me out. I'd expected that much. But our relationship continued, and evolved, and I never would have predicted that.

"I should've come by when you signed the lease," he said. "What was that, last month?"

"I didn't throw an office-warming party. How'd you wrap up with DeCanza? I left early."

I didn't want to tell him about Agent White unless I knew for sure there was a problem.

"You were there to see him flip?" Jim asked. I nodded,

and he went on. "After that, he followed me wherever I led him. Everything he said in Nammar's direct was a lie. He's Lorca. He ran the whole thing, from the top down."

"Did you finish with him?"

"Yeah, but Nammar doesn't know it. He's my witness tomorrow morning. I'll ask enough to make sure he didn't change his mind overnight, and then I'm going to hand him back to Nammar."

"Will they change his mind?"

Jim looked around the office. He must have been weighing the possibility that it was bugged. And he must have decided it probably wasn't.

"Would they change your mind, if it was your wife who'd go in the barrel?"

I shook my head. However Jim meant the question, the answer was no. They wouldn't change my mind for a hypothetical future wife, and they wouldn't change my mind for Juliette. I had no fond feelings for her, but no one deserved to go into one of Lorca's barrels.

"Will they let it go to a verdict?" I asked.

"This is Lorca. The man at the top. They're not going to risk an acquittal. Someone higher than Nammar will make a call tonight. They'll angle for a mistrial. If that doesn't work, they'll start offering pleas — and why not? They've already got him cold on tax evasion, so he's doing time either way."

"But you win," I said.

"I win."

I opened my desk drawer and got out a bottle.

"I was saving this."

"Keep saving it, Lee."

I was about to pull the cork, but his tone stopped me. I leaned the bottle on my knee and looked at him.

"I didn't come here to talk about the trial," Jim said. "I have another job for you — a client who needs a detective. She's a good client, and has been for a long time. So I think

I'd rather bring her a sober man. And a dry one, if you've got another set of clothes around here."

"What's this about?"

"Claire Gravesend."

He was watching to see if I'd react, but the name didn't mean anything.

"I'm supposed to know her?"

"You sold a photograph of her to a tabloid this morning. It's all over the internet."

It took me a second to figure out what he was talking about. I was still keyed up on Lorca and Agent White. Then I remembered my morning walk. My photo credit would have run alongside the picture. For good or ill, the whole world was going to know I took that shot.

"The suicide — what's she have to do with anything?"

"My client is Olivia Gravesend. Claire Gravesend's mother."

"You're talking about *the* Olivia Gravesend."

"Yes."

"The girl I saw this morning — she's the daughter?"

"I just said that."

"Your client's hiring me to do what?"

"Her girl's dead. She wants to know why and how."

"Aren't the police going to tell her that?"

Jim brushed a piece of cigar ash from his lapel.

"She doesn't trust anybody. They ID'd the girl with finger-prints, then sent a man out to her house with photos to make the formal identification. While he was there, he told her it looked like suicide."

"She's worried they're jumping to conclusions."

Jim nodded.

"It's pretty fast," he said. "If they start in that mind-set, they'll have blinders on."

"Did anyone see her jump?" I asked. "If there's a witness, if someone came forward —"

Jim cut me off with a wave of the hand.

"I don't know if there's a witness or not. And if they found someone to make a statement, how much do you trust that? You know how it works. You can buy a city councilman for ten thousand dollars. How much do you think a witness on Turk Street costs?"

I thought about how I'd spent the last several weeks, and what I'd watched this morning. Witnesses were as malleable as any other kind of person. Money wasn't the only thing that shaped testimony. Coercion was just as good, and cheaper.

"You said we're meeting her this evening," I said. "Is she coming here?"

"Her house — if you've got time."

"I was going to leave town for a while," I said.

"Because of today?"

"Mostly."

"Look, Lee — they were threatening him to get the testimony they wanted. We pushed back and he changed his story. We didn't have the same leverage as them, so we used different leverage. He could have been lying until we set him straight."

"Are you drinking the Kool-Aid, or just selling it?" I asked. "DeCanza shit his pants when you brought up Eagle Pass. So we both know what's true. He was terrified of your client, and that says it all."

Jim's silence was as close as he'd come to admitting I was right. Since that was all I'd get, I let it stretch as long as it would go. Jim found a paperclip at the edge of my desk, straightened it out, then bent the wire around his fingertip.

"Can you help Mrs. Gravesend?" he asked. "Or should I find someone else?"

Jim knew how to lure me in. As much as I hated to lose a shot at a client like Olivia Gravesend, I couldn't stand the idea of someone else getting the job. And maybe leaving town wasn't a great plan anyway. The government didn't need me around to make a case against me. If Nammar got a true bill out of a grand jury, someone would be at the airport when I came back. So I might as well just stay here and try to keep on top of it.

"When do we go?" I asked Jim.

"Right now," Jim said. "Go splash some water on your face. Try to look like the kid I used to know. I'll call Titus and tell him to pull around."

We were in the back seat of the Range Rover. Jim rolled up the black privacy screen, which closed us off from his driver, and then he leaned to the humidor built into the console between us. He selected a fat Cohiba. He began to roll the cigar back and forth between his fingers, but made no move to light it.

"What do you know about Olivia Gravesend?" he asked me.

"Public stuff. Whatever's in the papers. You fired me before I ever got to work for her."

Jim let that slide. He used a double-bladed cutter to clip the end off his cigar, then passed the tip a few times beneath his nose.

"She's not like other people in her position," Jim said. "She had family money, sure. And she might have married in to more. But if she'd been born in a shack and married a sharecropper, she'd still be where she is."

"You're saying she's smart."

"Smart doesn't cover it. You're smart. I'm smart. Olivia Gravesend is ruthless."

"But you trust her."

"She's been my client for thirty years. You know the first rule of managing a client like her?"

"No."

"Cover your ass," Jim said. "If Olivia wants something done, she tends to do it herself. If she brings in outside help, it's because she wants a cutout to take the blame. So see to yourself first. Then give her what she wants. But never, ever trust her."

We rode in silence down the length of Market Street. The driver pulled to the curb before we had to turn onto Embarcadero, and Jim opened his door.

"This is it?" I asked. "She lives in your building?"

"This is where I get out," Jim said. "I've got trial in the morning. I don't have time to go all the way out to Carmel and back."

So, as it happened, I left town that night after all, in the back of Jim Gardner's Range Rover, the privacy screen still up and the driver invisible as we raced south on 101. San Mateo, Palo Alto. San Jose just lights and highway signs, and then we were pushing into darker areas. I rested my head against the window and let the pavement glide past. When I smelled garlic I knew we were passing through the fields in Gilroy. After that, I must have fallen asleep for almost an hour.

When I opened my eyes, we were moving south on Highway 1. The curves kept our speed down, but not much. To the right, I caught fast glimpses of the Pacific between the trees. The water was smooth and silver-black in the moonlight. Ten miles like that, and then the road moved inland a little and the driver slowed. He turned onto an unmarked road and headed down toward the sea cliffs. We came to an iron gate, and paused. The gate began to swing open, and we rolled the rest of the way to Olivia Gravesend's house.

I got out of the car and stood looking up at it. It was made of rough-edged sandstone. Its many-tiered roof was covered in Spanish tiles. I counted six chimneys. The air smelled of lavender and eucalyptus and ocean spray. The house was built directly on the cliffs, and the waves were booming just a hundred feet below. Olivia Gravesend could have gone fishing out her bedroom window if she'd wanted to.

Jim's driver, Titus, stayed in the car but shut the engine off. I didn't know what else to do, so I walked to the front door and knocked. A butler met me. White hair, a white shirt beneath a black jacket. His hair was disheveled, and both his shirt and his jacket could have used a pressing. I doubted he always looked this way.

"She's waiting for you in the gun room, sir."

"Okay."

I had no way of knowing if she always met her visitors in the gun room. Maybe she saved it for the special occasions when she had violence on her mind. The walls were English walnut, lined with bespoke French shotguns. A table by the fireplace held an open wooden case with matched dueling pistols lying on green velvet. Olivia Gravesend sat by the cold fireplace in a pose so upright that her straight-backed wooden chair might have felt bad about its posture. She wore a black dress that went to her ankles. Her only jewelry was a small golden medallion. A saint I didn't recognize. She looked at me with eyes matched to the gunmetal all around her.

"You're Lee Crowe. Jim told me about you."

The butler took that as his cue to leave. After he shut the door, I could hear his footsteps moving off.

"Yes, ma'am," I said. "You can call me Lee."

"Don't *ma'am* me, Crowe — it sounds simple."

"All right."

"You photographed my daughter this morning. Why?"

"I saw her, and I shot the scene. I figured I could sell it to the paper."

"Why were you there?"

"It was just luck," I said, and regretted the word. "I was walking past, on my way to the office."

The woman stared at me in silence. Her nose was thin and sharp, like a hawk's beak. Her dark hair was up in a bun, and held in place with wooden pins the way her daughter's had been. Beyond that similarity, they looked nothing like each other.

"You live in that neighborhood — the Tenderloin?"

"No," I said. "I was doing something for Jim. For a different case."

"So you've been lucky today, Crowe," she said. "You got your picture, and you sold it. Now I'm hiring you."

"All right."

"Don't worry about your rates," she said. "Just send the bills."

"I can do that."

"Jim told you what I want?"

"You don't trust the investigation. You want to find out what really happened."

"Jim considers himself an ethical man," Olivia said to me. "Does that surprise you?"

"Absolutely not," I said.

"He looks in the mirror and what does he see? A pillar of the community. A lion of the law. I tell him I'd like to break the rules, so he finds the right man for the job, and stays home. His conscience is clear. We wouldn't want him to feel conflicted, would we?"

"You don't want me to talk about this with him."

"Correct, Crowe," she said. She pointed to another straight-backed chair on the opposite side of the fireplace. I sat down and smoothed my pant legs. "He mentioned you're quick. He also said you'd do whatever it took."

"I've been known to."

"But only if you have to. And you'll keep my name out of it, whatever it is you do."

"Tell me about your daughter."

"She was a good girl. Never mind how she grew up — she was kind."

"This morning, how old was she?"

"Twenty."

"Was she seeing anyone?"

"I don't know."

"What was she doing — college?"

"She'd left school. I don't know what she was doing."

"When was the last time you talked?"

"December, after Christmas. Her birthday."

"You fought?"

"Not at all. We had a glass of brandy. I was in this chair and she was in yours. It was cold; there was a fire. We spoke about her upcoming term. She was excited about a class, a professor she admired. She went back that night."

I looked out the window. Rain was streaming against the old glass. There were a few clear patches of sky, though, giving way to a view of the moon over the ocean.

"What school?"

"Harvard."

"She flew back to Boston?"

"Of course."

"Your plane, or a commercial flight?"

"Neither. My plane was in Vancouver getting a new engine. I hired a charter."

"And she made it there — you know that?"

"Yes," Olivia said. "I spoke to the driver, later. The man who brought her from the airport to our house."

"Your house?"

"My great-grandfather believed in many things. Most of all the utility of a pied-à-terre. You'll find a Gravesend foothold anywhere of consequence."

I tried to imagine how the Gravesends determined the cutoff for that. If I had my facts straight, Olivia Gravesend's great-grandfather had done with copper and gold what Carnegie had done with steel. But Gravesend hadn't pissed his fortune away on libraries for the common man. There could be a lot of houses.

"And after she arrived at her pied-à-terre?"

"She went to one class. And then she disappeared."

"How do you know she went to the class?"

"I talked to the professor, the one she was excited about. It was a journalism class."

"You went to Boston?"

"Twice. And no one's been in the house since January, except for me."

"You know that? There's an alarm system you can monitor from here?"

"I suppose I don't know that," she admitted. "I assume no one has been in but me."

"Is there a cleaning service?"

"She wouldn't allow one."

"Because she liked to take care of it herself, or because she wanted privacy?"

"I don't know."

"Did you take anything from the house?"

"Nothing—and I didn't search it. Both times, I went in and saw she wasn't there, and left."

"You reported her missing?"

"No."

She wanted me to ask why, but I waited her out. She needed to develop a habit of telling me things without a prompt. Her back was even more rigid now than it had been two minutes ago.

"She wrote to me," she finally said. "I hadn't heard from her for two weeks. I'd just started making calls. And then I got her first letter."

"Postmarked from where?"

"San Rafael. She'd come back to California."

"What did the letter say?"

"That I shouldn't worry. There was something she needed to do, and then everything would be fine again."

"Had she ever done anything like that?"

"Never."

42

"The letter was handwritten, and signed?"

"If it hadn't been, I can assure you I'd have done something more. Before you leave, I'll give them to you. There were six. The last one arrived a week ago."

"Postmarked from San Rafael?"

She shook her head.

"They were all different, but all within two hundred miles of San Francisco. The last was from Mendocino."

"Were the two of you close?"

"I want to think so."

"But you didn't know if she was seeing anyone. Was she guarded, or were you too busy to ask?"

Her eyes narrowed on mine, her sharp raptor's nose pointed down.

"It's easier than tiptoeing around," I said. "And I didn't think you were the kind to get offended."

She smiled with some bitter understanding.

"Did Jim call me the Iron Bitch? I know he likes that one. I've met at least three people he's said it to."

"I'm not the fourth."

"I'd fire him, but he's seen too much," she said. If she expected me to follow up on that, she didn't give any sign. "And your question? Claire was guarded. I know I have a reputation. Jim must have told you something. And maybe he's right about me, at least in some parts of my life. In business. In certain personal circles. But with Claire, I was her mother. First, and last."

"I don't—"

"Overwhelming love, Crowe. That's what it means, and it's what I felt for her. What I still feel."

"All right," I said.

"When she was under this roof, she wasn't so guarded. It started when she was eighteen. When she went to Boston."

"She was keeping things from you?"

"I think so," Olivia said. "She's my only child. I have no

43

nieces or nephews. I keep few friends — fewer still with children of their own. So the only point of comparison is my own youth. And I think whatever she was going through was more than the usual. She wasn't just a girl who'd turned eighteen, who'd gone off to college and decided to shut out her mother. There was something else. It got a little worse each year, and then it exploded."

The young woman I'd seen this morning had taken a long dive from a tenement window into the roof of a car, but when I'd found her, she'd looked like she might sit up, brush the blood from her ankle, and walk back to a cocktail party. I could only imagine what she must have looked like before she'd stepped off firm ground and into the air. Which is to say, she didn't look like she'd been on the lam from her mother since Christmas.

"Did she have money of her own?" I asked. "A fund she could tap in to, something to finance these last six months?"

"She had her own money. After she came of age, she got the first ten percent."

"Could you track how she spent it?"

"It was hers. So in a word — no."

"But you have the account information?"

"I *had* it. What it was when I handed it over to her. What she did with it after that, I don't know."

"How much are we talking about?"

"Enough to take care of herself, but not so much that she'd regret it if she made a big mistake."

I was sitting here because I'd photographed Olivia Gravesend's dead daughter, then sold the shot for a thousand dollars. That was money I'd use, regardless of my recent windfall from Jim. I've never had any real money. Being married to Juliette, I'd lived close enough to it that I know I'll never understand it. Take this room, with its rows of shotguns on the wood-paneled walls. Each gun was probably a year's worth of lease payments on my office.

"Mrs. Gravesend," I said. "I'm sorry, but I don't know what that means. I'd regret it if I lost the cash in my wallet right now — fifteen dollars. I know you're on a different level. Are we talking about a hundred thousand? Two hundred fifty?"

Her eyes tracked slowly from my shoes to my shirt collar. She was probably pricing everything I had on, which couldn't have added up to whatever she'd paid for her nail polish. I was glad I'd had dry clothes at the office.

"Twenty million," she said. Doing the math, she glanced at the oak-beamed ceiling. "Rounded down."

"That was a tenth of what she stood to get?"

"Yes."

"The rest came when?"

"Her thirtieth birthday. And that money was just a start. She was to receive the entire estate when I pass."

"That was irrevocable, or could you amend it?"

"I could do anything. And she knew it."

"Meaning she had every reason to stick around. To stay in your good graces."

"Certainly," Olivia said. She drew her shoulders together and held herself. "If that's what it took."

I glanced around again. To say this house was neatly kept would be an understatement. The air was filtered and scrubbed, and bore the antiseptic smell of eucalyptus. Beyond that, the place was curated. A long hallway held the portraits of Olivia Gravesend's humorless forbearers, each canvas framed in gold and lit from below with a single spotlight. Bronze plaques gave dates of birth and death. I'd been greeted at the door by a butler. He'd been worse for wear, but uniformed all the same. He'd escorted me through acres of the house before reaching the gun room. I wouldn't have guessed even one person lived here, let alone two. There were exhibits, like the dueling pistols, but there was nothing personal.

"Are you married, Mrs. Gravesend?"

"Occasionally."

"Now?"

"No," she said. "And not for the last five years."

"So . . . fair to say Claire wasn't having trouble with a step-father?"

"More than fair," she said.

"What about her own father?"

"She never met him, and she never asked about him."

"Were you married to him?"

"No," she said. "I wasn't. And what's that have to do with anything?"

"You didn't know if she was seeing anyone," I answered. "So I'm asking about the other men around her."

Olivia squinted into the fireplace.

"Because if you want to know who killed a woman," she said, "then you start with the men in her life. The ones she's closest to. Those are the odds."

I nodded, and we sat for a moment. It was the least uncomfortable silence we'd had so far. But I broke it with another question.

"Jim said someone from the medical examiner visited you today. Anyone else?"

"No one."

"Does SFPD know she'd been missing for more than six months?"

"They couldn't have had a clue," she said. "Unless she kept a diary in her purse."

Of course she'd seen the purse. It was in my photograph.

"But that's the kind of thing you can find out—what they really know," she continued.

"They don't hand that stuff out."

"But you could break in, and take the file. Or pay a bribe. Or find an inside man with a weak spot, and lean on him until he cracks."

Now I was the one wondering how much Jim had said.

When I'd worked in his firm, there wasn't much that set me apart from the hundred other attorneys on my floor. We wore identical suits and the same polished wingtips. Any one of us could recite the California Rules of Professional Conduct from memory. Our only crimes were our billable rates. I hadn't yet bought my Smith and Wesson. I didn't know how to bare-hand punch a man in the face without breaking all my fingers on his teeth. It wasn't until everything crashed down around me that Jim understood how useful I really was. I wasn't as clean as my brogues. I'd never belonged in a suit. He fired me, but he walked me out of the building himself. I was dirty, he said, to anyone listening. I was an embarrassment to the firm. I wasn't cut out for a corner office. In fact, I wasn't any better than my father. No one would ever forget he'd died in jail, after kiting a bad check.

But then we were in the elevator, alone. He told me if I wanted to work on the street and in the shadows—if I wanted to embrace my nature, be a blunt instrument—I could call him anytime. I don't know what I felt, but it certainly wasn't gratitude. By then I'd lost everything but an image of myself, and even that was disintegrating. I'd thought I was a fighter, the kind of guy who'd never run. But Jim was showing me to the exit, and when we got there, my plan was to keep on going.

Olivia Gravesend was watching me, waiting for me to respond.

"Maybe I could get the files," I said. It was actually a foregone conclusion that I would get the files. That would probably be the easiest thing about the case. "The fee will go up, of course. Either a little or a lot, depending on what I have to do."

"I'll pay."

"What makes you think they're hiding something?"

"What makes you think they're not? You know the place," she said. She paused long enough to give me the chance to

47

nod. "Most of them aren't working for the public—they're on the take. But you'd expect they'd pull it together and work for me. They sent an intern to me, with her pictures. A college kid. I called them, after—"

"Called who?"

"The chief of police. The mayor."

"They talked to you?"

Her laugh was a bitter cough.

"I got a runaround. I was leaving messages with secretaries. They had me talking to pageboys. They're talking to the press more than they're talking to me. The phone rang an hour ago, and it was a reporter. She called and asked for a comment. What do I think about my girl committing suicide?"

"What do you think is going on?"

"I don't know, Crowe. But it has to go way up. If that's how they treat me—Olivia Gravesend, the Iron Bitch who owns a piece of half the elected officials in this state—then whatever Claire got herself into was huge."

6

I SPENT ANOTHER ten minutes talking with Mrs. Gravesend in the gun room, and then she rang a bell and the butler came for me. He led me down a marbled hall and up a staircase to the door of Claire's childhood bedroom. He rocked the handle to show me it was locked.

"We cleaned it once after Claire left in December," the old man said. Before he'd answered the bell, he must have been doing something outside. He was wearing a topcoat now, and it was spattered with rain. "And then after the first letter came, Ms. Gravesend shut it up."

"Why?" I asked. "Did she think Claire wasn't coming back?"

"She didn't say that."

But she must have thought it was a possibility. Maybe she'd had other motivations, but either way, she'd taken steps to preserve evidence. That wasn't a guilty act, but it was an odd one. There must have been something about Claire's letters that set off alarm bells beyond what their text seemed to warrant.

"You knew Claire?"

"Since she was a little one."

"Were you surprised, what happened?"

"Of course, sir."

"Why?"

"Things like this, they shouldn't happen to people like the Gravesends, should they?"

"Who should they happen to?"

"No one, sir. But you wouldn't expect them here."

"You wouldn't."

He took out a key ring, sorted it in his palm, and then unlocked the door. He pushed it open but didn't step inside.

"What do you think?" I asked. "Was Claire in trouble?"

"I wouldn't have thought it in December," the old man said. "But knowing what I know now—that she ran away, that she jumped off a roof—I should imagine so. She must have been in trouble."

"But you don't have any idea what?"

"No, sir."

"Did you read the letters?"

"No, sir."

I went into the bedroom and switched on the light. The butler closed the door behind me.

I stood in front of an eleven-foot armoire, turned a little brass key that had been left sitting in the lock, and pulled the doors open. The thing was nearly empty; Claire must have taken all her favorite clothes to Boston. She probably took everything that meant anything to her. Diaries and letters. Gifts from the people who loved her, the people she didn't want to forget. I scanned the room again. Above the bed, a signed Klimt hung in a glittery frame. I doubted it was a reproduction. On the shelf above her writing desk, there were novels she might have read for a high school literature class. Tolstoy, Austen, García Márquez. There was also a sizable collection of books with misty cover art and gold-leaf jacket lettering. This was a teenager's bedroom. But in the time since Claire had moved out of this house, she'd grown into a young woman. A different person, perhaps. Boston would be the more interesting place to search.

Still, I turned back to the open armoire. There were a few school uniforms — white blouses, plaid skirts, navy blazers. I rifled through the clothes folded in the lower drawers but didn't find anything. Running socks that had been paired and rolled into balls; cotton panties; a few T-shirts.

At the matching vanity, I found half a dozen tubes of lipstick, the colors spanning a narrow band of the spectrum from coral pink to blood red. There was a mostly empty bottle of Dead Sexy perfume, a skull and crossbones emblazoned on its front. Two drawers held a collection of eyebrow pencils and assorted gold-plated grooming instruments. Nail clippers, tweezers, and scissors. There was a hairbrush, and when I held it up to the light, I saw a blond hair caught in the bristles. It had come out root and all. That could be useful. I took a receipt from my wallet and folded it around the blond strand, then tucked it behind a maxed-out credit card. I'd have it if I needed it.

The rest of the room yielded nothing, and the less I found, the more I searched. I lifted the mattress and checked under the box spring; I pulled the drawers out and checked underneath them. I opened the curtains and looked out the window, but there was nowhere to go there — a sheer drop to the ocean.

If Claire had wanted to jump out a window to her death, she didn't need to be in the Refugio Apartments in the heart of the Tenderloin. She could have just come home.

"Sir?"

I turned from the window. The butler was in the doorway, eyeing the tipped-up mattress and the drawers stacked on the floor.

"If you're finished in here, Mr. Garland's driver will take you back to the city."

I'd forgotten all about the driver. I looked at my watch and saw it was nearly midnight.

"Mrs. Gravesend said there were letters from Claire."

"They're in Mr. Garland's vehicle."

"Copies, or the originals?"

"The originals, sir."

"When can I see the Boston place?"

"You'd have to ask Mrs. Gravesend, sir."

"I'll do that," I said. I stepped past him and into the hall. "She's still in the gun room?"

"No, sir," the butler said. "I'm afraid she's left the house."

"Funeral arrangements?"

The butler studied his shoes as he answered.

"I believe she went to the Carmel Mission."

"I see," I said. I started for the stairs. When the man began to follow me, I waved him off. "Don't — I can find my own way out."

"I'm sure," he said. And then he tailed me to the door.

Back in the Range Rover, I turned on an overhead light and opened the packet Olivia had left for me. There was an envelope with the keys to the Boston house. The Beacon Street address was written on the back flap. I took that to mean I could go anytime I wanted. Then there were the six brief letters from Claire. She'd used plain white paper, and what looked like the same pen. For all I knew, she might have written all the notes in one sitting, and then mailed them over a span of six months. Olivia could attest to the handwriting, but that didn't prove the letters were written voluntarily. Claire could have been taking dictation, with a gun muzzle between her shoulder blades.

In any case, the first letter was exactly as Olivia Gravesend had described it.

Mother,
    I'm leaving school for a little while. I can always come back; what I need to do now won't

wait. Don't worry about me. Don't call the police.
I can take care of myself. You taught me how.
— Claire

The next five letters were variations on the original theme. *Don't worry, Mother, I've got this under control. I need to do this, and then I'll pick up where I left off.* And in the last note, one week ago, she'd hinted that she was almost done. Whatever she'd been searching for was within her reach. *Two days,* she wrote. *Maybe three.*

The letters were anodyne. There was no fear in them. They hardly contained any information at all. If she'd written them in the 1950s, I would have assumed she'd gotten pregnant, that she was disappearing to a home for unwed mothers and would be back in nine or ten months. It was still at least a possibility. Claire had pressures most young women didn't have to consider these days. Her mother could cut her out of a hundred and eighty million dollars for any reason at all.

But I'd seen Claire. I might not have been the last person to see her alive, but I was probably the last to touch her while she was still warm. She hadn't been six months pregnant. And for that matter, she wouldn't have needed to miss an entire semester to get an abortion.

Whatever she was taking care of, it probably wasn't an unplanned pregnancy. It could still be something in that neighborhood. A problematic boyfriend. A quickie marriage and wild honeymoon. But I was having trouble imagining how either of those scenarios would culminate in an heiress jumping from the roof of a Tenderloin tenement. The only thing that fit Claire's lifestyle was the Rolls, and as far as I could tell, that was just a freak coincidence.

I fell asleep somewhere north of Salinas and didn't wake again until the driver rolled to a gentle stop and tapped the horn. I looked out the window and saw the stairs leading up to my office. I thought about knocking on the privacy screen and asking him to take me to my apartment in Chinatown. But the guy's night had been long enough already. He'd have to be up early to get Jim to trial. So I got out, and stepped over a bum sleeping on my bottom step. He had bands of white medical tape on both his forearms, as though the only thing he had left to sell was his own blood. The sight of it made me think of Claire again, and how far she had fallen. At least the guy on my steps was still above the ground.

7

UPSTAIRS, I PUT Claire's letters in my safe and her house keys in my pocket. The last unsold seat to Boston was in first class, but Olivia Gravesend was good for it. The plane left at eight, which gave me four and a half hours.

I figured I could sleep in the air, and could buy whatever I needed once I got there. So with time to kill, I did what I'd become accustomed to that spring. I went out and walked down Turk Street, into the Tenderloin. But instead of the Westchester, this time I went to the Refugio.

The sidewalk out front was clear. Nothing left from the morning but a few pieces of windshield glass. Snowsuit Man was gone. At the corner, a car was idling beneath a darkened streetlamp. A man leaned through the open window, transacting business of one kind or another. Otherwise the street was dead.

The Refugio's front door was locked. I'd anticipated that. Every apartment building in the Tenderloin was locked, accessible only by an electronic keypad. I didn't know the code, but I had something just as good. The police were in and out of here on a nightly basis. They couldn't be expected to know the codes to all the tenements on Turk Street, so most doors in the Tenderloin had a code box that they could open with a squawk from their handheld radios. I didn't have a police radio, but I had a phone. I took it out and played my pre-recorded SFPD squawk, and watched the light on the box turn from red to green. I went in.

The lobby was dark enough that I had to turn on my phone's flashlight. I saw a desk, but I doubted there was a receptionist even in the daytime. The floor behind it was littered with needles and short lengths of surgical tubing. Glassine bags and dried vomit.

I found the mail room. There were no names on any of the steel boxes, so I didn't linger there. Both elevators were out of service, but I wouldn't have gotten into an elevator in a building like this anyway. I found a stairwell and began to climb, using my light to pick a path around the needles and liquor bottles and unidentifiable lumps. It was impossible to imagine someone like Claire Gravesend climbing these steps and not immediately turning around.

But she must have, and so I considered how I could narrow my search.

She'd hit the car hard enough to flatten it, and the Wraith was built like a tank. Either she weighed a lot more than appearance would suggest, or she'd had the vertical space to accelerate until her small frame packed more of a punch. So I skipped floors two through seven and started on the eighth. I came out of the stairwell into a wide hallway, which made an angular lap around the inside of the building. If Claire had come out of an apartment window, it had been a corner unit on the right side of the building. There was a wide crack under the door to Apartment 801, but it was dark. I'd broken in, and didn't particularly want to explain myself to the police. So I went up, floor by floor, until I found a light under the door of Apartment 1201.

I knocked, one knuckle against the wood. *Tap, tap.* I waited ten seconds, and tried it again. I wasn't really expecting anything, but then I heard a soft voice from behind the door.

"Yes?"

"Ma'am," I said. The gentlest voice I could manage after the day I'd just had. "I'd like to talk to you about yesterday morning."

The door opened until it jerked to a halt on the chain. I was looking at an eighty- or ninety-year-old woman in a wheelchair. Which meant she likely hadn't left the apartment since the elevators had gone out of service. That could've been years ago.

"Do you know about the young woman who fell outside this morning?"

"I saw her from my window."

"You saw it happen?"

"No — I saw after."

"What did you see?"

"She was on top of a car. A man came along and touched her neck. Then he took pictures of her."

It shouldn't have worried me that there was a witness to what I'd done. The photographs themselves were evidence that I'd come across her before anyone else, and that I'd done nothing.

"You heard her hit the car?"

"A loud bang — it woke me up," she said. Then she gestured at the wheelchair. "But it took me a while to get out of bed and to the window."

"Did you hear anything before the bang?" I asked. "An argument, or voices, or anything at all?"

"I was asleep."

"Right," I said. I only had one question left to ask her. "Did the police knock on your door this morning?"

"I told them everything I told you," she said. "They asked to come in, and they showed me their badges. So I let them in."

"Did you hear anything else after you let them in?"

"No."

"No commotion upstairs or downstairs — someone getting arrested?"

"Nothing."

She started to close the door, and I thought of one last thing. I put my hand on the jamb and stopped the door.

"Ma'am — did the police ask you how long the elevator's been out?"

"No."

"I could make some calls for you," I said. "The health department. The building department."

"Don't you dare," she hissed. I could see her small, sharp teeth. "If I make trouble, they'll kick me out. And if I lose this place, where would I go?"

"All right," I said, and thanked her again.

I kept going, and checked the two apartments above her next. They were both dark. I went back to the stairwell and climbed the last flight to the roof. The door that led out should have been locked, but the lock had been punched a long time ago. I put my hand on the metal and felt the fine grit of fingerprint powder. The cops were covering all the bases. I shoved the door open, and then I was out of the stench and into the rain, nothing above me but the sky.

I walked across the gravel to the waist-high brick balustrade, and stood where Claire would have if she'd gone off the roof and not out a window. The Refugio was five floors higher than any other building in the area. So I was looking down on Turk Street and over the dark roofs of a dozen other apartments and SRO hotels.

I didn't know what I'd hoped to find up there. Even if Claire had left a note on the railing, the police would have found it this morning. I wondered if I should go back and pound on the doors to all the corner apartments. It's what I would do if I were a policeman. But I wouldn't find anything they hadn't uncovered already, and I might get myself arrested in the process.

What I really needed were the police reports, and the work-up from the medical examiner. I looked at my watch. There was plenty of time. I could get the documents delivered by email and read them on the plane.

8

IF YOU EVER hire a private investigator, before you start complaining about his rates, consider that most of his money goes right out the door to keep up his overhead. Sources only take cash, and an investigator — a good one, anyway — has eyes everywhere. It adds up fast, and when tax time comes, it's not as though you can take a deduction on a bribe.

One of my earliest discoveries in cost-cutting was the nightshift. Either nocturnal workers perceive less risk, or they just have less to lose. Whichever it is, their monthly envelopes aren't as thick as their diurnal counterparts' payoffs, and they're usually eager for extra work for extra pay. All of which is to say I had the Hall of Justice, on Bryant Street, pretty well covered after dark.

My inside track to the Homicide Detail was a janitor who usually got to the sixth floor around three a.m. Elijah moved from office to office, and through the maze of cubicles, wheeling a trash can and a dust mop. When no one was watching, he was uncannily fast with a camera phone. In the medical examiner's suite, I had Cynthia Green. As the records custodian, she had a space to herself, and access to a scanner.

I was still up on the Refugio's roof when I took out my phone and started typing messages. I asked Cynthia for all the files on Claire Gravesend. I asked Elijah for anything on the woman who'd jumped off the Refugio Apartments and into a Rolls Royce Wraith yesterday morning. Both of my sources answered before I reached the ground floor; they'd get me what they could.

I headed toward Union Square, where you could find something to eat at any hour. I sat at the counter in the Pinecrest Diner, where I took my time with four cups of coffee and a Denver omelet. The man beside me left early on, abandoning his paper. I grabbed it, but set it aside when I saw it was already a day old. I had my phone, though.

The *Chronicle*'s website didn't have anything new on Lorca, which was fine with me. If that story could die in a dark corner, I'd send flowers. But there was a piece about Claire Gravesend, which included a photograph I hadn't taken: two patrol officers flanking a plainclothes inspector, all three of them exiting the Refugio. They wore latex gloves and had surgical masks pulled down from their mouths. The caption identified the inspector as Frank Chang. The story didn't contain anything I didn't already know — a young heiress likely had committed suicide by jumping off a tenement roof and into a parked luxury car. The police had no comment; the medical examiner's report hadn't been released at the time of writing.

I texted Elijah, who was probably almost done with his rounds in Homicide Detail: *Check Frank Chang's desk. It's his case.*

Compared to Elijah, Cynthia Green in the medical examiner's office had it easy. She was looking for an alphabetized file in a system that she maintained from the privacy of her own office. Elijah was looking for notes taken by multiple officers in an ongoing investigation. He was rifling through inboxes and inspectors' desktops. The documents he was looking for wouldn't be in one place; the investigation was too new. In the first twenty-four hours, documents and notes would be scattered all over the department. They'd be in patrol officers' notebooks, or sitting on a cruiser's dashboard, or filed in a cop's brain, not on paper yet at all. I could only cross my fingers and hope something had trickled up to Inspector Chang, and that Elijah would find it.

I put my phone away and paid my tab.

I found a cab and headed to the airport. Halfway there, I began getting one email after another. Elijah and Cynthia were coming through.

Outside of my boarding gate, I started my fifth cup of coffee and went through Elijah's photographs a second time. He had snapped an image of every piece of paper in Inspector Chang's inbox, and Chang was clearly a busy man. There was a ballistics report from an unsolved shooting on Valencia; a witness statement from that same shooting; a subpoena to appear at a deposition in what looked like a civil rights case against one of Chang's fellow officers; a handwritten letter from a Folsom inmate who claimed to know the triggerman in a 1977 North Beach hit — and buried in that, two pages of notes written by Sergeant Luke Gifford, describing the results of a door-knocking expedition in the Refugio.

Like me, the police had focused on the corner units on the right side of the building. Unlike me, Sergeant Gifford had gone inside every unit from 201 to 1401. He'd had the building supervisor with him, who unlocked any door that wasn't opened by a resident. Gifford's search might not have passed muster under the Fourth Amendment, but that hardly mattered. He hadn't found anything, so there was no evidence to exclude.

His notes opened the doors that had been closed to me that morning.

#201 — Estelle Ramirez. Wit. shows ID and invites me in. Tells mgr. to keep out. Makeshift beds on floors. Six children in one bdrm unit. All heard bang, but nbdy checked outside. Assumed car crash. Can't pinpoint time — no clocks / watches. Never seen vic. in building. Wit. consents to search — nothing of interest.

#301 — Unit vacant since April. Mgr. opens door. Trash from last tenant still inside. Rat nest under kchn sink. No items from vic.

#401 — Simone Anderson opens door. Mgr. says wit. is tenant and she is 19. Bruises on neck, face — not fresh. Mgr. says we need to check unit. She lets us in. One mattress in bdrm. Window blacked out with cardboard boxes. Wit. says: I work nights, need to keep light out. Never seen vic. in building or neighborhood. Out till 8 a.m. No one else lives in / uses unit. Mgr. confirms. Wit. consents to search — nothing.

Gifford went on, through ten more floors and ten more units. The wheelchair-bound woman in 1201 was named Leola Cummings. If the sergeant noticed she was effectively a prisoner, he didn't write it down. But I couldn't say I blamed him. Before reaching Leola, he'd been through eleven other apartments that were just as bad. Gifford had also searched the roof, noting the unlocked door. A forensics technician came up and dusted the entire building for prints.

Outside, along the balustrade where Claire would have been standing before she jumped, Gifford found an empty bottle of Seagram's 7. He'd bagged it for the labs. If the bottle had her fingerprints or DNA, then a story might slide into focus. It would neither prove anything nor rule anything out, but it would be suggestive.

Other than the bottle, Gifford hadn't taken any evidence from the Refugio. And except for the bottle, he'd found nothing, either in an apartment or on the roof, that might be connected to Claire. I was trying to decide what to make of that, when I turned to the preliminary autopsy report. The first ten pages were photographs. By the time I'd reached the second, I had forgotten all about Sergeant Gifford and his search.

For five minutes, I just looked at the photographs. When the airline's agents got on the PA to announce early boarding, I stepped away from the line of passengers and moved to the far side of the gate. This was a conversation I didn't want my fellow passengers to overhear.

"Did I wake you?" I asked, when she answered.

"This is Crowe?"

"Yes."

"You have news."

"The lead inspector on the case is a man named Frank Chang—"

"That was in the paper."

"And I have the notes his officer took when he went door to door in the Refugio, along with everything else in his inbox," I said. "I do more than read the paper. And I'm bringing him up for a reason. Expect him to come and see you today. He's at a dead end. His next logical step is to talk to someone who knew the victim."

"I see."

"Will you tell him about Claire's letters?"

"Absolutely not."

"They're the best lead in the case."

"Which is why I gave them to you, Crowe."

"He's got resources I don't," I said. "Forensics labs, DNA and print databases, document experts—"

"Whatever he has, you can buy."

Jim's other client, the upstanding citizen otherwise known as Lorca, had also given me carte blanche on my investigative activities. My rent at the Westchester hadn't amounted to much, but I had found ways to pad the bill.

When all this came to an end, I was going to have to get used to normal people again.

"All right," I said.

"Was there anything else?"

"I have a copy of the preliminary report from the medical examiner's office."

"Send it to me."

If she was impressed with what I could get in less than five hours, she didn't let it slip into her voice.

"It has photographs — graphic photographs," I said. "Including one of her back."

"Undressed, I presume."

"What made those scars, Mrs. Gravesend? The photos are very clear."

There was a long silence. From the overhead PA speaker, the gate agent announced that she was now boarding all rows and all passengers for Boston.

"Those are not your problem," she answered. "As far as Claire was concerned, she'd always had them. They didn't bother her. They didn't give her any pain. They didn't embarrass her. She was a beautiful young woman with everything to live for. I believe in my heart that she knew that."

"I can't do this if you're not straight with me."

"She didn't jump off that building," Olivia said. "Don't start on that path, not for one second. So unless you think somebody threw her out a window because he didn't like the look of her backside, the scars have nothing to do with it."

"What were they — some kind of medical procedure?"

"They are none of your concern, Crowe," she said, pausing between each word for emphasis.

"Was she sick?"

"She was as healthy as she looked in your goddamned photograph. And congratulations — the magazine you sold it to licensed it to every internet news site that ever hung out a shingle. I hope you get your cut."

That contingency was covered in a licensing clause on page three. But for once, I wasn't focused on the money.

"If there's a history of abuse, I need to know now."

"Under my roof — never."

"She left school and disappeared for six months. What was she looking for?"

"I already told you," she said. "I don't know."

"When Inspector Chang comes, he's going to ask about the scars. Don't sit there in your gun room and pretend he won't. You'll want a better answer."

"I'll take that into consideration," she said. "Was there anything else?"

"No."

There was another PA announcement, the final call for my flight. I walked across the now empty gate and handed my boarding pass to the agent.

"I gather you're at the airport," Olivia said.

"I'll call you again from Boston."

"Do that," she said. "And send me the documents."

She hung up.

I walked down the jetway, onto the plane, and found my seat in first class. I had been using my phone all night and all morning, and now it was dying. There was enough juice left to email the reports to Olivia, and then the screen went dark. That was fine with me. I could buy a charger in Boston, and for this flight, I just needed to think. And sleep.

I took the glass of orange juice the flight attendant offered me, and I stretched out in my seat. The jetway rolled back. I closed my eyes and saw Claire Gravesend on the crushed car, rain pooling around her. On a stainless-steel autopsy table, stripped of her dress and her jewelry and the dignity that she had somehow held on to until then. In the first of the medical examiner's photographs, she'd been face-up. In the second, they'd flipped her over. There'd been a deep red gash in the back of her head, and an even bigger one across

66

her buttocks, which must have hit the car first. Those were the only recent injuries, and none of them surprised me.

What I hadn't expected were the scars. I had never seen anything like them.

On either side of her spine, from the bottom of her head to her lower back, where the waistline of her panties would have almost hidden them, there were matched sets of old wounds. One pair for every vertebra. The scars were almost perfectly round. Some were the size of silver dollars, and others no bigger than dimes. There were smaller circles at the crest of each hip. An array of smaller dots had spread like unfolding wings across each of her shoulder blades.

Every wound had been perfectly placed, enhancing her body's bilateral symmetry. It might have been some kind of body art, scarification instead of a tattoo, but there had been no particular beauty in the wounds. They were ugly raised welts, wrinkled and pink. It was hard to imagine a scar like that could have come from a single wound. Someone must have cut into her over and over again.

And according to Olivia Gravesend, Claire had carried them all her life.

9

I WOKE UP somewhere over the Midwest. The plane was skirting a thunderstorm, the ride was bumpy, and I was thinking about Agent White. I'd left nothing behind in the Westchester. I was sure of that. But White might have seen me in the neighborhood. He might find residents of the hotel willing to identify me as the man who'd spent five weeks on the sixth floor. If he got far enough to search my former room, there was nothing. If he got a warrant and searched my apartment or my office, there was nothing. I'd dropped every piece of surveillance gear, and every memory stick, into a Tenderloin dumpster.

By now, they had almost surely braced DeCanza. They might have learned about the phone and the whiskey. The phone was a secondhand piece, paid for in cash. Like buying a gun on the street. They weren't going to trace its serial number to a store, then catch my face on a security camera. On the other hand, White didn't strike me as a quitter. You don't go after a man like Lorca if you're the type to shy away from a hard problem.

I'd boarded the plane hoping for some sleep. By the time we landed, I hadn't gotten much.

It was late in the afternoon when I stepped into a cab. I didn't have a hotel room, a return flight, or any kind of plan.

The closest I'd been to Boston was an eighth grade class trip to Washington, D.C.

Buying my ticket last night, I'd looked at a map of Boston, so I had a general idea of where we were headed. It didn't take long. We went into a tunnel and emerged into a warren of narrow streets, and in fifteen minutes the driver turned onto Beacon. The Common was on our left, and to the right, shoulder-to-shoulder brick and brownstone townhouses. Some of them had flower boxes under the windows, and some had Betsy Ross flags on poles that leaned out above the sidewalk, and I would have bet that every one of them was worth ten times what I would make in a lifetime.

I saw River Street up ahead. We were within a few hundred yards of Claire's place.

"Here's fine," I said.

The driver turned to the curb and stopped. Once I'd paid him, I got out and crossed the street to the park side. I walked the last block and a half to the Gravesends' Boston foothold, and then I lingered in the shade of a maple tree to take a look at the place. Most of the houses on this stretch of Beacon were redbrick, but the Gravesend place was built of smooth gray stone, the front wall gently curved like the top of a violin. The front door was above sidewalk level, reached by a set of stone steps. The place was five stories, with a pitched slate roof. It could have served as the consulate for some small European principality. A country with money to burn. Monaco, San Marino.

The windows were uncovered — no shutters and no curtains. There weren't any lights on inside, but there were polished brass lanterns on either side of the door, and each one softly flickered with a gas flame. I walked back to the intersection and crossed Beacon. Instead of going up the steps to Claire's door, I went to her next-door neighbor's. I rang the bell and waited. I didn't have anything else to do. After two minutes, I rang the bell again. The second time, the door opened, and a young woman stepped out. She was holding a naked baby, wrapped in a towel. The baby's hair was slicked down with water.

"Sorry," she said. "We were tied up."

"I didn't mean to bother you," I said. "My name's Lee Crowe, and I need to ask a couple of questions."

I held out my California private investigator's license. It was basically just a light green card with my name and registration number on it, but the California seal made it look official. I'd laminated it at a copy shop, and kept it in a leather holder with a passport photograph on the left, which made it look even better.

"Look," the woman said. The baby was squirming against her chest, hiding his face in her neck. "This isn't my house. I just work here, and so —"

"It's nothing to do with you. Or him," I said. I indicated the place next door. "I'm working for the next-door owner. Mrs. Gravesend."

"You mean Claire?"

"Have you seen her around lately?"

"Yesterday," the woman said. "But it was weird."

Weird was an understatement. Yesterday Claire had died, on the other side of the country. I kept my face even.

"I don't understand," I said.

"I was up there." She was holding the baby with both arms, so she couldn't point. She glanced upward. I followed her eyes to a three-paneled bay window on the third floor of her employer's house. "Sitting in the window. And Claire came up the steps, and knocked on her own door. And then she pounded on it. Like, slapping it really hard with her palms. She waited for five minutes, and then she went across the street."

I followed the woman's gaze a second time. She was looking at the maple tree I'd chosen earlier.

"And then?"

"I wasn't really paying attention. I was rocking him. I saw her there for a while, and then she was gone. I thought maybe she was locked out."

"What time was this?" I asked.

"I don't know. Yesterday afternoon. Sometime before six o'clock, because I was still here. I take a dinner break at six," she said. Her face tightened as she thought of something. "Is she okay? Why are you asking about her?"

"You're sure it was Claire?"

"I mean — yes."

"How well do you know her?" I asked.

"Not well," she said. She shifted the baby to her hip, and began to bounce him up and down. "But we talked now and then. And yesterday, when she was knocking on her door, she had her hair up. Like in a bun. So I could see the scars on the back of her neck."

"Round scars?"

"Yes."

"Did Claire ever tell you how she got them?"

"Are you — You said you were working for her."

"I'm working for her mother," I said. "Did she ever tell you how she got the scars?"

"I didn't know her well," she said. She was already retreating into the house. "It's really not my place to get into her business. Maybe this wasn't such a good idea."

She began to shut the door, and when I put my hand out, she slammed it quickly. I heard the dead bolts turn.

"Thank you for your time," I said to the door. "I appreciate it."

I found my way to a drugstore and bought a phone charger and a box of latex gloves, then walked around Beacon Hill. Soon, the nanny would go on her dinner break. Given the way our conversation had ended, I didn't want her watching through the bay windows as I entered Claire's house. If she'd been suspicious enough after our conversation to Google Claire's name, there was no predicting what she might do next.

For that matter, I had no idea what I should do next, or how I should catalog her statements to me. She hadn't struck me as a liar, so I'd been ready to write it off as a case of mistaken identity. But then she'd mentioned the scars on the back of Claire's neck. She must have mixed up the days. What she'd seen could have taken place the day before yesterday, in which case Claire would have had plenty of time to catch the last San Francisco-bound flight. She'd have arrived a little after ten p.m., leaving six hours to roam the Tenderloin until she found her way to the Refugio.

At least that was possible. The only other alternative was entirely improbable — that hours after Claire's death on the West Coast, someone was walking around Boston impersonating her.

I wandered down a narrow alleyway. The homes here were smaller. Carriage houses, maybe, or servants' quarters. I tried to picture what Claire's life in this city would have been like. She'd come when she was just eighteen, and all at once, she'd become the mistress of a five-floor mansion on Beacon Street. Twenty million dollars in the bank, and no one to answer to but herself. It was a miracle she'd held out as long as she did. Put me in the same circumstances at eighteen, and inside of two weeks, I'd have been broke, dead, or in jail.

At half past six, I turned back onto Beacon Street, walked to Claire's house with the key already in my gloved hand, unlocked the massive oak-plank door, and stepped inside. The street noise disappeared as soon as the door was closed. Light from the transom window illuminated a brick wall twenty feet in front of me. A portrait of Colonel Gravesend glared down at me. He had Olivia's dark hair and thin, sharp features. I reached back to lock the door, and then looked down. The hardwood floor had been waxed, but its polished surface was covered with a light layer of dust. I knelt to take off my shoes, leaving on my socks. There was a hint of perfume in the air.

I started at the bottom and worked my way up. The whole house had been thoroughly redone since Colonel Gravesend bought it or built it. The basement was a bar and lounge area. White carpet, furniture carved from clear maple. A set of retractable glass doors led to a sunken courtyard in the back, with an ivy-covered fireplace and a table with benches. Everything outside was made of quarried stone slabs as thick as railroad ties. I went back inside, behind the bar. The liquor shelves were ready to handle anything. So was the wine cellar, which I found by lifting a trapdoor behind the wet bar and climbing down an oak ladder until I was standing in a dimly lit grotto of arched brick. Every bottle was covered in dust. I pulled one out, at random, and turned the label to the overhead light. It was a 1922 Vale do Douro port. I set it back carefully. There were probably a thousand bottles in the cellar, and there were no empty spaces on the racks. Claire must have spent her free time developing other tastes.

It wasn't until the fourth floor that I found any sign that Claire had actually lived in the house. The lower floors were a museum, not unlike her mother's place in Carmel. A catalog kitchen, a formal dining room, a library and billiards room. Fireplaces in all the guest bedrooms, birch logs stacked artfully on the sootless andirons. The beds were made up, but smelled musty.

On the fourth floor, I found Claire's bedroom. Her clothes hung in the closet, and her toiletries were scattered in the bathroom. Lipsticks in subtle nude colors, a stick of clear deodorant, a prescription bottle with no label and three capsules of Adderall inside — the only indication I'd seen so far that an honest-to-god college student lived in this house.

I found a bottle of perfume and picked it up to smell the spritzer. It was the source of the scent I'd noticed when I first came into the house.

There was a narrower, steeper set of stairs that led from the fourth floor to the fifth. This had evidently been an attic before being reinvented as a sky-lit loft; Claire had turned it into her study. A desk was positioned in the center of the room, where it would get the most sunlight. All four walls were lined with bookshelves, and they weren't filled with leather-bound volumes printed and purchased to be displayed, like the shelves in the second-floor library. These books were meant to be read, and judging by their spines, they had been.

According to Olivia, Claire was concentrating in English, but from what I could see, that was only her opening bid. I circled the room, head tilted to read the titles. *The Making of the Atomic Bomb; Darwin: A Life; The Feynman Lectures on Physics; The Second Creation.* There was a clear trend in the titles. In her private reading, Claire was majoring in the physical world, with a minor in genetics.

I slid a volume off the shelf. *A Crack in Creation.* The author was a Berkeley professor, but we'd never crossed paths. She was in the Department of Molecular and Cell Biology, and I'd wandered through on a boxing scholarship. I thumbed the pages, hoping Claire had left notes, or underlined passages. But if the text had elicited any reaction from her, she'd kept it to herself.

I shelved the book and sat at her desk. There was a pencil drawer in the middle, the usual assortment of ballpoint pens and sticky notes and paperclips in a plastic tray. I lifted the tray and found an envelope taped to the bottom. I pulled it off and opened it over the leather blotter. A new brass house key and a smaller key tumbled out. There was no writing on the envelope. I put it back under the tray and dropped the keys in my pocket.

I opened the largest drawer and found a stack of lined composition books. I pulled them out, set them on the blotter, and counted them. Thirty-five notebooks, a hundred sheets each, and every page covered in the fine script I recognized from the letters Olivia had given me. Apparently, in this age of tablets and laptops, the heiress took her class notes by hand.

I looked at my watch, then checked the skylight above me. Nine p.m., and it was finally dark. I went down four flights of stairs. I'd seen a bag of coffee in the kitchen, and there'd been a grinder and French press in one of the cabinets. I could wash everything, send the grinds down the sink disposal, and there'd be no trace. That was important, because one way or another, this house would be searched eventually. When Inspector Chang found out about it, he'd want to come himself. Unless there was a budget setback, SFPD would get him here in a couple of days.

Whatever I did here I needed to do quickly.

I woke up sometime after three a.m. At first I wasn't sure what had pulled me out of sleep, and then my phone made its little chirp again. I'd fallen asleep in Claire's chair, and I was still in it. Sitting up, I pushed the open notebooks away and reached for my phone. The chirp had been a text message, sent by my home alarm system.

Motion trigger — 12:21 a.m.

It took me a moment to realize the system was texting Pacific Standard Time. Which meant it was warning me about something that was happening right now. A second text arrived: a photograph, from the webcam in my kitchen, which was made to look like a smoke alarm. I opened the photo and saw a man standing in the living room, next to my bedroom door. His face was invisible. Either the photograph was blurred or he was wearing pantyhose over his head. He was holding a cordless drill, and he'd set a black satchel on the edge of my couch.

Agent White. The sonofabitch.

I had no doubt I was witnessing a black-bag job, federal style. If those were pantyhose, White didn't have a warrant —but that wasn't stopping him from planting bugs in my apartment walls. I was thinking about calling SFPD and reporting a break-in, and then I heard a noise downstairs, the front door opening and closing. It was fast and quiet, one click and then another. I wouldn't have heard it at all if I'd been asleep.

I remembered my shoes. They were in the entrance hall, two feet from the front door. The house smelled like coffee because I had brewed three pots. Whoever had come inside either knew I was here or was an idiot. I scanned the room for a weapon. Claire had nothing but books up here. There were ballpoint pens in the desk, a pair of cobblestones she'd repurposed as bookends. But downstairs, in her fourth-floor bedroom, there'd been something better. I got up and moved as silently as I could, taking the stairs two at a time and hoping none of them would creak.

I entered Claire's bedroom, crossed to the fireplace, and took the iron poker from its stand. There was enough light from the street to see my watch. Twenty seconds had elapsed. I went back to the door, stood against the wall, and listened.

I heard him coming up the stairs. Soft steps, but he hadn't taken his shoes off. He reached the fourth-floor landing and paused. If he'd been watching the house from across the street, he'd have seen the reading lamp glowing through the skylights. And now, at the foot of the stairs to the fifth floor, he'd see the light spilling down from above. If he went up, then I could slip down.

I held my breath until I heard him heading up to the attic.

Then I crept out of the bedroom and waited by the stairs, the poker in my right hand. I could see a shadow, but not the man himself. I relaxed. I had him cornered in the attic, with the entire house — and the exit — at my back. And I was perfectly within my rights to be here. My client owned the house and had given me the keys. Whoever he was, he couldn't say the same.

While I was debating whether to call up to him, twenty-seven hundred miles away, in San Francisco, Agent White decided for me. He must have entered my bedroom just then, to plant a second bug. I had another smoke alarm camera above the dresser, set to alert me when it detected motion.

In my pocket, my phone chirped.

10

I HESITATED, but the man upstairs didn't.

He turned and charged me, raising something in his right hand. He didn't see the poker until it was too late. He barreled directly into my swing. The poker's hooked claw caught his wrist. I saw a flash of metal as a short-bladed knife flew out of his grip and tumbled down the stairs. The man didn't slow down. He just changed his tactics. He hit my chest with the top of his head, wrapping his arms around my waist and pushing with his legs. I went over backwards and he came with me. He'd have broken my spine on the stairs, but I was able to twist as I fell, and we landed together on our sides. He let go of me and punched me in the face, even as we were sliding down the steps.

We hit the third-floor landing. I tried to get up, but he swept my arms out from beneath me. My chin hit the hardwood. The tip of my tongue kept my teeth from smashing together. The man rolled me over and straddled my chest, and then he had his hands around my throat. My right arm was free. I could hear my hand slapping the floor, searching for the poker.

"Who else knows?"

His face was close enough to mine that our noses almost touched. Except that I couldn't see his nose. He was wearing a black ski mask. He spoke in a hoarse whisper.

"Who'd you tell?"

Even if I'd understood his question, it would have been impossible to answer. He'd tightened his grip, and was working his thumbs into my Adam's apple. Time turned into a series of broken thoughts and shutter clicks. I saw the bulge of his shoulders as he flexed and bore down on me. I wondered if I would still be conscious to hear my hyoid bone pop. On the floor, my fingers brushed something cold. Reflexively, they tugged the object closer and picked it up. The knife. My field of vision had shrunk to a pinpoint. Just before everything went black, my body made one final, adrenaline-driven leap.

I stabbed him in the lower back, hoping for his left kidney. The knife must have been honed to a razor's edge. My arm had no strength left at all, but I felt the blade sink into him. He grunted but didn't let up on me. I twisted the handle; instantly he reached both hands for the wound. I yanked the knife out, drew a gasping breath, and swung again. Harder and higher this time. The blade slammed into the side of his neck and didn't stop until it hit a bone.

The man fell sideways, sliding off the blade. He caught himself, and then slowly stood. His breath made a whistling noise out the side of his neck. I scrabbled backwards on the floor until I came to a wall, then pushed myself up.

We faced each other on the dark stair landing.

He was looking at my hand. I still had the knife. Its blade was short, but wide. Smooth on the cutting edge and roughly serrated along the back. My arm was slick with blood up almost to the elbow. None of it was mine.

"Get on the floor," I said.

Now I was the one whispering. He'd choked my windpipe down to the diameter of a coffee straw. I took a step toward him and raised the knife. One of us was going to pass out pretty soon. I didn't want it to be me.

"The floor."

The man lurched to the stairs and pounded down them,

one hand covering his neck and the other arm wrapped around his side. I leaned against the wall and listened to him go. At the first-floor landing, he must have collapsed. There was a crash, and then nothing. The house was entirely silent. Then he was on his feet again. He'd been built like a rock wall, and was using his strength to get out. But force would only get him so far. He was losing blood with every heartbeat. The harder he worked, the less time he had.

The front door opened, but I didn't hear it close.

I went into the guest bedroom on the third floor and reached the window in time to see the man limp across the sidewalk on the opposite side of Beacon Street. He leaned against the maple tree, nearly invisible in its shadows. A car passed, and the man waited until it was gone. Then he moved off, deeper into the park. I saw him fall and get up again. Twenty paces later, he was in the grass a second time.

When I turned away from the window, he was crawling.

I went downstairs, turning on lights as I went. There were no signs of the fight until I came to the main entry landing, where he'd fallen. He'd been down long enough for blood to pool there. He'd stepped in it, and left footprints on his way to the front door, which he'd left open. There was a dark red handprint on the top step, as though he'd slipped and caught himself. But after that, nothing. I shut the front door and went to the kitchen. I pulled off my shirt and put it in the stainless-steel sink, and then I washed my hands, arms, and face. My undershirt and pants were clean. I took hand towels from a drawer, and bleach spray from under the sink, and went after the blood on the floor.

I worked quickly, but thoroughly. Calling the police was not an option. I had every right to be in the house. The man attacked me, and I had stabbed him with his own knife. It was self-defense, pure and simple. But I didn't know who he was, or why he'd come. I could think of three possibilities. The worst was that Agent White had put a tail on me, which meant that the man could be a federal agent. Second to that, but almost as bad, was the chance that DeCanza had friends on the outside who didn't like what Jim and I had done to their man.

Or it could have had nothing to do with me. This could be about Claire. He could have come into her house to cover up the same things I'd been hoping to discover. If I wanted to shine a light on everything that led up to her fall, maybe he wanted to bury it. It was a decent theory, except that so far I hadn't found anything in the house worth killing for.

There was only one way to find out for sure. I didn't like it, but I couldn't think of any way around it. And I had a client to answer to. She would expect information. So I grabbed a flashlight I'd seen in the walk-in pantry, put on my shoes, and went out the front door. Standing on Claire's topmost step, I scanned the park. I didn't see the man I'd stabbed. In fact, I didn't see anyone at all. But he couldn't have gone far. And once I found the place where he fell, there'd be a trail to follow.

A hundred feet into the park, I found his blood on the grass. Where he'd been able to walk, the trail was harder to follow. The drips and spots were spread far apart, and hard to find in grass that hadn't been cut in a week. But where he'd fallen, and crawled, the trail was obvious. Long smears of blood darkened the grass. Walking or crawling, he'd moved in the same general direction, a track that took him diagonally away from Beacon Street.

Charles Street cut the park in half, and he must have lingered under a tree there for a while, resting, before he crossed the street. He'd dropped his ski mask on the side-walk, but I didn't even think of touching it. It was heavy with his blood, and had hit the concrete like a paint-laden sponge. By the time he made it across the street, he was getting weaker. The blood was one long streak now—he was crawling, and he never got up again.

The end, for him, was against a wrought-iron fence that surrounded the graveyard abutting Boylston Street. I saw the leaning headstones, and heard the wind in the maple leaves, and then I saw him. He was sitting with his back to the fence and his legs out in front of him. His chin was on his chest. I turned off the flashlight and crouched next to him. The longer I stayed here, the more certain it was that a jogger would come past.

"Hey," I said. I poked his shoulder with the butt of the flashlight. "Just tell me why."

He didn't answer. I nudged him a little harder with the light.

"Was it DeCanza that sent you?"

Again, he didn't answer. I was ready to knock him on the forehead, but before I could, he began to list sideways. Slowly, like an old tree going over. He hit the footpath face-first, and didn't move. I didn't need to put my fingers on his neck. He'd stopped bleeding, which meant his heart was done beating.

I'd never killed a man before, in self-defense or other-wise. I knew that later on, I'd be thinking about this. If I made it back to my apartment on Grant Street, and if Agent White wasn't there waiting for me, I'd lie in my bedroom with the door open and listen to the neon sign buzz through the night, picturing this moment. But right now, I needed to figure out what to do. I ran my hands over his pockets—he was wearing black mountaineering pants and a matching long-sleeved shirt—and found nothing but a subway card.

I took it, because I'd touched it and I wasn't wearing gloves anymore.

Of course he wasn't carrying a wallet or a driver's license. Which left one last option. Everything I knew about police investigations said not to do it. Common sense screamed no. But I needed to know who I'd just killed. I stood and turned him face-up with my foot. Then I used my phone to take a picture of his face.

I took the long way back to Claire's house, walking until after sunrise. I had an urge to call my ex-wife. Juliette Vilatte was closer to my age than to Claire's, and had grown up a hundred miles to the north, so she wouldn't have known her. But little else separated them. They'd likely gone to the same sorts of Parisian prep schools, had probably attended the same fundraisers and charity balls. Their parents' planes would have sat in nearly adjacent hangars in San Jose, from which they would have jetted off for their summers in Cannes and their weekends in Saint Vincent or Tahiti.

I hadn't spoken to Juliette since we'd signed the settlement agreement. I hadn't felt the slightest desire to talk to her until now. But maybe it was natural that I wanted to hear her voice. The first time I'd done real damage to another man, it had been Juliette who reassured me. Who had told me that it would be okay. Which was odd, because the man I'd attacked was the California Supreme Court justice who had been her boss. She'd begun her brief legal career as his law clerk, become his mistress somewhere in the middle of it, and ended it as his wife. Her father had smoothed that transition the best he could. Juliette had insisted. I stayed out of jail, and her father bought a son-in-law who was far more valuable and pliable than I'd ever been. I was still trying to figure out what Juliette had gotten out of the bargain.

But as much as I wanted to, I couldn't call her. That was impossible.

So before the sky grew too bright, I found my way back to Beacon Street. Even by daylight, I couldn't see any blood leading down the steps or across the sidewalk toward the park. I let myself inside. I couldn't detect Claire's perfume anymore. There was just the nasal-sting of bleach. It smelled like a cover-up.

11

I SPENT AN HOUR checking the house for blood I'd missed on the first sweep. Inspector Chang could be here as soon as this evening. I didn't want him to find a stray spot of blood on the wainscoting and decide to spray the floors with Luminol. If he did that, and then looked out the front window and noticed the Boston Police combing the park with K-9 units, it wouldn't take him long to put the two together.

I showered in Claire's bathroom, dressed in the clothes I'd been wearing, and went out. My phone's map led me to a department store on Boylston Street, where I bought a button-down shirt, a tie, and a sport coat. I put them on in the store, standing in front of a mirror near the entrance. My back was already black and blue from the fall down the stairs, and I was wearing handprints all the way around my neck. But after I fastened the top button and cinched the Oxford knot, the bruises were out of sight. My upper lip was a little bit swollen, and that was it.

Outside, I found a cab and got a ride across the river to Harvard.

From the notebooks, I'd learned that the professor who'd so excited Claire last December was a writer named Julia Forrester. She taught investigative journalism in what sounded like a mostly self-directed class, and she had a long trail on the internet. She'd started out writing online, at places like *Slate* and *Vice*, before stepping up to *Vanity Fair*, and nearly ten years at *The New Yorker*. There was a three-year gap in her bylines, and then she'd reemerged with a book about miners and death squads in Brazil. She'd learned two local languages while living in a string of Amazon villages, and had come out of the jungle with a major book deal and an even bigger price on her head. Two years later, she detailed the ties between an Uzbeki crime family and the CIA. A sticker on the cover of that book—which I'd found well annotated on Claire's shelf—announced that it was *Soon to Be a Major Motion Picture*.

Forrester had taken a visiting professor post last year, and Claire noticed. It was from Claire's notebooks, and not online, that I learned Forrester's office hours.

I got out of the cab at Harvard Square and backtracked on foot toward the Barker Center for the Humanities, following footpaths between the brick buildings and not making much eye contact with the kids I passed. I found a trash can and dropped in a rolled-up paper bag that contained my bloody shirt. I found a second one and dumped a sealed envelope with the knife.

Then I paused on a bench and checked the *Boston Globe* on my phone. There was a story, ten minutes old, about an apparent murder victim found next to the Central Burying Ground. There was no mention of the man's name, or the fact that he'd left a blood trail hundreds of yards long leading back to Beacon Street, or that he'd dropped a black ski mask in the middle of the park. Not a usual piece of jogging attire for a June morning that had started out at seventy degrees. If the police knew all those things, they'd have realized this wasn't an ordinary mugging-gone-bad. I wondered, not for the first time, about cameras in the park. No one had seen me stab him, but a camera might have caught me following

86

his blood trail and finding him. There was so much to worry about that the only solution was to let it all go. It would play out one way or another.

The building that housed Julia Forrester's office was a giant brick pile, a mix between Monticello and a London train station. I found my way up a broad staircase to the second floor, located her office suite, and went in past an empty secretarial desk. Forrester's door was open, and she was sitting behind a plain wooden desk. I recognized her from the jacket photos on her books. Curly brown hair, streaked with a little more gray than in the publicity shots. Horn-rimmed glasses in bright red, which drew attention away from the small scar just under her nose. There was a laptop in front of her, and she was writing. I knocked on the wall next to the door, and she looked up.

"Hi," I said.

"Yes?"

"My name's Lee Crowe."

I stepped into her office and shut the door behind me. I took out my investigator's license and handed it across the desk.

"I came out from San Francisco to see if I could meet you. I hope this is an okay time."

"You're not a student."

"No."

She pushed my PI card back without having given it more than a glance.

"If this is about something I wrote—"

"It's about a student of yours—a former student. Claire Gravesend." I saw her eyes refocus. She'd recognized Claire's name. "Her mother hired me to look into all this."

"All what?"

"You haven't heard?" I asked. "She was in your class—"

"She withdrew," Forrester said.

"So you haven't heard."

"Heard what?"

"I'm sorry," I said. "Her mother said Claire admired you, that she'd sought you out. So I guess you might've been close. But Claire was found dead in San Francisco. Two days ago."

I had no information that Claire had been close to anyone. Her class notes lacked any personal information. Olivia had told me that she'd spoken to Claire's journalism professor. As far as I knew, she was the only person in Boston that Olivia had reached out to when her daughter went silent.

"How did it happen?" Forrester asked me.

"She went off a building on Turk Street, in the Tenderloin."

"What do you mean, she went off a building?"

"Either she jumped or someone pushed her," I said. "There was a car on the sidewalk, directly underneath. A Rolls Royce Wraith."

"It was her car?"

I shook my head. But it was interesting she'd asked the question. She must have spent enough time around Claire, or done enough other research, to know about the money.

"It was there for a photo shoot," I said. "Part of a magazine ad. It didn't have anything to do with her."

"As far as you know," Forrester said.

I nodded.

"For all I know, she had a bone to pick with Rolls Royce and wanted to make an impression. But I doubt it."

Forrester closed her laptop and leaned back in her chair.

"Olivia — the mother — said Claire was seeing you during office hours, starting September?"

Forrester nodded.

"She wanted to take my class. It was full. So she came to persuade me to accept one more student."

"And she was successful?"

"She was very serious. Committed to it."

"What exactly was this class?"

"Investigative journalism. Getting all the way into a story. Telling it in full. Truman Capote goes to Kansas and comes back with *In Cold Blood*. That was the model."

"Or Julia Forrester goes to Brazil and comes back with a blockbuster, and a new scar," I said. "I'm guessing everyone in the class was supposed to come up with a story?"

"That's right."

"What was Claire's topic?"

"I know she had one," Forrester said. "But what it was, exactly, I have no idea. She left before she submitted a topic for approval. She'd taken a bioethics course. And she was interested in stem cell research—controversial stuff, depending on which circles you run in."

"That's medical treatments they get from fetuses?"

"Embryos," she said. "Totally different."

I could write everything I knew about stem cells on a grain of rice. There'd be room left over for what I knew about bioethics, and the difference between an embryo and a fetus.

"You think she was writing about stem cells?" I asked.

"I'm just telling you the sorts of things that caught her interest. If she'd stayed through the class, we would have developed the concept. And she'd have gone out in the field to work the story."

"Was she doing interviews?"

Forrester nodded, then pushed up her red glasses.

"What I knew about, it was all on background. Talking to professors here, and at MIT. Getting the lay of the land before she went out to ask hard questions."

"Is it dangerous, sending kids out to dig things up?"

"All journalism is dangerous. If it's any good."

"What was she asking the professors?"

"I don't know. I don't know who she was talking to, or even what departments they were in."

"Are all your student conferences that vague, or was she guarded?"

"She was guarded, and then some."

"But she must've told you something. Enough that you made an exception and let her into your class."

"She talked a good game," Forrester said. "She told me the books she'd been reading."

"The genetics stuff," I said. "That's what you're talking about?"

Forrester nodded again.

"Did she withdraw from school to work on her story?"

"I don't know why she left. She didn't stop by to tell me."

"But you talked to her mother?"

"That's right."

"Did she seem concerned?"

I saw her eyebrows arch up above the top of her bright red glasses.

"Isn't she the one who hired you?"

"I'm looking at every angle," I said. "Did she seem concerned?"

"She was worried enough to fly across the country and track me down," Forrester said. "She struck me as extraordinarily measured. Composed. But that doesn't mean she wasn't concerned."

"Did you ever see Claire's back?" I asked.

"Excuse me?"

"Her back," I said. "Maybe in a low-cut dress, or a tank-top. Something that would show her skin."

"I don't know what you're getting at."

"You don't know about the scars?"

"What scars?"

"So you never saw them?"

"I never saw her wearing anything but sweaters and jackets. She started coming to see me in September, and it was already fall weather. This is Boston, not California. What scars, Mr. Crowe?"

I took out my phone and found the autopsy photo, zoomed in on it to crop out the enormous impact wounds on her buttocks and the back of her head.

"Her mother wouldn't tell me what they were," I said. "And I don't have a clue. This is from her autopsy. The ME noted them in her surface examination. She didn't speculate on what they were — just well-healed old scars. Not a contributing factor in her death."

I handed the phone to her. She took off her glasses and held the screen close.

"Jesus," she said.

"I know."

"I never saw these."

"Not even the ones on her neck?"

She shook her head. She touched the phone's screen, zooming out to see the whole photograph. She winced and handed the phone back.

"I wouldn't have seen those," Forrester said. "She always had her hair down. Sometimes a scarf. You'll ask how I remember, so I'll tell you. She had very nice scarves."

"Always?" I asked. "Hair down, neck covered?"

"I never saw it any other way."

The nanny next door had given me a dead-on description of Claire. And she'd been wearing her hair up. Maybe she put it up in the summer, when it was warmer out. But Forrester was talking about sweaters and jackets and scarves. Indoors. As though Claire was deliberately hiding her skin.

"Did you have anything else, Mr. Crowe?"

"One thing — did Claire use a laptop?"

"Of course."

"She took notes by hand, but wrote papers on a computer?"

91

"I assume so," she said. "She brought one in here once, when she was trying to get into the class — she handed it to me and showed me her course transcripts."

I got up to leave, then paused and gave her one of my cards.

"Call me if you think of anything else. What she might have been writing about, where she might have gone after she left school. Anything."

"All right."

I opened the door and went back to the stairs. There was enough information from Forrester to keep me thinking for a while. At least I knew my instincts were still intact. I'd searched Claire's house from top to bottom but hadn't found a laptop. It didn't seem plausible that she wouldn't own one. If she'd left school to work on a paper, she'd have taken the computer with her. I had no idea where she'd been staying for the last six months. If I could figure that out, maybe I'd find the laptop.

12

I HAD NO INTENTION of returning to Claire's house. I'd cleaned it as well as I could, and I'd left with everything I'd brought in with me. I had her last five notebooks and the keys from the unmarked envelope I'd found in her desk.

I was sitting at an airport bar now, looking at an untouched beer. I had an idea about the keys. Olivia Gravesend said her family had a long-running respect for the value of a pied-à-terre. Claire must have grown up hearing that. So perhaps when she'd left Harvard and set out for California, she'd seen the need for her own foot on the ground. She had the money. And maybe she would have wanted a place of her own. You're never truly alone in a hotel room, after all. Your things are never entirely secure. She'd have traveled enough to know that.

I heard a call for my flight. I finished my beer and then went to the gate.

I landed in San Francisco before dark and took a taxi to Union Square. I didn't want to go home. And if White had bugged my apartment, he'd probably bugged my office. I hadn't put an alarm system in there yet, so I had no way of knowing.

I called Jim from a hotel payphone and reached him at his desk.

"Counselor," I said. "Have you had coffee?"

"I usually don't drink it after three o'clock, or I can't sleep."

"Then maybe you should go get a decaf. It's important."

"All right."

Jim was already in the body shop when I got there. He had two paper cups of coffee on the desk in front of him.

"How was Mrs. Gravesend?" Jim asked.

"Just fine. The Iron Bitch sends her regards."

"She heard about that?"

"Watch your back," I said, and he shrugged. Making an enemy of Olivia Gravesend didn't concern him, except for his bottom line. "But that's not why I'm here."

"Lorca?"

"There might be a problem."

"There's no problem. They dismissed it yesterday. What else could they do, when DeCanza had just confessed? They'll bring my client back next week and take a plea on the tax returns, and that's it."

"Agent White was in my apartment last night, planting bugs."

"White?"

"I'm pretty sure."

I showed him the photo from my alarm system.

"There's no face. You can't see anything. How do you know it's White?"

"I've got a feeling," I said. I held out my hand. "Give me that back — I want to show you something else."

He handed me the phone and I went to my camera roll. I pulled up the headshot of the man I'd killed. I hadn't looked at it since taking it. His face was paper white, and the reason for that was evident. His neck was covered in blood, the knife gash visible because of the tilt his head had taken. I palmed the phone so Jim couldn't see it.

"Representing Lorca and his friends, you've seen a lot of mug shots. Right?"

"Sure."

"And you've probably seen photo books of federal informants. People in the Witness Protection Program. Stuff you've compiled using sources like me. Stuff you got from your clients."

Jim conceded that with a slight dip of his chin.

"So just tell me this," I said, and handed him the phone. "Have you seen this guy?"

He looked at the photo. I saw his eyes moving back and forth as he worked something out in his mind. Then he tapped twice at the screen, turned the phone off, and handed it back.

"Did you just delete that?" I asked.

"You don't want it," he said. "Trust me. But where did you get it?"

"It doesn't matter — and I had a question you just dodged. Do you know him, or not?"

"Did you take that yourself?"

"You know him, don't you?"

"I couldn't tell you without breaking a privilege."

"That means yes," I said. "You know him."

"Is he dead?" Jim asked. He took the lid off his cup and sipped from the surface of the coffee. "Dead would be better."

"Who is he?"

When he didn't answer, I repeated the question. He put the lid back and stood up. His chair scooted backwards on rusty wheels. He brushed his rain-damp coat with one hand to flatten it.

"My advice to you, Lee, is really simple," he said. "If you were thinking about leaving town, that's a good idea. Go catch some fish in La Paz."

"What about Mrs. Gravesend?"

"Forget about her," he said. "Head south. Tonight."

"Fuck your privilege," I said. I stood up too. I loosened my tie and unbuttoned my shirt so he could see the handprints around my throat. "I know what they want to do to me, and I can handle them. I just need to know who they are."

"So he is dead?" Jim asked.

I nodded.

I didn't want to say it out loud, even here, where Jim and I talked about anything. But the guy was dead. Right now, if he was wearing anything at all, it was a toe tag.

"Good for you," Jim said. "But there's more of them. So go south. And don't call me for a while."

He stepped out of the office, and walked across the garage floor. Through the cobwebbed glass, I saw his phone light up as he brought it to his face. He was calling his driver to meet him out front. I gave him five minutes' lead, and then I walked out. The street was busy, and I didn't particularly want to be seen. I summoned a car with my phone and asked to go to Chinatown. I didn't want to go home, but I wanted to at least look through the windows as we drove past.

I ended the night at a backpackers' hotel in North Beach. From Chinatown, I took a streetcar, and then a cab over to Fisherman's Wharf, and then walked back to the hotel, where I paid for my room in cash. The bed wasn't much bigger than a cot, the walls were tissue-thin, and my German neighbors were deeply in love. I didn't care. I brushed my teeth with the travel kit I'd picked up, showered, and turned off the light. I lay on the bed and looked at the glow of streetlights on my ceiling. I was asleep long before my neighbors.

I also woke before anyone else in the hotel.

First thing I did was pick up my phone and check the *Globe,* and then the *Chronicle.* There was nothing new about the man I'd killed, and nothing about Claire. There was a three-inch article about Lorca. The government had voluntarily dismissed its case against Jim's client, who took a plea on a single tax evasion charge. Nothing about me.

I took the stairs to the front desk, paid for another night, and asked about the Wi-Fi password. Then I walked to a drugstore and bought socks, underwear, and a package of undershirts. I could get another day out of my pants and my Boston shirt, and after that, I was going to need to think about going home.

After I changed clothes, I caught a streetcar out of North Beach and over Nob Hill. I got off near Powell and Market, took the escalator down, and caught the first BART train to the Civic Center station. If Claire had bought a pied-à-terre in San Francisco, then the deed would be a public document, preserved on microfilm and stored in the Office of the Assessor-Recorder, in City Hall. Finding it would be as easy as typing her name into a terminal, getting the deed's microfilm reel and image number, and then asking a records clerk for the canister. If she bought the house under her own name, that is. If she'd bought it through a holding company, I'd never find it — I wouldn't know what name to search. And that was all assuming she'd bought a house at all, and that it was in San Francisco.

But Claire wasn't DeCanza or Lorca. She was a twenty-year-old woman. Though she had become secretive in the last six months of her life, deception wasn't ingrained in her nature. I walked from the station to City Hall, pushed through a crowd of protesters to climb the marble steps, and stepped into the entrance hall.

The records clerk on duty waved to me when I stepped into Room 190.

"Lee," she said. "*Hao jiu bu jian.*"

"Mae — long time no see," I said. "I've been busy. How about you?"

"Busy — but not now. What do you need?"

"I'm looking for a deed. The name is Claire Gravesend."

Mae was standing behind the counter but had a terminal in front of her. She typed in the name and then looked up at me.

"She's the grantor, or the grantee?"

"Grantee," I said. "And this would be recent. Within the last two years, but probably more like the last six months."

"Okay," she said. She hit return on her keyboard, and looked at her screen. "One second."

She took a scrap of paper from a wooden box and jotted down a number, then turned around and walked into the records room. I leaned around to look at the search result on Mae's screen.

GRAVESEND, CLAIRE
DOC. NO. J5989874-00
REEL: K919 / IMAGE 0956
RECORD DATE: 01/27/2019
DEED

Mae came out of the records room holding a reel of microfilm, presumably canister number K919. She set it on the counter.

"It's image nine-five-six," she said. The microfilm machines were behind me, and they were all empty at the moment. "Or if you've got a second, I can print it for you."

"Sure," I said. "That'd be great."

I left five minutes later holding a copy of Claire's deed. I sat down on the steps outside City Hall and read through it. The purchase price was hidden behind the usual language — she'd paid ten dollars, and other good and mutually agreeable considerations. There were no encumbrances to title, so it had been a cash sale. She owned the place outright, and the title was in her name alone.

The address was on Baker Street. I pulled it up on my phone's map to get a look. The house was a block from the

Presidio, near the foot of the Baker Street Stairs. That had to have taken a good chunk out of her coming-of-age money. It was a neighborhood of hillside mansions. The streets were shaded by cypress, were scented with eucalyptus, and you could see the Golden Gate rising beyond the Presidio. I folded the deed and put it in my pocket. Then I called a car and walked down to meet it on Polk Street.

I asked the driver to take me to the top of the Lyon Street Steps. I didn't want to give him Claire's address. After what had happened the last time I'd entered a house of hers, I wanted to minimize witnesses. Right now, Mae was the only person with any idea where I was heading.

When I got out, I walked over to the railing and looked down. The steps went from Broadway to Vallejo in two long pitches of stairs broken up in the middle by a stone pavilion. Half a dozen joggers were working their way up the steps toward me. I was the only person around not wearing bright leggings or headphones. I walked down to Vallejo, turned right, and went a block to Baker Street. Claire's house was down the hill, on the left. It was four floors high, with a wooden balcony that surrounded the top floor. The upper floors were clad in redwood shakes, but the street level was built from stone. Columns flanked the entrance.

It was the only house on the block without flower boxes, or ornately trimmed boxwood hedges, or carefully pollarded plum trees along the sidewalk. It was in good condition, but no one was doting on it. Claire was too private for house-keepers, and too busy to do yard work.

I walked down the hill and climbed the three steps to the door. I didn't ring the bell or lift the bronze knocker. I took out the larger key and slid it into the lock. It went in easily, and when I turned it, that went easy too. The dead bolt re-tracted, and I pushed the door open.

• • •

The entry hall smelled like a woman had walked through it five minutes ago. A touch of perfume, a hint of lotion. It was subtle, hard to nail down. And then I lost track of it. I took off my shoes and found the kitchen. The counters were bare. There was a liner in the trash can. I lifted the lid and found an empty cup of ramen noodles, a wadded paper towel, and a used pair of chopsticks. Beneath that, there was junk mail postmarked the day before Claire died.

But I was still thinking about Boston, and the last time I'd searched a house of Claire's. I'd had twenty seconds to find a weapon, and that had saved me.

I'd been lucky that time, and Jim's warnings to me were still as fresh as the bruises on my neck. I took out my phone and turned it off. Then I started opening kitchen drawers. They were mostly empty, but I found one with the basics: silverware, spatulas, a cheap-looking chef's knife. Claire hadn't come out here to play house. She'd picked up the minimum to get by, probably one trip down Grant Avenue to hit the Chinatown housewares shops.

I picked up the knife, and then I went to explore the rest of the house.

The living room was furnished, everything shrouded with white sheets. Same with the formal dining room, which looked out over Baker Street. The table was covered, along with each of the high-backed chairs.

According to the deed, Claire had purchased the house from an estate. The heirs must have unloaded it furniture and all. Which reminded me: I would need to tell Olivia about this house. If I couldn't do anything else for her, locating assets would be a service. I was thinking about that — how I could trace the source of the purchase money so that Olivia could reclaim whatever was left of the twenty million — when I went upstairs and opened the first door I came to.

It was a guest bedroom. There was a chair next to the bed,

and on it was a pair of slender-legged jeans. A black T-shirt was hung over the back of the chair. A pair of sandals lay on the floor, next to a small suitcase. The bed was covered with a heavy down duvet. I followed the shape under the covers up to the spill of blond hair on the pillow, and when I saw that I must have made some sound — a gasp, or a word or two spoken quickly, without thinking — and that woke her up.

Claire Gravesend sat up and swept the duvet to the side. She rubbed her fingertips against her temples, her eyes still closed.

She was wearing a bra and a pair of panties. Which meant that when she swung her legs to the floor and bent forward to stretch, I could see the scars running up her spine, two by two. As if someone had held her down and used her skin to grind out lit cigars. Box after box of them.

It was her. It could be no one else but her. Her body, her face, her hair. And now the scars.

Claire Gravesend.

I'd found her on Turk Street, had touched my fingers to her throat, where I found no pulse. I'd never forget her autopsy photographs: her body from every angle, stripped, washed with a hose, and laid bare on a steel table. The photographer had documented everything. Her chest cracked open, and her skin flayed out to the sides. Her skullcap lifted off, her brain tipping a fruit market scale to thirteen hundred and fifty grams.

And now she was looking up. Her eyes were meeting mine.

She yanked the covers up to her neck. When it came, her scream was so jarring that I dropped the knife. I stepped the rest of the way into the room and kicked the door shut. I knelt and put the knife behind me, out of her sight but not quite out of my reach.

"Claire," I said. "Claire — it's okay."

She just kept screaming.

13

"CLAIRE!"

It was the third time I'd said her name, and it finally seemed to get through to her.

For an interminable five seconds, we just stared at each other. She'd stopped screaming, and that was a mercy. This was a big house. The windows were probably double-paned. But we weren't on a block of Baker Street where women were supposed to scream inside houses. At least not out loud.

"Claire's dead," she whispered.

"Then who are you?"

"Madeleine."

"Gravesend?"

She shook her head.

"Adair," she said. "Madeleine Adair."

She had to be telling the truth. No matter what I'd thought in the shock of seeing her, the ME had identified Claire's body with fingerprints. California kept them on file with every driver's license application. There was no doubt that the girl I'd seen on Turk Street had been Claire Gravesend. That was beyond dispute. It was also impossible to believe she'd gotten up again.

"What are you?" I asked. "Her twin?"

"I don't know," she said. Then she shook her head. "It's hard to explain."

"I have all day."

"Not while I'm like this," she said.

I waited outside the door while she dressed. Before stepping out, I'd given her an exceedingly brief explanation of who I was and why I could open the door to Claire's house: private detective working for Olivia Gravesend, who had given me keys.

Now, standing in the hallway, I realized I'd left the knife on the other side of the door. I was still off-balance, acting as though the woman in the guest bedroom couldn't be trouble because she was Claire's mirror image. But that could be reason enough to fear her. I'd never seen Claire while she was alive—just the one moment on Turk Street, and then the autopsy photographs. Still, I'd have bet Madeleine Adair could fool anyone, Olivia Gravesend included. That would be a two-hundred-million-dollar trick, so long as the real Claire Gravesend didn't get in the way. Which seemed like a sound theory for a second or two. Madeleine might have had a reason to murder Claire, but leaving the heiress's dead body on a public street made no sense if the plan was to take her place.

I had less than a minute to think about it, and then Madeleine had slid into her jeans, pulled on her T-shirt, and stepped into her sandals. The door clicked open and she came out. She was holding the knife in her right hand, blade down at her thigh. She had a leather purse slung over her shoulder, and she'd put up her hair with a set of crosswise ebony pins. When she turned to pull the door shut, I could see the scars on the back of her neck.

"You were in Boston," I said. "The day Claire died, you went to her house and knocked on the door."

"You saw me?"

"Let's go downstairs," I said. "We can talk in the kitchen."

She nodded but didn't move. She was waiting for me to lead the way so that I wouldn't be behind her on the stairs. I went ahead, and she followed. If she'd wanted, she could have grabbed a handful of my hair, jerked my head back, and slit my throat. But by the time we reached the kitchen, I was still alive.

I pulled out a stool and sat at the counter, my hands in front of me. She stood on the other side of the stove. Behind her there was a laundry room and the back door. From there, wooden steps descended to a small garden. Madeleine never took her eyes off me as she backed through the laundry room to the door. She unlocked it and pulled it open. But she didn't turn and run. She just wanted a clear exit if she needed it. She came back to the kitchen and stood across the counter from me, knife in hand.

"Thanks for staying," I said.

She acknowledged that with a nod, but didn't speak.

"I'm just trying to get to the bottom of what happened to Claire," I said. "We want the same thing."

"Maybe."

"How long did you know Claire?"

"Two years. We met right after she moved to Boston."

"How did you meet?"

She shifted the knife from her right hand to her left, then rested its blade against the stone countertop. I could hear birds singing in the garden through the open back door.

"I work in the Harvard Book Store," she said. She didn't take her eyes from mine. They were light gray, the same shade as Claire's. "Two years ago, she walked up to my desk and asked where to find Oliver Sacks. We looked each other up and down and decided to get a drink instead."

She had a plainspoken Midwestern accent. She might have come to San Francisco from Boston, but I'd have bet she'd spent time in Minnesota before that. In any case, she didn't speak anything like Olivia Gravesend, whose untraceable inflection called to mind a Connecticut Yankee raised in a Gstaad chalet.

"You were a student too?" I asked.

"I was when I met her, but I graduated a year ago. From Emerson, not Harvard."

"You're older than her?"

"By three years, as far as we could tell."

"It's not rocket science," I said. "You take your birthday and subtract hers. She was born December twenty-ninth—"

"I told you, it's hard to explain. Dig in to things like that—when we were born, and where—it gets weird."

"I don't get it."

"I don't either," Madeleine said. With her free hand she was rubbing her elbow, kneading it deeply, as if she had to press hard to reach as far as the pain. "But I think Claire figured it out. She mailed me a ticket and a key to this house. She said we needed to talk. I got the letter the day she died. I saw her picture online and didn't know what was going on. I went to her house—the Beacon Hill house, in Boston—and tried to get in. But she wasn't there. I still thought it could be a mistake."

"You thought it wasn't her?"

"If there were two of us, why couldn't there be three?" Madeleine said, as if that question explained everything. "So I came to San Francisco but she didn't show up. I had to admit it was Claire. Not a third one, or a fourth, or whatever."

Madeleine might have been in the air while I was talking to the nanny who'd seen her knock on Claire's door. While I was following a blood trail through the park to find the man I'd killed, she'd been in this house waiting for a woman who was never coming home.

"Why did she ask you to come?" I asked. "What did the letter say?"

"I already told you—she wanted to talk. I figured she'd finally found something. But I still don't know what."

"Let's back up," I said. "This isn't making sense."

"I told you—nothing about us makes sense."

"So you met her in the bookstore, and you looked each other over and decided to go get a drink," I said.

"What would you do, if you looked up and saw your doppelganger?"

I was pretty sure I'd go get a drink. But I might not have invited my mirror image along. Drinking by myself was trouble enough.

"What did you talk about?" I asked.

"We found a quiet place," Madeleine said. "Somewhere we could be alone. And the first thing she did was pull up her hair and show me the scars. She'd seen mine already. I never tried to hide them, but she did."

I thought of the way Olivia Gravesend had shut me down as soon as I brought up the scars.

"Her mother was ashamed of them," I said. "Eventually it rubbed off."

"So she hid them," Madeleine said. "First for her mother's sake, and then it was second nature."

"What did she tell you about them?" I asked.

"She didn't tell me anything—she asked me what I knew. She wanted to know how I got them."

"And what did you say?"

"The same thing I tell anyone who asks," Madeleine said. "That I've always had them. The first time I used a hand mirror to see my back in the bathroom, they were there."

"But your parents—"

"I grew up in foster homes," Madeleine said. "In Seattle, and then in St. Paul. My parents adopted me when I was eight. Go ask them and they'll tell you—I know more about the scars than they do. And I don't know anything."

"Then who are you really?" I asked.

"If Claire were alive, you could ask her the same thing. Or you could go ask her mother. You don't really think Olivia Gravesend gave birth to Claire, do you? Claire didn't buy it."

Madeleine was right, of course. I'd noticed the physical difference, but hadn't questioned it. Olivia Gravesend looked nothing like her daughter. She was shorter, and her nose was sharper. Olivia had the Gravesends' dark hair. I'd seen portraits in two of their mansions, and raven-black hair was a family trait that went back to the 1700s. Olivia had told me she hadn't married Claire's father, and that Claire had never known the man. Those could both be true, if wildly deceptive, statements. I'd taken it as a given that Olivia had known her daughter's father, even if just for one night. But maybe she'd never met him either.

"You're the one standing here," I said. "Who are you?"

With her free hand, she reached behind her neck. I couldn't be sure, but I thought she was touching one of her scars.

"I never cared about any of this until I met Claire," she said. "I was too busy getting by."

"She changed that?"

"I was twenty-one — old enough for an adopted kid to ask the State of Washington for her original birth certificate. So I wrote to the Department of Health. As long as my birth parents hadn't requested anonymity, I'd be within my rights."

"And?"

"I got a certificate back," she said. "It lists my place of birth, and my residence, as St. John Catholic Church, in Yakima. Where my parents' names should be, it says *foundling child*."

"You were abandoned in a church."

"It says I was born October thirty-first, 1996," Madeleine said. "But the certificate was issued on October thirty-first, 1999. Which means the health officer took a guess and said I was three."

"What health officer?"

"It's Washington law," she said. "Someone finds an abandoned child, they're supposed to call the police. The police take the kid to the local health officer to figure out an approximate birthday. Then he fills out a foundling certificate."

"Who named you Madeleine?"

"The health officer, by law," she said. "Maybe it was his mother's name. When I was adopted, I got a new birth certificate. I became Madeleine Adair. But before that, I was Madeleine St. John."

"After the church where they found you."

She nodded.

"You don't remember any of this?" I asked.

"Nothing," she said. "At least nothing I can get my hands around. I remember sitting on a bed and looking at a blue curtain, and there was a woman on a chair next to me, and I remember knowing it was too late at night. I was supposed to be asleep, and I wasn't, and there were people coming in and out from behind the curtain, and I was afraid and thought maybe I was in trouble."

"That was the hospital?" I asked. "Where they took you right after the church?"

"I guess."

"Anything else?"

"I remember riding in a car. I think it was my first time in a car. Maybe my first time seeing a car. It was night, and there were bugs hitting the windshield — *splat, splat* — and everything was very fast."

"But you don't know who was driving?"

She shook her head.

"Do you know how many times I've tried to remember that face? How many times I got drunk in high school, and then lay down on the floor and watched the ceiling spin, and thought maybe — maybe this time — I'd remember?"

"I can guess."

"Claire tried to walk me through it. She tried to jog my memory—she picked me up once, at my apartment. Three in the morning, and she came up and knocked until I woke up. She made me come downstairs and get in her car, and she drove me out of the city and into the woods. A spring night, and she was on some winding back road that followed a stream. Going fast, so the mayflies would hit the glass. And I was crying, because I couldn't remember, and I knew how much she wanted me to."

"What about Claire?" I asked. "Didn't she have a birth certificate?"

Madeleine nodded. She began rubbing at her elbow again.

"I have a copy upstairs," she said. "In my suitcase. It says she was born December twenty-ninth, 1999. In St. Thomas."

"The Virgin Islands?"

"Yeah."

"Was she a foundling?"

"Not according to the certificate," Madeleine said. "It lists the mother as Olivia Gravesend. The father is unknown."

If everything Madeleine told me was true, then three months after she turned up in a Yakima church, Olivia went to the Caribbean and gave birth to a baby girl who would grow up to look exactly like Madeleine. Including the scars. I tried to imagine a pregnant billionaire, who could choose any hospital in the world, going to the Caribbean to deliver her child.

"I've never met Olivia Gravesend," Madeleine said. "But I've seen her picture. What do you think?"

I didn't answer that. I had a client to protect. What I thought about her was private, and when I dealt with her, it would be just the two of us.

"What about Claire?" I asked. "If she wasn't related to Olivia, were you related to each other?"

"We thought it was more than that," Madeleine said. "That day we met, after we left the bar? We went back to her house, got online, and ordered a DNA kinship test. It came in three days, and she called me. We used the swabs in front of each other, and sent them back by FedEx. A week later we got the results. We were the same."

"The same?"

"The lab tested seven hundred thousand genes against each other. They all lined up."

"What does that mean?"

"That we're identical," Madeleine said. "Monozygotic twins. There was one egg, fertilized by one sperm. The zygote split in two, and we grew into what we are — the same."

"That's not possible. Not if you're three years older than Claire."

She'd started shaking her head before I even finished the first sentence.

"You can freeze embryos," she said. "You can keep them on ice for years. Decades. And then you implant them. So we could have started from the same zygote. But I got implanted first. Claire stayed in the freezer. We might have been born from the same woman, or we might have had different birth mothers. Surrogates, I guess."

I studied her face. She stood across from me, one hand on her hip and the other tapping the knife's blade against the counter. Her eyes stayed on mine.

"You're not kidding, are you?" I asked. "You guys studied this. And you really believed it."

"I told you," Madeleine said. "Everything about us is complicated."

I couldn't disagree with that. She was certainly complicating my life. I wanted to verify the things she'd told me, which would mean hours on the phone and in front of a computer. I wanted to drive down to Carmel and talk to Olivia Gravesend. I didn't want to do either of those things with Madeleine looking over my shoulder. But at the same time, I couldn't leave her alone. She might run off, which would be even worse than having her around.

14

"WHAT DO WE do now?" she asked.

I looked at my watch, then at her knife.

"If you trust me enough to put that down, we could get lunch."

She unzipped her purse and put the knife inside it. It was long enough that its handle protruded from the top.

"Compromise," she said.

"Fine."

We could have gone on foot to a restaurant on Chestnut Street, but neither of us thought it'd be a great idea to have Madeleine walking around this neighborhood. If Claire had made any friends here, by now they probably knew she was dead. Seeing her stroll past would do more than raise an eyebrow. So she called a car. I sat next to the driver, up front, and she was behind me. The purse was in her lap, her fingers on the knife's handle.

We got sandwiches and mineral water at a coffee shop, and sat at a table near the back.

"Does Olivia know about you?"

"God, no," Madeleine said. "Claire didn't tell her anything about this."

"She was afraid she'd get cut out if she rocked the boat?"

"She never said it that way."

"What did she say?"

"*Mother's sensitive,*" Madeleine said. "*I shouldn't upset her.*"

When Madeleine imitated Claire, her easy Midwestern accent disappeared. Instead there was the Gravesend inflection. If you couldn't quite call it Old World, you could call it Old Money. I thought about the weight of the money that followed Claire wherever she went. It would have expanded her life, but it also drew a circle around her. She might have seemed like an easy target.

"So it was all about the money," I said.

"I don't know."

"What happened to your arm?" I asked. "You keep rubbing your elbow."

"It's nothing." She took her hand away and set it on the table. "It's arthritis. I've had it a while."

"At your age?"

"Claire had it too. So that makes two of us."

"Any other medical issues with you two?"

"Crap vision," Madeleine said. "I wear contacts but need reading glasses, if it's dark."

"And Claire?"

"She had laser surgery. Some specialist in Tokyo."

"Anything else?"

She shook her head, which was just as well. I wasn't sure what I could do with anything she was telling me. So I changed the subject.

"What about the San Francisco house?" I asked. "Does Olivia know about it?"

"I thought she gave you the keys."

"That was for Boston," I admitted. "I went there and found keys in Claire's desk. And I haven't said anything to Olivia yet. Was Claire secretive about the place here?"

"I'd never heard of it until I got the letter," Madeleine said. She took her sandwich apart and picked at it with her fork. "Why?"

"Claire's state of mind," I said. "I want to know how she was behaving at the end."

Which was partially true. I was also trying to figure out if her house was a safe place to stay. I didn't want to sleep in my apartment as long as it was bugged. And I didn't want Madeleine sleeping in Claire's place if there was a chance another masked man would break in during the night.

"Do you think she jumped?" Madeleine asked.

In truth, at that point I didn't know what I thought.

"Do you?" I asked.

"She wouldn't have done it," Madeleine said. She shook her head with some conviction. "She was getting close. She wanted to talk to me. This thing was her obsession, but it wasn't driving her mad. She just wanted to know where she came from."

"It sounds like it was more her obsession than yours."

"Why wouldn't it have been?" Madeleine asked. "I grew up knowing my parents weren't my own. I had a borrowed last name. My past was a black box. I didn't learn to accept it. It's how it always was. But for Claire?"

"How was it for Claire?"

"She had all her shit together, had her life tied up with a nice bow. Then she walked into a bookstore and met me."

"But you don't know what she found," I said. "Do you?"

"I don't."

"How are you?" I asked. "I mean, under stress. When things aren't going well, how do you hold up?"

"You're asking if I think about killing myself. You're thinking if it's a predisposition to act that way, and Claire and I were twins, then we'd do the same thing."

"Something like that."

"I've never thought about suicide," Madeleine said. "And

I haven't always had it so easy. I didn't have a staff. I couldn't jet to Europe for a different perspective on my problems."

Several times now she'd pointed out the contrast between her upbringing and Claire's. I wondered what lay beneath that. Jealousy doesn't have to lead to anything. Plans aren't the same as actions. Yet the motive was undeniable, and Madeleine's resemblance to Claire gave her an opportunity. Her plan might simply have been to erase and replace Claire, and walk into her millions. But it could have been even more complicated. There could be angles I hadn't imagined. I had to be cautious.

I pulled out my phone and lifted it, screen facing away from her.

"Sorry," I said. "I've got to take this call."

I stood up and walked outside, not looking back at her. On the sidewalk, with my back to the window, I dialed my source in Homicide Detail. Elijah answered on the fifth ring, his voice heavy. Usually he didn't get out of the Hall of Justice until seven a.m.

"Crowe?"

"That's right," I said. "You and Jeremiah want to make a little extra money this week?"

Elijah and his brother lived in an apartment above their uncle's Mission Street appliance shop. Jeremiah worked days to Elijah's nights, which meant they'd go a month at a stretch without seeing each other. They communicated via notes on the refrigerator, and when they ran surveillance jobs for me, they could patch together twenty-four-hour coverage with a couple of sticky notes, a delivery van, and a shared bus pass.

"What kind of job?"

"There's a woman up in Pacific Heights," I said. "I need her watched."

"Top rate?"

"Two thousand a week."

"Each?"

"That's right," I said. It was six times as much as I'd ever paid them, and Elijah paused to consider that.

"That kind of money isn't just a stakeout."

"She could be in trouble," I said. "So you wouldn't just be watching her. You'd be watching out for her."

"How soon?"

"We'll be back at the house in an hour," I said. "I'm going to leave her there and let you take over. But she doesn't need to know about you. If she leaves, you follow."

I gave him the address and then we hung up. When I came back into the café, I walked toward our table. Madeleine hadn't fled out the back door. She was staring at the deconstructed sandwich on her plate. She was working her left cheek between her back teeth, and didn't look up until I sat down across from her.

"We were talking about suicide," Madeleine said. "Assuming it's a predilection that runs with the genes. I don't know if it's inherited or not, but I'll tell you one thing."

"What's that?"

"Claire was afraid of heights," Madeleine said. "If she rode in a glass elevator, she'd stand in the middle and stare at the floor. She wouldn't lean on a windowsill if the window was open. She had falling dreams, the ones where you jerk awake right before you hit, and you're covered in sweat."

I thought of Claire's bedroom in the Carmel mansion, her window overhanging a sea cliff. I pictured a little girl, awake at three in the morning, every crash of the waves sending a subtle shiver through the house. It would be impossible to forget how high above the rocks she was, and the delicacy of her perch.

"You guys must have talked a lot."

"All the time."

"And you?" I asked. "You're the same about heights? The dreams?"

She nodded.

"So if you're going to look at what I'd do, and draw conclusions, then think about this. If I had to kill myself, I'd do anything but jump. *Anything.* I'd pour gasoline over my head and flick a match. I'd swallow rat poison. I'd run a hose from the exhaust pipe. I wouldn't jump."

But all of Madeleine's alternatives required equipment. Gathering equipment takes premeditation. You have to buy the gas and find the matches, and imagine your way past the bright flash of pain. You have to get the right poison, and not only swallow it but keep it down. You have to get a hose, and a car without a catalytic converter, and find a quiet place to park it. But to jump, if you live in a city, is a different proposition. All you need is a passing urge. There are millions of windows, and rooftops, and parking garages. There are bridges, stretching over dark water, beckoning.

In a city, the opportunity is everywhere. Which is what sets jumpers apart from most other suicides. They're more impulsive. They're plagued by voices and driven to desperation. The ones who survive long enough to see an emergency room all say the same thing.

I changed my mind on the way down.

I wondered what Claire had thought about, rushing toward Turk Street. Did she change her mind? Was the wind screaming out her error?

Or had someone else made the decision for her?

"What?" Madeleine asked.

"Nothing—just thinking."

"You're going to see her today? Claire's mother?"

"Yes."

"Will you tell her about me?"

"Not until I know what to say," I said. "Are you ready to go back?"

Madeleine put her napkin on her plate, covering the remains of her sandwich. When she started for the door, I turned around and traded my half-finished bottle of mineral water for hers. I held it from the bottom so my fingers wouldn't overlay her prints. Then I quick-stepped across the café in time to open the door for her.

We hailed a taxi and sat next to each other on the ride back to Baker Street. If I was calm about Madeleine, it was because I could barely spare time to think about her. I was still grappling with what had happened in Boston. I'd killed a man and left his body where it fell on the Common. I didn't know who he was or why he'd come after me on the stairs. I couldn't even guess what evidence might connect him to me. For all I knew, he'd written my name and phone number on a piece of paper and stuffed it in his shoe.

There were too many possibilities, too many potential enemies. Madeleine and Olivia. Agent White and DeCanza. My old friend Jim, who might not be my friend at all. I had no idea who Claire had been tracking, but those people might know about me — and it was all too much. More than I'd signed on for, cash notwithstanding.

I should have just gone to La Paz after the trial. I could have rented a room in one of the old hotels, where a ten-dollar tip to the desk clerk would let me pay in cash and write any name I wanted in the guest register. And if it had to happen, La Paz would have been a better place to kill someone. The desert was full of scavengers, the ocean churning with whitetips. If the body turned up anyway, it wasn't a big deal. The police there weren't like the Boston police. They were under constant siege, from men like Lorca. They had other things to worry about.

I stopped outside the front steps, and Madeleine looked over at me. She had to touch my elbow to get my attention. The weather had turned again. Her hair was misted with fine droplets of fog.

"You're going to see her now?"

"Yes."

"Am I safe here?"

"I could get some guys to come watch over you," I said. "People I trust."

In fact, I could see the Mission Appliance van parked at the top of the block. Elijah wasn't in the driver's seat. He was probably in the cargo area, where he could keep tabs on the house from a small screen connected to the dash cam.

"I don't need that," Madeleine said. "I'll lock the door and won't let anyone in."

"I'll be back tonight," I said. I handed her one of my business cards. "If anything happens, call me."

15

I OWN A CAR but I almost never use it. My work is too fluid, and moves too fast. If I can't find a parking spot in less than five seconds, it doesn't do any good to drive my own car on a tail job. It's pointless to have a car parked halfway up Nob Hill when my target is jogging down an escalator into a BART station. So I use taxis, and ride-sharing apps. I could draw a public transit map on the back of a bar napkin with my eyes closed. And my car, a black 1965 Camaro that Juliette gave me as a wedding present, spends most of its time in a belowground parking garage near Union Square.

I'm not sure where Juliette found the car. We came back from our honeymoon to a new house that was a gift from my ex-father-in-law. I had never seen the place, but Juliette knew the layout well enough. She immediately took me to the garage. It was two in the morning, and we'd been on her father's plane for fifteen hours, hurtling home from Hong Kong with a fuel stopover in Anchorage. And yet Juliette wanted me to take her for a drive. The keys were in the ignition. *Let It Bleed* was in the eight-track. A bottle of Wild Turkey, with an unbroken 1965 tax stamp, was in the glove box. My new wife, soon to be my ex-wife, bit my earlobe and whispered.

Take me to Half Moon Bay.

When Juliette is in the mood to please someone, she goes

all the way. She isn't one for half-measures. Not in any of life's arenas. She'll take you on a moonlit ride down Skyline Boulevard, and when you get to the cove she likes, she'll lead you down to the wet sand. You might not even notice the moment when everything else goes dark. There is just that single point of focus, a circle of light big enough to circumscribe two people. When you have her attention, you have it in full. The problem was that her attention didn't last.

Six years later, the only thing left is the car. And I've never even thought of letting her go.

Driving a hundred and fifty miles down the coast to see Olivia Gravesend was a chance to let the Beast stretch her legs. I hadn't taken her out of the garage in two months. I did have to consider the possibility that Agent White might have found her, though. If he'd broken in to my apartment, it was safe to assume he'd run a DMV search. So I had a choice between being paranoid and being realistic. Knowing my plate number wasn't the same as knowing where the car was. The parking garage was likely a mystery to him, because it was nowhere near my apartment or my office.

I turned off my phone, then went up the Baker Street steps at a jog. I caught a bus on Jackson Street, stepped off at Union Square twenty minutes later, and then backtracked up the hill to Bush Street and my garage.

I found the Beast where I'd left her: two stories below-ground, in a dark corner, beneath a nest of iron pipes. She was covered in a fine layer of concrete dust. There'd been some construction on the street above six weeks ago. I brushed my fingertip along her hood, exposing the glossy black paint beneath the dust. I walked around the car, checking for marks like that. But as far as I could tell, no one had touched her. I got down on my back and looked under both bumpers, and in the wells above the tires. People who know what they're doing will try to hide a GPS tracker where its antenna can get satellite reception. So I didn't crawl all the way under the car, or pop the hood and feel around behind the engine block. It was safe to assume White knew what he was doing, so it was safe to assume White hadn't found my car.

I opened the door, and sat down in the stitched-leather bucket seat. When I turned the key and gave the gas pedal a tap, the engine caught right away, hitting all eight cylinders with a roar that echoed around the subterranean garage.

When I reached the street, I leaned over and opened the glove compartment. Inside, on top of the registration and insurance envelope, there was an old-style flip phone. A pay-as-you-go model, not tied to any contract. Sometimes in my business, I need to make calls that can't be traced back to me. I turned it on and saw its battery was still full. Driving down the hill toward Union Square, I dialed Elijah.

"Who's this?"

"Crowe," I said. "I'm using this phone today. I need to keep the other one turned off for a while."

"Someone tracking you?"

I ignored the question. I didn't want to get started on the topic of who might be tracking me, or why.

"If anything happens with the woman, call me on this line."

"So far, she's just sitting tight."

"Good deal," I said. "You got the back door covered?"

"There's a birdhouse in the back, the kind up on a tall pole. I landed the quad on the roof, shut it down except the camera. There's a door from the first floor, and one from the basement. I've got them both."

Last year, I'd set up Elijah and Jeremiah with a couple of small camera-equipped drones. It was barely a five-hundred-dollar investment, and now one man could cover both sides of a house without getting out of his van. Of course it was illegal. But the rewards were high and the risks were close to zero.

"Think anyone saw it fly in?"

"Doubt it," Elijah said.

"Call me if something comes up," I said. "Neighbors with pitchforks, that kind of thing."

"Anyone from this block, I can handle."

"And if they call the cops?"

"I'll handle it," Elijah said. "I know most of those guys. I take out their trash."

I wished him luck and hung up. After crossing Market, I hit the entrance to U.S. 101 and let the Beast have some gas. By the time I passed the airport, I'd given in and pushed *Let It Bleed* into the deck.

I stopped for gas in Monterey, and spotted a payphone beside the service station. If I used my prepaid phone every time I wanted to make a call, pretty soon it wouldn't be a secret anymore. I dialed a number from memory and listened to the phone ring.

"Who's this?" Cynthia Green said.

"Crowe," I said. "I'm on the road, using a payphone."

"You got the autopsy report?"

"I did—and thanks," I said. "I need you to do something else."

"It'll be a slow night, anyway."

"Do you know anyone at the Boston medical examiner's office?"

"Not a soul," she said. "But I know someone out on the Cape, and she'd know someone in Boston."

"You know her well enough to get a favor?"

"It depends on what you want."

I paused. I'd trusted Cynthia for a few years now. I was about to find out how much that trust was worth.

"Some jogger found a dead man on the Boston Common a couple mornings ago," I said. "It was in the paper."

"This has to do with Claire Gravesend?"

"I don't know," I said.

"Because she had a Massachusetts driver's license in her purse," Cynthia said. "A Beacon Hill address."

The thing about Cynthia was that she read everything before she filed it. And she remembered everything she read. Usually that was an asset, but right now it was a problem.

"I just have some suspicions," I said, evenly. "I want to see where they go."

"So you want the Boston ME's report on a dead body found on the Common," Cynthia said. "I can get that."

"Keep my name out of it," I said. "And don't say anything about Claire. I don't want people thinking there's a connection if there isn't one."

"Sure, Lee," she said. "Count on me."

"Okay. Thanks."

I hung up the phone. From that point on, I had to count on her. Because now Cynthia knew I thought something tied Claire Gravesend to a dead man in Boston. Plenty of people knew I'd been in Boston. Olivia and her butler knew. There was Claire's journalism professor, Julia Forrester. The next-door nanny, who'd seen my PI license. My trail to Claire's house was a mile wide, and the dead man had drawn a line in blood that pointed back to her door.

A Boston cop could start at one end of this thing, and a San Francisco cop at the other, and they'd find me squarely in the middle.

I went back to the car, started the engine, and twisted the chrome knob to kill the stereo. I drove the rest of the way in silence.

Finding Olivia Gravesend's house was harder than I thought. I missed the private road the first time and wandered down the coastal highway for five miles in the wrong direction before I realized I'd gone too far. Driving back, I kept the speed down until I spotted a gravel road between a pair of overgrown bay laurels.

I nosed the car through the boughs, then coasted down the hill in neutral until I came to a locked gate. There was an intercom box on the left. I rolled down the window, hit the button, and waited.

"This is a private residence. You likely saw the signs, coming down the road."

I recognized the butler's voice. All he needed to round it out was a long-tailed topcoat and a monocle.

"It sure looks like it," I said. "Lee Crowe, here to see Mrs. Gravesend."

"Is she expecting you?"

"She expected me to keep her updated," I said. "Does that mean yes?"

"Wait a moment."

"Sure."

It was her dime. At least sitting in the car, listening to the engine's loping rumble, no one was trying to choke me. I wasn't getting blood on my hands. And I was getting paid the same. A minute passed before the intercom crackled again.

"Please come down."

I looked up. The gate was sliding open. I dropped the transmission into first and rolled down the hill toward the Gravesend place.

I thought she'd receive me in the gun room again, but I was wrong.

"She's waiting for you on the terrace," the old man said. "Follow me."

I found Olivia Gravesend in a redwood Adirondack chair, facing the ocean. There was a half-empty mug of coffee on one armrest, and an ashtray with three butts on the other. When she saw me, she exhaled smoke, ground out her lit cigarette, and set the ashtray on the stones by her feet.

"I've started smoking again, Crowe."

"It happens."

"This was older than Claire," she said. She held up a

pack of Camels. "I stopped the day I knew I'd have her. And started the day I knew she was gone."

There were no other seats near her. The nearest thing was a lemon tree in a tub-sized stone pot. I brushed the dirt from the rim and sat facing her. I looked her over. She was wearing tan slacks and a white sweater. Her hair was wound into a tight bun. Bare feet; a pair of tortoiseshell sunglasses perched above her forehead. I'd have said she looked good under the circumstances, except that with the sunglasses up, I could see her eyes. I guessed she hadn't slept in three days.

"You've found something," she said. "Haven't you, Crowe?"

"A few things."

There was no reason not to share some of it. So I told her about searching the Boston house and finding my way to Julia Forrester. I skipped the fact that I'd killed an intruder and spent the better part of an hour cleaning his blood off her staircase. Instead, I told her that Claire's computer was missing. And that based on my talk with Forrester, I believed Claire had left Harvard to pursue an investigative story. I didn't tell Olivia about the San Francisco house. I wasn't planning to tell her about Madeleine yet, and I didn't want anyone to know about that house as long as Madeleine was in it.

"She left to write an article?" Mrs. Gravesend said. "That's what you're saying?"

"I think so."

"What kind of article?"

"Claire was interested in genetics. Stem cells. Twin studies. Frozen embryos. That's all part of it."

"Part?"

I'd thrown in the comments about twins and frozen embryos to see how she'd react. But she just looked confused.

"She wanted to know where she came from," I said, nudging a little harder.

"I have no idea what you're talking about."

"Then I'll tell you what you're not telling me — Claire wanted to know where she was born," I said. "She wanted to know who she really was. And why she had those scars."

Olivia Gravesend opened the pack of cigarettes and looked into it. The lie was coming apart. I could tell from her posture. She'd been rod straight in defiance the last time I saw her. All that support had come out of her spine.

"She was my daughter. My Claire."

"Mrs. Gravesend," I said. "I can't help if you're not straight with me."

"I'll show you her birth certificate, if you don't believe me —"

"The one that says she was born in the Virgin Islands. That you're the mother and the father is unknown."

She looked up sharply, then nodded.

"You found a copy in Boston. Or got one from her school."

It would be easier to let her think that.

"Picture it from my point of view. I'm sitting here looking at the sixth-richest woman in the world —"

"Fifth."

"Okay. Fifth. You were forty-eight years old, and well educated. Why would you go to the Caribbean? The hospital in Charlotte Amalie sends anything serious to Puerto Rico."

"I brought my own doctor," she said. "It was a natural birth, at home. We have a place there, in the old town, overlooking the bay — I wanted —"

"It's bullshit," I said. I'd spoken quietly, but she stopped talking. So I went on. "I believe you've got a house there. And I'm sure you had a doctor who'd do anything you asked."

"Crowe."

"I'm not saying you did anything wrong," I said. "From a

moral perspective. From a legal perspective, it's a different story. You broke plenty of laws."

"You need to understand."

"I do," I said. "Driving down, I figured it out. You found Claire somewhere. She'd been abandoned, and was sick. You couldn't stand to let her out of your sight. You brought her to St. Thomas, and sent your doctor to the vital statistics clerk. He reported a home birth. You figured they wouldn't ask too many questions. If they did, so what? You could buy cooperation. And at the end, Claire would get a U.S. birth certificate."

My client had stopped looking at me. Quietly, she took a cigarette from her pack. The last one, I saw. She lit it, and blew smoke to the side. Then she turned to face me.

"And the Gravesend name," she said. "She got that, too. That was the main thing."

"So it's true?"

"My name is what mattered. It was supposed to right the wrongs that had been done to her."

She turned to face me, then held up her hands, twelve inches apart. The cigarette was between her left thumb and forefinger.

"She was this big, the first time I saw her. A tiny thing. Purple and screaming. And still perfect in every way. She glowed — you have no idea."

"I can picture it."

"You can't, Crowe. No one understands until they've seen it," she said. "Not unless you have one."

"I don't."

She blew smoke and nodded.

"I knew it the first time I saw you. Because I used to look the same way — as if I could put everything that mattered in one bag, and leave."

"But you wanted children."

"I did," she said. "And, god, did I try. Look at me. At who

I was back then. I could get anything I wanted. Except one thing. And then, just when I had given up, I had her in my arms. What do you think it would have taken to make me let go?"

"I don't know."

"And I'll tell you something else," she said. "The second I picked her up, I understood if I put her into the system, there was no guarantee I'd get her out again. It's not finders keepers. Not for little children. It's a labyrinth. Children get lost in it. Do you know what I was most afraid of, Crowe?"

"No."

"That whoever did that to her—drilled the holes in her back, abandoned her to starve—might someday come back. He could lay a claim on her. To keep her safe, to give her any kind of life at all, I had to change the rules."

"Break them, you mean."

"If it works, it doesn't matter."

"You made her vanish, and then reappear."

She took one last drag on the cigarette and flicked the butt over the railing. It spun out over the lower terrace, got a lift from the wind, and then plummeted toward the ocean.

"When she came back into the world, she was a Gravesend. And I was her mother."

"We're going to need to start over," I said. "You need to tell me from the beginning."

She stood up, and so did I.

"Do you want a drink?"

"All right."

16

WE RELOCATED TO a walnut-paneled barroom. Some
ancestral Gravesend had gone all out. There were batwing
saloon doors, and polished brass tap handles, and a view
across the Pacific that stretched toward a blue eternity.
The butler came from somewhere, summoned by a means
I hadn't noticed.

"Brandy for me," Mrs. Gravesend said. "And, Crowe —
what's yours?"

"Anything's fine. Brandy, if that's what you're having."

He poured our brandies and brought them to us at a table by the window. We sat with the snifter glasses between
us and waited for the old man to leave. When he had, Olivia drank a small sip and began without any sort of prompt
from me.

"I'd been involved in the Mission Carmel my whole life.
I'm talking about the minor basilica, on Rio Road — San Car-
los Borromeo del Rio Carmelo. I was baptized there, and so
was my mother. And I helped out whenever anyone asked.
To the point that if something came up — if they needed to
fix the roof, if some idiot came at night with a can of spray
paint — the bishop knew he could call me. And I would make
it right."

"Okay."

She took another drink of her brandy, and I did the same.

"On October twenty-ninth, 1999, the bishop called me with something else. The parish priest had been late in the chapel, cleaning up after a wedding. He heard a knock at the door, then cries."

"Where did he find her?"

"Right outside the chapel doors. Swaddled up, and in a box. He saw the taillights of the car, racing off."

"She was in a cardboard box?"

"The kind you'd keep files in, with cutouts for handles. A banker's box."

"Okay."

"I still have it," she said. "The swaddle, too. And photographs I took, to show how she was. What they'd done to her."

"You have all that here?"

"Yes."

"Why didn't you tell me the first time we met?"

She drank the rest of her brandy. Before she set the glass back on the table, the butler came in through a side door. He wiped down our table with a white towel. I'd hardly touched my drink, but he refilled both our glasses. I wondered how Olivia could stand to live in a house like this. She might have privacy if she snuck out a window and climbed onto the roof — but even that wasn't a given. Watching on my cell phone in Boston, I'd seen a man planting bugs in my apartment, and I hadn't been home since. I wasn't sure I could ever go back there again.

When the butler was gone again, she said: "I didn't tell you because it didn't matter."

"How could it not matter?"

"Claire didn't know. She never had any idea. She was my daughter, and that's all."

"There were at least five people who knew otherwise."

"The bishop died years ago," Mrs. Gravesend said. "Cancer. The priest never knew what the bishop and I arranged. And anyway, he was killed in Uganda. Less than a month later. I paid to fly him home."

"And the doctor?" I asked. "Did he die too?"

"No idea. He took other employment."

"When?"

"Claire was three. So I doubt he told her anything. And he never knew where I got her, or how."

"You had the same butler back then?"

She glanced at the door he'd disappeared behind.

"Mr. Richards would never tell anyone."

"Even Claire? If she asked him straight out?"

"Never."

"There's also the person who dropped her off," I said. "Maybe her father. What if you were right twenty years ago, and that person wanted her back? What if he was looking? If Claire wasn't the only one searching, that doubles the chances of one of them finding the other. Which is the kind of thing I'd need to know."

She spent a while considering that.

"I should have told you," she said. "And I'm sorry. You get so used to a story, it becomes the truth."

"I've heard that," I said. And then, when I saw her face, I tried to soften the blow. "But it doesn't make any difference. I haven't lost that much time."

"Then maybe I should have told her," Mrs. Gravesend said. "If she knew how I felt about it — that it was dangerous — maybe she'd have done everything differently."

"You were just trying to protect her," I said.

But I agreed with her. She should have warned Claire. If she had, her daughter might be alive right now.

"What was she like when you found her — aside from the wounds?"

132

"What do you mean?"

"Any other medical problems?"

"She was weak. She was malnourished and underweight. She had IV marks in her arms."

"Anything that didn't go away, with time and care?"

"No."

"When did she get arthritis?"

"What?"

"You didn't know?"

"She stopped running track in high school—her knees hurt. No one ever said arthritis. Who told you that?"

"No one," I answered. "When did she go to Tokyo to fix her eyes?"

"Two years ago. She hated wearing glasses."

"If she'd been diagnosed with something serious—cancer, say—would she have told you?"

"I think so. But how could she have been? The medical examiner didn't find anything like that."

"True."

"You don't think she jumped, do you?" she asked.

"At this point?" I asked. "Not really."

We finished our drinks, and then Mrs. Gravesend walked me through the house until we reached her cavernous bedroom. As in Claire's room, there was an armoire. My client took a key and unlocked the bottom drawer. Inside was a cardboard box. Brown, with a faux wood print on the lid. I knew the type well—they litter every law office in the country. They fill up empty offices and are stacked in hallways like building blocks. She lifted it out easily and handed it to me. There were no files in this box. I put it on the end of her bed and set the lid aside.

Inside, there was a thin swaddling blanket, striped with blue and pink. It was folded into a neat rectangle. She'd folded it so that a line of evenly spaced bloodstains ran down the middle. The blood was rusty with age. Next to the swaddle was an envelope.

"Those are the photographs?"

"Yes."

"Did you wash the blanket, or wipe down the box?"

"Of course not."

"How many people handled it?"

"The priest, the bishop, and me."

"And the guy who dropped Claire off," I said. "Assuming it's a man."

"And him."

"Okay."

I took out the packet of photographs, then put the lid back on the box. The photos were stuck together with age. They were three-by-five prints, clean at the edges and sharp at the corners. I gathered Olivia Gravesend hadn't looked at them in all the years she'd had them. When I pried the first photograph loose from the stack, and flipped it over to look at it, I could see why.

Claire had been such a tiny thing. I could have cradled her in two cupped hands. She was still young enough that her eyes were more black than blue-gray. From the front, she might have looked fine. But most of the photos didn't show her from the front. Olivia had rolled her onto her stomach and photographed her from the back. The wounds were all there, so fresh they might have been just cut. Some of them were still bleeding. Her back glistened with the sheen of antibiotic ointment. Claire's little face was to the side so it was framed in every shot. She was screaming.

I put the photographs back into the envelope and handed it to Olivia.

"I'm taking the box," I said. "I know a guy who does good forensic work. It'll cost you, but he's worth the money."

"What about the pictures?"

"If I need them, I'll call you."

The truth was I didn't think I'd need them, and they weren't the kind of thing I wanted to be carrying around. Better to leave them here.

There were still hours of daylight when I left the Gravesend place. Claire's box was in the trunk. Madeleine's bottle of mineral water was next to it. Between those items and the hair in my wallet, there was plenty to keep my forensics guy busy. But before that, I had one stop. In Carmel, I turned off onto Rio Road and drove down to the old mission. The chapel was still a Roman Catholic basilica, but the square of barracks-like buildings beside it had become a museum. There was a parking lot with room for fifty cars, and almost every space was empty. I got out of my car and went across the paved plaza toward the chapel. A fountain gurgled beneath a leaning stand of Spanish bayonet plants. The front façade of the chapel had a Moorish bell tower on the left, and a shorter tower on the right. It looked like the kind of place James Bowie and Davy Crockett would choose for a last stand. I went up to the door and found it unlocked, so I stepped through, into the cool shadows of the chapel.

Inside, it smelled of candlewax and smoke. Old wood and damp earthen walls.

A gray-haired man in workman's clothes was sitting in the front pew. He didn't turn around when I came in. There was no one else in the chapel. A couple of votive candles flickered in a niche along the side wall. I took a seat in the back row of pews, and waited.

After ten minutes, the man rose and started down the aisle. Now I could see that he had a white and wiry beard to match his ponytail. There were dirt stains on the knees of his jeans, and his forearms were torn up from working in the roses. A time-blurred tattoo marked his forearm. A crucifix that bore the silhouette of Christ, knees bent and head down. I watched him come toward the door. He stopped when he was even with me.

"You need me?"

"Do you work here?"

"Not for money."

"You're a volunteer?"

"Since I retired — fifteen, sixteen years."

That was a disappointment. He hadn't been at the mission the night Claire arrived. But in sixteen years, he could have talked to a lot of people. He could have picked up the institutional memories.

"You got a minute?" I said. "I'm trying to find out about a priest. Before your time, but not much."

"Let's go outside."

I followed him out, and we went to the parking lot. Aside from mine, there were three other occupied spaces. I thought he'd walk to the old Mazda pickup truck, but when he took out his keys and clicked on the fob, a BMW's lights flashed. The vanity plate said TOPDOC. The plate holder was made of polished pink metal. He leaned against the trunk, and saw me eyeing the car.

"My girlfriend's," he said. "I'm supposed to get the oil changed."

I handed him my card. Leland Crowe. Private Investigations.

"My client is a young lady, and she's looking for her family," I said. "When she was a baby, someone dumped her. Here, at the mission. A priest found her."

"When was this?"

"Twenty years ago. October of 'ninety-nine."

"I never heard about a baby."

"The priest went to Africa right after he found the girl. And he got killed there."

His eyebrows came together, rearranging the creases in his face.

"Why does he matter?"

"He saw the car that dropped her off. He's gone, but maybe he said something to someone. Maybe he kept a journal. I don't think he did anything wrong, if that's what you're getting at."

"You can go see him, if you want."

"What?"

"If you're talking about a priest who died in Africa, we must be thinking of the same guy," he said. He pushed himself up from the car's trunk and pointed back at the mission. "He's right around the side of the chapel, up against the wall. I cleared the weeds around his grave this afternoon."

I walked back across the courtyard and found the little cemetery alongside the chapel. Most of the older graves were unmarked except for abalone shell outlines. Those likely dated back to the eighteenth century. But I found one headstone from the 1930s, and then I found a small black stone with a bronze plaque. I knelt down and brushed some of the dust from the bottom lines:

> THE RIGHT REV. DAVID E. MARTINEZ
> Born August 15, 1964, in Salinas, California,
> This beloved pastor of Carmel gave his life in
>   defense of three children,
> Kibaale, Uganda, February 10, 2000.
>
> *Agnus Dei*

Olivia Gravesend's second story was holding together better than her first. I walked past the chapel's long shadow and found my way into the museum. A woman was locking up the front door. I asked her about the Right Rev. David Martinez. Though she knew he was buried beside the chapel, she hadn't known him. Nor had she heard of a little girl getting dropped off in the middle of the night twenty years ago. She did know that the previous bishop of the Monterey Diocese, Martin Pascutti, had died a while back. Cancer, she thought. I thanked her, and let her go ahead of me to the parking lot. Once her little Mazda truck was gone, my car was the last one left. I unlocked the Beast, swung into the low driver's seat, and hit the ignition.

It was easy to fit Mrs. Gravesend's story with what Madeleine had told me. They matched up, two pieces of a puzzle. Claire had been abandoned at Mission Carmel on October 29, 1999. Two days later, three-year-old Madeleine appeared at the St. John Catholic Church in Yakima, Washington. Yakima was probably eight or nine hundred miles north of Carmel. An easy two-day drive. He could have done it in a day, but maybe having a sick toddler in the car had slowed him down. Or maybe he'd lost time because, for whatever reason, he'd wanted to stay off the interstates. And maybe the roads were off-limits altogether during daylight hours.

But that was all just conjecture. I didn't really know anything at this point. At least some of the guesses felt solid. Madeleine must have been very sick, and her early years were marked with neglect and abuse. Her memories began in Yakima, when people started taking care of her. I couldn't fathom what had been done to her, but I could at least surmise a few things about the guy who'd done it. He was meticulous and purposeful. The pattern of scars proved that. And he must have started somewhere south of Carmel. He was headed north, and he was dropping off unwanted objects along the way.

Narrowing it to south of Carmel didn't help much, though. I needed to find another way in. I thought about the churches. The priest in Mission Carmel had heard a knock at the door, and then cries. Claire was swaddled, and left in a box. The man hadn't wanted to be seen, but he hadn't felt comfortable about a baby girl taking her chances. He'd made sure she was warm, that she couldn't roll off a step. He'd knocked, so her wait wouldn't be long.

And then there was the fact that he'd abandoned the girls in different places, on different days. Claire first, then, two days later, Madeleine. Why not both at once, and be done with it? Perhaps because the girls were the best clue to who he was. By abandoning them a thousand miles apart, he hoped their kinship and identical genes might go unnoticed. One abandoned child is an occurrence so common, it wouldn't merit a mention in a local paper. Two blond girls, with matching scars, might hit the front page. And if anyone had done a DNA test, identical twins with a three-year age difference would have been an international media circus. Maybe the man didn't think his secret could withstand that kind of scrutiny.

Or then again, it could be something simpler. He might have wanted to keep the girls. But the infant was sick and weak, and hard to travel with. So he dropped her off first, and kept the stronger one. Then, in central Washington, she began to slow him down. Maybe she was bleeding, or crying too much. Maybe she'd taken a fever and he was scared. Better to let someone else handle it. And both times, when it came to passing the responsibility, he'd chosen Catholic churches. Not hospitals, or fire stations, but priests. That had to say something about him, and what he was running from. If he wasn't the girls' savior, then he wanted to be. And there was someone else he was afraid of.

17

INSTEAD OF GOING back up the peninsula to San Francisco, at San Jose I followed the east side of the bay, dodging traffic on my way up to Oakland. My forensic guy, George Wong, lived in the hills to the east of town. He'd retired from the FBI Laboratory a decade ago, had left Quantico for his hometown, and was now teaching at Berkeley. He had access to good labs, and he took work on the side. I had hit the gas station payphone in Monterey again, so he was expecting me. He came out and met me in the driveway, already wearing a pair of latex gloves. Instead of shaking my hand, he waited for me to open the trunk.

"You touched the bottle?"

"Only on the bottom."

"And she drank from it?"

"Yeah."

"Who screwed the cap back on?"

"She did."

"Great," he said. "How about the box?"

"I picked it up from the bottom. Four other people might have touched it, too."

"You know their names?"

"Olivia Gravesend. A priest named David Martinez. And the most recently deceased bishop of the Monterey Diocese — Martin Pascutti."

"You said four."

"The fourth is the guy I'm looking for. Whoever dropped off the little girl."

"You said something about a hair to compare with DNA from the bottle?"

"Yeah," I said. I pulled out my wallet and extracted the receipt I'd folded around the hair I'd lifted from Claire's brush. "Here."

"Bring it inside," he said. "You can open the door for me."

He had balanced the bottle of water on top of the box. I shut the trunk, and we went into the house to talk payment and timing. I wanted everything as fast as he could turn it around, so I knew it wouldn't come cheap. But as long as Olivia Gravesend was still taking my calls, I wasn't too worried about that.

When we were done, I drove back down from the hills and waited in traffic to get across the Bay Bridge. There was more gridlock in the city, and it took me twenty minutes to get from the bridge to my parking spot. I was thinking about lost time, and my next steps, and not paying much attention to anything else. So I didn't notice the two uniformed cops waiting in the shadows beside my parking stall until I got out of the car.

"Leland Crowe?"

I looked up.

"Who's asking?"

"Inspector Chang," the taller cop said. "He's waiting for you at Bryant."

"He's with Homicide," the other one said. "If that rings any bells."

I glanced around. There was no patrol car parked down here, but then I remembered one on the street before I turned into the garage. I didn't see any choice but to play it cool. Better not to ask too many questions now.

"You guys want to pat me down, go ahead."

"Hands on the trunk."

"Sure."

They did a hand check, ankles to collar. One of them took my wallet and the leather case for my PI license.

"You fool a lot of people with this?"

"Hardly any."

"How come you carry two phones?"

"One to call my wife, and one to text my girlfriend. Better not to get mixed up, you know?"

"Lee Crowe," the taller cop said. He snapped my wallet closed. "I heard of you. You walked into a judge's chambers and knocked the guy's teeth down his throat."

"I've reformed."

"How I heard it, he had it coming. And I bet you don't call your wife much."

"I heard none of us likes to talk about it. Something in the settlement agreement. You guys driving?"

"Don't expect a ride back."

"I'd never."

They handed my things back. The shorter cop made a show of sanitizing his hands with a plastic bottle he pulled from a pouch on his hip. If he thought I was dirty, he didn't know the half of it. Or at least I hoped he didn't.

I followed Jim's favorite legal advice on the ride down to the Hall of Justice. I sat in the back of the cruiser, not cuffed but locked in all the same, and I kept my mouth shut. The shorter cop asked why Inspector Chang wanted to talk to me. I shrugged and looked out the window. I could think of three or four reasons Chang might want me under a hard light in a windowless room. But at least he was with the SFPD and not the FBI.

They parked in the garage and brought me into 850 Bryant from the back. Then up the elevators to the sixth floor.

I glanced at my watch. It was ten o'clock. If they kept me around long enough, I might run into Elijah as he made his nightly round. That would be a new one, for both of us.

They walked me past a cubicle farm, past a men's room that had a trickle of water running from beneath the door. Then we stopped at a scuffed-up metal door. The tall cop opened it. Inside was the requisite wooden table. Three plastic chairs with metal legs. A coned light above the table, a mirror on the back wall. There was an eyebolt on the floor, and another on the table. You could lock a man down, bind him hand and foot.

"Wait here," the short cop said. "He's on his way."

I stepped into the room and they shut the door behind me. I heard them walk off. Soft-soled shoes on linoleum, muffled voices. I waited until they were gone, then tried the door. It wasn't locked. I shut it, and thought about that.

This wasn't a custodial interrogation. I could walk out anytime I wanted, and if the camera in the corner was running, they could prove I knew it. Which also meant Chang wasn't going to read me my rights. He was hoping I'd get too comfortable, that a combination of casualness and confidence would lead to a mistake. I'd contradict myself, I'd slip out some damning admission. Whereupon the tenor of the interview would change.

I looked at myself in the one-way glass and wondered if Chang had been to Boston yet. He was probably on the other side of the mirror, watching me. I pretended I could see him, and I nodded. One investigator to another. Then I pulled out the perp chair and sat down with my feet on either side of the eyebolt.

A minute passed. The door clicked open and Inspector Frank Chang walked in. Gray suit, white shirt. No tie. He had a couple of file folders tucked under his arm, and a paper cup of coffee in each hand.

"Lee Crowe?" he said. "Thanks for making the time."

"Sure."

He sat down across from me and set one of the cups on my side of the table.

"What happened to your neck? My officers rough you up?"

"Not at all," I said. "They were pros."

"So what happened?"

"A scuffle in the Tenderloin. A basic misunderstanding — a guy in a parked car mistook me for a Peeping Tom. We sorted it out."

I didn't have to reach deep for the lie. It was the kind of thing that happened often enough.

"You reported it?"

"If I had, then the husband's name would be in a police report. Embarrassing, to my client. He was in a delicate situation."

"This was when?"

"Three, four nights ago."

He arched a black eyebrow. The gesture rearranged the shadows on his face. I noticed that his nose had been broken two or three times. He was built like a boxer. Short and wiry, the kind of guy who ducks the first punch and gets in close with jabs so fast his gloves are a burnt-red blur.

"This was the same night you took your famous photograph?"

"The same," I admitted. At least now I knew how I'd landed on his radar.

"You were busy," he said. "Seeing things, and not reporting them. You got assaulted, and then you found a dead girl. In that order?"

"Yeah."

"Two cell phones, no 911 call."

"Work comes first."

"Important client?"

"Sure."

144

"Important enough to have a name?"

"Mrs. Jane Doe. But she'll probably go back to her maiden name pretty soon."

"Your client's name isn't privileged."

"Let's agree to disagree. We'll get along better."

His eyebrow did its thing again. I was pretty sure it was an involuntary reaction, something he might not even be aware of. That made me like him a little more.

"Tell me about finding the girl," Chang said. "Time, location. The scene on the street."

"I was coming up Turk, on foot. This was after four a.m."

"Which way on Turk?"

"Toward Van Ness."

He nodded. He'd probably already talked to the advertising guy and his assistant. They would have told him about me.

"You were first on the scene?"

"The first conscious person."

"How do you mean?"

"There was a guy passed out, across the street. I call him Snowsuit Man. He's got this full body suit, and a smell like —"

"I know who you're talking about."

"So he was there, but he was out."

"Open windows, people looking out?"

"None I could see."

"Did you mess with the scene?"

"I touched the girl," I said. "On her neck, under her chin. To look for a pulse. She was still warm."

"You thought there might be a pulse, and you still didn't call 911?"

"There wasn't a pulse," I said. "And anyway, I could hear the sirens."

"So you touched her," he said. "Just on the neck?"

"Just the neck."

"Not her hands?"

"No."

"You're sure about that?" he asked.

Years ago, when I was fresh out of law school and Jim Gardner's newest associate, I'd watch him prepare his clients for cross-examination if they chose to take the stand. His rules were pretty simple. Just answer the question that was asked. No more and no less. Don't try to anticipate the next question. Don't overthink it. Simple rules to lay down, but hard rules to follow. Inspector Chang was interested in Claire's hands. He was pushing me on the question, either because he wanted me to change my answer or because he wanted to draw a box around my response. Something I couldn't get out of later. Don't think too much, Jim would say. But I wondered what he'd found out about her hands.

"I'm sure," I said. "I didn't touch her hands."

"Mind showing me yours?"

I laid my hands flat on the table in front of him, fingers splayed. There were no bruises or scratches. I turned my hands over and let him look at my palms and forearms. Now I understood why he'd started the interview by handing me a cup of coffee. He wasn't trying to be a good host. He wanted to trick me into giving him a DNA sample.

"Your medical examiner took fingernail scrapings from the girl?" I asked.

"What gives you that idea?"

"I have a television and a library card," I said. I picked up the coffee and took a sip. Then I handed him the cup. "If you're trying to rule me out, you could run that to the lab after you turn me loose. Maybe they'd get a decent sample and maybe they wouldn't. Or you could go get a DNA collection kit, and do it right."

"You're consenting to that?"

"If it'll keep your guys from following me around, I'm

happy to," I said. "You've got a man's DNA under her finger-nails? Is that it?"

That wasn't in the autopsy report, I almost said. They must have done additional lab work after the report was written. Or Frank Chang was just bluffing, to see if I got nervous about the idea.

"I'll be right back," he said. "I'll go get that kit. Enjoy your coffee."

He got up and left. If I hadn't been sure that a recorder was running, I'd have gotten out my phone to call Cynthia Green. She needed to check the Gravesend autopsy file again, to see if any lab reports had been added.

Inspector Chang came back a moment later. He'd put on latex gloves and was opening a DNA dry swab kit.

"You know what to do?"

"Sure," I said.

He handed me the swab and I ran it on the inside of my cheek and down against my lower gums, and then put it into its storage tube. I handed that to Inspector Chang, and he put it into a zipper-lock evidence bag. He took a fine-tipped marker from his pocket and wrote his name and the date on the bag.

"You take any photos besides the one you sold?"

"Plenty."

"You've been very cooperative, Mr. Crowe."

"Anything for my city."

"Do I need a search warrant to get the photos?"

"No, sir," I said. "You got an email address?"

"I'd rather have the original memory card," he said. "Chain of evidence."

He was in luck. I'd put a fresh memory card into the camera an hour before discovering Claire. There weren't any photographs of DeCanza or his FBI minders, so I wouldn't have to bargain with him about deleting the photos he didn't need.

"The card's in my office safe," I said. "You want to give me a ride?"

"You're over by City Hall?"

I nodded. The sooner I gave him what he wanted, the sooner I'd get rid of him.

Inspector Chang looked as glad to be out of the interrogation room as I was. He straightened up a little as we stepped out of the Hall of Justice and away from the buzz of its fluorescent lights. We went back to the garage, and to what I assumed was his personal vehicle. The city probably didn't loan out early-eighties Jeeps to its inspectors.

"You've got to give that door a good yank," he said.

I pulled it open and climbed up to the passenger seat.

"How'd you find me?" I asked, when he was inside and had the engine started.

"Same way you'd do it, if you're any good," he said. "I made a couple calls to set my lines, and then I waited."

He backed out of the space, his face impassive.

"What about Claire?" I asked. "After the photo, I followed the papers. You'd think it was simple. Suicide, case closed."

"You'd think."

"But you're still working."

"I'm still working."

"Did she go off the roof?"

"I have no idea," Inspector Chang said.

I reminded myself to ask Elijah to ransack Chang's office as soon as he got a chance. The SFPD might already have a preliminary report on the liquor bottle and cigarette butts collected from the roof. If Chang had Claire's DNA or fingerprints, then he could put her on the roof that night and he was lying to me now.

"She must have gone out a high window," I said. "That or the roof. No way she could have done that much damage to the car from a lower floor. Right?"

148

"I'm not sure about that either," he answered. "What's your stake in this?"

"Curiosity."

"Because you took a photo," Chang said. "Now you're in it for the long haul."

"I'm not in anything for the long haul. She just looked like a nice kid."

The light above my office door was out. We felt our way up the stairs in the dark. As I stepped up to the lock, key in hand, something crunched under my shoe's sole. Behind me, Inspector Chang clicked on a flashlight. I saw I was standing on shards of broken glass. I looked up, and Chang followed with the beam. The light fixture looked as if someone had shoved a broom handle through the frosted globe and into the bulb.

Then we looked at the door.

There were wedge-shaped impressions in the frame and on the face of the door itself. No subtle art with a set of thin picking tools. Someone had gone at it with a crowbar.

"It was like this when you left it?"

"No."

He moved me aside, reached into his jacket, and drew his gun.

"May I?"

"Go ahead."

He pushed the door open with two fingers. I hadn't even unlocked it yet.

"You got any enemies, Crowe?"

"A few."

"Anyone I should know about?"

"No one who stands out."

"Stay behind me so you don't get shot," he said. "I hate paperwork."

He stepped into my office suite, and I followed him. There

149

was a light switch to the right, and I hit it. The lights came on. Whoever had punched the door had wanted privacy on the stair landing, which was visible from the sidewalk. But once he got inside, he could shut the door.

"What's in there?" Chang said, pointing with the gun.

"A bathroom. Size of a phone booth."

"And there?"

"That's my office."

"Open the bathroom door."

"Okay."

I opened the door and stood to the side. Even cockroaches had trouble hiding in my office bathroom. It was that small. Inspector Chang looked at my toilet, my mop bucket, and my wall-mounted sink. Then we crossed the reception room and I opened my office door.

"Jesus," Inspector Chang said. "Is it always like that?"

I came from the wall and looked around the door.

"No," I said. "I keep it neat."

I stepped into the office. It had been thoroughly tossed. The desk drawers were on the floor, the couch was tipped over, its upholstery ripped open with a knife. The lithographs were off the walls, their frames smashed. My desktop computer was gone. I knelt and looked under the desk.

"Missing anything?"

"My safe."

"What was in it, besides the memory card?"

"Some evidence from a case — letters. My Smith and Wesson, a thirty-eight. My ex-wife's engagement ring."

"The gun was registered to you?"

"Yeah."

We were both kneeling by the desk, which sat on a knock-off Persian rug. The missing safe had left a square footprint in the pile, two feet by two feet. Other than my gun and Juliette's ring, everything in the safe was related to Claire Gravesend. The memory card, the letters she'd sent to reassure her mother. Of course, DeCanza didn't know that, and neither did Agent White. Whoever stole the safe wouldn't know what it held. Not until he got it to an empty warehouse and cut it open.

I thought again of the man I'd killed. Throughout our dark encounter, he'd spoken exactly six words.

Who else knows? Who'd you tell?

I looked at Inspector Chang. He holstered his gun as he got to his feet.

"I can get the guys here in ten minutes."

"I'll handle this on my own."

"I figured," Inspector Chang said. "But the safe had the memory card, and the memory card has my evidence. So it's not just your problem."

If I had put the same camera system in my office that I had in my apartment, I'd have known about the break-in. Which meant that fifteen minutes ago in the interrogation room, I'd have come up with some excuse about the memory card. But the office was so new, I hadn't protected it yet. Now Inspector Chang was here, and it would only make things worse to argue with him.

"Have at it," I said. "The place is yours."

He looked disappointed. Like he'd been ready to argue a point, or press me again on the ring of bruises circling my neck. I'd given him the only nail he could hang a hat on in the Claire Gravesend investigation. I'd admitted to being in the neighborhood just before she died. I'd been in a fight and I wouldn't give names. If he thought I was a liar, he might go a leap past that: It wasn't a coincidence that I found Claire, because I'd watched her fall. Not from the street, but from the top of the building. Just after peeling her hands off my neck.

So if he'd wanted to push me, he could have pushed hard, with search warrants. A deep dive into what I'd been doing that night wouldn't leave many great options. My alibi was that I'd been tied up in the Westchester. Too busy intimidating a federal witness to have killed an heiress. In terms of jail time, I'd get a better deal if I just confessed to bumping her off the roof in a drunken stupor.

But Inspector Chang decided not to push. Instead, he got out his phone, dialed a number, and turned his back on me.

18

IT WAS THREE a.m. before I got out of there.

When Inspector Chang said he could call his guys, he apparently meant two vanloads of forensic technicians, plus all the cops who could squeeze into seven patrol cars. The city must have been having a slow night. The crew crawled around on the floor, looking for fibers and footprints. They dusted every hard surface for prints; they shot a terabyte of raw data photos. A woman with a laser pointer and a digital protractor was calculating angles from the doorjamb. Another woman, with a tattooed crucifix peeking from her shirtsleeve, grilled me on the make, model, contents, weight, and progeny of the safe, of which I knew little, because the thing had been in the office when I got the place, its combination jotted on a sticky note.

Then they left, and I was still there, waiting for a locksmith. He arrived at two thirty, installed a new dead bolt, and told me I should look into a steel door. I paid him and waited for him to go. Then I turned my new key in my new lock and went across the landing. The broken glass from the light fixture was pulverized beneath my feet. A thousand footsteps, cop boots coming in and out, had turned it into powder.

At three a.m., I was out walking. There was nowhere I needed to be and no one waiting for me when I got there.

The usual state of affairs. Except that I was marked up with bruises, perfectly sober, and had a lot of money in the bank.

Across the street, a parked car flashed its headlights.

A big car. A Bentley so black, it almost disappeared into the night. I'd never seen it, but I knew in an instant who was driving it. She'd had a new Bentley every year since she'd turned sixteen.

The headlights flashed again.

I crossed the empty street, walking at an angle until I came to the driver's window. It slid down, beads of rain peeling off and running down the door panel.

"It's been a while," I said.

She looked up at me. It had been twelve years since I'd first met her, and six since the last time I'd seen her. I could say she hadn't changed at all. There was the pale face framed by dark curls. A dancer's taut curves half hidden by a jacket that hooked close to her throat, giving it the effect of a cape. The same perfume. But there was something in her face I'd never seen before. A shadow across her eyes, and a clench to her jaw. Maybe those were just the casual and indiscriminate marks of time gone by, but I had the idea that the last six years hadn't been easy on her.

"Get in," Juliette said. "Come on — it's pouring."

I walked around an acre of hood, then opened the passenger door and eased onto the leather seat. The heater wasn't on, but the seat warmer was. The rain picked up outside. The car was built so heavily, I couldn't even hear the drops pounding its metal skin.

"You were in the neighborhood," I said. "Just happened to be driving past."

"Something like that."

His Honor's courtroom was a block or two away. Maybe he was working late tonight. And since it was June, he'd probably just brought on his newest summer clerk. That could keep him after hours.

154

"You need a detective. You're wondering why's he working so late. It's not like he ever asks questions from the bench. It's been eight years since the chief justice let him write an opinion. And he doesn't need to read the briefs — he looks at his bank account, or calls your father, to know how he's going to vote. So what's he doing there?"

"Lee."

"But you probably have some ideas."

"I didn't come here to hire you. It's not like that."

"Then what's it like?"

"Some real detectives came to talk to me. About you. They made it sound like you were in trouble. Not like you'd done something wrong — the other kind of trouble. Like something could happen to you. I got scared, and I told them what I knew. And then, when they were gone, I thought maybe I'd messed up. I tried calling, but your phone's been off. And then I happened to come past here. I saw the police cars, so I waited."

"When they came to talk to you, you told them where I park."

"Yes," she said. She took her hands from the steering wheel and turned to me. "Did I mess up? Are you in trouble?"

"No."

"You're sure?"

"Just a break-in at the office. Not a big deal."

"Okay," she said. She paused, deciding what to say next. "But if you are in trouble, and you need some help —"

"I'm good," I said. It didn't sound like a lie. And I hoped my next question wouldn't give it away. "When did they see you?"

"It wasn't just once. It was two different times."

"Different guys?"

"Yeah."

"Describe them."

"A Chinese guy. Straightforward, city cop — he showed me his badge. Inspector Chang. And a white guy, the second time."

"Describe him."

"Blond hair, cut short. Like a military haircut. These eyes — I don't know. If you saw them, you'd remember. It's like you're standing in front of a searchlight."

"No badge on the white guy?"

"I didn't ask for it."

"You told both of them where I park?"

"Just the first guy," she said. "The white guy didn't ask."

"Then what'd he ask?"

"If I'd seen you. If we had any mutual friends. Whether I had some way of contacting you, something other than your cell or your email."

"No, no, and no."

"Which is what I told him," she said. She turned to face me. For a moment, I thought she might reach across the dark car and touch me. "And that's all I told him."

"When was this?"

"A few days ago," she said. "Right after you sold that photo."

"You saw that?"

"Everyone saw that."

"But they came when? The same day the photo hit the stands?"

"The same hour," she said. "But what's the photo have to do with your office break-in? Did you know her?"

"No," I said. "Did you?"

She looked through her rain-lashed windshield.

"Claire Gravesend," she said. "Olivia Gravesend's daughter. I must have met her. Or been in the same room as her. Not anytime recently — when I was a girl. When I had to tag along to my father's things. But she was younger than me, wasn't she?"

"A bit," I said. "A few years, anyway."

It was actually a twelve-year age difference. Not that Juliette needed to know how much I knew about the woman I'd photographed.

"So you know about her."

"What's in the papers."

"How about a ride to your garage?" she asked. "It's still pouring."

"Sure."

She shifted the transmission and we started to roll toward Van Ness.

"You're still driving her?" she asked.

"The Beast?"

"Yeah."

"No reason not to. She still runs."

"That's good," she said.

"I'm not the kind to walk away from something. As long as it works."

"Right. You'll just drive it into the ground. Until all it wants to do is die. And meanwhile, you're not having any fun either."

"That's the plan."

We stopped at a light, then took a right onto Van Ness. She had to slow in the middle of a block to let a man push his shopping cart out of the street. The old Juliette might have swerved behind him, not wanting to interrupt her schedule. So maybe she'd changed a little. I watched the row houses go by. A few lit-up stoops, a lot of dark ones. Silhouettes of men on concrete steps. Puffy rain jackets, bottles in paper bags.

"You been okay?" she asked.

"Sure — good clients, good jobs. You wouldn't like it. But it suits me. I follow cheating husbands around, with a gun and a camera. I can get salt-and-pepper shrimp at two in the morning, and all the Tsingtao I can carry up the stairs."

157

"Half of that sounds okay."

"And you? You've been doing good?"

She didn't answer right away. She sped up, to catch a yellow light before it turned. The car whispered along. Heavy as a battle cruiser, but quiet as the fog.

"Most nights, I wake up around now. Three, four in the morning. I hear his key in the lock and pretend I'm still asleep. That way we don't have to talk. And I don't have to think."

"They've got pills for that," I said.

"I take most of them."

"That's good."

We didn't have anything to say after that. I'd thought about this moment a thousand times, but I'd never imagined she'd say what she did. Or that hearing it would leave me so cold. I should have been triumphant, but I felt smaller than ever.

In five minutes, she stopped across the street from my garage. I got out and leaned down to look at her. She looked back. Neither of us had anything to say. The Beast was two stories beneath us. Juliette's blanket was still in the trunk. We could reach any of a dozen coves on Highway 1 before sunrise. So I imagined what it might be like if I got back in the Bentley. If I ran my fingertip along the fine line between Juliette's ear and her Botticelli chin. But I didn't do anything to find out. I just shut the door and went across the street. At some point, she must have driven off. The car was too quiet to hear, and I never looked back to check.

I stood behind the Beast and contemplated her. The garage's well-spaced lights gave a low hum.

If Inspector Chang posted men to watch her and wait for me, then he hadn't gotten a warrant to plant a tracking device. He was a by-the-book guy. As clean as you could be and still rise in the SFPD ranks. So I was safe from him.

I couldn't feel so sure about Agent White, who must have been the second man to come at Juliette. He was nowhere close to clean. If he'd known where to find my car, and if he'd had anything to do with Boston, then a planted GPS transceiver was the least of my worries. Considering the damage I'd done to the Lorca case, a block of plastic explosive wired to the ignition wasn't beyond the imagination. But White hadn't gotten anything out of Juliette about my parking space. So maybe the car was safe.

I took out my keys, unlocked the door, and sat down. To drive the car meant that I was trusting Juliette. Either I believed what she said about White, or I had no business using the car. I'd had six years to contemplate her trustworthiness, and had a pretty well-settled opinion on the matter. But tonight, the ground was shifting. She hadn't apologized, but she might have, if I'd stuck around long enough. She might have done a lot of things if I'd stayed in her car. I wasn't sure how far I wanted to pull that thread. So I hit the ignition and pumped my foot on the gas.

The Beast roared to life. There was no explosion. I backed out of my spot and headed up the ramps toward the street.

I took a roundabout route to Baker Street, driving through the park and across the bridge, then sitting awhile in the first pull-off, the city just an orange blur beneath the fog that smoothed out the hills. I crossed over again, parked on Chestnut Street, and walked back to Baker. When I finished climbing the hill, I could see the delivery van parked at the top. A good spot — they could survey the whole block. I pulled out my burner and called.

"What's up?" Jeremiah said. "That you, down at the corner?"

"Yeah."

"She's still inside. Three hours ago, she went upstairs. I saw her in the window. An hour ago it was lights out."

"Okay."

"You good, or should I stay?"

"I'm good."

"All right."

I hung up, then went up to the house and unlocked the door. I took off my shoes and walked around the entry level without turning on any lights. She'd had another bowl of ramen noodles. She'd found a bottle of wine but hadn't drunk much of it. The basement and garden doors were both locked. I went upstairs. Her bedroom door was open. I looked in and saw her beneath the covers. She was asleep on her side, facing me. There was a nightlight, low down, beneath the bedside table. I waited for my eyes to adjust, waited until I could see the slow rise and fall of her rib cage. Her hair was spread across the pillow as if, in the violent reaction to a dream, she had jerked her head forward.

Perhaps she'd been falling. Standing on the balustrade of a Tenderloin rooftop, unsteady in her black heels. And then a step off the edge. The city inverting itself as she somersaulted, the raindrops coming to a standstill as her velocity matched theirs.

"Lee?"

"Yeah," I said. "Hi."

"How long have you been there?"

"Not long," I said. "I was just checking. Making sure you're okay."

"What time is it?"

"Four thirty."

"You just got back?"

"Yeah."

"I'll get up," she said. "Give me a minute?"

"Keep sleeping," I said. "We'll talk in the morning."

I closed the door, then went upstairs.

I was too wired to sleep, and I hadn't properly searched Claire's study. Better to do that without Madeleine watching over my shoulder. And better to keep my hands and eyes busy so that I wouldn't start thinking about White, and the man in Boston, and my missing safe. Or, for that matter, Juliette Vilatte, and how she'd waited across the street from my office, freshly showered and lightly perfumed, at three in the morning. Better not to think of any of that at all.

19

MADELEINE DIDN'T SLEEP for long.

For ten minutes around sunrise, the sky was pink and underlit. Out the study window, the bridge's south tower was glowing a rich golden red. Then the sun got above the low clouds, the morning became gray and shadowless, and Madeleine woke up. Downstairs, she opened her bedroom door. Instead of going up, her footsteps led down. I listened for the front door, but she didn't head that way. I heard kitchen sounds: water running, beans in a coffee grinder. I gathered what I'd found in Claire's desk and went downstairs.

"Good morning," Madeleine said. "Again."

She'd ground the coffee and put a kettle on the stove. Now she was looking through the cabinets.

"I saw a French press," I said. "Up, and to the right."

"Thanks."

"Can I have a cup?"

"Of course," she said. "How was Mrs. Gravesend?"

"Upset, but understandably so."

"I meant, what did you learn?"

"At first she stuck to her story — Claire was her biological daughter, born in the Virgin Islands. But she opened up once I challenged her."

"Claire was a foundling too."

I nodded.

"She was left at the Carmel Mission, bloody wounds up and down her spine. This was two days before you showed up in Yakima. A priest found her after someone knocked on the chapel door. But he got killed in Africa. The only other person who knew about it was the bishop—and he's dead too. Cancer."

"So what now?"

"Coffee," I said. "And then I have some questions."

She finished making the coffee, and then when we each had a mug of it, I began to show her what I'd brought from upstairs. The first thing was a slim Moleskine notebook. It was dog-eared and bent, as though Claire had been in the habit of shoving it deep into her purse or her pockets to keep it out of sight.

"In Boston, I found two keys," I said. "One of them opened the front door. The other fit a lockbox behind the Dalí print in her study. And that's where I found this."

"What is it?"

"You tell me."

I passed the notebook across to her. She slid the elastic strap off its cover and opened it. For five minutes I drank my coffee and watched her read. When she looked up, I knew what she was going to say before she said it.

"This doesn't make any sense."

"Okay."

"Except, it sort of fits."

"How?"

"Look at this," she said. "She wasn't asking questions about police reports, or abandoned children, or child abuse rings. She was thinking about science, and research. Which makes sense, for Claire. She always leaned in that direction. One night we sat out in her back patio, by the fire—you saw that?"

I nodded.

"So we sat there, and she wanted to talk about experiments. As in, what if we were part of one?"

"And?"

"If we're twins, and I'm older, then she was frozen as an embryo," Madeleine said. "Where would you go if you wanted to find a lot of frozen embryos? Human embryos."

"A lab?"

"Not just a lab. A fertility clinic. They get dozens of fertilized eggs but only implant a few of them. They keep the rest on ice."

"But the scars?"

"That's where the experiments come in."

I pictured a fertility doctor who was running something on the side. Either pure research or an additional income stream. Something involving genetics, since that's where Claire had put her money.

"What did Claire think?" I asked.

"She didn't know. At least not then. But she must have gotten somewhere on her own, right?" She pressed her hand on Claire's secret journal. "These are her notes. She was interviewing people."

"Scientists, it looks like."

Whatever Claire was searching for was probably written down in this notebook. The problem was that she'd gone about her business as though she feared someone might be watching over her shoulder. Her first layer of defense was to omit her sources' names. On top of that, she'd veiled the substance of her discussions in an incomprehensible, but quaintly Victorian, code.

> Asked Doctor A about c —, and its effect on t —.
> He talked for an hour, showed me cross-sections
> of D —'s brain, some video taken before she died.

> He told me about Professor B, at Columbia. Went
> to New York on the next train . . .

She made it to Columbia, and found *Professor B,* who mentioned *Source C.* Source C was harder to track down, and she'd left Harvard to do it, but she eventually found him in California. She confronted him coming out of a dinner party in Santa Monica, and somehow talked him into meeting her at a bar. He was the one who told her about *Madame X.* The rest of the notebook — five entries spanning three pages — detailed Claire's apparently fruitless search for Madame X.

Madeleine read to the end, then closed the book and gave it back to me.

"Who are these people?" she asked. "And what did she want from them?"

The notebook wasn't giving any answers. I had more questions after I'd read it than before I'd found it. Who was D? Why did Doctor A have cross-sections of her brain, and video taken before she died?

"Columbia must have a faculty list," Madeleine said. "Why not email every male professor in a scientific field and ask if he met with Claire — or someone who looked like her, if she wasn't using her own name?"

"I think we should wait on that," I said. "It's a good idea, but if someone in this notebook is connected to Claire's death, I'd rather not telegraph our first punch."

"Then what?"

I gave her the second folder I'd found upstairs, which had been in an unlocked filing cabinet. It held a small stack of monthly statements from Claire's bank, and from her credit card company. All of the statements were addressed to the San Francisco house. Evidently she'd been living here long enough to have her mail redirected from Boston.

"So?"

"So other than cell phones, there's no better way to track a person than with a credit card," I said. "Claire didn't have a cell phone on her — it's not on the inventory schedule attached to her autopsy report. And she didn't have any credit cards, either. Which means this is a lead the police don't have. And if we can't follow the people in her notebook, then we can do the next best thing."

"Follow the money."

"Check this out," I said. I showed her the most recent statement. The account activity was already thirty days old. "She was getting cars from the rental places in North Beach, buying gas and lunches in towns up and down the coast. Look."

She read it. Then she pushed it back.

"These are weeks old — useless, probably. You should get the most recent transactions from her bank."

"I'm not like the cops," I said. "I can't serve search warrants. And if I call the banks and start asking questions, the only thing I'll get is a dial tone."

"So what do we do?"

I showed her the file folder where I'd found Claire's credit card statements. On the tab, she'd written her email address. Beneath that was something I didn't understand. I hoped Madeleine did.

"I think the top line, the email address, is her login name," I said. "So she can manage this stuff online. Which means this thing down here is a password."

I pointed to the second line of Claire's careful handwriting.

C x x x x x x x x x 99

"But wouldn't that account be shut down?"

"Why would it be?"

"Because she's dead."

"They don't know that."

"The coroner or the medical examiner or whoever did an autopsy — don't they issue a death certificate, and file it somewhere?"

"The only place they send death certificates is the Social Security Administration. But Claire probably wasn't getting Social Security, was she?"

"So all her accounts are still open?"

"Whatever she had, wherever she hid it, it's all still out there. All totally active. Bank accounts, credit lines, social media — everything."

Madeleine took the file folder, sliding it across the counter. I sipped my coffee, and watched as she studied the veiled password, tapping her fingertip against each *x*. Her lips were moving, spelling something out as she counted. She shook her head, and tried a different word. The second one must have been a better fit — she repeated it, whispering faster. Then she looked up at me.

"Claire Bear," she said. "It's what her mother called her when she was little. She liked it. Sometimes she'd call herself that, admonishing herself, in her mother's voice."

"She'd do what?"

"Claire Bear, if you have one more glass of wine, your head will assuredly ache tomorrow," Madeleine said. She sounded eerily similar to Olivia Gravesend. *"Claire Bear, your gentleman caller is waiting at the restaurant, and you're not even dressed — but I suppose it wouldn't be the absolute worst thing in the world if you were to stand him up."*

I pulled the folder back to my side of the counter, and tapped my finger along the spaces as I spelled out the words.

"And she was born in 'ninety-nine," I said. "Do you have your phone?"

She pulled it out, and I passed her one of the statements.

On the bottom of each page there was a website address. Valued Customers were invited to visit for more detailed information.

Madeleine used her thumbs to tap in the address. Then she paused, set down the phone, and looked up.

"It's okay to do this?"

"All we're doing is taking a look. And who's checking?"

She considered that a while. Then she typed Claire's login name, and the password. The screen went blank. Somewhere — I pictured a subterranean server farm in the Nevada desert — a computer was evaluating our credentials. Madeleine and I watched together, leaning from opposite sides of the counter.

> You're almost there! Because we don't recognize
> the device you're using, please identify yourself
> by answering the following security questions.

There were three questions, preselected by Claire when she set up the account. What is your favorite sports team? What was the name of your first grade teacher? In what city were you born? I glanced up at Madeleine.

"Did she ever talk about a sports team?" I said.

"We went to a couple of Red Sox games. She'd never been to anything like that. I think she had fun."

"So, the Red Sox. She went to Stevenson School, kindergarten through high school — right?"

"How did you know?"

"I searched her bedroom, in her mother's house," I said. "There was a ribbon from a fourth grade science fair. Second place. And a draft of something she'd written in her senior English class."

"But we need her teacher's name."

"She never told you?"

"How would that have come up?"

168

"I thought you stayed up all night, talking about every-thing."

"Come on."

I took out my burner, and dialed Olivia Gravesend. The butler answered on the second ring.

"Gravesend residence."

"This is Crowe."

"Mrs. Gravesend is out."

"You'll do," I said. "If you know the name of Claire's first grade teacher."

He paused, and I could picture the thought-wheels turn-ing. He didn't particularly like me, but I was the only per-son taking a serious look at Claire's death. And whatever the distance imposed by their peculiar relationship, he'd loved Claire.

"It was Mrs. Knore."

"Spell that."

"K-N-O-R-E."

"Thank you, Mr. Richards," I said.

He hung up. I turned to Madeleine.

"Type in *Mrs. Knore*. That's K —"

"I heard."

She typed with her thumbs, then tapped the screen to move the cursor to the input field for the last question.

"What about the place of birth?" she asked. "That's kind of up for grabs."

"Charlotte Amalie," I said. "For all she knew."

Madeleine grabbed the credit card statement. She flipped back to the first page, jabbed her finger into some text at the top that I'd paid no attention to.

> Congratulations! You've been a Valued Cus-tomer for one year, and you've already earned Gold Medallion Status! Log in to the website to learn more.

"I met her more than a year ago," Madeleine said. "By the time she got this card, and picked these questions, she had a pretty good idea she wasn't born in the Virgin Islands."

"Did she have any hunches?"

"She didn't have a clue."

"Then type in *unknown*," I said. "Let's see what happens."

She typed, hit the ENTER button, and then we waited. The screen went blank again. Signals traveled and servers churned. This time, it didn't take long.

> Welcome back, Claire! Did you know you've earned Gold Medallion Status? Click here to learn more.

"They're really pushing that medallion program," I said.

"If it was a card I could get, it'd just be a scam. But for her, it's probably legit. Free hotels in Monte Carlo or something."

I didn't take my eyes from the screen, but I didn't miss the fact that she had, once again, contrasted her financial situation with Claire's. Now she had the ability to log in to Claire's account anytime she wanted. It could be interesting to see what she did with that.

"Go to Account Activity," I said.

Madeleine tapped the link, and we both leaned in close to the phone, to read through the mundane transactional history of Claire Gravesend's last twenty-six days on earth. If she had known the days were running out, she hadn't done a lot to treat herself. And for a multimillionaire, she appeared to have a remarkable ability to scrounge a five-dollar lunch from a gas station. But maybe that was just because she'd been on the road a lot. She'd rent a car for a few days, and stay in motels up and down the coast, then be back in the city long enough to need a thirty-dollar trip to the grocery store. She hadn't been going crazy. If she'd been blowing money on diamonds, on cars like the one she'd flattened, she hadn't been doing it with this card. Though God knows she could have, with her available credit.

We scrolled to the bottom of the list. Her second-to-last charge was a five-hundred-dollar credit hold for a room at a Mendocino bed-and-breakfast. The B&B had never undone the hold, and had never charged her for the room. That probably meant she'd never checked out, and the B&B didn't know what to do.

Her last charge might have been in a bar. She'd bought something for twenty-six dollars and change at a place called the Creekside.

"Click on that one," I said. "I want to see more."

Madeleine clicked on the link and we read the few lines of text that came up. There wasn't much information. The date of the transaction, and the address and phone number of the business that had submitted it. The place was up a forest road to the northeast of Mendocino. About as remote as you could get, in that part of California. Madeleine touched the screen, her fingertip tracing beneath the date and then the address.

"That's impossible," she said. "Isn't it?"

"We don't know the time. Just that it happened the day she fell."

The transaction had gone through sometime after midnight, the same morning Claire had died. At least the drink fit — her autopsy report noted a blood alcohol level of point-zero-five. She hadn't been legally drunk when she died, but she might have been when she left the bar. Mendocino was three hours north of San Francisco. A hundred and fifty miles. Some of the roads were so curvy that you couldn't speed if you wanted to. And I'd found Claire just before five in the morning.

"The timeline works," I said. "She might've had a couple hours to get to the Refugio."

Madeleine shook her head.

"And then what? Pick the lock, run up the stairs, and jump off the roof? For what?"

"I didn't say it made sense. It's just possible."

"Yeah, but it really doesn't make sense," Madeleine said. "And if the police didn't find her credit card, where was it? In the rental car still? At the bar?"

"I don't know."

I scanned the credit card transactions and found the rental car. Like the bed-and-breakfast, the car company had put a hold on the account. And that hold, too, hadn't been lifted. I ran my finger under the transaction and watched Madeleine scan it.

"So where's the car?" she asked.

"Maybe somewhere in the Tenderloin."

"What do we do?"

"We go up to Mendocino and ask around. At the bar, and the bed-and-breakfast."

"We?"

I had a feeling she'd come in handy, but I didn't want to explain that to her. She might refuse to play along. Either on moral grounds or for simple considerations of safety.

"You've got something else to do?" I asked.

Apparently she didn't, because she put her phone away, set her coffee mug in the sink, and spoke to me over her shoulder while she was rinsing it.

"Give me a minute. I'll grab some things."

As soon as she was upstairs, I took out my burner and texted Elijah. I told him I'd be out in an hour, mystery blonde in tow. He and Jeremiah needed to cover the empty house and follow anyone who broke in. It had taken me about twenty minutes at City Hall to find the place, and my only clue was an unmarked key. If I could do that, so could anyone else.

20

WE REACHED MENDOCINO just before noon and
passed through the town without stopping. Fifteen miles up
the coast, past Fort Bragg and the village of DeHaven, we
turned off Highway 1 and onto the forest road. Madeleine
had been using her phone, but turned it off and set it aside.

"This place, the Creekside — it doesn't have a website."

"Okay."

"And it's not like she was just wandering past and saw it."

"So she was meeting someone," I said. "Maybe she found
Madame X."

"Look at this — a one-lane bridge. And the curves," Madeleine said. We were following a creek through the woods.
The road was a coiled ribbon, barely the width of the Beast's
wheelbase. "What do we have? Ten more miles?"

"Twelve."

"If she was so desperate to die, why drive all the way back
to the Tenderloin?" Madeleine asked. "It'd be hours. She
would've had time to cool off. She could've called someone
— she could've called me."

"I know."

"The whole idea that she jumped . . . it's bullshit."

A fair point, but I didn't answer. I drove. It was a road that
took some concentration, and I gave it what it asked for.

• • •

Our initial sighting of the Creekside wasn't what I'd pictured. I'd imagined a ski lodge the size of a shopping mall, the kind of place that had gazelle on the menu and strung-out rock stars wandering in the lobby. But after we passed over another wooden trestle bridge and turned onto a gravel driveway, Madeleine's phone announced that we'd arrived at our destination. That was it. There was nothing else that indicated we'd arrived anywhere. Just the gravel drive.

I stopped the car in the middle of the road. As soon as we were still, the air around us filled with winged things. Mayflies, maybe, hatched from the creek. They thumped gently against the car. Soft bodies and cellophane wings.

"What do you think?" I asked, looking up the driveway.

Madeleine looked at her phone.

"It's up there. Or it doesn't exist."

"Do you have cell reception, or is that offline?"

"Offline."

Which meant we had a minimalist map and no possibility of a satellite view. We couldn't see what we were getting into. We'd just have to drive up and see.

I put the car in gear and took the turn. We rolled upward along a right-hand curve. Midway up, there was a small bronze sign on the left, mounted on a post so that it would be at eye level for a driver.

MEMBERS ONLY

That was more like it. Back in the trees, where the shadows were already long, I caught a flicker of red light from between the needles of a young redwood. I focused, and saw a telltale ring of LEDs. The kind of near-infrared lights that circled the lens of a night-vision-equipped closed-circuit camera. I pointed it out to Madeleine.

"Nice little club," I said. "All the precautions."

"They could've just put up a fence."

174

"Then everyone would know they were here."

After the sign, and the camera, the driveway changed. The muddy ruts disappeared. The gravel was raked, proceeding up the hill between two rows of well-tended rosebushes like a Zen garden. Pale yellow blossoms drew butterflies and bees. I saw three more cameras in the woods. I wasn't sweating yet. This was Northern California. Squatters lived elbow to elbow with billionaires. A forest clearing could be a place to park an Airstream trailer, or a landing pad for a twin-turbine helicopter. So far as anyone watching the camera footage knew, we were just a couple of road-trippers who took a wrong turn.

In a quarter of a mile, we came to a parking area made of crushed black slate. A low stone building sat at the far end, dwarfed by the old-growth redwoods that rose behind it. The trees were so tall, they were catching the sea breeze, drawing a cloak of fog to the ground.

I eased the Beast between a Tesla and a Land Rover. There were half a dozen other cars parked around the side of the building, where a stone-lined path led into the woods. Someone had set oil lanterns at ten-foot intervals along the path's wooden handrails. At night, they would give just enough of a glow to allow a person to walk comfortably down the path, but beyond that it would be pitch black, the woods full of mystery.

"What is this place?" Madeleine asked.

"No idea."

"Best guess, then."

"A spiritual retreat," I said. "Yoga for rich ladies. Cooking classes and paint-by-numbers in the moonlight."

"And they get their chakras tuned. While they kick a stubborn pill habit."

"Was Claire into that kind of stuff?" I asked.

"Not in the slightest. And she didn't need rehab."

She opened her door and got out. I followed her across

the parking lot, over the oak-planked porch, and through the front door. The inside of the Creekside looked like the tasting room at a Napa winery. Untreated wood floors, a stand-up bar, a few tables made of wine barrels. There was a big fireplace at one end — not big by Gravesend standards, but by mine — and a slim woman in an equally slim black dress waiting behind the bar.

"Welcome," she said.

"Yeah. Hi."

She reached beneath the bar and brought out a pair of tall wineglasses. Maybe it really was a tasting room. The vineyard could be on the other side of the hill, assuming they'd cleared the forest.

"And will you be staying with us?" she asked.

"Staying? No."

She looked relieved.

"I didn't see any new names on tonight's list," she said. "I thought there'd been a mix-up."

"No mix-up."

"But you are members?"

"Members?" Madeleine asked.

"I'm sorry," the woman said. "But this is a private club."

She picked up the glasses and put them away. I glanced to my right. Madeleine wasn't paying any attention to the woman. She was looking at the fireplace. Set into the wall above the mantel was a rectangular piece of black stone, bigger than a king-sized bed. Carved into it, in careful bas-relief, was a snake. Or maybe it was a dragon. It had what appeared to be wings. Legs sprouted from its scaled belly. It was bent into a circle, so that its long-fanged mouth could swallow its own tail. The building was relatively new, but the carving looked ancient. As though it had been chiseled free of its original site by Egyptian temple robbers.

Madeleine reached back and touched one of the circular scars on her neck. Her skin had broken out into goose bumps.

I turned back to the young woman.

"We don't want a drink," I said. I showed her my investigator's license, the kind of open-and-closed flash that every detective does on TV but none of the real ones ever use. "You don't have to serve us, so it doesn't matter if we're members. I have a couple of questions about some credit card fraud. I'm sure it's not a big deal, but we need to clear it up."

"Wait. Credit card fraud?"

"Yes, ma'am," I said. "I'm investigating a charge that was claimed by this business. Four nights ago."

"I don't know anything about that," she said. "I was on vacation all last week. Look, you should really go."

"But that's where it gets complicated," I said. "Because I need to write a report. And right now, I can't say that there wasn't fraud. Or criminal activity. So there will be an escalation. Then you won't be talking to me, but to the feds. So help me out."

"And you'll go?"

"You take credit cards here?"

"Of course."

"And you're open past midnight?" I asked.

"Not usually."

"What's that mean?"

"It depends on the members. On what they want."

"But sometimes you're open that late?"

She nodded.

"If someone asks."

"A member asked, four nights ago?"

"I don't know," she said. "I wasn't here."

"Is there a list?"

"Of members?"

"Members, what they request. All of that."

"I couldn't show that to you."

"So you have it."

She backed up until her shoulder pressed against the door behind the bar.

"I don't know if we have it. I didn't say we had one."

"But you couldn't show it to us if you did."

"I don't know anything about our members," she said. "It's a private club."

"A private club for what?" I asked.

"For our members."

"Who come here to do what?"

"Whatever they want."

"It sounds like a great club," I said. "How do I join?"

"You need an invitation."

"Can you invite me?"

"I'm not a member. I just work here."

"Is Claire Gravesend a member?"

"No."

"But you didn't look at the list. So how do you know?"

"I don't recognize her name."

"You know all the members' names? No exceptions? I thought you didn't know anything about the members."

She looked at the front door. Maybe she was hoping I'd give up and leave.

"Maybe there are one or two exceptions to the rules?" I asked.

"I didn't say that. I didn't say anything. You're putting words in my mouth."

I rested my fingers on the edge of the bar. The young woman glanced at the door behind her but held her ground.

"Let's make sure I've got this straight," I said. "You're not usually open late, but you might be if a member asked. You don't know if anyone asked four nights ago, because you weren't here last week. But you're not ruling it out. And you take credit cards."

"Yes," she said. "If we're done, I think you should go."

"What can you buy here for twenty-six dollars?"

"This is about a twenty-six-dollar charge?"

"Fraud is fraud. And with a credit card, you're looking at wire transmissions across state lines. Put that with a pattern of activity—"

"A glass of Cabernet."

"That's what you can get?"

"Or two glasses of Chardonnay."

"You ring that up and it'd be what? Tax and everything."

"Twenty-six fifty-seven."

Which was the last amount charged on Claire's card.

"When can I come back to see the manager?"

"You need more?"

"I need to write a report. The people who read it will have certain questions. You want me to have the right answers."

"Tomorrow. He'll be in tomorrow."

"This time tomorrow?"

"Yes."

"So he's not here now?"

"There are a lot of people here now," she said. Again, she glanced at the door behind her. "Just not him."

"Thanks," I said.

I turned and walked out, and Madeleine came along beside me.

The Beast didn't idle quietly. She rumbled, and shook. I could feel the vibrations moving up my spine. We sat in the parking lot, facing the forest and the path that led away into the woods. Whatever secrets this club had were down there.

"What was going on in there?" I asked Madeleine. "The minute we walked in you were staring at the fireplace."

"I've seen it before."

"The fireplace?"

She shook her head.

"The snake. That carving, or something like it. I can remember it."

"Where?" I asked. "When?"

"I don't know—of course I don't know." The look on her face was pure fear. "Let's get out of here."

I put the car in gear and we started down the rose-lined driveway. I checked the rearview mirror just before the building was out of sight. The young woman had come outside. She was standing next to a man. Blond hair, cut close. His chest was the width of the Beast's engine block. I guessed he wasn't the cook. Then they were out of view, and I drove the rest of the way to the road.

I waited until we'd crossed the second trestle bridge, and then I slowed and turned to Madeleine.

"Tell me," I said. "What happened just now, and what you remember."

"I don't remember anything but what I told you. I think I've seen it before, but I don't know when, or where."

I started driving again.

"We need to find out more about this place," I said.

"What is it?" Madeleine asked. She was breathing deeply and slowly, and rubbing hard at her elbows. "A members-only hotel?"

"It's whatever the members want it to be."

"It's what?"

"She told us," I said. "The members can do whatever they want. And back there, they have a lot of privacy."

She thought about that for a while. The pain in her joints didn't seem to subside. We crossed the creek three more times, and then came into a clearing where a down-blast of wind had leveled the forest. Suddenly we were in sunshine. Around us were the rotting trunks of fallen trees. Trees that would have lived five thousand years but for one unfortunate night.

"What now?" Madeleine asked.

"There's the bed-and-breakfast, in Mendocino. The last place she stayed the night."

"We're going there?"

"We'll get a room," I said. I heard myself say it, and I glanced at her. "A couple of rooms. We'll wait until midnight, and then come back here."

"To do what?"

"Find out what's down that path, for starters."

"I don't know how safe that is," Madeleine said. "There's something about that place that isn't right."

"I know it."

"But you know Claire was there, don't you?" she asked. "It's not like someone stole her credit card and then drove out to a cult compound to buy two glasses of Chardonnay. She went there herself. There must have been something she wanted."

We drove the rest of the way to Mendocino without talking. It wasn't dark and I wasn't going easy on the gas pedal. But it took close to an hour. Which got me thinking again about Claire, and her last drive. In half an hour, when we arrived at the Discovery Cove Bed and Breakfast, we got some new information. It compounded the problem exponentially.

Claire hadn't gone straight from the Creekside to San Francisco. She'd made a stop. And her rental car had never made it out of Mendocino.

21

WE WERE JUST NORTH of Mendocino, at a rocky inlet marked on the map as Slaughterhouse Cove. Claire had meant to spend the night here, at a bed-and-breakfast that faced the ocean. The geographical nomenclature was clearly no good for business, and so the owner of Claire's lodgings had invented a more inviting name. The Discovery Cove Bed and Breakfast. Which wasn't bad for the place. The cove was beautiful — a broad finger of deep blue water dotted with rocks and islets, and surrounded on three sides by grass-topped cliffs. The grounds of the B&B were even better. There were cypress trees and Spanish dagger plants, and roses twined around stone birdbaths and white lattice archways — landscaping flourishes my ex-wife would have called bride magnets. She'd married me under such an arch near Point Reyes, so I suppose she knew what she was talking about.

The main house was a Victorian gingerbread affair, with big porches and a lot of hand-painted scrollwork under the eaves. The rooms were all individual cottages, six or eight of them spread out on the parcel. According to the website, which I'd checked out after finding the credit hold, some of them came with their own porches, some of them with hot tubs or fireplaces. All of them had views of the ocean and the waves breaking on the cliffs up and down the difficult coast.

I parked in the small lot and we got out. We walked side by side up the steps and past the rocking chairs that lined the porch. I opened the door for Madeleine and we walked over to the concierge desk at the far end of the room. There was a silver push-button call bell on the blotter. Behind the desk was a doorway with a velvet rope across it, and a sign that said STAFF ONLY.

I gave the bell a double-tap, and then we waited. Above us, there was a creak of footsteps coming down a set of wooden stairs, and then a woman appeared in the doorway, lifting the rope from its hook so she could step through. She had silver-black hair tied up in a perfectly round bun at the top of her head, and she wore a neat floral print dress that seemed to reflect all of the colors in her yard.

She looked at me, and opened her mouth to begin either a question or a note of welcome, but whatever she was about to say never came out, because she saw Madeleine. Her eyes widened, and she reached out and took hold of the doorjamb for balance. Then she turned and looked back the way she had come, and shouted so she could be heard from upstairs.

"Larry! She's back!"

Next to me, Madeleine was backing up. I reached out and took her hand, to keep her from bolting. This was exactly what I'd wanted. The kind of break I'd been hoping for when I'd asked Madeleine to come along. I gave her fingers a quick squeeze. *Play it cool,* I was telling her. And she must have gotten the message, because she eased up. From upstairs, there was a muffled response. The voice of an old man who'd been roused from rest and wasn't especially happy about it.

"Larry!" the woman said, again. "She's come back! Get her things!"

There was another grunt from upstairs, this time a little louder. Then the woman turned to us. One lock of hair had come loose, falling across her forehead. She brushed it back.

"I'm sorry," she said to Madeleine. "You were only registered for that one night, and you didn't come back. I had a wedding the next night — every cottage booked — and we didn't know what to do. So we packed up your things in the morning, and made up the room. I haven't run your card yet."

"I'm not —" I squeezed Madeleine's hand again. A little harder this time. "I mean, I apologize."

I let go of her hand and she stepped forward.

"Some things came up and I had to leave in a hurry."

"We saw you go with those people."

"It was a family emergency."

"Three in the morning, and peeling out of the lot. It must've been an emergency."

"I can take my things back," Madeleine said. "And if you have any rooms —"

Larry came through the doorway. His left foot dragged a bit, but he held his back straight. He was carrying a black roller bag, the kind that could fit into any airline overhead compartment without too much fuss.

"Thank you so much," Madeleine said.

Larry didn't look at her, or at me. He simply set the bag down and turned to go.

"And her car keys," the woman said. "Don't forget her keys, Larry."

He pointed at the bag's outside zipper pocket, and then he went back upstairs without saying anything.

"As for rooms," the woman said, "we opened up, after the wedding. I can give you the Drake Cottage again."

Madeleine looked at me, and I nodded.

"Sure," she said. "We'll take it."

"Then you're all set. You're already registered — I can just charge you for the night you had, and add this one," the woman said. "And you know your way."

The woman gave a weak smile, then glanced down at the

bag. She was waiting for Madeleine to take it and for us to walk away. Probably only a few seconds passed, but they stretched out a long way and became uncomfortable.

"The key?" Madeleine asked.

"You don't have it?"

"No — I — I'm sure I must have left it in the room," Madeleine said. Her voice took on the same tone as her imitation of Claire imitating Olivia Gravesend.

"We didn't see it when we cleaned the cottage," the woman said. She took a key from her pocket and unlocked the cabinet on the wall behind her. Inside were small cubbyholes, labeled with the names of the cottages. Her hand moved past Vancouver and Cook, then stopped at Drake. She took the key, which was on a heavy pewter fob cast in the form of a sailing ship. She handed it to Madeleine. "Have a look for yours tonight. Or we'll have to charge you the replacement fee."

"Of course," Madeleine said. "And I'm sorry about this — all this confusion."

Madeleine took Claire's bag and we went back out the way we'd come. When we were outside, in the parking lot, I began looking for cameras. There were none that I could see, and that was a pity. Because I saw tire tracks memorializing a particularly rapid exit from the B&B's asphalt lot. The marks led all the way out to the road. The car had skidded out of the lot in a hard right turn. Which would have taken it to the north. Away from San Francisco.

"We won't find the key in the Drake Cottage," I said. "The autopsy report had a schedule of personal property. One of the things on it was a key on a pewter fob."

"She left all her things but she took her key — she planned to come back."

"But now the timing's even harder," I said. "Claire got picked up at three. That gave her an hour and a half, max, to make it to San Francisco."

"Could they have done it?"

"They were definitely in a hurry," I said. I nodded toward the tire tracks. "But they didn't go the right way."

I unlocked the Beast's trunk and took out my backpack. It had my laptop and my toothbrush, and that was about it. Before I could shut the trunk, Madeleine stopped me with her hand at the small of my back. She leaned close to speak.

"We're going to go wandering all around this place looking for the right cottage," she said. "Trying our key in every lock. Larry and the Bun Lady are going to look out an upstairs window and figure out something's wrong — if they haven't already."

She had a point there. The Bun Lady had accepted Madeleine as Claire. And Claire would know the way to her cottage.

"No," I said. "I'll go wandering, with the key and the suitcase. Because I don't know this place. You stay here a bit. You need to make a phone call."

"Okay."

I took the key and the roller bag and set off. I looked back, once, and saw Madeleine leaning against the Beast's hood, talking into her phone. She was gesticulating with one hand.

It looked real enough that I wondered if she'd actually called someone.

There were little signs in front of every cottage, which made it easier. I didn't have to go up to every door and try the lock. I just walked past Magellan and Vancouver, and then went down the stepping-stone path to Drake. I climbed the steps to its porch and unlocked the door. Turning the dead bolt took a bit of effort, as though the replacement key hadn't been ground to quite the right shape. I leaned to look at the lock, and saw bright scratches in the otherwise dull bronze patina. I'd picked enough locks to know the telltales.

I turned back to the parking lot. Madeleine was still

talking on the phone, but acknowledged me with a two-fin-gered wave. If she was faking it, she was exceptional. Her lips were moving, quickly and purposefully. I went in and closed the door behind me.

It was a three-room bungalow. A living room, a bedroom, and a bathroom. The bed was a canopy job, and the bath had claws on its feet. There was a door from the bedroom that opened onto a small deck, where a cedar hot tub hid from the road behind a low trellis of clematis. Peek over the top and you'd have an unobstructed view of Slaughterhouse Cove.

The entire cottage was spotlessly clean. Whoever had hit it must have come after Larry and the Bun Lady had cleaned out Claire's things. Which got my mind sprinting down a half-dozen twisting paths all at once. Claire had left this room at three in the morning, and was dead on Turk Street an hour and a half later. The B&B's owners had cleaned out the room sometime after eleven. Someone else had checked in later that day. Sometime during that window, a person had come and picked the Drake Cottage's lock. And barely twenty-four hours later, someone had picked the lock to Claire's Beacon Hill house in Boston.

I believed that the man I'd killed in Boston was related to the men who'd bugged my apartment and trashed my office. And that all three break-ins were connected to Agent White.

But now I had to accept another possibility. Everything that had happened could be about Claire. I could be a tar-get because of that alone. Because I had taken a photograph. Because Jim Gardner had sent me to Olivia Gravesend, who had hired me to find out the truth. Someone had found out about that and had set out to shut me down.

"Lee?"

I turned toward Madeleine, who had just come into the cottage and shut the door.

"Everything okay?" I asked her.

"No trouble yet," she said.

She'd pocketed her phone.

"Were you actually talking to someone?" I asked. "You looked good out there."

"My boss, at the bookstore. Telling him I needed a few more days."

"Family emergency."

"It's true," she said. "It is a family emergency. But I needed to tell him something, to buy a little more time."

I hadn't given much thought to Madeleine's life. She was more than just a connection to Claire, and there was an entire world of things I didn't know about her — a swirl of family, friends, jobs, pets, leaking faucets, and rent to pay. All the triumphs and the minor annoyances. The only thing I knew for sure was that when she'd heard from Claire, she'd dropped all of it to come to San Francisco.

I picked up Claire's suitcase and set it down on the bed.

"We were lucky to get this," I said. "If Larry hadn't cleaned the room the next morning, it'd be gone."

"What do you mean?"

I told her about the lock, and waited while she went over to study it. When she was back, I unzipped the suitcase, and opened it.

Judging from her credit card transactions, most of Claire's journeys had lasted twenty-four hours or less. Out and back, in a single night. But she must have expected this one would take longer. She'd brought a few changes of clothes. I began to unpack the suitcase, lifting things out and setting them on the bedspread. Two pairs of jeans, folded carefully. A zippered mesh sack contained three pairs of panties and a bra. There was a crimson Harvard sweatshirt, in case the nights got cool. The only thing that wasn't neatly folded was an empty hanger bag. Larry must have stuffed it into the suitcase when he was cleaning out the room. But if it had held the dress she'd worn to her death, Claire had probably traveled with it hanging from the hook in the back seat of her rental car. She'd died wearing heels, but she'd packed sandals to wear with her jeans.

Beneath all the clothes, in matching leather cases, I found her laptop and her phone. I took out the phone and tried to reach its home screen, but it was locked. I needed either the six-digit passcode or Claire's thumb. I held it out to Madeleine.

"Do you know the code?"

"No."

"And you can't use your thumb?" I asked.

"Identical twins don't have the same fingerprints," she said. "The patterns aren't genetically coded."

"For real?"

"We tested it," Madeleine said. "We tried unlocking each other's phones. It didn't work."

I took out the computer. When I folded the screen back, it lit up and invited me to enter a password. I typed in *ClaireBear99*. Most people use the same password across a dozen accounts. It's wildly insecure, but it saves some time. But apparently Claire wasn't like most people. When I hit the return key, the screen's image shook side to side as if I'd fed it something bitter. It invited me to try again.

"Any idea on this?"

"None."

I closed the computer and put it back into its case. I probably only had a couple more tries and then the thing would lock itself for eight hours. I didn't want to waste my chances on random guesses as long as there was a chance Madeleine might remember something. If I'd known how short our time together really was, I might have done things differently.

22

BY AGREEMENT, AFTER a discussion in which I laid out more of my plans than I wanted to, Madeleine kept a low profile in the room. I went out to the parking lot to search Claire's rental car. I found nothing, but not for lack of trying. I searched under the spare tire, and under the hood, and I got down on my back and looked underneath the frame. But it was just an empty rental car. The only trace of Claire was a lingering hint of perfume that I noticed when I sat in the passenger's seat to look through the glove box.

When I was done, I walked back to the main house, taking my time so that I could look again for security cameras. The gingerbread trim along the eaves would have been a perfect hiding place. But I didn't see anything.

I went into the house and crossed the lobby to the desk. I tapped the bell and waited for the Bun Lady to come downstairs. When she arrived, I had my investigator's license out and waiting for her.

"The lady's resting in her room," I said. "But I have a couple of questions."

"You're a detective?"

"She's upset and embarrassed about what happened the other night. And she's outraged."

"Outraged?"

190

"Not at you," I said. "I'm helping her look into what happened."

"It wasn't a family emergency?"

"No, ma'am," I said. I came a little closer, and lowered my voice. "She doesn't remember a thing about that night. She doesn't know who she left with, or when, or why. Or what they did to her."

"Did they drug her?" the woman asked. "One of those . . . like, a date drug?"

"Date rape drug," I said. "We can't rule it out. Did you see the people she left with?"

The woman's face had flattened in shock. I could guess what she wanted to tell me. Guests at the Discovery Cove Bed and Breakfast didn't get drugged and kidnapped. Let alone raped. This wasn't that kind of place.

"Larry saw them," she finally said.

"He did?"

"He doesn't sleep well. So he sits up," she said, and pointed toward the porch. "Out there. That's why we have all the rocking chairs."

"Can you go get him?"

"All right."

We spoke on the porch, side by side in wooden rockers. It was a good view. I wouldn't have minded sitting out there on the nights I couldn't sleep. Without turning my head, I could see the path that led down to the Drake Cottage. The parking lot was in front of me. Beyond it, there was the road, and then the cove.

"They came at three a.m.," Larry said. He was hoarse, and the skin underneath his eyes looked bruised. "I'd been out here a couple hours by then."

"Doing what?"

"Sweating it out."

191

"Excuse me?"

"I'm trying to quit these pills," he said. "My doctor's had me on them since I don't know when. It got so they were worse than the pain. Which is worst at night. So I come sit out here. I don't want to wake her up."

"You keep the porch light on?"

"She wants me to, for business. But I usually turn it off so I can see out."

"That night?"

"I'd turned it off."

"So it was pretty dark."

"Really dark, yeah," Larry said. He reached back and fidgeted with his shirt collar. The red flannel looked like it had been through the wash about a thousand times. "They came in a black car. It wasn't a limo, but if you stretched it out, it could've been. I couldn't tell you the make and model. European, I guess. If it was American, I'd have recognized it. And I never heard of cars that big coming out of Japan."

"Okay," I said.

"They pulled around, like they were using the driveway for a U-turn," he said, and pointed to the other side of the road. "You see how it is. It happens all the time."

The highway was narrow, a thin strip of asphalt that fell away to the ocean on the west side. If you'd missed whatever you were trying to find in Mendocino and suddenly found yourself heading out of town, you'd need a driveway to turn back.

"But then they stopped," Larry said. "Just sat there and waited, with the engine running."

"Nobody got out?"

"Not then. Not till she came walking out."

"Claire walked out, on her own?"

He pointed up the stepping-stone path that led back to the cottages. It wound past benches and archways of roses.

"Came through there. I heard her before I saw her. Black dress, so she blended in. It was the shoes that gave her away. Those high heels."

"Was she steady on her feet?"

"She could've walked a tightrope," Larry said. "Didn't look to me like she'd been drugged."

"She just came out? They didn't honk or anything like that?"

He shook his head, then reached back to rub his neck. There were scars behind his ear, a curved line of old staple marks in his scalp.

"She came out like she'd been waiting on them. Or like they called her."

"You keep saying *they*."

"When she got up to the car, a chauffeur climbed out of the front. Big guy, in a suit and a thin black tie. And one of those hats every chauffeur's got."

"How well could you see him?"

"When he opened the door, the dome light came on," Larry said. "So when he stood up, I could see him from the chest up, over the car's roof. Clean-cut white guy, blond hair. If I ran into him in West Hollywood, I'd say he was Russian. Up here, who knows?"

"What'd he do?"

"He came around and opened the back door, and a woman got out. When she stepped out of the way, I could see a man sitting on the other side."

"What'd they look like?"

"The woman had long blond hair. All done up in a thick braid, like a rope. She looked to be in her forties, maybe, though she seemed more fragile than that."

"How so?"

"She moved like someone used to being careful. Like she might trip and that'd be the end of it," he said. "And she was covered in jewelry — she had enough gold and stones to weigh down a dead body. You don't see that on many young people."

"I guess you couldn't see her face."

"Not really," Larry said. "She went up and the driver opened the front door for her, and she sat down up there. That girl of yours was coming across the parking lot. She got up to the car, and I don't think she knew the man was in the back until she bent to get in. Then she stepped back, real quick, and said something."

"What?"

"I couldn't make it out, and if any of them answered her, I couldn't hear that either."

"Okay," I said. "So what then?"

"The chauffeur put one hand on her shoulder and she got in the car. He shut the door behind her."

"Did he push her in?"

"If he did, it was gentle."

"A slow push, with a firm grip?"

"Maybe."

That seemed possible, given what happened to Claire a few hours later. But then again, I'd seen the autopsy photos. There hadn't been a handprint on either of Claire's shoulders. A big guy clamping down on a young woman and muscling her into a car would likely leave a mark. Maybe all she'd needed was a little nudge. Walking across the parking lot, she would have seen the woman get out and take the front seat. Larry hadn't said anything about her pausing when she saw the woman. So she was expecting her, but not the man — and she wanted to talk to the woman badly enough that the man wasn't a deal-breaker.

Maybe he should have been.

"What'd he look like?" I asked. "The guy in the back seat?"

"Blond hair, past his collar. A little bit curly. Nordic-looking guy, like a Viking — except he was clean-shaven."

"What was he wearing?"

"A suit, but he'd taken the jacket off. It was on his knee."

"Big guy?"

"More or less like his chauffeur."

"After she got in, what happened?"

"The driver shut her door. He went back around and got behind the wheel. And then they peeled out. I don't know what kind of car it was, but it must've had a big engine. Ten, twelve cylinders. Thing had to weigh a couple of tons, but it went out of there like a rocket."

Larry leaned back in his rocking chair. He'd rolled up his shirtsleeves. Faded tattoos ran up and down his forearms. Green ink blurred into sun-hardened skin. I couldn't read any of it, but I guessed they'd been unit numbers and insignia. Which might explain a few things about Larry.

"What'd you do before you got this place?" I asked.

"Ten years in the navy. Then twenty with LAPD," he said. He indicated the house with a nod. "My wife was in real estate, so this thing was her deal."

"How long since you retired?"

"Nine years."

"But you still know how to look at a guy in the dark and take down the details."

"You got that right."

"It's not a skill you forget."

"It isn't."

I stood up, and he didn't. I was about to thank him and walk off, and then I thought of something else.

"You ever heard of a place twenty miles up the road?" I asked. "Something called the Creekside?"

He looked up at me, paused, and seemed to consider an answer.

"The Creekside?"

"That's what they call it."

"Who's they?"

"The members. It's supposed to be a private club."

"Never heard of it."

"You get people stopping through who talk about a secret club? Something way out in the woods?"

Again, his eyes went far away. He was weighing an answer.

"If it was a secret, why would they talk about it?"

"I don't know."

"Neither do I," he said. "But I never heard about anything like that around here."

Instead of going back to the cottage, I walked across the highway and climbed out on a ledge of rock that hung fifty feet above Slaughterhouse Cove. The waves were breaking just beneath me, but there wasn't much of a swell today. I got out my flip phone. Reception was down to one bar. I dialed my forensics guy, George Wong.

He picked up on the fifth ring and said, "Who's this?"

"Are you in the lab?"

"Lee Crowe?"

"That's right. Can you hear me?"

"Mostly. I didn't recognize the number."

"I'm just using this phone awhile," I said. "You done anything yet?"

"You didn't get my email?"

"It's been hard for me to check it—can you run me through it?"

I turned to look south, then glanced to the left. I could see the Drake Cottage on the hill above the road. The curtains in the bathroom were drawn. Claire's rental car was still in the parking lot. It looked like Madeleine was settling in.

"I'll start with the old stuff," George said. "Because, frankly, it makes more sense."

"Okay."

"I found six prints on the box. I ran them all, but only got two hits."

"You actually got IDs?"

"Yeah, but it's not what you want," George said. "I called a friend at Quantico, and he ran them through all the archives I'm not supposed to have. The hit came off a military database. Your priest, David Martinez, was a GI before he took the collar."

"What was the other hit?"

"You — from the California DMV database."

"So prints are a dead end."

"Sure," George said. "So then I went to town on the blanket."

"I think it's a swaddle."

"Same difference. The stains are blood, and the DNA matches the hair you gave me."

"So we know it was Claire in the box. She was bleeding when she got dropped at the church."

"Yeah," George said. "We know that. But I went over the blanket with a magnifying glass and a fine comb. And I found a hair."

"What kind of hair?"

"Short, black, and straight. It might've come off a man's head — but don't get excited, because this wasn't like the hair you gave me. It didn't have the root and follicle attached."

"So you can't get DNA from it," I said.

On the highway, a tan SUV slowed as it approached from the north. Its turn signal lit up, and then it went into the B&B's lot. It parked in front of the main house and a man got out. I didn't think much of it. The place was bound to get another customer eventually. Another truck was coming down the highway, and I turned to face the ocean so I could hear George over the cacophony of diesel engines and air brakes.

"That's not totally true," he said. "The nucleus gets destroyed in the cornification process—when the cell transitions into hair. But you can get mitochondrial DNA from a hair because the mitochondria are preserved."

"Run me through what that means."

"Every cell has mitochondria, right? They're like the power plants for cellular life."

"Okay."

"And they have their own DNA. Your mitochondrial DNA comes entirely from your mother. So yours would be identical to hers, and hers would be identical to your grandmother's and so on, with only the usual variances for mutation."

"So you can't use it to identify people, is what you're saying."

I turned around and scanned the bed-and-breakfast. Larry was still on his rocking chair, watching me. I nodded at him, but couldn't tell if he responded. The tan SUV was still parked out front, but the driver was gone. He'd either gone to his room or he was in the main house, checking in.

"That's right," George said. "But you can tell other things."

"Like what, for example?"

"Like that whoever left that hair on the blanket was probably Korean."

"Korean?"

I looked up the hill to the Drake Cottage. Madeleine was out on the deck, leaning on the rail. There was a glass next to her elbow. She waved to me, and I waved back.

"We don't have any of the priest's DNA, but unless his mother was Korean, you can rule out Martinez. Same for the bishop, for your client, and for the little girl."

"And me," I said. "My mother wasn't Korean."

"So there you go," George said. "A clue."

"I'm looking for a Korean. That narrows it to what— eighty million people?"

George ignored me and went on.

"And in a way, it might fit with the other thing I found. Which is where it gets weird," he said. "You got time for this?"

"Go ahead," I said.

"It's about the girls," George said. "You gave me the hair and the bottle, and asked me to compare them. I did, and I've never seen anything like it."

I looked up again. The door to the deck was open, as were the windows in the sitting room. The white curtains fluttered inward on the gentle wind.

Madeleine was gone, and the tan SUV was racing out of the driveway and onto the road. Heading north.

23

"ACTUALLY, I MIGHT not have much time," I said. I was climbing off the rock ledge and scrambling back up to the road. "So if you can run it quick, that'd be good."

"I can lay it out in one sentence," George said. "They're identical twins, but they have different mothers."

"What?" I asked. Now I was moving across the road. Not quite running, but walking fast. "How is that possible?"

"Remember what I told you about mitochondrial DNA? I tested that, too, because I had to rule them out for the hair. Their nuclear DNA is identical, so they're twins. But their mitochondrial DNA profiles are completely different, which means their eggs came from different women."

"I thought identical twins came from one egg. That the egg splits in two and makes copies of itself."

"That's right. That's where twins come from — real twins, I mean."

"You're not making sense."

"How much do you know about cloning?"

It took me a few seconds to even come up with a response.

"I thought that was just sheep and dogs," I said. "Or crops. I thought they hadn't ever tried it on a human."

"Until this morning, I was right there with you," George said. "If you think the scientific hurdles are hard to clear, just imagine the legal ones. But look — the way cloning works is you take the DNA from the nucleus of a host cell and implant it in an egg. That's really all there is to it. And if you did that a couple of times, with the same nuclear DNA, but eggs from different women, then you'd have exactly what I'm looking at. Identical twins with nonidentical mitochondrial DNA."

"Isn't there another explanation?"

"Not that I can think of, unless you want to rewrite everything we know about mitochondrial DNA inheritance."

There was a truck coming, and I was still partially in the road. It swerved around me, its horn blaring. I got off the road and started down the driveway.

"You said something about Korea making sense," I said. "That it fit with what you'd found."

"Maybe it's not a big deal. But imagine that twenty years ago you wanted to have a dog cloned. Maybe some other complex mammal. Where would you have gone?"

"I don't know," I said. "Korea?"

"That's right — the South Koreans were pioneers. Their reputation took a hit ten years ago. One of their scientists got caught faking his research and got booted out of Seoul National University. But still — and I mean, to this day — if you want to lay out a small fortune and clone Fluffy and Rufus, it's Korea or nowhere."

"You're saying the hair on the swaddle might have come from . . . what? A scientist? Some kind of genetic engineering expert?"

George paused, which was unusual for him. I started walking again, staying on the far side of the lot so that I wouldn't have to acknowledge Larry, or even look at him. I made it to the stepping-stone path before George stopped me midstride once again.

"I'm going to go out on a limb here," he said. "I'm not just saying it's some random Korean scientist. I might actually know the guy's name."

"What?"

"I might have even met him once," George said. "Before he disappeared."

I could see the Drake Cottage up ahead. The front and back doors were open. I could look straight through the little house to the ocean.

"What are you telling me, George?"

I started walking again, getting off the stepping-stones and onto the grass so that I could approach the cottage without making noise.

"It's not a sure thing. It's just a guess. And I think the dates fit," George said. "When did you say the older woman was born?"

"'Ninety-six," I said.

"Then it's almost perfect," George said. "Look, in the nineties, there was one guy in Seoul who was writing paper after paper on nuclear transfer, and gene synthesis, and some things closer to my line of work, like DNA sample amplification. His name was Dr. Park Kwung-ho. You heard of him?"

"Why would I have?"

"It made the papers here, when he disappeared. In 1994."

In 1994, I was still in high school. I was dividing my time between a pair of places I wasn't supposed to be: a Tacoma boxing gym and a girlfriend's bedroom. I sometimes read the paper, but my mind was entirely occupied with concerns more immediately at hand.

"What did you hear about it?" I asked.

"There was some chatter in my circles. You know those old stories about the North Koreans, how they used to kidnap people off the beaches in Japan?"

"Sure."

"People thought maybe it was something like that. They wanted him — God knows what they could do with his skill set — so they came and grabbed him."

"You believed that?"

"I didn't give it much thought," George said. "But if there was one guy in the midnineties who could have cloned a human being, it was probably Dr. Park."

"What are you saying?"

"Maybe he didn't end up in North Korea or get lost in the woods. Maybe he took a job."

"In California."

"If he wasn't kidnapped, somebody hired him," George said. "Brought him over here to set up a lab."

"A lab for what?"

"Something secret enough that he had to fall off the map. And lucrative enough that he'd agree to do it."

I thought of the woman Larry had seen the night Claire died. A woman with a chauffeur, and enough jewelry that even an old cop noticed it. I didn't know her real name, but Claire had given me something to call her.

Madame X.

"He never turned up?" I asked. "This guy, Dr. Park?"

"Not that I know of. The FBI had a file on it."

"How do you know?"

"A couple agents interviewed me about it, in 'ninety-four or 'ninety-five. Because I'd had some emails back and forth with him, and they were going through all his contacts."

"Why was the FBI involved?"

"He was prominent, and the North Koreans might have had a hand. So of course there was a file. We had a file on everything like that."

"If they'd found something later on, would they have told you?"

"I don't know . . . maybe not."

"Could you ask around?"

"Sure."

Without climbing the steps, I peered inside the cottage. The cushions from the little couch were on the floor. Out on the deck, a drinking glass lay on its side, ice cubes and water spreading out in front of it.

"Thanks for this, George," I said. "But I've gotta go."

"Sure."

I folded the phone and pocketed it. Outside the cottage, in a bed of peonies, I spotted a small concrete statue. Neptune, maybe, or Zeus. It was eighteen inches tall. I picked it up by the head, hefted it so that I could swing it one-handed like a hammer, and went through the front door.

Inside, it took about ten seconds to see I didn't need a weapon. There was nowhere to hide except the shower, and that was empty. Claire's suitcase was gone, along with her computer. My backpack, which had held my own laptop, was also missing. The room had been haphazardly tossed. Drawers were open, the bedcovers had been ripped off and thrown to the side. In the bathroom, the lid had been shoved from the toilet's tank, and it had shattered on the porcelain floor.

I walked out onto the deck and looked back at the ocean. I could see the ledge where I'd been talking to George while this had happened. It must have gone down in under a minute. The question was how they had taken Madeleine. Larry, sitting in his rocking chair, would know if she'd been dragged to the SUV or if she'd walked to it willingly. The thing had been parked thirty feet from him. He must have seen me walking back across the parking lot. If he'd seen the same blond girl get kidnapped from his parking lot twice in one week, wouldn't he have said something to me?

There was nothing to do but go and ask him. I stopped outside the front door and set the statue back where I'd found it. Then I walked back down the path, under the lattice arches, the roses at full blossom and drawing bees.

I was thinking: *She played me.*

She'd used me until she got to Claire's computer, and then she'd called her friends. She tossed the room to make it look

204

like she'd been taken by force, but she'd relaxed once she'd left the cottage. Larry had been sitting right there; if anything had seemed strange, he would have raised an alarm. He hadn't said a thing.

In the confusion of that moment, it made sense. It seemed wholly logical. Or, at any rate, it explained all the facts as I knew them. She must have stolen Claire's things, taken my computer to hobble my investigation. I still didn't know who she was or what she wanted. But I was sure, right then, that she wasn't on my side.

At which point, I turned the corner and mounted the steps to the main house, and looked up. In one glance, my story fell apart. The facts had changed.

Larry's shirt was red, and the flannel was absorbent. From across the road, I hadn't been able to see what was now plainly visible. He'd been shot dead center in the chest. He was still in the rocking chair, hands gripping each armrest. His chin was resting against his sternum. There was a pool of blood in his lap and on the wooden seat.

From that point, and for the next ten minutes, I was on full automatic. I began climbing the stairs toward him, and stopped when I felt something underfoot. I'd stepped on a white towel. I must have stooped to pick it up, because I remember powder burns stippled down its center, and light shining through a series of holes. As if it had been folded like a Chinese fan and wrapped around the muzzle of the gun. A makeshift silencer. The man must have pulled the trigger seconds after exiting the car. The towel had covered some of the noise, and the rest of it had been blocked by the truck passing in front of me.

I crossed the porch, went right up to the rocking chair.

"Larry?"

Of course he wasn't going to answer, but right then I didn't understand that. I knelt next to him, and for the third time in nearly as many days, I put my hand on another person's throat and felt for a pulse that was nowhere to be found. Doing that must have tipped the rocking chair back, because when I let go and stood up, the chair tilted forward and Larry tipped out. He fell onto the porch, his head making a hollow *thunk* on the old redwood.

I looked for help, with Larry spilled around my feet. But there was no one else around. A mixed blessing. On the one hand, there was no one who could point an accusatory finger at me. On the other hand, there wasn't anyone else who could take over.

It was just me, and I knew what I had to do next.

The front door was wide open. I stepped over the threshold and into the lobby and crossed to the desk. I didn't need to ring the little bell. I could see the woman's feet protruding from behind the reception desk. I'd never learned her name, and now there was no point. A thick mist of blood dotted the wall. Clumps of hair lay on the carpet and the desktop. Even in my state, I could imagine the bullet's trajectory. I went around the desk, but didn't kneel beside her. It only took a glance at her head to see that there was no point in searching for a pulse.

I know there's very often a shortfall between a man's achievements and his aspirations. Between who he is and who he wants to be. And I'm hardly a special case. Look at me, and what I've done with my life. If there was a measure of my progress it was this: I was shocked. I didn't think about taking a picture. It never even crossed my mind. Or if it did, I don't remember it: Within a few hours of leaving Slaughterhouse Cove, I went through a second trauma, and one that was much more personal. From what I know about head injuries, it's fair to assume there are details about that day I don't remember.

But this is what I do know.

I caught my breath out in the parking lot, leaning against the Beast. When I could think again, I looked around. There were two cars in the lot — mine, and Claire's. Which probably meant the other cottages were empty. I had the place to myself, except for a couple of corpses. My name wasn't on the register, and my credit card wasn't on the system. We'd taken Claire's room, picking up where she'd left off. But my fingerprints were in the main house, and in Claire's cottage. And the last thing I needed was for some Mendocino County sheriff to call Inspector Chang and tell him that my fingerprints were in Claire Gravesend's cottage, a stone's throw from a pair of corpses. I unlocked the Beast's trunk and opened the toolbox. There was a clean engine rag on top of the socket wrench set.

I started in the main house, then went to the cottage, and finished with Claire's rental car. I moved quickly, and purposefully, and I left no traces. In all, it took ten minutes. And then I was ready to move, and I knew where I needed to go.

24

I LEFT SLAUGHTERHOUSE Cove fast enough to lay down a new set of tire tracks in the parking lot. I hit the road and pulled hard to the right, and went north as fast as the Beast would take me. I wasn't sure what I'd do if I caught up to the SUV. Rear-end it, run it off the road. Then bluff hard like I had a gun until I could get in close enough to try my fists. I didn't know if that would work or not, but I knew I had to try. Madeleine's life counted on it.

Assuming she hadn't planned the whole thing. I still couldn't say for sure it hadn't been her finger on the trigger.

It was close to dusk when I turned onto the forest road. I hadn't come upon the SUV yet. I drove the last twelve miles a little more slowly, letting the sky could bleed out and go dark, so that I could make a plan.

In the end, I spotted an overgrown pullout a mile from the last wooden trestle bridge. Loggers might have cut it a century ago. I backed the Beast into the narrow gap between the trees, going far enough back that she'd be out of view from the road, but not so far that she'd sink in the mud. I killed the engine, then went to the trunk and selected a long-shanked flathead screwdriver from the toolbox. I'd already taken a flashlight from the glove box.

I started toward the Creekside on foot, staying in the

woods, well away from the road. I crossed the creek beneath the bridge, hopping stone to stone until I was in the middle, and then wading through knee-high water to a log that tilted onto the opposite bank. Just before I hit the driveway, I turned deeper into the woods.

From here on, I knew there could be cameras. I hoped they were mostly pointed at the driveway, and that the club didn't have some other layer of security. I pictured laser trip lines. Motion sensors. And, worst of all, dogs.

It was getting darker, and now it was starting to rain. Overhead, the evergreen canopy blocked out the sky. The trees caught most of the drops before they reached the ground. But I could hear the prolonged *shush* of rain in the boughs above me. Ahead, in the failing purple-gray light, I could see a clearing: the parking lot, and the low-slung reception building. There were four vehicles in the lot. Three of them looked like they cost more than my Chinatown condo.

The fourth was a tan SUV.

I knelt on the forest floor, as close as I could get to a redwood trunk. I watched the clearing and I waited for full dark, which was a long time coming. It was early summer. The sun was setting at a steep angle. I spent the time looking for cameras in the trees and on the reception building. There were three in plain view. There were probably others I couldn't see. I was just going to have to live with them.

The reception building had big windows facing the front. Even from my spot in the woods, I could tell there was no one inside.

I got up, walked out of the woods, and stepped into the clearing. I didn't try to duck or take cover, and when I reached the crushed slate, I didn't try to hide the sound of my footsteps. I walked to the SUV and came around the back, where I committed its license plate to memory. Then I walked around the side of the building and turned the corner to the back. There was firewood stacked along the back wall. Seeing it made me realize that I could smell smoke. The air was sweetly tinged with burning hardwood. It wasn't coming from the fireplace in the reception building, but from somewhere else.

I walked beside the stacked wood and reached the back door, which had a window. I cupped my hands on either side of my eyes and looked in. It was dark, but for the green light of a digital clock. Enough to see that I was looking at a commercial kitchen. Steel worktables, a giant gas stove, a stainless door that likely opened to a walk-in refrigerator.

There was nothing for me there, so I went back around the building and found the path we'd seen earlier that day. No one had come to light the hurricane lanterns. The boardwalk led away into the woods, disappearing in the shadows. From ahead, in the darkness, I heard a sharp pop. A knot cracking in an outdoor fire. There was a murmur of low voices. I started down the path, trailing my fingers on the handrail so that I could keep my balance in the dark.

In two hundred feet, a set of wooden stairs came down the hillside and intersected with the main boardwalk. Looking up, I could see the outline of a cabin. There was a kerosene lantern on the porch rail, and a dimmer light filtering through the stained-glass window on the door.

But I could still hear the voices ahead of me, so I continued on my course. I passed five more cabins, each one bigger than the last, and then I saw a clearing. Firelight illuminated redwood trunks the size of buildings. I'd come through the younger woods to a grove of giants. Ten or more of the trees had to be a thousand years old. They stood in a circle, and within that natural enclosure, the members of the Creekside had built their gathering place. I crept closer until I could look down into it. It was a stone amphitheater, built into a natural basin in the center of the grove. At the bottom was a fire pit, and the logs burning in it were the size of wine casks.

Two men sat next to each other on the stone bench nearest the fire. One was in faded jeans and a checked flannel shirt. The other wore dark slacks and a sports jacket. They both had full heads of hair, but neither had the blond curls that Larry had described.

"No, it wasn't like that," Sport Jacket was saying. "It wasn't nearly as close a call as the historians say. They blow it out of proportion in the retelling."

"It sells more books," the other man said. "But I heard you were there for the whole thing?"

The fire cracked again. A fountain of sparks swirled upward. The men were holding wineglasses. A bottle stood on the bench between them. I stepped into the amphitheater and moved laterally until I was behind the men.

"Where'd you hear that?" Sport Jacket said. "That I was there?"

"Here, by the fire."

"You're pretty new here, though."

"A couple of years."

"And how are you finding it?"

"So far, so good," Flannel Shirt said. "If you're anything to go by, then I'm all in. Look at you. And seriously — is it true you were there? Right in the thick of it?"

Sport Jacket took the bottle and held it toward the fire to see how much was left. He poured, first for his companion and then for himself. Then he tossed the empty bottle into the fire.

"Not just that. I knew them. All the players — Khrushchev, in particular. Now, you take LeMay — Curtis was crazy, but at the end of the day, he followed orders. And Jack wasn't going to give that order unless Khrushchev went first."

"Sure."

"Nikita didn't want to die. He liked his dogs too much."

I couldn't see his face. Just his broad shoulders and his thick hair. Which was enough to know that what I was seeing and what I was hearing couldn't possibly add up. Anyone old enough to be on a first-name basis with Jack Kennedy and Nikita Khrushchev would count his years with three digits. This guy didn't look like he was much past fifty. I was figuring out what to do with that when a woman's soft voice spoke in my ear, a whisper that was as intimate as it was familiar.

"Turn around, Crowe."

Her hand on my shoulder urged me around, and I turned. Madeleine. My body went rigid with anger. But when she stepped out of my shadow and stood in the full glow of the fire's light, I saw that she wasn't really Madeleine. Her face was the same, but her hair was a foot longer, and she wore it in a thick, intricate braid. There were a few more lines on her face than Madeleine's or Claire's. A looseness under her eyes, and small creases, as if she'd been squinting into the sun. I guessed she was about forty. Which pegged her point by point to Larry's description.

She even had the jewelry, colored gemstones that sparkled around her wrist and on her trigger finger. I saw the jewels with complete clarity. In fact, I couldn't stop looking at that hand. She was holding a small automatic pistol, and it was pointed at my chest.

"My son and I had a bet," she said. "He said you'd never make it this far. I said otherwise. And I love being right."

"Congratulations."

"Same to you," she said. "But there's one thing I've been dying to say to you. Since we got the first report about you."

"Which is?"

"Goodbye."

I'd been focused on the gun. I hadn't noticed the men who'd emerged from the darkness on either side of me. But suddenly there was a man on my left, grabbing my arm. As I was turning toward him, I saw the second man in my peripheral vision. His arm was a blur of motion.

A couple of years ago, I was sitting in court after testifying in an uncommonly bitter divorce proceeding, and the next witness was a medical doctor, who proceeded to opine that it was impossible to remember the blow that rendered you unconscious, and that anyone who claimed such recall was a liar. At the time, because of my allegiances in the case, I wasn't inclined to believe him.

Now I'm not so sure.

I have no recollection of the impact. I have no memory of falling, but I must have. I have two chipped teeth I can't explain, and there is a hard lump on the right side of my chin that feels like a splinter of bone.

The first thing I remember — and this has to be an hour or two after the fact, judging from what I now know about the back roads of Mendocino County and the time it takes to drive them — is the sharp taste of vomit in my mouth, and then the smell of it, and then the cold wetness of it down the front of my shirt. Then I remember my head, the pulsing agony of the lump growing off the crown of my skull. When I tried to reach up and touch it, I couldn't move my arms. My hands were bound behind my back. It was this realization that woke me up entirely.

I opened my eyes. My right eye wasn't pulling its load. Instead of a clear picture, I was just getting bright fog. I closed it, and then the view made sense. I was in the back seat of a moving vehicle, on the right-hand side. It was still dark. We were bumping down a poorly graded dirt road, making ten or fifteen miles an hour. The forest around us was completely dark. I turned my head to the side and saw that I shared the back seat with a man. Young, fit, clean-cut, and not anyone I knew. The driver could have been his twin brother.

The man beside me leaned across and jammed the barrel of a gun into my ribs.

"Hey," he said, but not to me. "He's awake."

"So?"

"You want him back asleep?"

"He needs to answer questions when we get there. You think he can do that?"

"I don't know."

"Then let him be."

The man withdrew his gun from my ribs and held it just under my left eye.

"You hear that?" he said. "You're lucky."

I closed my eyes again and slumped forward until my forehead kissed the front seat. With my hands bound behind my back, it was an easier posture. Minutes passed. The SUV pounded down the road. It must have gone this pitted route a thousand times before. Its shocks had long since given up. The ruts and potholes didn't matter. I rode them out. I didn't feel them any more than a blackout drunk feels the rumble strip, or the sudden lurch as his car pitches off a cliff.

And beside me, the man with the gun didn't say another word. I gathered he approved of my unconsciousness.

Of course, I was entirely awake.

I was riding out the bumps and thinking through my options. They didn't look good. My one bit of hope was that they needed me alive long enough to answer questions. Since these men weren't asking me anything, their role was probably minimal. They were just taking me to my interrogator. If their only job was to deliver me alive, then maybe I had a chance. When I made my move, they might hesitate to shoot.

The SUV slowed down, and the road surface changed. We hit a smooth patch, followed by a rattle of metal, and then another smooth patch. A cattle guard set inside a concrete skirt. We continued down a gravel road for ten more minutes, but the grade was better. The driver sped up considerably. The tires were kicking rocks into the undercarriage. Then he slowed, made a right-hand turn, and we were on pavement again, accelerating rapidly.

As an experiment, I moved my feet a few inches apart. My hands were bound, but my feet were free. On top of that, they were bare. They felt bloodied up, which was a mystery for a moment, until I realized what must have happened. After they clubbed me unconscious in the amphitheater, they'd had to move me somehow. They probably grabbed me by my hands and dragged me. Somewhere along the way, my shoes had come off. My socks, soaked from the creek crossing, wouldn't have lasted much longer.

I cranked the new facts into the formula and recalculated my odds. In the end, my conclusion was simple. I could work with this.

25

WE WERE ONLY on the paved road for a minute or two, and then my opportunity came. The driver braked, and laid his hand on the horn. I opened my good eye. We were coming into a small town. Ahead of us, a fuel tanker was pulling out of a parking lot and onto the highway. It must have been hauling a full load. It was moving at a walker's pace, tracing a broad curve that took it all the way across our lane and the turning lane, and a couple of feet over the last solid yellow line. Its exhaust stacks were spewing black clouds. We came skidding to a near-standstill just before we hit it. My driver craned to the left to see if there was anything coming at us from the opposite direction, and the man beside me did the same thing.

I knew I wouldn't get a better chance than this.

I pitched myself forward, put all my weight on my right leg, and kicked sideways with my left. I gave everything to that motion. My bare foot caught the man next to me in the back of his head, rocketing his face into the window. The impact was like an ice block getting smashed with a sledge-hammer. The tinted glass became an opaque spider web. Instead of shattering, it bulged outward.

I didn't need to see what would happen next. The way a hitter knows where the ball will land at the instant his bat connects, I knew the man wasn't getting up. If I hadn't dealt a fatal blow, I'd given him something so close that the distinction didn't matter inside of my time frame, which wasn't long. I fell back onto the seat, swiveled until I faced my own door, and brought my bare feet up. I got the lock with my big toe, then pulled the door handle with the toes on my other foot. I kicked the door open and was sliding out of the moving vehicle when the driver finally reacted. He hit the gas, which accelerated us in a fast jolt toward the tanker, and then he slammed on the brakes. My open door swung forward, rebounded at the end of its arc and would have slammed shut except that my right foot was in the way. The small bones of my ankle stopped it. I cried out, then kicked it open with my left foot.

Again, I lunged for the opening, focused on nothing but the blur of pavement. But I made it nowhere.

The driver had reached around and grabbed my shirt collar. He began to haul me back in. I flipped around, my shirt twisting with me. He didn't let go. Both my feet were outside the door now, dragging on the asphalt. With bound hands, there was only one option. I bit his forearm, clenching down as hard as I could. I shook my head back and forth until my mouth filled with his blood. He bellowed, and I gagged. Then he let go.

I fell out sideways and hit the road.

I felt the SUV's rear tire graze my back, and then I was skidding on rough asphalt. I hit a divot, tumbled ankles over shoulders, and wound up on my knees. In that moment, I was beyond injury. Pain would come later. Right then, every nerve in my body was laser focused on one thing. Survival.

Fifty feet away, the SUV skidded to a halt. The tanker was already receding into the distance. It was just a pair of red lights, moving away. Its driver either had no idea what had happened behind him or he'd correctly assumed it was safer not to be involved. So I was on my own. I did a one-second scan, making decisions as I saw things. On one side of the road there was a steep hill. At the top, dark trees stood out against the moonlit clouds. There'd be great cover at the top, but getting up the incline would be impossible. On the other side, where the tanker had emerged, there was a long parking lot and a wooden building. I saw a sign, letters etched in neon. Boomer's Saloon. The parking lot was empty.

The SUV's reverse lights came on — my cue. I stood up and sprinted.

I ran the first hundred steps in darkness, listening to an engine revving behind me, to tires spinning on rough pavement. Then, suddenly, my shadow was stretching out in front of me. I could see bits of broken glass in the parking lot. Cigarette butts and bottle caps. The SUV had backed up and swung around. It was coming at me.

I was steps away from the saloon's porch, and didn't dare look back to see how much of my lead was left. I focused on the building, chased my shadow across the porch, and hit the front door with my shoulder. It probably had to be pulled open, not pushed, but with my hands bound behind me, I was just doing what I could.

Of course the door didn't budge.

The headlights swung again to catch me, lighting up the door and the walls. I turned and faced the SUV, which was now idling twenty feet away. The driver's door swung open. I saw a leg step down. He'd have a gun, of course. If he hadn't been carrying one of his own, by now he'd have reached into the back seat to take his companion's.

I waited until he had both feet out of the vehicle and then began to run again, down the dark corridor of the porch. The first gunshot was a sharp crack. The bullet missed my face by inches, hitting the barred window beside me. The glass pane didn't shatter, but inside, the neon tubes of the saloon's Budweiser sign exploded in a spray of sparks.

I ducked and kept running.

A burglar alarm was going off. I heard a second shot. I couldn't tell where the bullet went, but it hadn't hit me. I reached the end of the porch and turned around the building's corner.

I saw another business: Anna's Asian Palace. I hit the dark glass door with my shoulder, hard enough to crack it. A second alarm joined the first. Maybe somewhere, a sheriff's deputy was getting a radio call. Not that I was going to stick around and find out. I was running toward the back of the building. If there were any other shots, I didn't hear them. I reached the end of the parking lot, where high weeds grew from scrabbly ground and an overfilled dumpster sat amid a glittering sea of broken glass.

I dashed toward it, then ducked behind it. I didn't see the man. The SUV was on the other side of the building — if it was still there at all. The man could have cut his losses after the second shot. I didn't know if this town had a police department, but if it did, maybe he didn't want to linger while two burglar alarms were going off.

I looked behind me. There were a couple of houses on a back street, and a long cinderblock wall, which must have been built to shield the neighborhood from the highway's noise.

The dumpster, all alone at the rear of the parking lot, was the most obvious place to hide. I made a run for the wall. The vision in my right eye was getting better, but that improvement was counterbalanced by screaming pain. My head throbbed, my shoulders felt like they'd been broken on a wheel, and my bare feet were getting shredded.

I reached the wall and tucked up into its shadows, and not a moment too soon.

The SUV rolled around the side of the building. It paused and the driver switched on his high beams, then sped toward the dumpster. He skidded to a halt in front of it, jumped out, and ran around the rear with his gun out.

I pressed against the wall and knee-walked backwards. There was some kind of thornbush growing here, climbing the cinderblocks. I got myself wedged between the wall and the twisting branches, and lost my balance. With my hands behind my back, there wasn't much I could do. I fell flat on my chest, and then I had a rat's-eye view of the world in front of me. If it hadn't been for the burglar alarms, he might have heard me. But he didn't react at all. He opened the dumpster's lid, fired two shots inside, leaned up on his tiptoes, and looked inside.

Apparently, questioning me was no longer the priority.

The man dropped the lid and looked around, contemplating the path I might have taken. He studied the houses, and then the wall. He looked right at me. I tensed, ready to roll sideways and struggle to my feet if he raised the gun.

But instead, he tucked the gun inside his jacket and got out a phone. He'd seen the shadows and the thorn branches, but not me. I watched his phone's screen light up, watched him type out a message. He stood a while longer, looking at the screen, waiting for a response. Then he put his phone away and went back to the SUV. I had a cloudy memory from earlier in the night. I'd walked across a clearing and approached the same vehicle. I'd knelt to look at its plate. But whatever I'd stored in that memory slot had been beaten to a pulp. It was too dark, and I was too far away, to read the plate now. I watched the man climb into the vehicle, slam the door, and peel out of the lot. He went back to the highway, turned right, and disappeared.

When the man was gone, I embarked on a minutes-long ordeal of extracting myself from the thornbush, rolling to my side, scissoring my legs until I was sitting up, and then bracing my shoulders against the wall so that I could stand. By the time I finally got to my feet, I was so winded that I wanted to lie down again. Instead, I walked down to the end of the wall, where I could rub my bound wrists against the rough-edged corner.

Five minutes later, I had my hands free. I brought my wrists around and looked at them. I used my teeth to pull off the remaining tape, then swung my arms until I could feel my fingers again. When that was done, I checked myself. No wallet, no phone. They hadn't taken my watch. It was two thirty in the morning. It had been nine thirty or ten last I'd looked. I'd been out a long while. I had no idea how much of that time we'd been driving. No idea where I was now.

I began to limp along the wall. I didn't want to cut back through the parking lot, in case the police showed up. The adrenaline was fading now, and it was getting harder to walk. I wanted to sit down, to hold my bare feet and ball myself up against the cold, but I kept walking. I reached the end of the wall, and then went along the side of an auto body shop. There were pickup trucks in various states of disrepair. An abandoned-looking school bus. They all had California plates. That didn't do much to narrow my location.

I could still hear the burglar alarms, but they were fading now. I rejoined the highway, and walked on its shoulder. I told myself that if I saw headlights, I'd run for cover. But the road was quiet for five minutes. Enough time for me to walk halfway into town. There was a coffee shop that looked like a barn. A used car lot across from it, deflated balloons hanging on the chain-link fence. Later on, I passed a sign that pointed down a dirt track and unconvincingly beckoned passersby to a dairy.

The air was cold and smelled of fallow land and pine needles. In the distance there was the silhouette of rising hills. I passed a hand-painted sign for Paco's Tacos, and after that was a closed-down gas station, everything dark except the pumps.

I was about to move on, and then I stopped.

There was a phone booth next to the building. I wondered if it worked. I wondered who I would call. I looked at my watch again. It was three in the morning. There was one number I knew by heart, and one person who would almost certainly be awake.

The woman on the other end of the line had been reluctant to place my call. She warned me, twice, of the time. Now we were listening to the phone ring. Two times, three times, four.

"Hello?"

"Good morning, ma'am, this is the operator," the woman said. "Will you accept a collect call from a Leland Crowe? You will incur charges."

There was a pause. It went long enough for me to wonder what I'd do if she hung up.

"Lee? I mean — yes, I'll accept. Put him on."

"Thank you, ma'am. I'm putting the call through."

The operator vanished with a click.

"Lee?"

"I hope I didn't wake you."

"You know my schedule," she said. "Are you in trouble?"

"A bit."

"Are you hurt? You sound — I don't know. You sound bad."

"I'm okay," I said. "But I need a ride."

"I'll come get you," Juliette said. "Just tell me where."

"That's the thing. I don't know."

"Jesus, Lee. What happened?"

"Look up Boomer's Saloon," I said. "And Anna's Asian Palace. That's where I am."

"Hang on."

I waited, and after a while she came back on the line.

"Laytonville," she said. "You're in Laytonville. That's like three hours north, on 101."

222

"Can you still come?"

"I'm walking to the garage," she said. "I'll meet you at the saloon?"

"Not there — it'll be crawling with cops."

"What?"

"You don't want to know," I said. "I'm at a Chevron next to Paco's Tacos. There's a hill with some pine trees behind it. I'll go up there and lie down. If you've got a first-aid kit, bring it."

A car appeared on the highway. It was moving fast, but when it passed, I didn't miss the Mendocino County Sheriff's seal adorning its side.

"Lee?"

"Yeah?"

"Nothing — I'm coming."

At the top of the hill, after scanning around to make sure I wasn't in someone's backyard, I sat down against a tree trunk. My feet were caked with blood and debris. In the darkness, probing carefully with my fingers, I found a few slivers of glass that hadn't come out during my half-mile walk from the saloon.

I swept a pile of pine needles and forest loam over my feet. Not much of a blanket, but better than nothing. Down below, another sheriff's car went past. Engine racing, but no siren and no rooftop lights. They wouldn't find much at the saloon beyond a couple of bullet holes and a broken glass door at the Chinese restaurant. Around here, that was probably enough intrigue to keep them busy for hours.

I thought of Juliette because I didn't want to think about Madeleine. It had been bad enough to think that she'd double-crossed me. The alternative, which now seemed infinitely likelier, was worse. So I pictured Juliette, walking barefoot through her house, slipping a jacket over her shoulders and stepping into a pair of sandals. She'd hit the lights in her garage, then press a button to open the door. I could picture it easily, her path from the bedroom to the car. I'd lived in that house, briefly, and when I'd moved out His Honor had moved in. He'd had his own divorce to contend with, and anyway, Juliette's place was better than whatever he could afford.

I had to admit: After this, I would owe her. Two days ago, that would have been unthinkable. Now it didn't seem so bad. I fell asleep thinking about her, the possibility of us falling together again. But once I was asleep, that was all gone.

Toward the end, I dreamt of Claire Gravesend.

She was walking down a mirrored hallway, unclothed. Copies of herself stretched to infinity on either side. A hundred million perfect selves, just out of reach beyond the glass. She came right up to me, her eyes unseeing. Then she stepped into me, a ghost passing through a wall. It felt like a cold breeze. I turned. The scars on her back had opened again. New blood poured from fresh wounds, trickling down her naked skin.

"Lee."

She was walking away from me, leaving bloody footprints on the cracked glass floor.

"Lee!"

I opened my eyes and saw the dawn sky above the trees. Gray and overcast. Juliette was kneeling over me, her hands cupping each side of my face.

She let go and moved back when I sat up. I looked at my watch. It was five thirty in the morning.

"You said three hours."

"So I sped," she said. "Jesus, Lee—look at you."

"I know."

"What happened?"

"Did you bring the first-aid kit?"

224

She nodded, then shook her head. She'd always had big eyes. Right now they were as wide as I'd ever seen them.

"It's not enough," she said. "We'll have to stop somewhere. What happened to your head?"

"I don't know," I said. "A club. A shovel. I guess it doesn't matter."

"Can you stand?"

"I got up here, didn't I?"

But it turned out I needed her help to stand, and needed her arm around my waist as a steadying force before we could pick our way down the hillside to her Bentley. She didn't hesitate to offer it, and I didn't think twice about taking it. It was all perfectly natural, the way people act toward each other when everything is stark and the line between life and death is visible to the naked eye. It's the easy patches we need to watch out for.

She drove a mile to a grocery store, and left me sitting in the car while she went in. I struggled to stay awake. The passenger seat was wide and deep, and it was warm. Juliette was back in ten minutes with a paper sack and two cups of ice. I briefly wondered if she was going to mix us a couple of cocktails, but the paper sack was full of first-aid supplies, and the ice was for the lump on my head. She had butterfly bandages and big gauze pads. Rolls of white tape and tubes of antibiotic ointment. She helped patch me up, right there in the parking lot. She cleaned my feet and plastered them with bandages, and helped me out of my shirt so she could dress the wounds I'd gotten sliding along the road. She put Band-Aids on my chin and my right cheek — covering cuts I didn't even know I had — and then she filled an ice pack and handed it to me.

"I'll take you home now."

"I can't go home — it's bugged."

"Your apartment is bugged?"

I nodded.

"I thought it was an FBI agent I crossed. Something to do with a case I was working for Jim — you remember Jim?"

"Of course I remember."

"Okay — sorry. I thought it had to do with a trial. This guy Lorca. But I was wrong. It's something else. You remember I took that picture —"

"Claire Gravesend. The girl who jumped."

"I don't think she jumped."

"If you can't go home, where am I taking you?"

"I need to talk to Frank Chang," I said. "A homicide inspector with SFPD."

"So, Bryant Street?"

"Yeah."

"We'll have to stop somewhere first. You can't go into a police station like that."

I didn't want to disagree with her so early in the day. Between here and San Francisco lay a hundred and sixty miles of highway, and at least as many opportunities to get into an argument. But the fact is that you can walk into any police station in San Francisco with a bloody shirt, and no shoes, and your pockets turned out, and fit right in.

"We don't have to stop," I said. "Nothing will be open, and anyway, they took my wallet."

"I can make a call," she said. "And don't worry about the money. You can pay me back later. If you want."

"Okay."

She put the car in gear and did a sharp turn out of the lot. We passed back through Laytonville, rejoined Highway 101, and began to speed south. For several miles, we didn't speak. We sped through the woods and the low hills, walls of trees on either side moving past in a green blur. I closed my eyes because it was making me dizzy.

"Do you want to tell me about it?" she asked.

"Okay."

So I sat there, in my ex-wife's Bentley, with my eyes closed, and told her everything that had happened to me since stepping out of the Westchester Hotel on the last day of Claire Gravesend's life.

26

WHEN I FINISHED, we were just outside of Santa Rosa. Juliette pulled off the highway and into the parking lot of a coffee shop. She went in and came back a moment later with two paper cups. She handed me mine, then dug into her purse and took out a prescription pill bottle. She shook two pills into her palm, took one, and held out the other for me to take.

"What is it?"

"It'll pep you up."

"You know it's a federal offense to share prescription drugs?"

"Just shut up and take it. Don't be such a prig."

"Okay."

I took the pill with a sip of the coffee. I figured I could use some pepping up, illicit or otherwise.

"Are all your cases like this?"

"Hardly," I said.

"You know that carving of the snake eating its tail — the one you and Madeleine saw in the Creekside?"

"Yeah."

She'd driven to the edge of the parking lot. Now she checked her side-view mirror to be sure the lane was clear. She punched the gas and we accelerated onto the highway.

"I've seen that."

"What?"

"Well, not that one specifically, but ones like it. It's called an ouroboros."

"A what?"

"An ouroboros," she said, pronouncing it slowly. "It's an Egyptian symbol. It was adopted later by alchemists, in like the third century."

"How do you know that?"

"High school in Paris. Unlike you, I was generally awake in class."

Her purse was on her lap. She tapped its side so that her pill bottle rattled. I got the point. Juliette's doctor had been fine-tuning her attention span since she was thirteen.

"They teach that crap in French high schools? Egyptian symbols and alchemy?"

"It's called art history," Juliette said. "There's an ouroboros carved into the east façade of the Louvre."

"Okay," I said. "But what's it mean?"

"The magnum opus."

"The masterpiece?"

"No — in alchemy it meant something else. Literally, 'the great work.' The pursuit of the philosopher's stone."

"You mean the quest for eternal life."

"Yeah."

"And that's what they've got over the fireplace at the Creekside."

We sat on that for a mile or two.

"Maybe it's what the club is all about," Juliette finally said. "Looking for immortality. It's all the rage right now, in some circles."

"Your circle."

"I don't go for that kind of thing."

"But you've heard of it."

"People talk," she said. "Of course, a lot of it sounds like bullshit. Blood transfusions. Supplements. Calorie restriction. Some people will try anything."

"And some people will go too far."

We reached San Francisco at nine thirty in the morning. She had driven above the speed limit most of the way, but our pit stops had eaten up time. The Chinatown stores where I bought most of my clothes would be open, but Juliette would have none of that. She parked illegally at the corner of Geary and Grant, just east of Union Square. Her regular haunts should have been closed until ten, but as promised, she'd called ahead.

For my ex-wife, no door was ever truly shut. Rules were just the opening offer in a negotiation.

"Wait here."

"Okay."

She got out but left the car running. I watched her trot up Grant, purse swinging from her left arm. She hooked a right onto Maiden Lane and went out of sight. She'd left me her phone, its screen unlocked. I opened a web browser and searched, but found nothing on the murders at Slaughterhouse Cove. Surely by now someone had discovered the bodies and called the police. But news moved slower up there. Small towns could keep secrets for years, and places like the Creekside, unambiguously in the middle of nowhere, could hold on to them forever.

At least with Juliette's phone I could search Mendocino County property tax records. As a licensed investigator, I had subscriptions to a couple of public records databases. I logged in to one, then entered the address I'd first seen in Claire's credit card statement. A link popped up, and I tapped on it. The thousand-acre parcel was owned by a limited liability company called Creekside Management. I went to the California Secretary of State website and looked up the LLC in the business registry. It was a Nevada entity but was registered in California because it owned property in the state. Its local agent was a blandly named company in Sacramento — probably a one-room office in a low-rent strip mall, with a single employee whose chief responsibility was to know as little as possible.

A Nevada limited liability company is the corporate equivalent of a Liberian-flagged cargo ship. You find them all over the world, but they have no connection to their home state. They chose their flag for the anonymity it offers. Without kicking in a door to serve a search warrant, it's impossible to tell who owns them or what their true purpose is. They come and go in the night; they change hands in under-the-table transactions. Still, I went to the Nevada Secretary of State website and looked it up. There was a manager listed — some guy named Terry MacAllen. But he was probably just a shill. A dodgy attorney or an ex-paralegal who made a living registering companies and serving as a manager on paper only. I could probably find his name associated with a couple hundred other companies.

I was at a dead end. But I knew Inspector Chang could go a lot further. He could get warrants. He could brandish a badge that hadn't been laminated at a twenty-four-hour copy shop. I was prepared to do something I'd never even contemplated. I was going to walk into the SFPD headquarters, ask for a cop by name, and tell him everything. Before I did that, though, I might as well know where I stood.

Cynthia's name wasn't on the San Francisco Medical Examiner's website, but there was a phone number for Records. I called it, and was lucky. She hadn't gone home yet, even though the sun was up.

"Hi, Cynthia. It's me."

"Lee?" she said. She must have been giving her Caller ID a double take. "You're always on the move, aren't you?"

"I stay busy. Did your friend on the Cape come up with anything?"

"You didn't get my email?"

"I'm having a hard time checking it."

"I sent you the report last night."

"Did you look at it first?"

"You know me."

"You got time for a quick summary?"

"There wasn't much — the guy bled out from a two-inch stab wound in his neck. It missed the jugular, but it cut his carotid in half. He had some defensive marks on his forearm. Meaning, before he got stabbed, someone took a swing at him with something. Maybe a pipe."

I could have corrected her about the weapon. And I wasn't sure it strictly counted as a defensive wound if he got it while trying to stab me.

"What about an ID?"

"None, but that was the interesting part."

"How so?"

"They ran all the databases for prints and DNA. No matches except in the unsolved files."

"Say that again?"

"There was a thumbprint at a murder scene, eight or ten years ago. That was in New York. A banker or somebody, killed in his house. Then, they got a match on his right index finger — it was identical to a print from a different scene in Nevada, four years ago. Different fingers, so until last week, no one knew those two prints came from the same guy."

"So they don't have a name," I said. "But they've tied him to two priors."

I tried to feed that information into the mix. If his prints didn't match anything in a government identification database, he couldn't possibly have been an FBI agent. That didn't rule out the possibility that Agent White had paid an informant to do something off the record. But when I considered the fact that Claire's vacant room in Mendocino had been hit at nearly the same time as her Boston house, it seemed like it was time to rule out White once and for all.

"He was bad news," Cynthia was saying. "Maybe not such a big loss, in the grand—"

Right then, Juliette opened the door and got back into the car.

"Hey, Cynth . . . I gotta go."

I hung up and handed Juliette her phone. In return, she gave me a suit bag and several paper-wrapped packages. There was a pair of pants, a good shirt, a belt, shoes and socks. The suit bag held a two-button jacket. I hadn't told her any of my measurements, but if she remembered the ouroboros story from the tenth grade, then it was no surprise she could recall my shoe size.

"You mind if I dress while you drive?"

"Go ahead."

At the first red light, she dipped her hand into her purse and came out with a stack of twenties. She set it on the seat next to my leg.

"That's five hundred. The most I could get from the ATM."

"I'll pay you back."

"You know what you could do?"

"No."

The light turned green, and she began driving.

"Drop by sometime. Anytime, really. You know the way."

"Drop by."

"Yeah," she said. "And if you ever get your car back, bring it. We could go for a ride."

I looked to see if she was joking. She reached across and touched my elbow.

"Put the shirt on," she said. "I think it'll look good on you."

• • •

Of course there was a bank of payphones close to the city lockup, which was adjacent to the police station. I stood in a light rain in my new clothes, dropped in change from Juliette's purse, and dialed the Homicide Detail. A secretary answered the phone, and I asked for Inspector Chang. I gave her my name and said it was urgent. Something about my voice must have convinced her, because she didn't mess around.

"I'll transfer you."

I listened to a new line ring, and then Chang picked up.

"Crowe?"

"That's right."

"I was hoping you'd call — in fact, I was trying to call you."

"What?"

"We need to talk. Now."

"Okay."

"Where are you?"

"Right outside the station. Over by the jail."

"Those payphones?"

"Yeah."

"I'll come down," he said. "We'll walk around. Give me two minutes. It's got to be fast, because I'm leaving town at noon."

We hung up and I leaned against the jail's outer chain-link fence and waited. In about a minute and a half, Chang came jogging around from the Bryant Street side. He looked like a guy who spent most of his downtime either running or hitting a speed bag. He slowed down when he got a look at me.

"All that just happened?"

"A couple hours ago."

"You're working the Gravesend case," he said.

It wasn't a question, and he wasn't looking for an answer. But I nodded.

"You were driving out of the mother's estate when I was coming down to talk to her."

"Okay."

I thought back. After I'd seen Olivia Gravesend the last time, I'd stopped at Mission Carmelo, then at George's house in Oakland. Chang's men had picked me up in the garage the minute I got back to the city. Which meant that the first time we talked, he was freshly back from seeing Olivia himself. Having seen me down there that morning, he'd known I was lying about my involvement. He hadn't let on at all. I'd thought I could read his face like an upturned card, and I'd been dead wrong.

"Sure," he said, as if he could read my train of thought. "I knew. And remember when you let me take a DNA swab?"

I nodded. You don't forget doing something like that. Not if the guy taking it is a homicide inspector and you're in an interrogation room.

"You're not a suspect. Not a match at all," he said. "And here's something else. You were right — we found some skin scrapings under her nails. We compared that DNA to hers, to make sure she hadn't clawed herself somehow. I just got the results back."

"There was a familial relationship," I said. "The DNA came from her father."

"Or her son," Inspector Chang answered. "It could go either way, is what the lab said — father or son."

"She didn't have a son. But she was looking for her father. So she must have found him."

"And that's why we need to talk. Because you're still on the case, and I'm not."

"What?"

"Let's walk," he said.

He pointed in the direction he wanted to go. If we'd gone north along the cracked sidewalk, we'd have reached the underpass and some shelter from the rain. But there were

235

groups of men camped out down there, and Chang wanted to be alone. So we went east, in the rain. He at least obliged me by walking slowly, which was about all I could manage.

"The word came down last night," Chang said. "I got it from my lieutenant, and she got it from the chief. And I've got no idea where he got it from."

"What was the word?"

"Claire Gravesend was a suicide. End of story. Case closed. Then my lieutenant handed me this."

He passed me a piece of paper. It was a printout of an airline reservation. Inspector Chang was flying to Anchorage this afternoon.

"Alaska?"

"They've got me sitting in on a jailhouse interview. Guy says he's going to confess to some cold cases here in the city."

"Nothing to do with this?"

"Not at all. They weren't even my cases."

"Your bosses are getting you out of the way?"

"If that's what they wanted, Alaska's pretty far. I'll be gone twenty-four hours."

"You don't think it was a suicide?" I asked.

"I don't," he said. He stopped. "I'll tell you something. You know the NTSB?"

"The National . . . what is it?"

"The National Transportation Safety Board."

"Okay."

"They've got a full deck of experts on car accidents. They work with the manufacturers, and their engineers have stats on every car for sale in the country. You tell them the make and model of a car, and they've got a guy who can answer any question about how it'll hold up in a crash."

"I don't get it."

"I had a guy from the NTSB come out to the warehouse and examine the Wraith. He had Claire Gravesend's autopsy report. So he had the car, and he had her measurements. And what he told me is that it didn't add up."

"Didn't add up how?"

"She hit the car so hard, she put the roof down to the door handles."

"Yeah — I saw that."

"She weighed just north of a hundred pounds. The highest place around was the roof — a hundred and forty-one feet. You take her weight and the distance she had to accelerate, and you can calculate the force. The NTSB crunched the numbers and compared it to what they know about Rolls Royce Wraiths, and they said there's no doubt."

"She couldn't have done that much damage?"

"Not even close."

"So what do you think?"

"Something else fell with her, right? That's what it has to be. She was holding on to it and hit the car with it. It wasn't just her weight. It was Claire, plus something extra."

"You think — what? She had a suitcase full of gold bricks?"

"Whatever it was, it was heavy."

"And you think whoever pushed her off the roof was trying to get it. After she hit the car, he ran down and took it."

"It's the only explanation," Chang said. "The only way the facts make sense."

We were walking again. Two blocks up, there was a taxi. Its driver was leaning against the trunk, finishing a cigarette. I was starting to get an icy feeling in my stomach. I'd been chasing leads all over Northern California, but I was beginning to realize that I'd fundamentally misunderstood the story.

"That's what you wanted to tell me?" I asked.

"I was hoping you'd run with it. Because I can't."

"Okay," I said.

Telling my story to Chang and dumping the case on him

wasn't an option. He was out. It hadn't been much of a plan anyway. If Madeleine had a chance, it was me.

"You'll run with it?"

"I'm all over it," I said.

I needed to go. I needed to get back out there. I waved to the cabdriver. He took one more drag on his cigarette, then flicked it into the gutter.

"I'll see you, Inspector."

We shook hands.

"Good luck," he said. I was barely listening to him. "I'll help you if I can. But it'll have to be on the down low."

"Sure."

I got into the cab's back seat and shut the door. The driver pivoted around in the front seat.

"Turk Street," I said. "You know the Refugio Apartments?"

Ten minutes felt like an hour. Finally, the driver rolled down Turk Street, past my erstwhile digs at the Westchester, and then to the Refugio. I paid him with some of Juliette's cash and limped across the street.

I'd gotten in here the first time by using my phone to play a police radio squawk. I didn't have a phone now. But on the wall next to the door, there was a code box and an intercom. I knew there was at least one person who'd be at home. The woman in the wheelchair. As long as the elevators were out of service, she wasn't going anywhere.

I punched *1201* into the intercom, not sure if the thing was even functional.

Beside me, the speaker crackled. I was struggling to remember her name — I knew it when I'd talked to her. I could remember her face. But her name had been smashed to a pulp up at the Creekside.

"Yes?"

I closed my eyes and pictured myself standing at her door. There had been a smell coming from inside. Like someone had spent forty years cooking onions and boiling vegetables with the windows closed. But the apartment wasn't triggering her name. Which is when I remembered: she hadn't introduced herself to me. I'd found out her name by reading the notes Elijah had photographed.

"Yes?" she said again.

"Leola Cummings?"

"Speaking."

"We talked a few nights ago about a young woman who jumped."

"I remember."

"Do you have a moment?"

"I suppose."

"Any chance you can buzz me in?"

She didn't answer. The intercom clicked twice and I thought she'd hung up. But then I heard the door's dead bolt slam open. I grabbed the handle, pulled the door back, and stepped into the lobby.

If the cab ride from Bryant Street had been painfully slow, climbing the stairs was agonizing in every respect. It took about two minutes per floor, and by the time I got to the roof I was so dizzy I had to lean against the wall and close my eyes until my heart finally caught up. Then I pushed the door open and went out into the rain. I crossed the littered gravel and went to the balustrade on the building's right corner.

Claire had hit the street directly beneath me. But I wasn't looking there. I was looking at the roofs of the lower buildings. There was an apartment next door, only three or four stories tall, and a run of low tenements across the street. Their roofs were mostly flat gravel, with street-facing façades, all decorated with empty malt liquor bottles, and fast food containers, and the rat-picked remains of dead pigeons, just like the Refugio's.

I wasn't really sure what I was looking for until I saw it

on the roof directly opposite me. It was a hundred feet away, in the middle of a two-floor building on the other side of the street. There, alone in the gravel and black roofing tar, was a woman's high-heeled shoe.

Claire had been wearing one shoe when I found her. Her other foot was bare. The police had collected everything from the scene, and from the Wraith. Every piece of her personal property had been itemized on a page of her autopsy report. There was the handbag, and the pewter key fob, and the evening gown. A fine watch. And one high-heeled shoe. The other one was missing.

The police hadn't found it because it wasn't where it was supposed to be. If Claire had fallen off the top of the Refugio Apartments, her shoe couldn't have landed on the building across the street. It was impossible. But now, all of the impossible things made sense. The timeline of Claire's journey from Mendocino to San Francisco; the fact that there was no trace of her in the Refugio; the excessive damage to the Rolls Royce. And now the impossibly placed shoe.

I looked up, into the clouds.

Claire hadn't fallen from a low height, carrying an extra weight. She had fallen from a great height, a point high enough that her body alone was capable of destroying the car. There were no fingerprints in the Refugio Apartments because she had never been inside the building. She had made it from Mendocino to San Francisco in record time because she hadn't been troubled by roads.

She'd come by air, in a small plane or a helicopter. And then she'd been thrown out.

The ground would have been invisible, the streetlights blurred away to an orange glow as she plummeted earthward. It had all come to this, these final seconds portended again and again in her nightmares. She would have been screaming. Thrashing her arms so that she'd wake before she hit. Somehow, surely, there could be a second chance. A soft landing among sweat-soaked sheets, her breath coming hard and fast against her pillow, her heart like a wounded animal caught in her chest.

The only mercy is that the end, when it came, would have been instantaneous. Like hitting a switch. No pain, no fear. Just the eternal dark.

27

I WALKED ALL the way to the Powell Street BART station before I found a working payphone. There was no directory, so I had to dial the operator to get the number for A-Star Appliance on Mission Street. With that in hand, I called the shop and spoke to Elijah's uncle, who told me Elijah was out. That was no surprise, since Elijah was sitting in the back of a van on Baker Street, watching Claire Gravesend's house on my dime. The uncle eventually agreed to give me Elijah's cell phone number.

Elijah answered on the first ring.

"Yeah?"

"It's Crowe."

"Every time you call, it's a different number."

"Things have been complicated," I said. "Any trouble at the house?"

"Dude came to the door about six this morning and rang the bell. Nothing happened, and then he walked off. There was a car waiting at the bottom of the hill. He got in and they took off."

"You follow him?"

"No, man, because he just rang the bell. If I'd followed him, I would've left the house sitting empty. And he hadn't really done anything."

"Okay," I said. "Good call. What'd he look like?"

"White guy. Six foot tall. Buzz-cut hair."

"Blond?"

"Yeah."

"You're still in the van?"

"Yeah."

"New plan, double the pay. Can you come pick me up at Eighth and Market, at noon?"

"Do I bring in the drone or leave it sitting?"

"Bring it in."

I hung up and descended farther underground. I took the train from Powell to Civic Center. I needed to learn about air traffic control. Surely there were people tracking every object in the sky, and keeping records. I just needed to know who and where, but since I didn't have a phone, I'd have to do it the old-fashioned way. I reemerged from the station and entered the library. Half an hour later, I had it: Elijah and I needed to go to Rancho Cordova, outside of Sacramento. And somewhere along the way, I needed to cook up a decent cover story. Something plausible enough to get me through the door of a locked federal facility, and so compelling that the people inside would have to help me. I didn't have time for bureaucratic bullshit. I needed help, and it had to arrive the minute I got there.

At one minute past twelve o'clock, a battered A-Star Appliance van coasted to a stop in front of me, and I got in. I glanced in the back. There was a sleeping bag, a pair of video monitors, a set of headphones connected to a handheld directional mike, and a cooler.

"Got any food in the icebox?"

"Just Red Bull."

"When we get out of the city, let's hit a drive-through."

He looked me over. If the sight of me gave him any second thoughts about his involvement, he didn't voice them.

"You sure you can eat?"

"I'm going to try."

"Where we going?"

"NorCal TRACON," I said. "Rancho Cordova, outside Sacramento."

"Rancho Cordova—where the junkyards are. What's a track'em?"

"TRACON. Radar. Air traffic control for most of Northern California."

"This is about the girl who jumped? Or are we on a different case?"

I told him everything. I was going to need his help from there on, so it was only fair to deal him in and let him decide how much further he wanted to go. The story took longer than what I'd told Juliette, because now I had more facts to deal with. The NTSB's report on the damage to the Wraith, and the high-heeled shoe I'd spotted from the roof of the Refugio.

By the time I got to the end, we were past Oakland and Richmond and heading into Vacaville on Interstate 80. Elijah was contemplating what I'd told him. He nodded, one dip of his chin. He'd been on stakeout duty long enough that he'd grown the beginnings of a goatee.

"The air traffic control place makes sense."

"You think?"

"She had to come from a plane," Elijah said. "Your friend Chang had a good idea, but he didn't know about the shoe on the roof."

"Someone saw her in Mendocino at two or three in the morning. He didn't know that, either."

Without lifting his right hand from the wheel, Elijah pointed at a cluster of fast food joints built around an upcoming overpass.

"How about it?"

"Looks good."

. . .

While we were in the drive-through line, I borrowed Elijah's phone and tried calling Olivia Gravesend. I had three misdials before I got the number right.

"Gravesend residence."

"Mr. Richards," I said. "This is Crowe."

"A new day, a new phone. We haven't heard from you in a while."

"I like to keep moving," I said. "Can you put Mrs. Gravesend on?"

"A moment."

"Sure."

Elijah elbowed me and I looked up. We were at the pay window. A young woman was leaning out, looking at Elijah but speaking to someone else in her headset. I handed Elijah a twenty.

"Crowe?"

"Good afternoon," I said. "Sorry it's been a while."

"You've had difficulties?"

"Yes and no."

"Start with the difficulties."

"My apartment's been broken into, my office has been tossed. I've lost my car, my wallet, my computer, and my phone," I said. I'd also lost her dead daughter's twin sister, but I wasn't ready to get into that. "Someone tried to crack my skull, and took a couple shots at me. I had to call my ex-wife at three in the morning and borrow her money to buy clothes that weren't covered in blood."

"All right," Olivia said. "I take it you're getting somewhere."

"Yes, I am. I'll fill you in face to face. What I need right now is a favor."

"What favor?"

"You've got to throw your weight around."

"And do what?"

"Do you know anyone at the Federal Aviation Administration?"

"No."

"What about Homeland Security?"

"Why don't you tell me what you need and I'll tell you what I can give?"

"I need to get inside an air traffic control facility."

There was silence, but it didn't last long.

"Let me call a friend," Olivia said. "Go ahead and tell me what you need from her — I've got a pen."

"We're going to NorCal TRACON. Someone's got to let me through the front gate and give me radar data that covers the city last week. I need the tracks and altitudes, and the time stamps, and I need them to lay it over a city map."

"And?"

"We're coming in an A-Star Appliance van —"

"We?"

"I'm with my colleague, Elijah," I said. "We'll be there in about an hour."

"Then let me make my call," she said. "If there's a problem, I'll call you back."

"Wait a minute, Mrs. Gravesend."

"Yes?"

"You don't have to tell me your friend's name," I said. "Just tell me she isn't in the FBI, the SFPD, or the mayor's office. And that she isn't anyone I know."

The list of people I didn't trust was getting pretty long, but I thought that basically covered it.

"I assume if you knew this person you'd have called her yourself."

She hung up. I set Elijah's phone on the dashboard so I'd see the screen light up if she called back. But it was dark for the next hour, and then we were in Rancho Cordova.

The radar facility was on open ground across from a marsh, wedged between Mather Field's runways and a sprawling mess of auto wreckers and outdoor shooting ranges. Elijah stopped at the security booth and rolled down his window.

The guard stood up and stepped out of his little booth.

"Mr. Crowe?"

"That's me."

"The director's waiting for you," he said. "You drive in, straight up to the front. You can park in the VIP space and he'll come out and meet you."

"Okay."

"Clip these on."

He passed a pair of laminated visitor badges through the window, then reached inside the booth and punched the button to open the gate. Elijah put his window up and rolled through.

"Lady must have some good friends," he said.

"She spends her money well."

"Place looks like Fort Knox."

I nodded toward the front of the building. A man in a navy suit stood next to the glass entryway. He lifted his hand to greet us. Elijah parked and killed the engine.

"Let's go," I said.

We got out of the van, and then the director of NorCal TRACON was shaking our hands. He paused, but only for a second, when he saw my bandaged face. Then he pushed on, shaking my hand with both of his.

"Mr. Crowe?" he said. "A pleasure. I'm Warren Reese. Let's go to my office. I can get you anything you need from my terminal. I was told you need tracking data from last week?"

"That's right," I said. "Thanks."

He led us into the facility. We skipped the metal detectors and went through a marble and concrete lobby, and then he brought us into the heart of the building: a huge circular room, with workstations laid out like the spokes of a wheel.

It looked like Mission Control in Houston, except that the people in here were guiding every plane in Northern California that wasn't inside an airport tower's zone of control. We went across the room and up a flight of metal stairs to a glassed-in office that overlooked the floor below.

He motioned for us to sit in the chairs that faced his desk, and then he sat down and pulled his keyboard toward him.

"I'm looking for a small plane that went over San Francisco on Tuesday morning. Sometime between two and four thirty."

"Easy," he said. "Not a lot of air traffic then."

"It probably would've been coming out of the north."

"Narrows it even more."

His fingers began to move on the keyboard. I couldn't see the screens, just their reflection in his glasses. He sorted through files and archived radar tracks for about a minute, and then he turned one of the screens toward us.

"This is a helicopter," he said. "You can see its track here —it took off north of Mendocino. Must've been a private field, because there's no airport there. It came south, over Marin and just west of the Golden Gate, and entered San Francisco city limits at three forty-nine a.m.—that's what you're looking for?"

"Can you zoom in on that?" I asked. "So I can see where it went, over the city?"

"Sure."

He toggled his mouse and zoomed in on the radar track. The underlying map didn't have streets, but I knew the lay of the land well enough. The helicopter had come in just west of the Presidio. It would have flown directly above China Beach, over the Richmond District, and then Golden Gate Park. But before it reached Mount Sutro, it took a sharp turn to the northeast. It did a few tight circles, then wandered across the Lower Haight and Hayes Valley. It straightened out over the Tenderloin, and then headed south again.

"What happened here?" I asked, pointing at the screen.

Reese shrugged and pushed up his glasses.

"Maybe the pilot spilled hot coffee on his pants."

"Maybe so," I said. "Can you tell his altitude?"

"Where?"

"Here," I said, touching the screen where the radar track crossed the Tenderloin.

He clicked on the track there and a box popped up.

"Two thousand feet. Going ninety knots."

I looked at the screen.

"Is that his registration number?"

"His N-number, yeah. The tail number."

"Can you look that up and see who owns it?"

"Easy."

He began to tap at the keyboard again, working on a screen I couldn't see. Beside me, Elijah had taken a pen from his pocket. He opened his wallet and found a receipt, then handed both the pen and the paper to me. I wrote down the registration number and looked up when the director spoke.

"Creekside Management, LLC."

"Goddamn it."

"I'm sorry?"

"Nothing—it's another dead end."

"I could pull the eighty-fifty they filed with the FAA," the man said.

"Say that again?"

"The eighty-fifty—you can't register an aircraft in the U.S. unless you meet certain residency requirements. And you need to certify that, so there'd be a signature."

"You can get that?"

"Easy," he said. "But not from this desk. Would you mind waiting here?"

"Sure."

He got up and left the office, fast-walking down the metal stairs. Elijah and I went to the windows and watched him cross the control room floor and disappear down a broad hallway.

"Dude's working it," Elijah said. "Really wants to impress you."

"Or whoever called him and put him on the spot."

We watched the big tracking screens at the center of the room. Planes cutting paths all over the northern half of the state, lining up and coming in to San Francisco, to Oakland and Beale Air Force Base.

Then the director was jog-walking back down the hall, a folded piece of paper in his right hand. He came up the stairs and opened the door.

"I don't know if this helps or not," he said. "They had their attorney do the certification. So it's his signature on the document."

"Who?"

He held the paper out to me.

"Some guy named Jim Gardner."

28

I SHOULD SAY a word or two about Jim Gardner. I'd met him in my first year of law school, at an on-campus interview at Boalt Hall, in Berkeley. I was a green interviewee then, with a borrowed suit, a broken wristwatch, and a negative net worth, and when I looked at Jim I saw power. I didn't think much about where it came from. All that mattered to me was that he had it. Not how he'd acquired it or how he sustained it over the years. Only that he had it, and that in time, if I impressed him, he might pass some of it over to me.

In his bones, Jim is a trial attorney. Which is to say, he operates in the moment, and his natural element is the courtroom floor. He's reflexive, not contemplative. But he knows his limitations. He hires squads of associates to write his briefs. A dozen paralegals shepherd his evidence toward trial. His secretary plans his day, down to what he orders for lunch and what route his driver takes to go home.

While his area of expertise is trial work, over the years he's put together a team with other skills. One of those specialties is tax work, and it's that practice that's allowed him to build a client list that boasts every mogul, magnate, titan, and rock star north of Tijuana. And more than a handful south of it. His team of lawyers digs in to and then restructures their clients' finances. They build nonprofits and sham charities, and figure out ways to move money offshore and back. He has a reputation for looking the other way, for leaving certain questions unasked. He lets his results be his advertisements, and word of his achievements spreads easily within the rarefied circle of his target clientele. All of which meant that when I saw Jim Gardner's name on the Form 8050 aircraft registration, I didn't exactly hyperventilate and faint.

Jim's business is servicing rich people. In the last twenty-four hours, it had become clear that the man behind Claire Gravesend's death was as wealthy as a man could be. If he was behind the company I'd found in the land records, he owned a chunk of Northern California the size of San Francisco. He had a chauffeured car and a twin-turbine helicopter. If George was right, he had enough draw to make a top scientist in South Korea fall off the face of the earth. A phone call from him and the SFPD dropped a case. I didn't know who he was or what his intentions were.

But I knew the man who could point the way.

I dialed from the road while Elijah drove us back to San Francisco. I knew I was taking a risk, of course. Rosemary Townsend had been Jim's secretary her entire adult life. Loyalty was her first instinct, but discretion was her second. I had to fall on the right side of the line or Jim would know I was coming for him. Surprise would be the better option. Jim didn't want to talk to me, and would have a particular objection to the questions I wanted to ask. He had more enemies than all of his clients put together. As a consequence, he was careful. His life was set within rings of security, the final bit of which was a California concealed carry permit and a .40 automatic that he brought everywhere but court.

The phone was still buzzing. Rosemary must have been behind Jim's desk, updating his calendar by hand. She answered on the seventh ring.

"Mr. Gardner's office."

"Rosie — how are you?"

"Lee?"

"The same," I said. "Is Jim in?"

"Yes, but he's in a meeting."

Of course he was. He lived in meetings because he didn't like to talk on the phone and he didn't like to write emails. Rosemary spent most of her day lining up a stacked series of audiences. Jim and a client. Jim and a witness. Jim and a disbarred attorney who'd become a private investigator.

"Do you know when he's going to be home?" I asked. "He wanted me to swing by and show him my file on Natasha, but I forget when."

"I didn't see that on his calendar."

"I've been working on something for him — I guess it's more of a personal project. Maybe I shouldn't have said anything about her."

I'd made up the name Natasha. She sounded like the kind of woman Jim would get involved with and then want chased off. It was believable fiction because it had happened before.

"It's all right," Rosemary said. "I won't say a thing. He'll be home at eight."

"The condo?"

"No — he's working from home tomorrow."

"He's going to Skyline?"

"That's right."

"Thanks, Rosie."

"Don't mention it — and I won't mention anything either."

We hung up, and Elijah drove another ten miles while I thought about what to do. Then I picked up the phone and called Olivia Gravesend. The butler gave me his usual icy barrier and then handed me off to Olivia.

"Mr. Crowe?"

"I've got a good lead now," I said. "So I wondered if I could borrow Mr. Richards tonight."

"You were just talking to him."

"I thought maybe if you told him, it'd go better."

"You want me to tell him to do what?"

"Get a car — a big one — and meet me at half past seven."

"Where?"

"The Saratoga Gap trailhead, off Skyline Drive. And before he gets there, he should line the trunk with a plastic sheet."

"And?"

"And I'll have him home by ten."

"At which point I'll get answers?"

"I'm hoping we all will."

"All right, Crowe," she said. "I'll send him."

Skyline Boulevard followed the peninsula's wooded spine, miles of curves and hairpin turns, with chances to pull out and look down at the towns below. San Mateo, Menlo Park, and Palo Alto — the sorts of places that had no use for someone like me until things went wrong. Then I was welcome, as long as I remembered to park down the street and ring the bell at the service entrance.

At the intersection with Highway 9, where that road crossed the mountains on its roundabout route from San Jose to Santa Cruz, there was an open space preserve, a trailhead, and a parking lot with room for twenty or thirty cars.

"Ten bucks that's him," Elijah said.

He used his chin to point at a silver-gray Jaguar parked at the end of the lot. A white-haired man sat in the driver's seat, both hands on the wheel.

"That's him," I said. "Pull up alongside."

We got out of the van and into the back of the Jaguar, and then I explained what we were going to do. Mr. Richards listened to everything, nodding in all the right places. He didn't ask any questions until I was done, and then he only had one.

"Did James Gardner kill our Claire?"

"No," I said. "But he knows who did."

"That's enough for me."

I looked at Elijah. He'd called work ten minutes ago, coughing hard into his fist while he explained he wasn't coming. If the only question was the money, it would've been an easy choice. I'd offered him a couple of months' pay for a few hours of work. But he also had to think about the consequences. Five thousand dollars for five hours of work was one thing. Throw in twenty-to-life for aggravated kidnapping and it was another consideration.

"Same," he said. "I'm cool."

"Then I'll see you guys in about half an hour."

Mr. Richards pulled back his cuff-linked sleeve and looked at his watch.

"At five after eight."

"On the dot," Elijah said.

"Or more or less. This isn't a precision operation."

I got out of the car and opened the van's sliding side door. I grabbed the black pillowcase that Elijah and I had filled with the supplies I'd need, then swung it over my shoulder, shut the door, and started walking.

At first, the trail clung to the top of the ridgeline, but then it dropped down. I began by walking through damp, golden grass. Then I was passing beneath mossy oaks and short bay laurels. Ahead, the path descended still more, and grew darker. My new shoes, with their smooth leather soles, weren't made for this kind of thing. Twice I slipped on slick patches of rock and went down hard. Maybe it wasn't just the shoes. I still hadn't regained my equilibrium after the Creekside.

When I descended a little more, into the shadows of the taller trees, the highway noise disappeared, as though everything but the forest had vanished. There was the sound

255

of the wind. From somewhere higher up, where the woods thinned out to allow a meadow, an unmated mockingbird was winding up to sing all night. I walked another mile listening to him.

The trail had been leading down into a hollow. I reached the end of the little valley, where two ridges joined each other like the delicate curve between a pair of fingers. I stopped there and took Elijah's phone from my pocket. I pulled up a satellite view and checked my position. I was in the right place. If I bushwhacked up the slope toward higher ground, in a quarter of a mile I would cross from state land to private property. Jim's woods.

I closed out of the map and called Mr. Richards. Elijah answered right away.

"What's it look like?" I asked.

"Flying in now."

He was in the back of the van, guiding the drone and watching its camera feed on the small flatscreen displays.

"The gate's shut," he said. "I'm going over the driveway now — looks like it ends in a turn circle."

"Any cars?"

"None outside. There's a garage."

That meant his cook and his housekeeper were off for the night. Jim's secretary had told me that Jim planned to work from home tomorrow morning. Those two facts should have told me something, but I didn't make the connection. Otherwise, I might have changed my plan, or called the whole thing off. I had a lump on my head the size of a baseball, and I was still jittery from whatever Juliette had given me. If I'd been playing chess against Death, I would have lost in three moves. My one advantage was that chess has rules and real life doesn't. And anyway, I've always had a flexible attitude toward rules.

"I'll fly around the house and peek through the windows," Elijah said.

"Do that."

I shifted the pillowcase off my shoulder and began to climb, pulling myself up the steepest places by hanging on to tree trunks. I had to stop every fifty feet to catch my breath. I heard Elijah talking and brought the phone back to my ear.

"I didn't see anything — place is dark inside."

"Okay. I'm coming up. Be ready."

I hung up the phone and checked the time. Ten to eight. Jim hated being early as much as he despised being late, so I could count on his driver to deliver him to the house in ten minutes. I'd need to hurry if I wanted to be in place when he got there. I opened the pillowcase and dug through it until I found the black ski mask. I slipped that over my head, tugging until my eyes were lined up. Then I started up the hill again.

29

AT THREE MINUTES to eight, the slope flattened out, and when I emerged from the trees, I was looking up at the concrete pylons that held the rear half of Jim's house aloft. I went under the broad back deck, then came out along the side of the house and went toward the front. I looked up, checking the gray sky and the tree limbs. It took me a moment to find the drone. I'd never have noticed it if I hadn't known it would be there. It was hovering a hundred feet up, behind a screen of younger redwoods.

I went over to the same copse of trees, knelt in the soft red mulch that had built up beneath them, and opened the pillowcase again. Inside was a basic kidnapper's toolkit. There was a high-voltage stun gun the size of an electric razor, capable of delivering a crippling jolt with the push of a button. Assuming that put Jim on the ground, I had duct tape. After my experience in Laytonville, I wasn't planning on cutting corners. I'd brought enough tape to bind Jim like a mummy. Once the pillowcase was over his head and cinched around his neck, he'd be as easy to move as a suitcase.

I knew I had to do more than scare Jim. I didn't have any other choice. No cover story was going to get him into Olivia Gravesend's car. If he came with me, he'd be bound, gagged, and riding in the trunk. That was a line I'd never crossed. I picked up the stun gun and held my thumb over the button. The anodes looked sharp enough to pierce clothing, delivering their charge directly into his musculature. The way I imagined it, I'd come up quietly behind him and press the thing into the back of his neck. He'd go down, and then I'd have his keys and the remote for his house alarm. I would own the situation.

I was thinking through the angles and the approach when I saw lights wash over the driveway and heard the swish of tires over smooth pavement. I thought I was ready, but ten seconds later, when the black Range Rover stopped in the circular drive, everything changed.

I watched Titus step out from the driver's side and open the rear door. That was normal. That was what I expected to see. Then I watched a shapely bare leg step down, a high heel click onto the blacktop. I saw a knee, a pale thigh, and then the hem of a crimson dress. The woman stood up and stepped away from the door. She brushed her red hair off her right shoulder, then stepped back and waited as Jim came out through the same door and slipped his arm around her waist.

I still had the stun gun in my hand, but my grip was failing. I hadn't planned for this at all. Jim was supposed to step out alone, and his driver was supposed to clear out, leaving us alone. That was how it worked every time I'd visited Jim's house. That was the scenario I'd prepared for. I wasn't prepared to do to this woman the things I was ready to do to Jim. I wasn't going to zap her with a couple hundred thousand volts and take the risk of whatever that might do to her heart. I wasn't going to move in on her with my fists if the electricity didn't do the job. So I froze. I knelt there in the grove of trees and watched Titus drive away, and watched Jim use the remote on his keychain to disarm the house. He used his key in the lock, led the woman into his house, and hit the door with his left foot.

I watched it slam shut, and watched my window of opportunity vanish.

I stood up and put the stun gun back into the pillowcase. Before I could start my creeping retreat toward the back of the house, I felt Elijah's phone vibrating in my pocket. I pulled it out and answered it.

"Damn," Elijah said. "Who's the lady?"

"You saw that?"

I looked up. The drone was still hovering directly overhead, nearly invisible now except for the small red light on its side.

"Sure — but now what? You got a plan?"

"Not really."

"He's in there with a girl, right?" Elijah said. "Quiet night, all by themselves. So you need him to come out, alone."

"It's not like I can go ring the doorbell."

If I did that, he'd see me on a closed-circuit camera, or through a peephole. He wouldn't open the door for a masked man. If he saw my face, his reaction would be no better.

"Hold tight," Elijah said. "I got an idea. Just watch."

"Watch, and do what?"

"Be ready."

Before I could answer, he killed the connection. I looked up. The drone hovered for another second, then whirred off toward the south. Elijah was calling it home. I shifted so that I could lean out. Lights were coming on in the house. Downstairs, outside. The upstairs was still dark. As far as I knew, Jim's bedroom was on the second floor. That was the only level I hadn't really seen. His study was in an all-glass cube on the third floor, and that was dark too. No surprise there. He had company. He'd be entertaining her downstairs before he —

My thoughts stopped with a screech of rubber, a long blast from a car's horn, and then a crash of bending metal.

I whipped around. I could only see part of the driveway.

As it rose up the hill toward Skyline, it curved out of sight. The sound had come from somewhere up there, in the invisible distance. Still, I knew what I'd heard.

Elijah.

I turned back to the house and watched Jim step through the front door. He closed it behind him and walked purposefully up the driveway. He'd taken off his jacket and tie. He was holding a semiautomatic pistol in his right hand, down near his hip. As he walked up, he passed within five feet of my hiding place. Close enough that I could smell the woman's perfume as he went by.

While I waited for him to get out of sight, I untied my shoes, slipped them off my feet, and put them in the pillowcase. Then I stood up, pillowcase in one hand, and stun gun in the other. I followed Jim up the driveway in the failing light. My socked feet were silent on the blacktop.

I stopped where the driveway began to curve, and listened.

"Dude crossed right over the centerline," Elijah was saying. "I didn't have no choice."

"You dumb shit—let me see your license."

"My license?"

"Your driver's license."

"C'mon, man—"

I took another ten steps. Up ahead, there was the gate. It was ten feet high and made of cast-iron bars. Elijah had driven the van into its center so that it buckled inward. It must have been well built, though, because it hadn't come open. Or he'd only hit it as hard as he needed to. Just enough to create a ruckus outside and set off an alarm in the house.

"—what's my license got to do with it? The dude, he came over into my lane."

"You're the one who hit my gate. You got any fucking idea how much that's going to cost?"

Jim was fifty feet away, standing with his back to me. I

261

was in Elijah's line of sight, but he didn't acknowledge me. I kept walking. I imagined I was walking on water, each step so gentle that my weight wouldn't break the surface tension.

"I got two hundred bucks in my wallet," Elijah said. "There's a Viking stove in the back of the van."

"Not even close."

"It's a good stove. You put it up for sale, you'd get four thousand. Easy."

Jim stepped to the side so he could see the van over Elijah's much taller shoulder.

"A-Star. That's where you work?"

"You don't gotta get my boss into this, man. He's not in this. This is just you and me."

"You want to keep your job?"

"C'mon."

"You think you're getting out of this? You haven't got a clue, son."

"What's that for?" Elijah asked, nodding toward Jim's right hand. "I'm just a guy had an accident. Let's kick it down a notch."

Jim looked down at the gun in his hand as though he'd forgotten it was there. He seemed to consider it for a moment, and must have decided it was an escalation this confrontation didn't need. He tucked it into his waistband. I was ten feet away from him.

"All right," Jim said. "We kicked it down a notch. Now let's see the license. The gate camera already got your plate. So what've you got to lose?"

"Really? You're not kidding?"

"I'm dead serious."

Elijah took out his wallet. He began to slowly thumb through it. I was five feet away. Elijah handed Jim a card and took a step back from the gate.

"This is a library card."

"It's got my name."

"It's got *a* name."

I was three feet away now.

"Just do it," Elijah said. "Go for it."

I shoved the stun gun into Jim's back, hard enough to bury the anodes in the muscles next to his spine. At the same time, I pushed the button. There was a loud crack, like a fuse blowing. Jim stiffened. I hit the button again, and he tipped forward into the gate. I pulled the gun out of his waistband and slammed its butt between his shoulder blades, and he went down.

"Damn," Elijah said.

Jim was on his side. I kicked him so that he was facedown, then straddled his waist, his hands pinned to the pavement under my knees. I put the gun into my own waistband, then took out the first roll of duct tape, pulled his hands together behind his back, and started binding them. Fifteen, twenty wraps. Jim stirred and I punched the back of his head, which flattened his nose into the pavement.

"Damn."

"You could help me."

"Gate's closed."

"Fine."

I moved down and began taping Jim's ankles. When I was done with that, I put the pillowcase over his head and taped it in place with a loose wrap around his neck. I patted down his pockets, found his keys, and took his wallet and phone. Then I stood up and looked around. On Elijah's side of the gate, there was a code box and an intercom mounted on a low stone column so that a driver could reach it through a rolled-down window.

"Check his keys," Elijah said. "There'll be a button on the alarm remote."

I found the right button, tapped it, and the gate began to swing open, coming toward me on its hinged arc. Elijah saw the problem and slipped through the widening crack, trotting toward me. I took Jim's ankles and Elijah got his shoulders, and together we lifted him up and moved him back before the opening gate hit him.

"We better load him up quick," Elijah said. "Someone's gonna drive past."

We started toward the van, Elijah carrying most of the weight.

"We've still got the redhead to worry about," I said. "It'll screw everything up if she stays in the house."

"I got an idea about that."

"That makes one of us," I said. "But it better not be anything like this."

We reached the van and Elijah shifted his half of Jim's weight into one hand and used the other to slide the door open. We shoveled Jim into the cargo space and he began to let out a weak groan. Elijah slammed the door, and then it was quiet again.

"C'mon," he said. "You know me better than that. She's gonna get a ride home in a fine car with a professional butler behind the wheel."

Which, in the end, is how it worked out. Thirty minutes after I headed south, driving an increasingly frantic Jim in the A-Star Appliance van, Mr. Richards rolled up to Jim's front door, rang the doorbell, and told the redhead that Mr. Garland had been called away. An unexpected emergency. It had thus fallen on Mr. Richards, the backup chauffeur, to take the young lady wherever she wanted to go. Elijah watched all this from the trees, narrating it to me over the phone. When the butler and the redhead drove off, he stepped out of the woods, opened the front door with Jim's keys, and had the house to himself. We were back in business.

30

WE WENT SOUTH, Jim flailing against the duct tape. He hadn't seen my face yet, and I hadn't spoken to him. I rolled down the windows as we passed through the garlic fields surrounding Gilroy. The night air blew in, cool and damp and fragrant, like a cellar full of onions.

"Carl?" Jim asked. "It's you, isn't it?"

I put the windows back up so I could hear him.

"If it's about the trust account," Jim said, "it's not a problem. I can fix it."

I said nothing.

There was a sheriff's car ahead, parked on a pull-off. The driver's window was down. I kept a steady pace, sixty miles an hour. I didn't look at the cop as I passed him.

"If this is about DeCanza, I don't know anything," Jim said. "I got that information in the mail — no return address. All I did was ask the man some questions."

I had to smile at that. The back of the van had become his confessional. I was his invisible priest. And he was telling flat-out lies, though at least on this point I was ready to absolve him. If he thought he was talking to a rogue Agent White, he could have offered me up as a sacrifice.

I checked the rearview mirror again and saw only darkness. The sheriff had stayed put.

"If this is just about money," Jim said, "we can work something out. It'd be easier if we could talk, and if I could have my phone. I know people who could help."

Again, I said nothing.

Jim may have had an impaired sense of right and wrong, but there was nothing else defective about him. I didn't discount his intelligence because he hadn't figured out who I was or where I was taking him. He had enough enemies to fill a midsized sports arena. Picking one from that crowd while bound and hooded in the back of a van would be hard.

"Lansdale — right? You got out last month," Jim said. "Keep in mind, I told you not to move the cash that way. Twice. In writing. And you did it anyway. You should be thanking me. You only got ten years. Could've been more."

He wasn't speaking out of guilt, but out of fear. If he'd had half his wits, he would have shut up. He could advise his clients all he wanted about remaining silent, but he'd never been bound and blindfolded and thrown in the back of a van. I hoped he'd keep talking. The more he ran his mouth, the more afraid he'd become, which meant he'd be all the weaker when I finally asked him a question.

And he obliged me.

In the hour it took to reach the Gravesend place, he scrolled through half a Rolodex of his transgressions. Clients screwed, witnesses thrown to the wolves. Frame jobs and cover-ups. There were a few married women, and more than a few of their daughters. Claire Gravesend must have been at the very back of his ledger, because by the time we reached Olivia's gate, he hadn't mentioned her. I got out of the van and shut the door before I hit the intercom. I didn't want Jim to hear us speak. I listened to the ringer's low tone, and then my client came on the line.

"Yes?"

"It's Crowe."

266

"What's that you're driving?"

"A van."

"Where's Mr. Richards?"

"Seeing a young lady home," I said. "Meet me out front. Mr. Richards mentioned a wheelchair—"

"It was my father's. It's in his dressing room."

"Bring it."

She cut the connection and then the gate began to roll. I opened the door and leaned in to check on Jim. He was curled on his side. It was the only viable position since his hands were bound behind him. I got in and drove the rest of the way up to Olivia's house. When I killed the engine and switched off the lights, she opened the front door and came out pushing a wheelchair. There were stone stairs leading up to the front door and she came up to the edge of the first step and then stopped.

I got out of the van, shut the door, and went up to her. She looked at my face, with its bruises and bandages. Then she looked at my clothes, probably pricing everything and wondering if I planned to expense it on her invoice.

"What is going on, Crowe?"

"You'll know in a minute," I said. "Go wait for me in the gun room and unlock the French doors. I won't be long."

"All right."

I took the wheelchair from her and carried it down the steps to the van. When I heard her shut and lock the front door, I opened the van's door and grabbed ahold of Jim's shoulders. I slid him out and let him drop into the wheelchair. With his hands behind him, he was liable to tip out. The only thing I could do about that was to hold on to his shirt collar while I pushed him with one hand.

We went down a flagstone path that led around the side of the house, into the gardens. A fountain trickled somewhere, out of sight. The waves were louder over here, the wind a steady force coming up from the edge of the cliffs. We reached the terrace and I wheeled Jim up to the threshold of the French doors. He was shaking. I leaned close to the pillowcase and whispered.

"Try not to wet yourself," I said. "She'll think less of you."

Then I opened the door and pushed him into the room. Olivia was waiting in the straight-backed chair. The fireplace was as cold and as dead as the first time I'd met her. I wheeled Jim up until he was between the two chairs, and then I put my hands on his shoulders. He flinched away from my touch.

"Would you like some answers?" I asked her.

She looked at the bound and hooded prisoner I'd brought into her house. Her face displayed no horror at all. Merely curiosity. She lifted a glass of brandy from her chair and sipped it.

"He told me you were flexible about rules," Olivia said. "That you're a dogged sonofabitch. Now I understand."

"Who said that?"

"Jim Gardner."

"Jim said that? That's the nicest thing he's ever said about anyone."

I unwrapped the tape that held his black hood in place, and then I pulled the pillowcase away.

Attorney and client looked at each other in silence. As far as I could tell, neither of them even took a breath for the first ten seconds. I could hear the waves washing against the rock faces. I thought of Claire. Spinning downward, into the dark. It was Olivia who spoke first.

"Jesus, Jim."

For once, he had no answer. He looked from her to me.

"You've got a conflict of interest, don't you?" I said. "A pretty big one."

Jim swallowed, and found his voice.

"I don't know what you're talking about, Lee."

"You've got two clients. Olivia, and the man who killed her daughter. You know his name."

"I don't know who killed Claire."

"You do," I said. "I know you do."

I turned to Olivia then, because she hadn't heard this next part. But I was speaking to Jim, too.

"When I was up in Boston, in Claire's house there, a man broke in and attacked me," I said. "I killed him — not because I'm any good at that, but because I was lucky. I thought it had to do with one of Jim's other cases — that the man had followed me to Boston, and that he came into the house for me. Not for Claire. But I was wrong."

"A man broke into — You killed a man?"

"Yes, ma'am."

"Don't *ma'am* me, Crowe," she snapped. "You killed a man in my house?"

"I stabbed him in your house. He died outside, in the park."

Jim was looking at the fireplace. A study in silence.

"What's this have to do with Jim?" Olivia asked.

"I followed the blood trail, through the park. This was at night, so you can relax. No one saw. I found the man and pulled off his mask, and took a picture. When I got back to the city, I showed it to Jim."

"And?"

"He erased it. He told me to forget you and go to Mexico."

Olivia got out of her chair and walked within a foot of Jim. She looked down at him.

"Why, Jim?"

He hadn't just been staring at the fireplace. He'd been thinking. Trying to come up with a way out of this situation. I knew him well enough to guess the route he'd take. He'd try to paint himself as Olivia's savior.

"I had to protect you," he said. "You asked me for a detective. One who'd go all the way. I set you up with Crowe, and he went too far. I don't know what you told him to do. But taking the picture was stupid. It was evidence. It would convict him and bring you down with him."

He'd walked into a trap he'd taught me how to set. He'd started lying before he knew how much I had on him. It was a classic mistake, one he exploited every time he walked into court. He didn't know about the NTSB report on the impact damage to the Wraith. He didn't know about the shoe on the roof, or my trip to the radar facility. There was an aircraft registration document in my pocket with his signature. It wasn't just a helicopter anymore. It was a murder weapon. And Jim knew who owned it.

"Here's what I think, Jim," I said. "When Olivia came to you, you didn't have a clue. She wanted a detective, and you sent her to the best one you knew. If you'd had any idea she was trying to find one of your own clients, you'd have sent her to a loser. Some guy who couldn't put two and two together if you wrote it out on a chalkboard. But you sent her to me. So the way I'm looking at it, you were in the clear."

"I am," Jim said. "I am clear."

"You were. Back then," I said. "And then I showed you the picture. You recognized the face and you put it together. You knew one of your other clients killed Claire. You might not have known how, or why. But you knew you had a problem. So you did what you do best—what you're famous for."

Jim said nothing.

"What did he do?" Olivia asked.

"He looked the other way. And asked me to do the same."

"Jim?"

Olivia had taken a step back. I saw her gaze go to the side of the fireplace. She was eyeing the poker, considering its heft and the arc of its swing. She and I weren't so different.

We were in a room full of guns, and she wanted to bludgeon someone.

"It's bullshit, Olivia," Jim said. "He's playing you for more money. He's gone off the reservation. I'm sorry I brought this man to you."

"How did Claire die?" I asked. "Quick, Jim. Tell your client."

"I know what I read in the paper. She jumped off a roof in the Tenderloin."

"Wrong."

"Says who?"

"Physics."

"Now he's a physicist. Olivia, do you know how dangerous this man is?"

Olivia backed toward the fireplace and took the poker off its stand. When she stepped forward again, Jim was within the reach of her swing. So was I.

I knew I was in the right. I just had to explain myself before she took a swing.

"Before he got called off the case, Inspector Chang got an NTSB report on the car," I said, struggling to keep all the facts straight through the lingering fog of concussion. "Long story short, Claire couldn't have done that much damage falling from the roof of that building. She only weighed so much. The Refugio is fourteen floors high, with nothing higher around. Did you know one of her shoes was missing? I found it on the building across the street."

"You — what?" Olivia said. "You're not making sense, Crowe."

I knew I was stammering. I had to show her what I meant. Moving slowly, I took the sheet from my pocket and unfolded it. Olivia scanned it with a couple flashes of her eyes. I saw her focus alight on Jim's signature, and stay there. Then I turned and held the page in front of Jim's face.

"I went out to NorCal TRACON," I said. "Because, as you said, I'm a dogged sonofabitch. We tracked the helicopter over the city. It flew directly over that block of Turk Street on Tuesday morning."

"What are you saying?" Olivia asked.

"She didn't jump off a roof," I said. "She was thrown out of a helicopter. Jim's client's helicopter."

"It's purely circumstantial," Jim said. "And you can't prove anything without a time of death."

"I've read her autopsy report," I said. "Have you?"

He stared at me in silence, and I spoke to Olivia without looking at her.

"What kind of watch did Claire have?"

"A Rolex. I gave it to her."

"A Pearlmaster," I said. "It's listed on the property schedule, in the appendix. A good-quality watch, right, Jim? But could it survive a fall from two thousand feet? Do you really think they don't know the exact time of death?"

"The radar—"

"Be real, Jim. When someone hits a pop fly in Pyongyang, they know it. They know where the helicopter was. It's all in the record."

He looked at the fireplace again. I waited for him, wanting to see what he'd come up with. Ten seconds stretched to twenty. An eternity in front of a jury, which in this case was Olivia Gravesend.

"Jim," she said.

When he spoke, it was slow and firm. He could put on his confident, courtroom voice like another man puts on a jacket.

"I registered a helicopter for a limited liability company. You're asking me to divulge the name of the member. Which is attorney-client privileged information. No judge would compel me to answer."

"I'm not asking a judge," I said.

I took out Elijah's cell phone and made a video call.

31

"HOW YOU GUYS doing?" Elijah said.

He was sitting in Jim's kitchen, holding the butler's phone at arm's length. He'd helped himself to a glass of wine from Jim's refrigerator. There was a plate of hors d'oeuvres next to the glass. The cook had probably left it so Jim could offer something to the redhead. Elijah used a little knife to slice off a piece of foie gras. His state of repose was what I wanted to see. It meant he'd found what I needed.

"We're just fine," I said. I was holding the phone so that Jim and Olivia could see the screen. "Just three people sitting by the fireplace, in a gun room, talking about murder. All we're missing is the butler."

"He's not back yet?"

"Maybe he hit it off with the young lady," I said.

"You wanna see what I found?"

"Sure."

Elijah turned the phone around so the camera faced in front of him. He began to walk, going through the kitchen, down a set of broad stairs to the den, past a wet bar, and to the antique cage elevator that Jim's architect had scrounged from a bankrupt Kansas City hotel. Elijah stepped inside, pulled the brass gate shut, and hit the lever. We watched as he rose up through the den, past the second floor, and into the all-glass room at the top of the house. He stepped out and panned the camera around. There were wooden filing cabinets surrounding the central desk. Their drawers were open, and empty. Stacks of paper were arranged in neat rows on the carpet, and on the desktop.

"How many clients did you find?" I asked.

"Seventy-two."

"That many?" I said. "Complete information—bank account numbers, Social Security numbers, everything?"

"And emails, printed out," Elijah said. "And tapes. Your boy is old-school. He tapes his phone calls."

On the phone's screen, Elijah's hand came into view as he picked up a small envelope at the top of one of the paper stacks. He opened it and shook a miniature cassette tape into his hand.

"You found a lot of those?"

"Thirty, forty. Who does that?"

I looked at Jim and shrugged. I'd known about the tapes and Jim's habit of making them. He did it in case he needed to blackmail his own clients. If they balked at his invoices, he'd get out the recordings. That was page one of the Jim Gardner playbook. In making them, he'd never imagined that they might all fall into the FBI's inbox in a bulk delivery, whether his clients had paid their bills or not.

"Can you imagine what they'd do if my friend boxed that up and left it on Agent White's doorstep?" I asked. "You've got a lot of clients. Lorca's not the only one who can make a man disappear."

"You're on some of those tapes."

"And you're on all of them," I said. "So your clients won't wonder where they came from."

I watched him while that sank in.

"I just need a name, Jim. The guy doesn't have to know where I got it."

He looked from me, to Olivia, and then back at the phone's screen. Elijah panned around again. There were

274

tens of thousands of pages of documents. Bank statements. Wire transfer requests. Sham invoices. Swiss accounts and numbered lockboxes in the Cayman Islands. Entire empires could fall overnight. Most of them would file lawsuits, but a few of them would think of stronger measures.

"The name," I said.

"It's not going to mean anything to you," Jim said. "He does everything through shells and holding companies. He puts on two pairs of gloves before he touches an elevator button. He's a ghost."

"So tell me the name."

"Stefan Larsen."

"What's he worth?"

"Plenty. More than anyone in this room."

"How'd he get it?"

"I don't know."

"Jim."

"I really don't. I think he's got a science background."

"In 1994, you helped him recruit a Dr. Park Kwung-ho, out of South Korea, right?"

Jim's face showed a rare flash of surprise. He suppressed it, but not fast enough. I caught it, and so did Olivia. She was watching me as closely as she was watching him. She had no idea where this was going.

"Recruit . . . no."

"Then what?"

"Larsen asked me to help track Park down. After he recruited him."

"He wanted you to track him down after Park went missing the second time. In 1996. Is that what you're telling me?"

"Yes."

"What are you talking about?" Olivia asked. "Who is Park?"

I raised my hand, signaling her to wait. I wanted Jim to talk while he was in the mood for it. If he had a break, he'd sit there and figure out some backdoor strategy to avoid the damage I was threatening to unload on him.

"You put him in touch with a detective?" I asked Jim. "The way you set me up with Olivia?"

"In a sense."

"In what sense?"

"Larsen wanted to find Park. But he also wanted certain things to happen after he found Park. So he needed a very specific kind of guy. I put him in touch with somebody, and I think they got along fine. I heard Larsen made him into a regular employee."

"He wanted a hit man, is what you're saying. And you helped him find one."

"You'd have to ask Larsen what he wanted."

"Or the hit man," I said. "He'd know."

Jim shook his head.

"You missed your chance. He's dead."

"When, and how?"

"You know better than I do," Jim said. "You killed him in Boston."

It took me a moment to absorb what he meant.

"When I showed you the picture, you said, 'Good for you.' And then you told me there were more of them. I thought you were talking about feds. But you meant Larsen's men."

He gave the slightest of nods.

"How many?"

"I wouldn't know. I just sent the one man. But he got more. After a while, they all looked the same to me."

"What did Larsen want with Claire?"

"I don't know."

"Do you know what Dr. Park was doing for him?"

"Not a clue, Crowe. You know me better than that."

"Sure," I said. "Your client hands a briefcase to a guy who flies to Nassau and wires money to a pilot who ferries a plane full of cocaine over the Rio Grande. And you don't know what your client does for a living. No clue. Maybe he owns a luggage store."

"As far as I know, Larsen never handed a briefcase to anyone."

"Then let's just cut to the chase," I said. "Where do I find him?"

"I don't know."

"Where do you send the invoices?"

"An email address."

"That's not good enough, Jim," I said. I looked at the phone. The video call was still connected. "How soon can you box that stuff up and get it to White's house?"

"You took the van," Elijah said. "But don't worry. Your boy's got a Porsche in the garage. I can put it all in there and give White the keys."

"Put a bow on top."

"You got it."

Jim was watching the screen. Elijah had set the phone down, propped so we could see as he knelt and began to gather the stacked documents.

"Now you've got another choice," I said. "It's a tough one — do you call your clients and tell them what happened? Or keep your head down and wait for them to find out from the feds?"

Jim gave it some thought. Maybe he was thinking through his chances of skating out of this with a motion to suppress. There was a break in the chain of evidence. The conversations were protected by privilege. No way the government could use any of these documents in court. Valid points, but Jim knew the flip side, too. Which was that whether the government used the files or not, it would know everything. The feds would never forget what they saw. And Jim's clients wouldn't forget either.

"Jim, did you hear that?" I asked. The call's audio feed had blanked out for half a second. "You know what that is, right?

His battery's running down. When it dies, I won't be able to call him back. Not even if I wanted to."

"I gave you the name."

"Tell me where he is and I'll keep your files safe."

"I don't know where he is right now. But I know something almost as good," Jim said.

He put his head down and brought his eyebrows together. Pausing the way he would in court when he wanted the jury to lean toward him, hanging on the suspense. It was just how he was. He couldn't help it.

"I know where he'll be tomorrow night."

"Really."

"He invited me to something down in Beverly Hills."

"What kind of something?"

"A gathering, is what he called it," Jim said. He cleared his throat. "An opportunity. *Not just the chance of a lifetime, but the chance of many lifetimes,* if you want the exact words."

"It sounds like a sales pitch."

"Exactly what I thought," Jim said. "So I said I might drop by. And I might've, just to meet his friends. Fresh blood and all that."

"When, and where?"

"At nine o'clock tomorrow. In a house, up in the hills. He didn't need to tell me the address — it's Meredith's place."

"Whose?"

"Meredith Miles. The actress."

"She's your client?"

"Olivia sent her to me."

I glanced at Olivia and she nodded.

"You've got her address?"

"Of course."

I brought the phone close to my mouth and spoke to Elijah.

"Pack up the Porsche. Go any direction you want. Switch

cars when you can, and find a hotel room somewhere. Bring in the files and sit tight till I call you."

"You got it."

I killed the connection, then glanced around the gun room. It would be wrong to say that the things in here were priceless. There were rows of English shotguns. Matched dueling pistols lay in velvet-lined cases. Their value could be ascertained, and traded upon. And from a security perspective, that was the problem. The entire house was a lure. What was in it could be stolen and fenced. Surely Olivia had thought about what a target she was. And I'd be willing to bet she'd taken some steps to protect herself.

"Do you have a panic room?" I asked her.

"Off my bedroom."

"Can you lock it from the outside?"

She nodded.

"With a key," she said.

"If we let Jim go, he could change his mind. He could warn Larsen," I said. "You'll need to keep him as a guest for a couple of days."

I didn't care for the way Jim was looking at me, so I dropped the pillowcase back over his head.

32

IT WAS TWO in the morning, and I was in Olivia's Jaguar, heading south. I was going to the Beverly Hills house of an Oscar-winning actress, to crash a party I had no business dropping into. I had about four hundred dollars in cash and a semiautomatic pistol that belonged to my former boss. I had a good suit but no tie. I had Elijah's phone, but no wallet and no ID. I had three hundred miles to work out a plan.

Behind me, back in Carmel, Olivia and her butler were keeping watch on Jim Gardner. We'd taken the phone out of the panic room, then cut him loose inside. There was a kitchenette and a well-stocked freezer, and a little bathroom. I figured Jim could last two or three weeks in there, if he had to. Cozy and safe behind four feet of concrete and a steel door thick enough to stop a tank round. After Olivia closed it and turned her key in the lock, we couldn't even hear him yelling.

I hadn't told Olivia everything I'd seen and learned in the last forty-eight hours. She knew the main thing — that a man named Stefan Larsen had murdered her daughter by throwing her out of his helicopter. But she didn't know about Claire's twin, or the Creekside. She didn't know everything Dr. Park had done for Larsen. For that matter, neither did I.

But I was starting to get a picture. Jim had said it himself: Larsen was selling an opportunity.

The chance of several lifetimes.

I watched the sun come up while I sped down the Central Valley, irrigated fields stretching forever on either side of the interstate, a morning haze hanging over them. The air coming through the vents smelled of fertilizer and manure.

I was in no particular hurry.

I pulled into a truck stop and had a good breakfast, then went into the bathroom and washed up at the sink. I took the bandages off my face and checked out the damage. Just some abrasions high on one cheekbone. The lump on my head was going down. It was bad, but it wasn't even close to the worst beating I'd ever taken. Mentally speaking, there was still some fog. But it was lifting. Nothing I couldn't fix with ten hours of sleep in a dive motel, a shot of bourbon, and a Tylenol.

But first, I did a bit of rolling surveillance. I drove the rest of the way to the city, came over the mountains and through Century City, and then I turned toward the heights. Meredith Miles lived on Deseo Lane, near the top of a canyon. I drove past houses that made Claire's Baker Street home look like a caretaker's cottage. And then, a little farther along, I must have come to the real money, because I couldn't see the houses at all. Just the fences and the walls.

Meredith's place was at the end of the road. Her wrought-iron fence was tall enough that she could have kept loose tigers and chimpanzees on the other side if she'd wanted to. The house was invisible, but there was a guard booth at the gate. Considering who lived on the other side of the fence, I was surprised there was only one man inside. But he was alert, and watched as I slowed down. At least I was in the Jaguar and not the Beast. The guard might remember a '65

Camaro, but Olivia's car was perfectly anonymous in this neighborhood.

I turned around, slowly. Just a guy cruising around, passing the time. An L.A. tradition if ever there was one. I went back down the canyon. I didn't know L.A. any better than I knew Boston. I just drove until the buildings looked squat and sun-beaten, and then I got off the freeway and found a motor court, where I got the Manager's Special without any fuss. Double the posted rate for a ground-floor room. Cash up front, and no need to sign the guest book.

The room was everything I expected. There was a rusted-out window unit air conditioner. One chair, one cigarette-burned table. The dull purple bedspread covered a thin, pilled blanket. The place was directly beneath the flight path to LAX. In the two minutes I spent looking over the room and turning down the bed, four jets roared overhead.

I turned the air conditioner all the way down and pulled the vinyl-lined curtains closed. I hung my shirt and jacket on the back of the chair and laid my pants across the table. I took a shower, reconsidered that shot of bourbon, but went ahead with the Tylenol. Then I got into the bed without really toweling off. I put Jim's gun on the bedside table, and fell asleep.

I woke at six p.m., and sat for a while on the edge of the bed. I counted what was left of Juliette's money, then counted the bullets in Jim's gun. Altogether, my situation wasn't bad. I could buy thirty cups of coffee and kill nine people. And by ten o'clock, the chances were good that I'd be on my way to the nearest jail, if I was lucky, or tied up in the trunk of a car if I was less so.

I didn't have a solid plan for preventing either option. I suppose I could've given up, but I had a paying client. And I had some skin in the game too — they'd hit my office, they'd broken into my apartment, and they'd tried to kill me twice. Not to mention, I wanted my car back. The Beast had sentimental value, more so in the last twenty-four hours than in the last six years. But still.

Plus, there was Madeleine. Maybe I'd been avoiding her, steering my thoughts well and clear. If she and Claire had been the products of some kind of laboratory experiment, then she was a victim just as much as Claire. If they'd taken her, and if they'd killed two people to cover their tracks, then she probably didn't have a chance. That was the brutal probability I hadn't wanted to consider.

By a quarter to eight, I was at the back of a three-car line waiting to get into Meredith Miles's compound. The car in front was alongside the guard booth, window down. I couldn't see the driver, or the guard. They must have been talking to each other, but I had no idea what they were saying. After thirty seconds, the gate rolled open, and the car drove in. Now I was second in line, and there were two cars behind me, close enough to my bumper that it would be hard to get out quickly. I'd made no promises to Olivia about how well I'd take care of her car, though, so at least there were some possibilities.

The second car's window came down. Again, I couldn't see the driver's face. I could see the guard's left arm. He looked like a big guy. Thirty seconds, and the gate opened. The car went inside, and the gate began to close. I took my foot off the brake and idled up to the booth. My window was already down. I got my first real look at the guard. He wasn't really sitting in the booth. He was wearing it, and it was a size too small. Maybe he was moonlighting from his regular job in the NFL. His suit didn't hide the tattoos on his neck and the backs of his hands.

"Good evening," I said.

"Your name, sir?"

His voice was curiously high-pitched. Maybe he'd started taking steroids before he'd hit puberty.

"Jim Gardner," I said.

He looked at me, squinting like a man who needs glasses but isn't wearing them. I wondered how often, if ever, Jim had come down here. He usually liked to make clients come to him. But this was Meredith Miles. He might make exceptions to the usual rules. The guard eased back into the booth and extracted a clipboard. He consulted a piece of paper, moving his nail down a list. His fingers were the size of paper towel tubes. If he'd wanted to, he probably could've reached out, grabbed my hair, and ripped my head off my shoulders.

"There you are," he said, in his child's voice. "All the way at the bottom."

"Where I belong."

"Have a good night, sir."

He hit the button and the gate rolled open. I nodded to him, put up my window, and drove inside. The driveway went up a hill, past stands of dry-looking pines. I'd driven two hundred yards before I caught the first sight of the house. It looked like something that belonged in the Tuscan hills. Smooth standstone and stucco, columns and cupolas, and big arched windows that served the dual purpose of looking out over the grounds while allowing someone on the outside to appreciate all the lights hidden in the high half-timbered ceilings. There were cars parked on either side of the driveway, and I pulled up behind the last one.

It was an SUV. A tan one, with mud still crusted around its wheel wells. One passenger window was badly cracked and held together with an X of duct tape. I would have known it anywhere. In a way, it was almost a relief. It's always easier showing up at a party when there's a familiar face. Someone you know, who you're looking forward to catching up with.

I killed the engine, then the lights. For a moment, I sat

in the car and looked around. There were people on the house's broad front terrace, but the grounds were empty. I got out of the car, lifted Elijah's phone, and called him. I walked slowly, not toward the house but out at the edge of the lawn's lit-up perimeter. Just a man who wanted to finish a private conversation before he joined a group of his peers.

"What's going on, Lee?"

"I'm at Meredith's place," I said. "Walking around outside, using your phone to hide my face while I look for someone."

"You got in?" he said. "Good deal."

"That was the easy part."

"What's the hard part?"

"Whatever comes next."

"Sounds like you got it all figured out," Elijah said.

"If I don't call you by tomorrow morning, toss the documents in a dumpster and call the FBI from a payphone."

"What about the Porsche?"

"Keep it. Or fence it. By then, I won't care."

"Okay," Elijah said. "You gonna ask how I'm doing?"

"How are you doing?"

"Great—I got a suite at the Drake, on Union Square. Just me and ten boxes of documents, and a mini-bar you wouldn't believe."

"You're at the Drake?" I asked. "Seriously?"

"I'm pulling your leg." He paused. "I'm at the Ritz."

I'd come around the side of the house, and now I could see the back. It was built up the side of a hill. There was a terrace midway up, with all the usual accouterments: hot tubs, sectional furniture, umbrellas. There was a man leaning against the railing, doing what I was doing: talking on the phone where he'd be out of sight and beyond earshot. I wouldn't have noticed him except he'd turned to take the call. As he brought the phone up, I saw his face in profile.

My driver. The man who'd brought me from the Creekside to Laytonville. Who'd objected to my early exit so much that he'd tried to put a bullet in my back. He was alone, and that made sense. His buddy from the back seat was either on ice in a Mendocino County morgue or looking at a long hospital stay.

"Hey, Elijah," I whispered. "Have a good time at the Ritz, or wherever. Go nuts. I gotta go."

I hung up and put the phone away. When I pulled Jim's gun out of my waistband, I liked the way it felt in my hand. Compact and heavy, like a claw hammer's head. I made sure the safety was on, and tucked it back under my belt. I started walking up the hillside again, following the shadows of trees. I reached the terrace and edged around until I was behind him.

"That's not a problem," he was saying into the phone. "That'll happen tonight."

He listened for a moment, and then he said, "Yes, sir."

I waited until he hung up, and then I cranked my right arm around his throat and pulled him tight to my chest. The stiff cartilage of his windpipe was up against the crook of my elbow. I used my left hand to push my right fist inward, and I flexed my bicep to tighten the pincer. It was a classic blood choke, a crushing squeeze that cut off all arterial flow in and out of his brain. He lasted about five seconds, which was half as long as I'd hoped for.

His knees buckled, but I didn't ease him to the ground. I wasn't going to fall for such an obvious ruse. I leaned back, taking his full weight, and let him dangle. He kicked once, the hard-edged heel of his shoe scraping down my shin. My mouth was right next to his ear, close enough to bite it off. I'd already had a taste of the guy and didn't want to repeat it. So I doubled the pressure on his throat. We could be headed toward irreversible damage. A shattered hyoid, a ruptured eyeball. That was all just fine with me.

He stopped moving. I held on another three seconds and then I let go and shoved him hard. He went sprawling onto the flagstone terrace, landing face-first behind the hot tub's raised deck. He wasn't even twitching.

I knelt beside him and patted him down. Wallet, phone, car keys. A slim handgun that might have been a Walther PPK, but in the dark I couldn't tell. In the opposite lapel pocket, there was a screw-on silencer, twice as long as the gun it was built to fit. I rolled him over and put two fingers on his throat. It took nearly a minute to find his pulse, and when I did, I couldn't be sure it wasn't just my imagination. Finally, I brought my head up and looked around. There was no one on the terrace, no one visible in the sprawling grounds to the side of the house. Up above, there were lit-up windows, but there was no one standing in them. The party was up front.

My problem was mostly solved, but I still needed to figure out a place to stash the guy. There was no way I could drag him back to the front of the house, down the driveway, and into the Jaguar's trunk. Not without getting noticed, anyway. I leaned over and checked the hot tub. It had a wooden lid, hinged down the middle. I unlatched the side nearest me, lifted it, and looked in. The tub was empty, but I won't lie. If it had been full of water, I'd have gone ahead anyway. I folded the hinged lid in half, grabbed the guy underneath his shoulders, and muscled him up onto the deck. Then up over the hot tub's lip, until gravity could do the rest. I dropped him, closed the lid, and latched it.

I spent a moment on a deck chair, getting my wind back. Long, slow breaths. Eyes closed. Then I stood up, tucked in my shirt, straightened my jacket, and walked back around to join the party.

Which was like nothing I'd ever attended.

Even when I was Juliette Vilatte's husband and I had to show up at penthouses and Marin County weekend homes and shake hands with people I had no business ever meeting, I never saw anything like what I saw that night in Meredith Miles's house.

I climbed up the steps to the front porch and looked around. If I'd had a camera with me, and if no one tackled me, I could have made a killing selling the shots to *Just Now!* There was the director, the mobster-film guy who'd started our hostess's career. His arm was around the actress from *The Scars at Night*. They were talking to a woman who'd made headlines for bringing down a secretary of state. There were other faces, eight or ten, that I recognized but couldn't place.

"You must be one of his friends," a voice said, to my right. "You're not one of mine."

I turned and was standing face to face with a woman I'd seen on theater screens and billboards for a decade. She was barefoot, wearing a dress that seemed to consist of a small black sheet and maybe a safety pin. She had a glass in each hand.

"White, or red?"

"Whichever you want less," I said. "And yeah — I'm one of his friends."

She handed me the glass of red wine and I clinked its rim against hers.

"Nice to meet you," she said. "I'm Meredith Miles."

"Lee Crowe."

"What do you do, Lee?"

"Every day's a little different," I said. "I follow people around and take pictures. Sometimes they don't like it, and then stuff like this happens."

I touched the bump on my head, and brushed my fingers along my scraped-up cheek.

"Pictures?"

She took a step back.

"No," I said. "I'm not one of them. Mostly I work for Jim."

"Jim?"

"Gardner."

She came back. Two steps this time, so that she was closer than before. She took ahold of my elbow and dropped her voice.

"You work for Jim? Really?"

"Since I got out of law school. He's been like my father — what I imagine it'd be like, having a father."

"He's coming tonight?" she asked. "He said he might be here."

I shook my head and frowned a little. Keep it simple, Crowe. She'd know bad acting if she saw it.

"Something came up — he's trapped at another client's house. He couldn't get out."

"I needed to talk to him."

"You could try his cell," I said, which was also true. She could try anything she wanted. "Or if he doesn't pick up, you could tell me. I'll be seeing him tomorrow morning."

"It's about all this," she said. She dropped her voice. "I'm having second thoughts."

"And?"

"And I wondered what Jim thought. If he could look at the contract — is it safe? If something goes wrong, is there any recourse? Is it even legal?"

"I don't know. I haven't seen the contract."

"Neither have I. It's all so secretive, isn't it?"

"Why wouldn't it be? It's the chance of many lifetimes."

"He told you that too?"

"Larsen?" I said. "That's his pitch."

"How do you know him?"

"Jim put me in contact," I said. "I've been helping stream-line his organization. Trim it down. Cull the herd. However you want to put it. I can't really get into it without breaching a client confidence."

"Does it touch on this?" she asked me. "On what he's selling us? If he's got legal problems, and it relates to . . . to whatever this really is . . . then I'm not letting him get any-where near me. Not with a needle."

"You're careful."

Her eyebrows arched, ever so slightly.

"How are you going to live forever if you're not careful? You could have all the right genes. You could get all the best upgrades. Whatever money can buy. But if you don't look two ways before you cross the street, it doesn't matter," she said. "Here — come with me."

She took my arm and led me into the house.

We stopped three times on the way through.

The first time, it was to say hello to a New York producer and a Spanish actress. The three of them exchanged air kisses, their cheeks half a foot apart. The producer shook my hand, and the actress simply nodded. Meredith intro-duced me as Lee, one of her lawyers. Not too long ago, that would have stung. Because it could have been true. I could have been Jim's partner, and then I would have been stand-ing here without any subterfuge. An invited guest.

But by now I knew enough about myself to know that if I'd ever actually attained what I'd wanted, I'd have been miserable. I'd be here on the clock, taking orders from Jim. Invited because I was useful and helpful, like the caterers. I wouldn't have arrived under a false name. I wouldn't have a gun in my waistband and another in my lapel pocket, both of them stolen. I wouldn't have locked a man in Meredith's hot tub.

I was deceiving everyone but myself. And that was just fine. I was happy with what I was doing because I was call-ing the shots, and interpreting the rules, deciding which ones to simply toss out.

Meredith led me away. We made it halfway across a sunken den before she stopped a waitress, who relieved us of our wineglasses. Then we went through a showpiece kitchen where water had probably never been boiled, and through a door to a second kitchen that wouldn't have been out of place in a busy restaurant. There were six people at work, uniformed in white. Meredith went to the largest man in the room and tapped his shoulder.

"Harry," she said. "I'm going to be in my study for a minute. Tell Leon if Stefan shows up, call me right away."

"Okay."

She pushed through a side door and we walked down a hallway, and then through a door at the very end of it.

"Leon's the guy at the gate?"

"That's right."

"Where'd you find him, the Chargers lineup?"

"I don't think he ever played football," she said. "At least, not for money. Maybe for cigarettes, in the exercise yard."

She walked halfway across the study, and then stopped. She turned and looked at me.

"The whole house is wired up. I can shout out anywhere. Leon and Harry will come running."

"I see."

"Modern technology to get them here, but once they show up, it's strictly fifteenth century," she said. "Fists and knives. So who are you, really?"

"Lee Crowe."

"There's no Lee Crowe on the list—" She broke off and studied my face. "You're not surprised I can memorize lines, are you?"

This room was decorated with film posters. Some vintage, some from her own work. There was a drafting table in the center, unbound scripts strewn across it. A laptop computer sat in the middle, its screen dark. She'd gotten her first Oscar for acting, but her second for writing. She'd pressed on with both.

"No," I said. "That doesn't surprise me at all."

"Whose name did you use to get in here?"

"Jim's — who else's?" I said.

"Did he send you here?"

"Of course he did," I said.

Which was sort of true. Jim had told me where to go and when to be there. Perhaps in doing so, he'd been engaging in an act of emergency room triage. Or a simple weighing of interests. Olivia Gravesend and Meredith Miles were good clients, and powerful women. Stefan Larsen was throwing people out of helicopters. Jim may have lacked any sense of morality, but he understood optics. Regardless of his reasons, I needed to turn this conversation around.

"Stefan Larsen scares you, doesn't he?" I asked.

"A little bit," she said. "But that's why you're here?"

"We're worried, Ms. Miles," I said. "And from what I've seen since I got here, you should be too."

I reached into my jacket and took out the slim handgun I'd taken off the man outside. I'd already screwed its suppressor into place. I held it on my outstretched palm, so that its muzzle faced me. Then I offered it to her.

"What is that?"

She made no move to touch it.

"I took it off Larsen's man, five minutes ago. He was on your back deck."

"What do you mean, you took it off him?"

"I came up behind him and put him on the ground. And then I went through his pockets."

"You did what?"

"It's okay — he's not getting up."

"You killed —"

"I knocked him out and locked him in your hot tub. Which was empty. He won't drown."

"You're talking about the blond guy — Michael? He was here to set up the presentation."

"With this?" I asked. "A silenced Walther PPK? Loaded

with hollow points? Larsen told you about this and you were cool with it?"

I had no idea what kind of ammunition was in the gun. I wasn't sure hollow points would be worse than any other kind of bullet. But they sounded bad.

"He never told me anything about that," Meredith said.

"Larsen and his men have killed three people, maybe four. And that's just the ones we know about."

She spent a long moment looking at me, at the gun on my palm.

"Put that down," she finally said. "You don't want your prints on it."

"They're all over it."

"Regardless."

I set the gun on the corner of her drafting table.

"Did Jim really send you?"

"Yes."

"How can I trust you?"

I glanced at the gun on her drafting table and took a couple of steps back. Anyone in her position knew how to handle one. Directors arranged classes with retired military guys and sent their actors out to ranges and pop-up shooting galleries, the same training courses the cops used. It was all about realism. Little details of mechanics and stance made a difference once the cameras were rolling. Or so they believed.

"You've got the guy's piece. And if you want to ask him what he was doing, he's probably starting to wake up now. You could take Leon off his post and let him do whatever he does."

I still had Jim's gun in my waistband. But I hadn't really lied to her. There was a bottom line. She could trust me, whether or not I could explain why.

"Leon's good where he is. And if Larsen's man is where you say, then he's fine there, too."

I watched as she pulled a tissue from a box on the desk and, with that in her hand, picked up the gun. I must have been right about the classes, because the first thing she did was click off the safety. Then she picked up a tissue with her other hand and used that to rack the slide. An unspent bullet ejected onto the carpet.

"You've got the safety off. You're one round down, but you know from the weight you've got plenty more," I said. "You're cocked and locked. Six pounds of pressure on your index finger and you'll put a hole through my forehead. No one will even hear it."

She held the gun down at her side, and looked at me. She was breathing hard, but not so hard that she couldn't shoot straight.

"Would you like to call someone who can vouch for me?"

"You said Jim's tied up."

"We have another mutual acquaintance. Someone you trust a good deal. And she's got more of a stake in this than Jim."

"Who's that?"

"Olivia Gravesend. She says you've got her number."

She was silent for a long moment. Her finger was still on the trigger.

"We go back a few years."

"I hear you do fundraisers."

"What's she have to do with this?"

"Call her and ask."

She backed to the drafting table and picked up a cell phone. She used voice commands to dial so she could keep her eyes on me the whole time. She'd made the call on speaker, and I could hear the phone ringing. Three hundred miles to the north, Mr. Richards picked up.

"Gravesend residence."

"Meredith Miles, calling for Olivia."

"Yes, ma'am," he said. "Of course."

294

They must have been standing in the same room; Olivia was on right away. He'd just handed her the phone.

"Yes, darling," she said. "I thought you'd call."

Meredith switched off the speaker and held the phone close to her ear.

"Who is Lee Crowe? Did you send him here?"

Then she was silent, listening. I couldn't hear Olivia's answer at all, but it must have gone on awhile. Meredith's mouth compressed into a tight line. Her index finger tapped on the Walther's trigger guard.

"Why?" she asked.

This answer was just a short beat, but Meredith must not have understood.

"Say again?"

As she listened, her eyebrows pulled together. Then she began to nod, as people do on the phone even when the object of their sympathies can't see or appreciate the gesture.

"Something happened to Claire?"

Another short explanation, and this time Meredith looked up at me.

"Olivia . . . okay."

She took the phone away from her ear and put the call back on speaker.

"— and then he killed her," Olivia was saying. "He'll never answer for it, because he owns more people than I do. Which is where Crowe comes in."

Meredith Miles considered that.

"What would you like me to do?" she said.

"Trust him," Olivia answered. "Give him some latitude."

"I see."

"He's a little rough around the edges," Olivia said. "Not really the sort of person you'd usually want to —"

"I'll call you back."

Meredith used her thumb to hang up.

In the movies, her face was an open book. She could telegraph her emotions with a matchless luminosity, her every thought flashed to the world at forty-eight frames per second. Hundreds of millions of people probably thought they understood her.

In real life, at close range, I was getting a different perspective.

I was on the other end of a silenced Walther PPK, and I couldn't read her face at all.

"What happened to Claire?" she finally asked. "She never said how, or why."

"You hung up on her."

"Let's hear it from you."

"Claire went looking for him — for Larsen. I think to confront him. But it didn't go so well. He tossed her out of a helicopter."

"You're serious."

"He's got secrets. And if anyone gets close to figuring them out . . ."

But I didn't need to finish that thought.

"Did Claire get so close?" she asked. "What did she know?"

I couldn't answer that. At that point I didn't know exactly what he was selling. I had a lot of pieces of the puzzle but they hadn't quite come together. There were the cloned girls and the men up at the Creekside, with their loose talk around the fire about Kennedy and Khrushchev. And then there were the scars. If Larsen had been experimenting on the girls, maybe he'd taken it a step beyond that. Maybe he was harvesting something from them.

"Tell me this — how did you meet him, and what did he promise you?"

"I've never met him," she said. "I started hearing his name from people I trust. People in certain circles. They said he had a cure. That it really worked."

"A cure for what?"

"For time," she said. "It ticks a little faster for some of

us, doesn't it? And none of us will ever have as much as we want. The people in this house can buy anything they want, except one thing."

"And Stefan Larsen is selling it to you."

"But there are needles, and contracts, and some secret retreat up in the north where you take the treatments," she said. "Half the people in this town wouldn't eat a cucumber if they heard it was genetically modified. And we're lining up for this?"

"You don't even know what it is."

"It's either too good to be true, or it's true and it has consequences no one's worked out."

"What do you think?" I asked.

"I want to know about Claire Gravesend. Why did he kill her?"

"That's part of what I'm trying to find out, Ms. Miles," I said.

I saw her look me over. There were the cuts from spilling out onto Highway 101, and the fading bruises from a life-or-death fight on a stairway in Boston. There could have been new marks, from the scuffle on her terrace.

For the first time in six years, I wasn't embarrassed by any of it.

"It's Meredith," she said. "Ms. Miles sounds like someone's grade school teacher."

33

THERE WAS NO time to tell her more. Her phone rang, and she answered it. It wasn't on speaker, but I could hear Leon's small voice just the same.

"I let them through the gate," he said. "They're driving up now."

"Who else was with him?"

"His mother."

"Thank you," she said. She hung up and looked at me. "Tell me what you want. Then I'll tell you what I'm willing to do."

"He's going to make a presentation, right?"

"That's right—a sales pitch. When you were a kid, did your parents ever go to a Tupperware party? It's like that, except the cheapest package is ten million dollars."

"That's a lot of Tupperware."

"What do you want?"

"To watch, and listen. When he leaves, I want to follow him."

"That's it?"

"I won't do anything in your house."

"You already did—that man, outside."

"Aside from that."

"Anything else?"

"Larsen sent a man to kill me in Boston. That same day, he

had people toss my office and bug my apartment. He knows my name and my face. It'd be better if I didn't mingle with your guests."

"Agreed."

"So what can you do?"

"This is a take-it-or-leave-it proposition, and you've got about thirty seconds."

"Go ahead."

"I told you the house is wired up."

She picked up a remote control and pointed it at a flatscreen television on the far wall. She sorted through an onscreen menu and hit a button, and then we were looking at the sunken den. The camera was hidden somewhere high up, so we were looking down at her guests. The volume was low, but I could hear the murmur of half a dozen conversations. People who had come to rub shoulders with their peers, drink wine, and listen to a devil's proposition.

"You can watch from here," she said. "And you'll leave before he does. Out the door, turn right, and go to the back of the house. You already know about the terrace."

"Yes."

"Agreed?"

"It'll do just fine," I said. "But there's the matter of the guy in your hot tub."

"Leon will take care of him," she said.

"If you just kick him loose, he's going to come after me again."

"Leon's dealt with prowlers. Larsen's man won't be doing anything for a couple of days except taking aspirin."

"And if he reports you to the cops?"

She was turning to leave, but stopped before opening the door.

"He won't," she said. "They never do."

"If it works for you, then it's fine with me."

"I won't see you again, Mr. Crowe. So this is goodbye."

Then she opened the door and left. I locked it after her, then went back to the drafting table. Meredith Miles wrote her scripts while perched on a teak and canvas director's chair. I pulled it out and sat down, then picked up the silenced pistol and looked at it. It was in good shape. A well-maintained and well-loved tool. I could smell the burnt sulfur of recent shots. It had been fired since the last time it was cleaned. The right thing to do would be to hand it over to LAPD, who could take it to their ballistics lab. They'd probably tie it to unsolved crimes from coast to coast. But that was never going to happen. There was a good chance I'd be using it tonight.

Larsen and his mother came into view five minutes later. She was the same woman I'd seen in the redwood grove at the Creekside, just before getting knocked cold. A tall blonde, her hair braided carefully and pinned up at the back of her head. She could have been Claire or Madeleine, visiting from the future. They all had the same face, the same curves, the same smooth skin. But this woman moved carefully. Not with the lissome grace of a dancer, but with the fragility of the infirm. She crossed the room and sat down at the end of a low couch, aloof and alone. A waitress came by with a tray of wineglasses and scurried off just as quickly, dismissed with a glance.

Larsen took the opposite approach. He worked the room, moving easily from group to group. Of course he'd press the flesh. He'd made big claims that came with an equally outsized asking price. If a third of the people present bought his cheapest package, he'd leave here fifty million dollars richer. He wore a dark suit jacket over a black, collarless shirt. His blond hair reached his shoulders. The body beneath his jacket looked broad and muscular. He was exactly what Larry had described to me. And he and his mother could have passed as siblings. Which is to say that there was no visible age difference between them, and it would have been impossible to state how old either of them was.

After he'd met and greeted everyone in the room, he stepped into the empty space by his mother and pulled out his phone. I watched him dial, watched him hold the phone to his ear. And then a phone began to vibrate in my pocket. It wasn't Elijah's, but the one I'd taken from Larsen's man.

I pulled it out and looked at the screen. The incoming number had no name attached to it. Larsen had instructed his man well. He didn't want to be listed in the contacts. Which meant that the phone Larsen was using was probably a burner, or registered through some hopeless trail of limited liability companies. I grabbed one of Meredith's pens, took a page from the untitled script, and wrote the number down. There was no way I was going to answer, but the phone was giving me a couple of other options. I could tap a button and send a preset text response.

Sorry, I can't talk right now.
I'm on my way.
I'll call you later.

I knew I couldn't talk to Larsen, but I could needle him a little bit. I picked the last option, because it sounded the least subservient. I wasn't up to my ears in some big problem that I was solving for him. I wasn't rushing to his side. I'd let him down in Laytonville, but that wasn't really on my mind. *I know you're calling, boss, but I'm ignoring you. I'll call you when I feel like it. Until then, fuck off.*

I turned the phone off and put it back in my pocket. Meanwhile, I was watching the TV screen. Larsen read my text, and stiffened. He leaned down and whispered something in his mother's ear. Then he turned and looked around. Meredith Miles had just appeared, joining a group at the other side of the den. Larsen came to her. They did the requisite

301

air kiss. One side, then the other. No touching at all, but not because Larsen didn't try. I couldn't hear what he said to her; there were too many other conversations going on at once.

But after he finished speaking, Meredith signaled the nearest waitress. Time to go. In fifteen seconds, every uniformed person in the room had cleared out. Remaining in place were fifteen Hollywood power brokers, plus Larsen, and his mother, whose look of cold disdain hadn't changed since she'd walked into the room.

I watched Meredith tap the rim of a champagne flute with a cocktail fork. The room fell silent, and faces turned toward her.

"I guess one way or another, we all know why we're here," she said. "And I think you've all met Mr. Larsen by now. The servers are gone, so if you want anything else, you'll have to pour your own drink — but everyone here probably lost that skill long ago."

Her crowd responded with a polite laugh.

"So, Mr. Larsen," she said, turning to him. "Go right ahead."

Larsen reached into his jacket and came out with a slim black remote. He stood looking at it, his head down, then looked up and hit a button. His advance man had installed equipment around the perimeter of Meredith's sunken den, and now those machines were whirring to life.

There was a bank of angled mirrors mounted to black motor housings on the ceiling. They began to spin, and from around the room, a dozen laser projectors, placed on all the walls, cast their beams upward. What appeared next was pure sleight of hand. A carefully orchestrated miracle of light and interference.

A tiny star appeared, floating four feet above Meredith's floor. It rotated slowly, showing its light pink corona, pulsing, growing larger. The gathered guests stepped back and gave it space.

"This is how you began — how we all began," Larsen said. "A single cell that split in two."

The star was now the size of an orange. It began to contract in the middle, as though unseen hands were tightening a belt around its equator. One orb became two, pressed tightly against each other.

"From that moment, the clock was ticking," Larsen said. He looked at his audience, making eye contact with anyone who wasn't focused on the hologram. "We have only so many days in this life. Time slips through the glass. You've been dying since the moment you were born."

Floating in front of them, the holographic cells began to divide at an exponential rate. An embryo was taking shape. It grew into a fetus, and then into a newborn. The infant descended to the floor. It lay there, naked and shivering — and aging. There was a child, who grew into a woman. Just as her beauty was in full blossom, she aged into a centenarian, gray-skinned and shriveled.

Larsen hit a button and the presentation paused. The naked old woman lay frozen on the floor. She was shimmering. A sculpture in light.

"This is the path you're on. The only one you thought was possible. You didn't choose it. There was no choice. At best you're resigned to it — to grow old, to wither, to die."

He looked around again.

"Or maybe you're not so resigned, are you? You're here, after all. You heard something. A rumor. And as much as you ever wanted anything, you wanted to believe that there might be another way."

He lifted his remote. On the floor, the shimmering woman began to stir. She stood up. Naked, and hunched. Her skin sagged with age. She hugged herself against the cold. Her face was turned down, hidden behind ropes of unwashed hair.

"Any clock can be reset. With just one minute to midnight, you can still turn it back."

The woman was standing taller. The wrinkles were disappearing from her skin. She dropped her hands from her chest and revealed full breasts. She pushed her suddenly blond hair aside and raised her clear face.

We were looking at Madeleine.

Except that it wasn't Madeleine. Not quite. The holographic woman appeared to be older by ten or fifteen years. She turned around once, slowly. And then, like a light bulb going out, she disappeared. Larsen took her place at the center of the sunken den.

"I think you've all met my mother."

All eyes turned toward her, but she didn't look up. She sat at the edge of the couch, face turned to the side, looking at nothing.

"About twenty years ago, she was diagnosed with an aggressive form of leukemia," Larsen said. "She had less than a year to live. Her doctors proposed a course of chemotherapy that would have destroyed her bone marrow. She'd have to replace it later, with transplants from donors. A process that comes with its own complications and risks. Not to mention considerable pain. But I had a better idea. It wasn't just a cure for cancer. It was a cure for everything—a way to turn back time."

He looked around the room. Most of his audience had taken seats. Meredith was next to her first director, whispering something to him. Larsen cleared his throat.

"How many of you have heard of the young blood movement?"

Most of the hands in the room went up.

"And how many of you have tried it?"

304

Only two people raised their hands this time, including the director at Meredith's side.

"It's a simple concept," Larsen said. "A child could have come up with it — draw blood from the young, and transfuse it into the old. The idea came from a study done on mice. They linked the circulatory systems of young mice and their older peers. New blood into old arteries. The older mice thrived. As much as you can thrive with another organism grafted onto you."

Meredith leaned forward. The director put his hand on her bare knee, and she swatted it off, but didn't take her eyes from Larsen.

"What did you do to your mother?"

"Almost exactly what her doctors recommended. We wiped out her bone marrow and replaced it with transplanted tissue."

"Whose tissue did you use?"

"Her own," Larsen said. He glanced at his mother. "We used bone marrow from her childhood. It's what's called an autologous haematopoietic stem cell graft. Replace the sick tissue with healthy tissue from the same patient. There were no complications from rejection. And because the tissue was harvested in her earliest youth, there were other benefits you couldn't begin to imagine . . . Allow me."

He stepped away from the center of the floor and triggered his projectors. A swirl of blue light began at the ceiling and descended toward the floor until it hovered at eye level. The light coalesced and took a new shape. We were looking at a concrete building. It stood alone in a snowy field. The image began to rotate. At the side of the building, there was a crude portico above a set of double doors. An ancient-looking ambulance was abandoned beneath it, all four of its tires missing.

"My first laboratory," Larsen said. His voice had taken a

hush of nostalgia. "It was nowhere near here. The powers that be frown on free thought. At least in this country, and particularly when it comes to stem cells."

The hospital dissolved. Now we saw the inside of a lab. A man with blond hair to his shoulders worked at a bench, going between a microscope and a set of flickering computer screens. We couldn't see his face, but didn't need to.

"A stem cell is an amazing thing," the real Larsen was saying. "It can differentiate into any kind of tissue. It can regenerate and renew."

Light bled out of the microscope's eyepieces and took a solid shape in the illusory laboratory's air, allowing us to see what Larsen was looking at in the microscope. Cells in a suspension pulsed and divided.

"The stem cells in your bone marrow generate your blood. But that's not all they're capable of. With just a few modifications, they can travel through your circulatory system and renew whatever they touch. Heart tissue. Your liver. Your eyes. As healthy as they were when you were a child. And it's not pills, or chemicals, or trendy diets. It's your own body, turning back time."

We saw a gray heart grow firm and healthy, a mottled liver become slick and brown. Next there was a child playing in a meadow. A lithesome teenager diving from a cliff toward the ocean. And then, in a flash, the sunken den became a sepia-toned morgue. The floor and the walls were made of small white tiles, like a subway station. Steel carts bore crude-looking instruments. There were shears that looked like they'd been forged in a blacksmith's shop. Scalpels and bone saws. In the center of the room, beneath coned lights, was a gurney. A shrouded form lay upon it. Larsen walked through his illusion and stood next to the body.

"I imagine most if not all of you don't have bone marrow from your childhood sitting in a freezer somewhere, ready for use. Well, what if someone found a way to harvest your

DNA and implant it in a cell?" he asked. "And what if we could give that cell a spark of new life, so that it was born again, its clocks started from zero? All of the marks of age erased. Imagine what it would be like if those stem cells — your stem cells — were waiting for you in a vessel, growing in a perfect environment, until you were ready to harvest and receive them?"

He paused and let his audience study the morgue.

"If we could do that — if we could have a limitless supply of our own stem cells, but as fresh and vibrant as they were in our youth — we would have a wellspring inside us. A fountain of youth, inside our bones."

Now the morgue disappeared. We were treated to a long hallway. A man was pushing the gurney through the gloom. Far ahead, there was a door. White light blazed from the crack beneath it, from the jamb, from the keyhole.

"I can open that door," Larsen said. "I can take you to the other side. I can —"

"What are you saying?" Meredith asked.

"I found a way," Larsen said. If she'd thrown him off, he rediscovered his balance quickly. He'd given this presentation before and expected questions. "I can take a tiny sample of your DNA. I can transfer it into the nucleus of a cell. I can plant it where it will grow. In less than a year — ten months, give or take — I can start to harvest bone marrow. Your bone marrow, but with the cellular clocks reset."

"Is this cloning?" Meredith asked. "Human cloning?"

"Of course not." His voice was serene. On the other side of the room, his mother still hadn't moved a muscle. "This is just for stem cells."

"How are you getting them?"

"I have a proprietary process. After I transfer the DNA — your DNA — I cultivate the cells inside an entirely disposable vessel."

"What does that mean — a disposable vessel?"

"That's the proprietary part."

"Proprietary as in patented?"

Larsen shook his head.

"Patents are part of the public record, and the protection lasts only so long. But secrets last as long as you can keep them. And I keep them very well."

"You need to give me more than that. You're asking for ten million dollars."

"Which is a quarter of what you made last year."

"But more than I'd want to lose," Meredith said. "I want to know what I'm really buying."

"It's not so simple to show you," he said. "After all, we can't cut my mother in half and count the rings."

His mother glanced up but didn't move beyond that.

"Then how are you going to prove this all really works? That you can really do this?" she asked. When Larsen began to raise his remote, she shook her head. "That's just smoke and mirrors. Everyone here knows how to make a movie."

"I can't show you my facilities," Larsen said. "But I can give you the next best thing."

"Which is?"

"People you trust," he said. "I did this for my mother two decades ago. There were complications, initially. I was trying to make new cells from old DNA — chromosomes that carried all the mutations and damage you'd expect after a long life well lived. Some of those imperfections carried through my vessels, even through the process of rebirth. Since then, technology has outpaced the problems. I can edit genes like a line of text. I can take your DNA and make it the way it was when you were born. I can —"

But I had heard enough. I knew what Larsen was doing, and I knew why he could never explain himself to Meredith Miles. He was talking in circles about rebirth and disposable vessels because he couldn't tell her that he was inviting everyone to dinner and serving them human flesh.

I opened the study door and stepped quietly into the hallway. I could hear the presentation continuing in the front of the house, but I didn't go that way. I went toward the back, the way Meredith had told me to go. I stopped on the terrace, next to the still-latched hot tub, and caught my breath. Then I went on. I wasn't finished yet, but I was getting close.

34

I DID A three-point turn in the driveway and drove back down the hill toward the gate. The last car in the lineup was a black Maybach. My now dead acquaintance Larry had described a car just like this. Long and powerful, a European make that he couldn't quite put his finger on. A chauffeur was outside it, buffing the exterior with a white cloth. It was at the end of the line of parked cars, and Larsen had been the last person to arrive. I looked the other way as I drove past the chauffeur, and then I waited for the gate to open.

I followed Deseo Lane down the canyon for three hundred yards until I came to the first cross street. It was just a short cul-de-sac. I took a right and parked at the end, facing out. I turned off my headlights but kept the engine running. I watched the intersection ahead of me, and I waited.

I passed the time by making a phone call to George Wong.

"What can I do for you?" he asked, once we'd gotten past the rote beginnings of most phone conversations.

"Is there bone marrow in a person's spinal column?"

"You're just all over the map, aren't you, Crowe?" he said. "Yes. There's bone marrow. Generally speaking, the bigger the bone, the more it'll have."

"How do you harvest it?"

"With a big needle."

"Can you harvest bone marrow from a baby?"

"You could do a lot of terrible things to a baby—the question is, why would you want to?"

"But if you did it over and over again, it would leave scars, right?"

"Of course it would leave scars. What are you getting at?"

"Let me ask you something else," I said. "Last time we talked, you were telling me about Dr. Park. He was doing cloning by nuclear transfer. Let's say you can clone a human—"

"Judging from what I saw in the lab, that's not just a hypothetical."

"Okay, sure. So if Dr. Park started with the DNA of an old woman, when he transferred that into an egg, then what?"

"Assuming you had a surrogate mother to take care of the gestation, you'd get a baby."

"Would she be eighty years old at birth?"

I imagined a baby born with white hair and wrinkles. Falling apart before she ever got started.

"No, that's the miracle of cloning—when the egg divides the first time, one cell into two, it restarts the clocks."

"What clocks?"

"Cells have all kinds of clocks, but here we're basically talking about telomeres. The caps on the end of your DNA strands. When a cell divides, your DNA copies itself, and the telomeres help keep that process tidy. The older you get, the more worn out they are, and the more mutations creep in."

"Things fall apart," I said.

"The center cannot hold," he answered. "But cloning sets the timer back to zero. Don't ask me how. I'm way out on a limb here already."

He paused, and I watched out the windshield. A car went past, but it was nobody I needed to worry about.

"Do you remember Dolly?" George asked.

"You're talking about the sheep?"

"The sheep," he said. "Dolly was cloned from a six-year-old ewe. That's middle-aged, in sheep years. So people wondered if she'd fall apart faster than normal."

"Did she?"

"She got arthritis at age four. She died of lung cancer at age six."

"Is that a yes?"

"It's a definite maybe. Because on the other hand, she lived indoors and ate a lot of treats."

"What do you think?"

"I think if I were a clone, I'd be careful," George said. Another pause. "I wouldn't miss my annual physical. If prevailing wisdom said to get screened for something at age fifty, I'd get the screening at twenty-five. Or at least, if I'd been cloned when Dolly was, I would."

"But today would be different?"

"About five or six years ago, a new system was developed that lets you rewrite genes letter by letter. It's called CRISPR. If you made a clone today, and you knew what you were doing, then yeah, you could definitely write out any anomalies. You could make a perfect replica."

"Thanks, George," I said.

I hung up without taking my eyes from the road ahead. I tried to keep a leash on my thoughts so I could stay focused on the task at hand. My job for Olivia Gravesend was basically over. She'd asked me to find out what happened to her daughter, and I thought I could tell her. She might not believe the story, and it might destroy her to hear it, but there was no other tale to tell. I could drive back to Carmel, make my report, and submit my invoice. But if I did that, any chance Madeleine had would disappear.

I couldn't quit yet.

An hour later, Larsen's unmistakable car rolled past the mouth of the intersection. It was in my line of sight for three seconds, and then it was gone. I waited ten more seconds before shifting into gear and following him. I had to assume Larsen's driver was checking for tails. His boss knew I was gunning for him. The only way to follow a quarry like Larsen is either to take the risk of getting burned or accept the possibility of losing your man. I chose the latter. If I lost him, I could find him again. But if he saw me now, he might never lead me where I wanted to go.

I looked at the car's GPS. I was heading down Deseo Lane again. This street was about to take a sharp right curve and terminate on Angelo Drive. Larsen was going to have to turn — but I wouldn't be there to see which way he went. If he went left, he'd head up into the hills for a quarter of a mile and hit a dead end. If he went right, there were a dozen possibilities. I could rule out all the dead ends. I was looking for exits. Escape routes. If he wanted to come down from the heights, there was really only one option — Benedict Canyon Drive. And if you took that road in the other direction, you'd get to higher ground. Up to the top of the ridge and then over, into Sherman Oaks, Van Nuys, or North Hollywood.

From the intersection ahead, there were two ways to Benedict Canyon Drive. The short way and the long way. I assumed Larsen's driver would take the fastest route. His boss was a busy man. So when I got to the intersection, I took the long way, which shot me out on Benedict Canyon one street north of Larsen. If I sped back down toward the city, and he was going that way too, I'd come up on him from behind. If he was heading to higher ground, he'd pass me going the other direction. I downshifted, and found out what the Jaguar could do on a one-lane road as crooked as a broken spine.

The neighborhood wasn't built for drag racing, and probably wouldn't tolerate it. Getting pulled over would be a disaster. I had no ID, had two stolen guns within reach, and was driving a car registered to Olivia Gravesend. One of those guns was likely linked to multiple homicides, including deaths at a bed-and-breakfast I had recently visited. Yet I didn't slow down.

I skidded around a right-hand turn, bumping over the curb and nearly scraping some guy's rock wall. Then I had a relatively straight stretch, heading downhill, where the land on the right was too steep to build anything. I could see a stop sign up ahead, and I sped toward it. There was another home on the right, and someone had left a gray trash bin halfway out into the street. I didn't swerve in time and clipped it with the front bumper. It flew into a boxwood hedge, white trash bags exploding out its top.

I slowed for the stop sign, then took a nearly 270-degree right turn onto Cielo Drive. This street went down, pushing through the contour lines as it plunged out of the hills and toward Benedict Canyon. I passed a sign that warned me to watch my downhill speed. I was watching it, all right. I was doing about seventy on a road built for fifteen or twenty.

A car coming up the hill in the other direction dove to the side. I heard its horn as I passed, and then it was gone. I sped on through the dark. There were no streetlights here. Just the overhanging trees — willows and scrubby oaks, and silhouettes of century plants, in the Jaguar's high beams. There was another stop sign up ahead, and I ignored it, blasting past the mouth of Beverly View Drive without even kissing the brakes.

Another three curves and I was at Benedict Canyon Drive. I slowed and came to a stop at the white line. I put on my turn signal. Just a good citizen out for a drive. I turned right, and drove about a hundred yards before I saw a pair of headlights coming toward me. My skin prickled. It was the Maybach, passing me as it headed the other way. I waited until he was out of sight, and let one other car pass. Then I did a U-turn and went after him.

. . .

Mulholland Drive sits at the top of a ridge in the Santa Monica Mountains and goes east to west, winding between parks and some of the most expensive real estate in California, and ending as a dirt road at the edge of a wilderness area half the size of San Francisco.

I had a feeling that's where Larsen was headed. When he got there, he'd either have to take a right or a left. If I could beat him there, I could use the same trick that had just worked for me a moment ago. I'd either come up innocently behind him, or I'd see him pass in the other direction.

I looked at the map and saw there was a way to do it, but I'd have to move if I wanted to get to the top in time. It was another race, this time going up instead of down. The streets were just as narrow, and just as winding, and I had to deal with oncoming traffic on five occasions. I was certain someone would pick up a phone and call the cops, but I reached the top of the ridge without being chased. I turned left onto Mulholland, toward Benedict Canyon Drive, and I took my time, driving fifteen miles an hour until I came to the intersection.

I reached it without seeing the Maybach. He must have turned left when he'd reached the top. So I sped up — forty, fifty miles an hour — and caught up to him after six curves. I saw the taillights first, then the Maybach's distinctively sloped back end. I eased off the gas but kept him more or less in sight. The best time to spot a tail is in the first half mile of a drive. I hadn't given him that opportunity. Now I could be anyone. I was just a guy driving west on Mulholland, headed toward Interstate 405. Maybe I wanted to see the city lights. Maybe I was headed to Malibu.

After that, things happened pretty quickly. We drove about two miles, which took around four minutes. Mulholland crossed the interstate on a high overpass. I saw a ribbon of red lights headed north, and another of white lights coming south. Then we came up a low rise. There was a church school on the left, and an empty parking lot on the right. The Maybach turned right, into the parking lot. I saw that there was a view of the city to the north. The edge of the parking lot fell away in a steep slope. Far down below, there were lights spread out to the horizon. I wasn't sure what I was looking at. Van Nuys, or Northridge. I didn't have time to look at the map, and it didn't really matter. Because at the same moment the Maybach entered the lot, a helicopter appeared from the lower part of the slope. It must have been hugging the hillside as it came up toward the ridge.

It flared back, then settled onto the parking lot. The Maybach drove straight toward it. I broke every protocol of surreptitious surveillance and stopped the Jaguar in the middle of the road so that I could watch.

The pilot jumped out and opened the helicopter's side door. Simultaneously, the chauffeur exited and opened the Maybach's two rear doors. Larsen got out, and then his mother. They walked to the helicopter and stepped inside. The driver got back in the car, looped back onto Mulholland, and passed me without making eye contact. I wasn't his problem, and he wasn't mine. I was watching the pilot, who was shutting the door and climbing back into the cockpit. I was watching him strap in and adjust his headset, then flip switches. The dual engines' whine became a roar. Ten seconds later they were airborne, and ten seconds after that, the helicopter was just a blinking red light. It gained altitude and disappeared above a low-hanging cloud.

And just like that, Larsen was gone. I punched the steering wheel, hard enough to feel my knuckles pop. I should have anticipated this.

Behind me, a car was honking. I was blocking the lane. I took my foot off the brake and did a U-turn. Larsen had gone off to the northwest, so I needed to get to the interstate. I wouldn't be able to keep up, but I could try my best.

When I used Elijah's phone to call Inspector Chang, he picked up on the fifth ring, slightly out of breath.

"Good evening, Inspector," I said. "Are you back from Alaska?"

"I just walked in."

"You have something to write with?"

"Yes."

"Take this down," I said.

I read him Larsen's cell phone number, which I'd written on a page from one of Meredith's scripts.

"What is that?"

"The cell phone of the man who killed Claire Gravesend."

"Are you serious?" he asked. "Where are you?"

"L.A.," I said. "So, listen — our window is going to close fast. Unless you've got some way of locating that cell phone and telling me where he is."

"I couldn't do that without a warrant," Chang said. "And I can't get a warrant without an investigation. And I don't have an investigation because the case is closed."

I nearly ran into the car in front of me. When I hit the brakes, it was hard enough that I dropped the phone. I had to fish it up from the floor.

"That's it?" I said. "You can't do it?"

"I can't do it."

"All right," I said. "Then wish me luck. Or don't — you should probably forget we had this call."

I hung up and went with the flow of traffic. It was a mile before I realized that I wasn't out of options. With one eye on the road and one eye on the phone, I started searching the internet for a phone number. It took a minute to find it, and then I dialed and listened to it ring.

A woman answered.

"NorCal TRACON," she said, and waited. So calm and professional that for a moment I thought she was a recording. I was waiting for an options menu, but she spoke up again. "Yes?"

"I need to speak with Director Reese right away."

"He left at six."

"Then you need to call him at home, and transfer me."

"Who is this?"

"Lee Crowe," I said. "I met with him yesterday."

The pause went long enough that I thought she might write me off as a crank and hang up. Every UFO nut in Northern California had probably called her desk at one time or another. But after a long moment, she came back on the line.

"Hold, please, Mr. Crowe," she said. "Transferring now."

The line went silent. I put the phone on speaker so that I could drive with both hands on the wheel.

"Hello?" Reese said. "Crowe?"

"I need one more favor," I said. "It should be quick."

"Go ahead."

"You remember the N-number on that helicopter we were looking at yesterday?"

"I can pull it up."

"Good—because the thing just took off from a parking lot at Mulholland and Interstate 405, and it's headed to the northwest. I need to know where it lands."

"Mulholland and 405? You're talking about Los Angeles."

"Yeah."

"That's not on our watch."

"You mean you can't do it?"

"That's not what I said. I just need to call SCT—our sister facility in San Diego. Can I call you back on this number?"

"Please," I said.

He hung up and I drove for ten minutes in silence. The freeway was raised above the surface streets, and the traffic was moving fast now. I saw signs for U.S. 101. I could take it north, toward Ventura, which would put me closer to the coast. Or I could stay where I was and catch Interstate 5, back through the Central Valley. I chose the coastal route, and as I was lining up for the exit, the phone rang.

"Yes?" I said.

"He's still in the air," Reese said. "He's going a hundred and fifty-four knots west-northwest. Altitude is six thousand feet."

"What's west-northwest of L.A.?"

"Santa Barbara, I guess. Then a bunch of little towns as you head up the coast."

"Can you call me when he lands?"

"If I can."

"What's it depend on?"

"He's in a helicopter, so he can land anywhere," Reese said. "California isn't exactly flat, and topography and radar don't get along."

"You'll lose him if he goes below the mountaintops, is what you're saying."

"But he's nice and high now. And his transponder is on."

"So call me if he changes course or goes off your screens," I said.

35

LARSEN WAS FLYING toward Santa Barbara at a hundred and fifty knots, and I was following on the ground at a fraction of his speed. He'd reach his destination well ahead of me, assuming I ever ended up in the right place at all. Near midnight, I stopped for gas in Ventura, fifty miles outside of L.A. I didn't want to slow down, but the Jaguar's tank was so close to empty that the engine was shuddering. Reese hadn't called me back, which meant that Larsen was still in the air. Every minute I spent pumping gas, Larsen gained another three miles on me.

After Ventura, the highway hugged the coast again and the traffic thinned to nothing. I had a full tank, so I gave the engine whatever it wanted, crossing my fingers that the California Highway Patrol was somewhere else tonight. I didn't realize there were railroad tracks adjacent to the highway until I chased down, and then overtook, the Pacific Surfliner train making the run between Carpinteria and Santa Barbara.

One hour and twenty minutes after the helicopter dusted off, the phone rang. I glanced at the screen, then answered.

"Did he land?"

"Five minutes ago," Reese said. "Looks like the middle of nowhere. You ever heard of San Simeon?"

"Hearst Castle."

"Close," he said. "Do you have a pen?"

"I'm driving."

"Pull over," he said. "I'm going to give you some GPS co-ordinates."

I let the car's momentum fall off. Then I drifted over to the shoulder and braked to a stop.

"Okay," I said. "Go ahead."

He read out the digitized longitude and latitude coordinates. I typed them into Elijah's phone, thanked him, and hung up. Then I opened the map and pasted the coordinates into it. It pinned a location a hundred and thirty-seven miles to the northwest.

I drove through the night. Around three thirty in the morning I got to the turnoff. I slowed to thirty miles an hour and flicked on my high beams.

The land was treeless. Barren, except for waist-high grass. The ocean was somewhere nearby on the left, but I couldn't see it. I could smell it, though. That, and the wet grass, and the late-spring flowers that grew along the roadside. There seemed to be hills on the right, but I couldn't see how high they were or whether there was anything up there. It was a while until dawn.

I had the phone on the dashboard so that I could see the map. When I drew even with the pinned spot, I saw an un-marked gravel driveway. The wooden gate was ten feet high, and made of planks so thick that a truck might not have been able to ram through it. But the stone wall stretching off to either side was only five or six feet high. I had tried to sneak into the Creekside on foot, with disastrous results. I imag-ined it'd be about the same this time. I parked the car so that it blocked the gate. Then I called Elijah. I might have woken him up, but I didn't think he had hit the minibar too hard.

"Yeah?"

"You got something to write with?"

"Sure. Hang on."

"Take this down," I said.

I gave him Larsen's phone number, and then GPS coordinates.

"What is this, Lee? Insurance?"

"Pretty much. If you don't hear from me by noon, leave a note on Frank Chang's desk next time you're going through Homicide Detail. Tell him the man he's looking for is named Stefan Larsen."

"You going to be okay?"

"We'll see. Hopefully he doesn't have a dozen guys on the other side of this wall."

"Be careful."

"Sure."

I got out of the car and locked it. Then I went to the wall, boosted myself to the top, and slipped off the back side, into Larsen's property. The driveway led away from the road and then curved behind a hill. I walked as quietly as I could up the driveway, following its curve, and stopped when I saw the house. It was all cantilevered concrete and plate glass. Like something stacked together by a toddler. A little way up the hillside, there was a landing pad for the helicopter. It was sitting there, rotors tied down to concrete chocks. Next to the landing pad was a small storage building. Tools and parts for helicopter maintenance, I imagined. Perhaps a bunk for the pilot. I turned my attention back to the house. A flagstone turnabout circled around the front. There was a three-car garage, and a koi pond with lilies floating in the center. I remembered reading somewhere that koi could live a couple of hundred years. I supposed Larsen might want company, aside from his mother.

As I approached the house, a pair of lights flicked on to

illuminate the path to the driftwood front door. I walked up, not sure what I was going to do until I actually got there. What was clear, walking up, was that this was the man's house. It might have been his office, too, but it was foremost a home. I could see through the glass wall into the living room. There were low black leather couches lit from above by lights recessed in the concrete ceiling. A painting hung above the wet bar: driftwood strewn along a fogbound beach. The fireplace was an open-air affair, like a rock garden in the middle of the vast room. A half-empty tumbler of whiskey sat on a low boulder near the gas-fed flames.

Larsen must have turned in before finishing his drink.

There was no doubt he had an alarm, and cameras. No matter what I did, he was going to be coming downstairs. Probably with a gun.

I already had the Walther PPK in my hand, so I raised it and fired three shots at the floor-to-ceiling window next to the door. The glass went opaque around the bullet holes, and webs of cracks shot out all around. I picked up a rock the size of a volleyball and used it to smash the glass out of its frame.

I stepped through, dropped the rock on the floor, and crossed the living room. I went behind the bar, because it was made out of polished concrete and would be the best place to stand in a gunfight.

I didn't hear any alarms. I didn't hear the cavalry charging. I waited a minute. Then I picked up a bottle of Stolichnaya vodka from the rail, unscrewed the cap, and pitched it into the center of the fire pit. It shattered on the rocks, and there was an instantaneous *whoosh* as a blue fireball went as high as the ceiling. Next up was a bottle of Bacardi, which did the same thing. If Larsen's burglar alarm wouldn't bring him running, maybe his fire alarm would.

But everything above the flames was made of poured concrete. There was nothing to catch fire. I waited a full minute and watched the flames die out. Finally, I heard footsteps coming down a set of stairs.

Larsen came into the room. His curly blond hair was disheveled. He was wearing flannel pajamas, and had a sleep mask pushed up over his forehead. He also had a slender automatic pistol in his left hand. He surveyed the broken glass on the floor, then the misplaced rock, and finally the window. He had his back to me.

"Drop it, Larsen," I said.

So he knew I meant it, I fired the Walther and put a bullet into the floor between his feet.

Larsen was a quick study. He dropped the gun and put his hands up without having to be told twice.

"Turn around."

He turned, seeing me face to face for the first time.

"What's my name?" I asked him.

"I haven't the faintest."

"You bugged my place and tossed my office. I already talked to your mother, up at the Creekside. So come on."

"I don't know what you're talking about."

"You also murdered Claire Gravesend, and you'll answer for that tonight. How you answer for it depends."

"On what?"

"On how quickly you give me Madeleine."

He did his best to look at me with pity.

"Do you need money for drugs?" he asked. "Is that why you're here?"

"I'd take an Excedrin if you've got one. But I'm doing fine for money. Maybe not by your standards."

"What do you want?"

"I already told you," I said. "Let's cut the bullshit. Give me Madeleine and I'll make it easy. I'll call the cops. Otherwise, it's just you and me."

Just in time to shift my stance and change my aim, I saw a

flash of movement behind him. A man came hurtling through the broken window, and after that, everything happened at once. I saw a muzzle flash and heard the suppressed *bang* of a silenced handgun. A bottle exploded behind my head. I ducked, and fired back.

I didn't miss.

My bullet caught the man in his chest. He didn't scream or fly back like in the movies. It was as though a puppeteer had cut his strings. He ended up on his side, so that his back was to me. He had blond hair, like the men who'd driven me from the Creekside. On the back of his neck, above his T-shirt, there were two circular scars. I had no doubt what the coroner's assistants would find when they cut his clothes off and turned him over.

Three seconds had passed. It would have been plenty of time for Larsen to grab his gun off the floor and dart outside. But he was frozen where he stood, hands still in the air. I turned the gun back to him.

"That was your pilot?"

He nodded.

"He's you, isn't he?" I asked. "A younger you. A disposable vessel."

"You don't know what you're talking about."

"How many of them did you make?"

"You'd never understand. I could show you everything and it would be beyond you. Intellectually. Financially. You're out of your depth."

"And somehow I keep one step ahead of you," I said. "Starting with that guy you sent to Boston. I killed him with his own knife."

He just stared at me. Behind him, embedded in the concrete wall, was another ouroboros stone. A black snake curled into a circle so that it could consume itself.

"You know, Meredith Miles said something interesting to me about all this," I said. "How can you live forever if you're not careful? If you don't watch where you're going, you could get hit by a bus, or a train — or a bullet."

Before he could process that, and maybe think to dive out of the way, I adjusted my aim and pulled the trigger. I'd hit the other man dead center in his sternum, but I got Larsen midway between his right knee and his hip. He went down hard, scrabbling in a circle as his other leg kicked. I stepped around the bar and used my foot to sweep the nearest gun away from him.

Then I stood over him and put a bullet into his other leg. His cry was far louder than the gunshot. I wasn't worried about it. We were a long way from the road, and the nearest house was probably Hearst Castle, eight or ten miles to the south.

"You won't live forever if you bleed to death, Larsen." I sat down on one of the larger rocks by the fire pit. I rested my elbows on my knees but kept the gun trained on his face. "And I'll make sure you bleed to death, if that's what I have to do. I'll just sit here and watch."

For a moment, the only sound was the wind. It came off the ocean and through the high grass, and it parted roughly around Larsen's concrete house — the first real obstacle it had encountered in five thousand miles.

"What do you want?" he asked.

It was just a whisper. His jaw was a vise. His teeth might have cracked under the pressure.

"I already told you. I want Madeleine. Get her to me and I'll give you my belt for a tourniquet. We'll figure out something else for the other leg."

"I don't know a Madeleine."

"And I don't know anything about anatomy," I said. "No clue how many arteries are there. Maybe I got lucky and a bullet hit your femur. You got any idea what that would do? Because I don't."

"You can't get her without me," he said.

"Then you'd better hurry up."

"Get me the tourniquets."

"Not a chance," I said.

"If I die, so will she."

"Okay."

He looked past me, his eyes going unfocused for a second. I thought he might start to cry. If he had, it wouldn't have surprised me. He wasn't supposed to die on the floor with a two-bit private investigator looking down on him. He was supposed to outlive the redwoods in his Creekside grove. He was going to watch the pyramids turn to sand.

"You're really just going to sit there," he whispered.

"As long as it takes."

It took about ten minutes.

He never wept openly, but there were tears running down his cheeks. I didn't talk to him at all. He knew what I wanted, and he'd give it to me if he felt like it.

"Please," he said, once.

That was the last thing, and then he closed his eyes. I stood up and nudged him in the hip with my foot. He didn't move. I tapped on his knee with my toe. Nothing.

I stooped and grabbed him by the ankles, then dragged him away from the mess of his blood. I wanted to be able to kneel and work without ruining my new pants.

I took off my belt and looped it around his right leg. I pulled it as tight as I could get it, then roughly cinched it off. I looked around. The man I'd shot was wearing a pair of sweatpants. There was a cotton-rope drawstring around the waist. With a hitch knot, it could work just fine.

Tending to his other leg took about two minutes. I checked his pulse, and put a finger under his nose to feel his breath. At the moment, he was alive. I had no idea how much trouble he might have been in. At least I could be certain he wasn't going to come sprinting after me if I left the room. I picked up the dead man's silenced pistol, which was a match to the one I was already carrying. Then I took Larsen's slender automatic from the floor.

By then I was pretty well armed. I had four guns, and would have taken a fifth or sixth if I'd come across one, but I didn't. And I searched the whole house.

I wasn't looking for guns, though. I was looking for Madeleine. Barring that, I was looking for a paper trail that might lead me to her. I gave the kitchen and the dining rooms cursory tosses, and spent a little more time in the study. The problem with the study was that, unlike Jim, Larsen was not a paper collector. He did everything on his computers, and without the passwords, they were useless to me. Ultimately, this room was more interesting for what it lacked than for what it contained. There were no diplomas, or family photos, or decorative pen sets with the names of appreciative companies stenciled on a plaque. There was no desk drawer full of knickknacks — in fact, there were no drawers. Just a glass desk and a floor-to-ceiling window. There were four big screens and two keyboards. There was a sleek-looking camera, for running video conferences.

The rest of the house was the same. Larsen may have wanted to live forever, but he had no desire to hold on to the past. He didn't keep mementos. He must have traveled, but he brought home no souvenirs. I could have debated him about the value of prolonging a life that wasn't worth remembering. But he was unconscious in a pool of blood, and I had a house to search.

36

LARSEN'S BEDROOM WAS VAST, clean, and cold. Polished concrete, tinted glass. The sheets on the surprisingly narrow bed were dark burgundy. It looked like the kind of prison cell a deposed fascist might have designed for himself. There were no clocks, and no mirrors, even in the bathroom.

I left that room and went to the other end of an enormous walkway that overlooked the kitchen and den from thirty feet up. There was a door at the end. I pushed it open and stepped inside, my gun's muzzle leading the way.

I was face to face with Larsen's mother.

She was asleep, flat on her back with her arms beside her. She wore a white bra, matching underwear, and an entire display case of jewelry. Her hair was combed out onto the white sheet. There was a small white device clipped to her index finger, a blue light slowly blinking at the tip. Her head was tilted to the side.

But none of that compared to the bed itself, if you could call it that. She lay inside a glass tube, capped at either end by heavy steel doors. The tube sat on top of a metal box about the size of a coffin. There was a small control panel on the outside of the box. Dials and lights, and what might have been an intercom speaker. I walked carefully up to the machine. A digital display showed barometric pressure. Another showed O$_2$ saturation.

I tapped the barrel of the gun on the glass. She didn't stir. I thought about taking her out of the machine and asking her questions, but I wasn't sure what would happen. If I'd read the display right, she was in there under several times the normal atmospheric pressure. If I popped the door open and yanked her out, she might die of the bends on the floor in front of me, her blood bubbling up like a can of warm soda. And if she didn't, then I'd have an even less savory range of choices. I couldn't picture myself shooting a woman to make her talk.

The oxygen chamber's round hatch could be opened from the outside by turning a heavy chrome handle. I didn't see a lock, but there was another way I could keep her from getting out. I chose a pistol, ejected its magazine, and jammed the gun between the door handle and the chamber's steel rim. I backed out of the room, never taking my eyes off her. If Claire had lived a little bit longer, she might have looked like the woman in front of me. Which made my skin crawl in ways I couldn't begin to explain.

I searched the rest of the house, and then the garages. I found no trace of Madeleine, no hint as to what might have happened to her. The only places left to search were the helicopter, and the little maintenance shed built up against the hill next to the landing pad.

I checked on Larsen once more — still alive, and still unconscious. I tightened his tourniquets. Then I went outside. I followed the path up the hill and slid open the helicopter's side door. There was nothing inside it that I didn't expect. Supple white leather upholstery. Flatscreen televisions and burled walnut trim. I found life jackets and fire extinguishers under the seats. There was a compartment with an inflatable life raft, and a canister with an orange plastic flare gun. I left the doors open and went to the maintenance shed.

The man I'd shot must have come running when he'd realized his boss was in danger. In doing so, he'd left the steel door ajar. I peered inside, then stepped in and turned on a light. Half of the space was an apartment. There were two sets of bunk beds, a kitchenette, and a circular table. There was a bathroom with a stall shower and two sinks. I saw three toothbrushes on the counter, three sticks of deodorant in the cabinet behind the mirror.

Three brothers must have lived here. Identical triplets, with the same genes, the same scars, and different birthdays. Two of them were now dead, and the third was somewhere south of here, engaged in a long chat with Meredith Miles's ex-con front gate guard. I'd shut them all down, but ultimately they were Larsen's victims. Not mine. Maybe he had a way to justify what he'd done to them, could explain it to himself if not the world at large. After all, he wasn't enslaving other people. Just copies of himself.

I went to the other side of the room and found the helicopter maintenance logs. There was a fifty-five-gallon drum of Jet-A fuel strapped to a dolly. A backup, I supposed, in case the chopper ever landed here without enough gas in its tanks to safely fly out again. There were metal shelves stocked with engine parts and tools, and an entire bookcase of manuals.

And between two of the shelves, in a concrete wall that directly abutted the hill outside, there was a solid steel door. The door had no handle, and no keyhole. There was a small black box on the wall next to it. A tiny camera was positioned at the top of the box, and a blinking red light sat at the bottom.

I leaned and put my ear against the door. I could hear the long, low hum of something running on the other side of it.

Exhaust fans, maybe. The metal was thick and unyielding, and cold to the touch.

I needed to get in there, and I thought I knew how.

Five minutes later, I was back in the main house with the dolly and straps from the fuel drum. Larsen wasn't quite where I'd left him. He'd come back to his senses. After flipping over onto his stomach, he'd pulled himself along the floor about five feet. He was trying to pull himself up on the end of a couch.

He hadn't heard me come in, so I walked right up to him, knelt, and grabbed his arms before he even knew I was there. I pulled them behind his back and tied them together with one of the fuel drum straps. Then I hoisted him up, leaned him against the dolly, and put another strap around his chest to keep him up.

"How are you doing?" I asked him. "Can you feel your toes?"

He didn't answer. Which was fine, because I didn't care in the slightest. I tilted him back, then wheeled him out of the house and up the path to the maintenance shed. We rolled inside and I brought him past the metal shelves, over to the door. I undid his chest strap and held him up by taking a fistful of his curly blond hair, and then I lowered him down to the black box to present his face to the camera.

Nothing happened. I reached around and slapped him with my free hand until he opened his eyes.

The red light stopped blinking. Then it turned green, and the door clicked open. There was a hiss of cold air rushing out, the dusty scent of oxygen, and a sharp tang of rubbing alcohol. And underneath that there was a lower smell, the odor of old bandages festering in a trash can.

I pulled the door the rest of the way open and looked in.

• • •

I was standing at the mouth of a cave. The entrance tunnel sloped gently downward, and was lit overhead by high-wattage LEDs. Up ahead, the tunnel curved out of sight.

I brought Larsen fifty or sixty feet inside, and then I laid down the dolly and left him there. I walked onward, still following my gun sights. Before I reached the curve, I heard something that almost stopped my heart.

A baby crying.

First there was just the one. The hungry, fearful wail of a very young infant. The cries came in waves of three, as though the baby had to draw a new breath after each effort. The sound must have awoken others, and they began to join the first. I couldn't tell how many. It sounded like I was coming up to the NICU ward in a children's hospital. I lowered the gun and clicked the safety. I looked back at Larsen, and he turned his face away from me. He couldn't meet my eyes. So I went on. I had to be a witness. I had to see what he had done.

My new shoes made a sticky sound on the freshly painted floor. I looked down and saw that I was leaving bloody prints, each one a little fainter than the last. Overall, I'd left quite a trail behind me, in reaching this point. But it ended here. I knew that as I turned the corner, went through a double set of glass doors, and saw the first domed room in front of me.

The room was a circle, fifty feet in diameter. The perimeter was lined with heavy lab tables. Microscopes were wired to laptop computers. I saw bench-mounted equipment that I couldn't begin to identify, and several things the size of industrial photocopiers in the center of the room. There were shelves of glass bottles and plastic jugs, and racks of test tubes, and miles of thin plastic tubing. Larsen was bringing his clients' DNA here, perfecting it with his CRISPR machines, and transferring it into human eggs. After that, it was just a matter of gestating a disposable vessel.

There was another tunnel on the far end of the lab. The

crying was coming from down there. This passage had doors all along one side, one every ten feet, for a hundred feet. The doors were steel, and had tiny square windows in their centers. Thick, wire-reinforced glass in the windows. There were steel-flapped slots midway down each door. Like mail slots, but wider. As wide as a metal food tray.

I went to the first door and looked through the window.

I was looking at a tiny cell, carved out of the solid rock. In its thirty-six square feet, it held a cot, a steel toilet, and a sink. All of them were low and small. The toilet was a foot high. The sink was eighteen inches off the floor. The cot was four feet long. Someone had drawn on the wall with crayons. Nothing I could make out. Just random, sad scribbles.

I hadn't thought my stomach could sink any lower. I'd been wrong.

That cell was empty, but there were nine more. I found Madeleine behind the fourth door. The first time I'd seen her, she was nothing but a lump under the covers. A spill of blond hair across a pillow. This time, she was curled into a fetal position on a too-short cot, with her back to me. She had no pillow and no blanket. She was wearing an open-backed hospital gown. The scars on her back were gone. In their place were open wounds. Larsen meant to tap her for all she was worth. It had been his plan all along, interrupted by two decades. She might have been in the same cell, on the same cot, on the night that Dr. Park had his crisis of conscience and broke her out.

I used the butt of the gun to tap on the door. Madeleine didn't move, so I tapped harder. Finally, she sat up. She moved to the end of the cot and put her knees up to her chest. She hadn't looked at the window.

"It's me," I whispered. "Lee Crowe."

"Lee?"

She looked up. When she saw my face, she started crying. I held the gun to the window.

"I'm going to get you out," I said. "Stand all the way to the side, face against the wall."

She nodded, and moved.

There were two locks on the door. A dead bolt, and a simpler lock on the doorknob. I put two bullets into the top lock and one into the knob. Even after that, it took five kicks to get the door open. She came tumbling out of the cell and into me. She held on to me, but I didn't put my hands on her. I didn't know where her wounds were.

"The babies," she whispered.

"Have you seen them?"

I felt her nod against me.

"Whenever they take me out. For the harvesting."

"Who was doing it?"

"His name is Larsen. And he had other men helping."

"I took care of them," I said. "Is there anyone else — besides the babies?"

"Follow me. I'll show you."

She took my hand and led me down the hallway. I looked into the windows of the remaining cells, but they were all empty. Madeleine pointed toward another, up ahead.

"Look," she said.

I leaned in. I was looking into a large domed room. It was the same size as the first lab I'd walked through, but it was being put to a very different use. There were six metal stands arranged in a semicircle. Each stand held a clear plastic bin. Inside every bin was a swaddled baby. Most of them were screaming. Their faces were red and pinched, like dried apples. There was a woman in there with them. She had matted brown hair that stuck out in all directions. Her eyes were heavily lidded, half closed from sleep deprivation. She wore a sweatshirt and a pair of surgical scrub pants. Neither looked like they'd been washed recently. She was barefooted, and her toenails were long.

As I watched, she picked up a baby. I cringed, not knowing

what to expect. But she cradled him gently and began to rock him. I watched her mouth make shushing noises, impossible to hear over the wailing. She walked to a shelf and took a bottle of premixed formula from a box. The room was crammed with supplies. Diapers. Bottled water. Creams and wipes. There was an unmade bed and an overflowing trash can.

I moved away from the window and looked at Madeleine.

"She's a prisoner too," Madeleine said. "At night, when we're alone, we talk. We can hear each other if we shout."

I could believe that. The sound carried well down here. The steel doors shut in everything but the screams.

"How can he trust her with them?"

"She was a surrogate — that's how he gets the babies in the first place. Surrogates, from online ads. But he tricked her, and brought her here. So one of those is hers. What can she do, but take care of them? They're just babies. What would you do?"

I had no idea. The question was beyond any circumstance I had ever imagined. But it was a more personal matter for Madeleine. Twenty years ago, her own birth mother might have been locked in that room.

"We need to get her out," she whispered. "Get all of them out."

I looked at the door. There were more locks on this one. The other cells were for children who had graduated from the nursery. This one had the infants, and so it was built to hold their adult caretaker.

"We'll need to find another way," I said. "With them on the other side, I can't just empty a clip at the locks."

"There has to be a key."

"Come with me," I said, and we walked back down the hall to see if Larsen was still alive.

But Larsen wasn't where I'd left him.

The dolly was there. And there was a long smear of blood

336

along the floor, leading to the wall, where it stopped. He couldn't have stood up. That was impossible, with gunshots in both his legs. Someone had to have helped him. Maybe Larsen's chauffeur had driven home. He might have stopped for a drink somewhere, or dinner. A little bit of freedom — enough that I'd beaten him to the compound.

"Stay here," I whispered. "And take this."

I handed her the gun I'd been using, and drew two others from my waistband. Jim's and Larsen's. I began to walk up the tunnel, toward the maintenance shed. Halfway up, I noticed something else. A trickle of straw-colored liquid was running along the tunnel floor from up above. I knelt and touched it, brought my finger to my nose.

Fuel. Jet-A, from the fifty-five-gallon drum. I had moved it when I'd taken the dolly. But I'd left it upright, and sealed. It hadn't been leaking. I thumbed the safeties on both guns, pulled back their slides, and checked that each chamber held a cartridge. Then I looked back at Madeleine. I nodded for her to move back, out of sight. When she had, I went up.

I stepped out of the tunnel and into the maintenance shed. I swept right, and then left. The room was empty. But the drum of Jet-A was on its side, fuel still spilling out. It was puddled on the floor, half an inch deep. Some of it was spilling into the tunnel, and the rest was flowing out the front door.

Now I could hear the noise outside: the building whine of a twin turbine helicopter starting up. I knelt in the puddle of fuel by the door and looked out, to the side. The helicopter's rotor was beginning to spin. I couldn't see into the cockpit, but the sliding side door was still open, and I could see into the main passenger compartment.

Larsen's mother stepped out. She was wearing a flowing white dress. It blew around her in the building rotor wash. Her hair did the same. She had something in her hand and I couldn't tell what it was until she turned. By the time I understood, I only had a second to make a choice.

I could run out of the building, dive into the high grass, and roll down the hill. In which case I would live. Or I could turn around and go back into the tunnel, to Madeleine and to the babies. In which case I would almost certainly die with them. Because what Larsen's mother was holding was the helicopter's flare gun, and even as I watched she was raising it up and pulling the trigger. I didn't hesitate, and I didn't even try to shoot back. Not when I was standing in a pool of gas. I pushed off the doorjamb and sprinted back into the tunnel, pulling the steel door shut as I went.

"Run!" I shouted. "Run, now!"

I pounded down the tunnel. I caught up to Madeleine at the first set of doors and saw that the fuel had already made it that far. I shoved her through the doors, and then grabbed her wrist and started pulling her across the room.

The maintenance shed exploded when we were halfway across the domed lab. We were pulled backwards as the ignition sucked air out of the cave to feed the flames. Then the shock wave hit us and flung us forward. The double set of glass doors behind us probably saved us from being incinerated outright. We got up, pushed through the next set of doors, and ran past the line of children's cells until we reached the nursery.

We might have survived the explosion, but it was the fire that would surely kill us all. Madeleine pounded on the steel door and looked through the window. The kidnapped woman was already there, on the other side of the glass. I could see her eyes, wide with terror. I looked back and saw that the entire lab was in flames.

"Tell her to move all the babies. Now — now!"

Madeleine started shouting, and then I pushed her aside. I gave the woman fifteen seconds, and then I began to shoot the locks. I emptied every gun I had. Fifty shots in all, maybe.

Two of the guns had no suppressors. When I was finished, I could see Madeleine shouting at me, but I couldn't hear anything but ringing. I kicked the door and it didn't budge. The air was already full of oily smoke, and it was starting to get hot.

I kicked three more times. My head was spinning. I stepped back, and kicked a final time, and the door swung open. Madeleine went in first, and I followed. I shut the door, and looked to my right. The woman was huddled on the floor. She'd stacked the swaddled babies in her arms the way a person carries firewood. She was cradling all six of them while rocking back and forth on her knees.

Their faces were wailing, but I couldn't hear them.

Madeleine went to the woman and I went to the storage shelves. I found a stack of clean swaddles. Another shelf had jugs of water, for mixing powdered formula. I took an armful of both and went back to the door. I began soaking the swaddles and stuffing them into every crack I could find.

Before I was finished, the overhead lights went out. Red lights came on above the door, and then they faltered too. There was a boom from outside, from somewhere above us. The backup generator, or maybe the battery bank.

Now there was just a square of orange light from the door's window. Dim and smoky and distant. I crawled across the room until I found Madeleine in the dark. She passed me a warm bundle, then another. We sat there with the woman, whose name I didn't know, each of us with two babies in our arms. I had never held an infant before. I cradled them on my lap and put my face against their heads, breathing into their soft hair. The air was thick and choked with smoke. The babies were panicky and jerking, and coming out of their swaddles.

My eyes started to sting and tear up, so I closed them. I lay down close to the floor and held the babies next to me. I reached out, first in front of me, and then behind me. Madeleine and the woman had gone prone as well. Madeleine squeezed my hand in the dark.

Her palm was warm and sweaty, and I could feel her heartbeat pulsing against my skin. She let go of me, and then I was alone in the dark with the two babies. I could feel the floor slipping, tilting back and back, the way a room begins to spin six or eight drinks into a bottle. I thought about the grass outside, cool and wet from the fog and rain. I could have been out there, watching the flames rise upward from the hillside, a bright flare in a dark landscape. I saw myself there, kneeling on the wet earth. In front of me, smoke rose up, and curled around in a convection current, eating its own tail. For just a moment, I thought I understood eternity. What it meant to live forever, and what it meant to die. But there was no choice on the table, no offer before me. I had already chosen. I lay there in the dark, and felt nothing but acceptance.

37

IF YOU WATCH a few men die, you start getting some fairly solid ideas about what it might be like. How it would feel to slide off into the dark while your fingers go cold and your limbs get stiff and your last words are lost forever. You think about the sorts of things that might be waiting there, on the other side.

None of it was going the way I'd imagined.

For one thing, I hadn't expected all the pressure on my face. Something was pinching the bridge of my nose and something else was digging into the back of my head. Dusty-smelling air burned my nostrils. It burned all the way into my chest, and I coughed, and then I realized I had it all wrong. I opened my eyes to a blur of pulsing red light and roving shadows. Someone was squeezing my hand. I jerked, and swept my arms around. I couldn't find the babies. When I tried to sit up, someone pressed me back down.

"Easy, Crowe."

I looked around, and my eyes struggled to focus. I thought I saw stars. Then Inspector Chang was leaning over me. He just looked at me, and waited until I put things together on my own.

"You ran the phone number," I whispered. "You tracked it."

"I got curious," he said. "I called a friend in LAPD — easy, don't get up — and he added it to an existing Amber Alert. So it was fast tracked."

I tried to sit up a third time, and he didn't stop me. I lifted the oxygen mask from my face and dropped it. I was on the ground, two hundred yards from the hillside. There was an ambulance parked next to me. Three fire engines had left tracks in the grass leading up toward the shed.

The fire was out, and the ground around the shed was covered in white foam.

"What about the others?"

"The women are being treated in the house. The babies already left in a different ambulance," he said. "They're no worse off than you. Except the babies —"

"You saw the wounds?"

"Yeah," he said. "I saw them. After the firefighters brought you out, I asked them to leave you here. So I could talk to you alone."

"Okay."

"Your phone rang. I took it out of your pocket and answered it. It was Director Reese, at NorCal TRACON. He said they picked up the helicopter on their screens, forty-five minutes ago. It took off and went west."

"Out to sea?"

"Until it disappeared," Inspector Chang said.

"You mean it crashed?"

"That's what I asked. But Reese didn't know. It could have run out of fuel and gone down. It could have landed on a ship. Or it could have passed out of radar range and then gone north or south."

"But he doesn't know."

"He doesn't," he said. "You want to tell me what's going on?"

"On one condition."

"What's that?"

"When I'm done, if you don't arrest me—you'll let me take Madeleine and go."

"Madeleine's the blonde? The Claire Gravesend lookalike?"

I nodded.

"Go ahead," he said. "And don't leave anything out."

An hour after sunrise, I was driving again. Madeleine was sitting next to me. We were going forty-five miles an hour on Highway 1, headed north. If I went any faster, the Jaguar began to shimmy and fishtail. Which was my fault. I had left it parked in front of the gate. Chang had arrived when the flames were still five stories high. He'd called the fire department in Cambria, fifteen miles away. So now the Jaguar's rear end was badly dented and the wheels were out of alignment, having been shoved aside by the first engine to arrive on the scene.

We were halfway to Carmel before Madeleine said anything.

"He never planned to throw her out," she said. "They were going to bring her to that place, but she figured it out, in the air. She knew what they were going to do to her, and she fought. That's why they tossed her out."

"He told you?"

"One of them did," she said. "They all looked the same. They were all the same."

I didn't answer. I drove us through the morning mist, taking the curves carefully. The land sloped sharply to the ocean, everything either green or blue or gray. Lichen-covered rocks and wind-sculpted cypress trees. The ocean met the sky with no discernable horizon.

"When we started, we thought we were going to find out who we were," Madeleine said.

"Didn't you?"

343

"It wasn't worth it. I don't want to know all this. I don't want to be this."

"You're whoever you want to be."

"Is that true?" she asked. "Is that true for anyone? For you? Can you just be the person you want to be?"

"I think so," I said. "I hope so."

And we left it at that.

At nine o'clock, I turned into Olivia Gravesend's driveway. Mr. Richards opened the gate, and I drove up to the house. Madeleine stayed in the car, and I went inside and met Olivia in the gun room.

She hadn't slept, but I'm certain she looked better than I did.

"You've got blood on you, Crowe."

"None of it's mine."

"And?"

"And I have answers for you. The whole story. As well as something else — someone else."

"Tell me."

"You must have known from the beginning that Claire wasn't like other people. That she was special."

"Yes."

"Which was truer than you think, and also untrue. By which I mean that there's one person who's almost exactly like her."

Olivia frowned at me. She was holding a porcelain teacup, and set it down on the little table next to her straight-backed chair. The only other item on the table was an antique Colt pistol. I supposed she had armed herself with it in light of the fact that she had a prisoner locked in her panic room.

"I know," I said. "I'm not making sense. What I'm trying to do is warn you. I'm going to have Mr. Richards bring someone in. And you're going to want to believe that she's someone she's not. You'll know things in your heart and in your head, and you'll be right and wrong. And you and she will have to sort it out."

"What are you talking about?"

I opened the door and nodded to Mr. Richards, who was waiting outside. He went away through the cavernous house. I closed the door and came back to the fireplace.

"I could explain all sorts of things to you, Olivia, but you're not going to believe me until you see it for yourself. Claire wasn't just a baby who'd been abused by her birth parents. In fact, strictly speaking, she had no birth parents. Or if she did, they must have died fifty or sixty years before she was born. But she had a family."

"I'm her family."

"It's true," I said. There was a knock on the door, and I went and put my hand on the knob, but didn't open it. "But there was someone else she loved too."

I opened the door and looked out. Madeleine was wearing her hospital gown underneath a wool blanket courtesy of the Cambria Fire Department. Standing next to her, Mr. Richards looked as though his legs might fall out from underneath him.

Madeleine stepped into the gun room.

"This is Madeleine Adair," I said. "She's—"

But Olivia had already crossed the room, had already taken Madeleine into her arms. She was sobbing against Madeleine's shoulder, gripping her tightly.

I went out and shut the door behind me. I walked away before I could hear any of their conversation. I could imagine what they might be saying to each other, but even that felt like a trespass. I brushed past Mr. Richards and headed for the front entrance, for the sunlight outside.

345

38

I WASN'T DONE for the day, though. I still had to drive a sullen and silent Jim Gardner back to his house. I let him sit up front, in the passenger seat of the A-Star Appliance van, which was a far more comfortable arrangement than he'd had coming down.

I let him out at his damaged gate.

"My gun?" he said.

As far as I knew, it was sitting outside the nursery's steel door in the burned-out shell of Larsen's cave.

"If the police ever come and ask you about it, say it was stolen."

"And my files?"

"I'll give them back. Your Porsche, too."

"Are you keeping copies?"

"What do you think?"

He thought about it, and nodded.

"What about us?" he asked.

"What's there to ask about?" I answered. "I'll still take jobs if you've got them. Starting tomorrow, I've got a clean plate."

He closed the door, and I drove off. Up Skyline Boulevard and back to my city. I had no keys to my apartment, but I had just enough of Juliette's cash left to pay a locksmith. There was even enough change left over to get a Tsingtao from the restaurant downstairs, which I carried up and brought with me to the shower.

A week later, I had mostly put my life back together. I had keys to my house and my office. I had a new wallet, with new bank cards to go in it. A towing service brought the Beast down from the forest service road in Mendocino County, and once I dug the spare key out of a kitchen drawer, I even had a car again. I found Larsen's planted cameras and tossed them in the street, so I had my privacy, too.

But what I didn't have was anything to do.

I cleaned up my office, putting my files and furniture back together. I bought a new computer, and a new safe, and a new gun. And then I sat there, behind my too-big desk, with my empty reception room out front. I went to the window and pulled the blinds apart to check across the street. I did it three times before I admitted I was looking for something in particular.

I was hoping to see a black Bentley. A car so dark it blended into the night. I wanted her to be there, but she wasn't. Not that night, or the next, or the one after. I hadn't heard from Madeleine, or from Inspector Chang. Elijah was back to work at 850 Bryant Street. Olivia had sent a check, but nothing else. But maybe it didn't matter. Talking to any of them would have dampened my loneliness but couldn't extinguish it.

Finally, on the fourth night, I couldn't stand it anymore.

Drop by sometime, she'd said. *Anytime.*

The moon was out, and I still had the blanket in the trunk.

At two in the morning, His Honor's car was in the VIP slot outside the courthouse. Which meant that she was at home, awake. Waiting for the sound of his key in the lock so she could pretend to be asleep.

Of course I knew the way. I used to live there. Driving up, I felt light in my stomach. A fine balance point between excitement and fear. I was remembering the way she smelled, the way her body felt against mine. The way we were together in the beginning, before everything came apart. My hands were damp on the steering wheel.

I pulled up across the street from her house. I had the windows down and could hear the wind in the eucalyptus trees. And when she opened the front door, I thought it was because she'd seen me. Her perfume made a river through the air. Maybe it was just my imagination, a memory sparked by her profile in the open doorway. But it was real enough that it filled up the car and left me breathless.

I watched her come down the walk, and through the gate. A car pulled up just as she reached the sidewalk. A man got out and came around to her. They embraced, and then she turned her face up to him. The kiss that followed was long and slow. He opened the door for her and she slid inside. I turned off my headlights and put my forehead against the wheel. I didn't want them to see me when they drove past. I didn't want anyone to see me.

I waited until the car was gone, and then a long time after that.

Maybe Larsen had it right after all. Maybe there was no point in holding on to anything from the past. All it can do is hurt you.

39

IN THE END, the past had too much momentum. My old habits had gathered too much weight. Which meant that three days after I saw my ex-wife wrap herself around a stranger and ride off in his car, and ten hours after Jim's last check cleared my bank account, I was at the end of Baja California Sur, in La Paz. I checked into the Hotel Miguel Hidalgo and got my old room. I had two windows with rusted screens and no glass. They overlooked Paseo Alvaro Obregon, then a thin strip of beach, and then the Sea of Cortez. If the wind got to be too much, I could close the slatted wooden shutters, turned silver by the sun.

There was a ceiling fan, and a cast-iron bed with springs that creaked every time I rolled over. There was a bar downstairs, and a restaurant next door. I remembered it from last time too. There were the same block letters painted on a pastel wall.

MARISCOS, the wall said.

I didn't cut myself off as much as I wanted to. I had a new phone, and I made a point of checking it. I'd sit at the bar at ten in the morning, with a sweaty bottle of Pacifico next to me, and read the news.

The Coast Guard had long since given up any search for Larsen's helicopter. They'd never spotted any debris at sea. No one saw a fuel slick riding on the waves. If they'd doubled back and returned to the coast, they'd come in low, with the transponder turned off. There was no way to know what they'd done. They could have landed at the bottom of the ocean, or on a ship. Without refueling, they could have reached any spot on the coast from Mexico to Oregon.

By now, they could be anywhere. Their bank accounts were untraceable and thus intact. They'd have other homes, and other aircraft. There could be more labs. They could regroup, assess the damages, and then think about next steps.

Which meant that even in La Paz, I didn't feel safe.

I'd come by air, so I'd left my new gun in a new safe. On my first night in town, I talked to my bartender. He remembered me from six years ago, and told me to wait in my room. Sometime before sunrise, there was a knock on my door. I handed the man three hundred U.S. dollars and he passed me a rusted snub-nosed revolver. Its wooden grips were held together with electrical tape. I opened the cylinder and dumped six bullets into my palm. The brass cartridges had green pits of corrosion. The lead was powdered with oxide.

So long as it didn't blow up in my hand, I'd be fine.

On the fourth day, I came downstairs and ordered a beer. There was no wind, and it was already ninety degrees. I sat at the bar and looked at the news on my phone. There was a new report about the fire in Larsen's lab. Most of it was flat-out wrong. The rest was missing so much information, it meant nothing. The reporter didn't mention the holding cells, or the nature of the lab equipment, or the contents of the nursery. But he quoted Frank Chang, who said that investigators had finished searching the debris. They'd found no human remains. Which was something I was willing to hang on to, and take as true. There were rooms I'd never searched. If there had been other screams during the fire, I would never have heard them.

. . .

I looked up from my phone. The bartender was waiting across from me, both hands on the wooden plank.

"Yeah?"

"There was a woman," he said. "This morning."

"A woman."

"She asked about you."

"By name?"

"She asked for Lee Crowe. She asked if you're staying here."

"And what'd you say?"

"I said I wasn't sure," he said. "I said maybe she could come back later and I'd let her know."

"And then she left?"

He nodded toward the door with his chin.

"She'll be back."

"Describe her."

He held his hand five and a half feet off the floor.

"This high," he said. "American. Young."

"Blond?"

He shook his head.

"I don't know. She had her hair under a baseball cap. And she had big glasses. Sunglasses."

"You didn't get her name?"

"No."

I finished my beer and paid my tab. I already had everything I needed in my pockets. My wallet and passport. My phone and my gun. I could lose everything upstairs and it wouldn't matter. I left the hotel and went to the restaurant. It wasn't open, but I sat at one of the tables on the patio and waited until it was.

Then I ordered lunch, and bottled water, and I passed the time looking at the entrance to the Hotel Miguel Hidalgo. I couldn't think of any woman I wanted to see who'd know to look for me in La Paz. I thought about hailing a cab and going to the airport, or the bus station. I could charter a boat and go to Cabo. I could do anything I wanted. There was nowhere I needed to be.

So I stayed, and watched the hotel's entrance.

At a quarter past six, I saw an American woman in a black baseball cap and tortoiseshell sunglasses. She had pale skin, and was dressed like she'd planned a safari on Rodeo Drive. Light khaki pants, a thin silk blouse cut to look like a jacket. Low heels. I couldn't see if she had any scars. Her hair wasn't blond, but with dye for sale in every drugstore, that meant nothing.

She went into the hotel. I put cash on the table and left the restaurant. I walked back to the hotel and leaned against the stucco wall next to the door. I was in the building's long shadow, but the wall was still hot from the day's sun.

I waited five minutes, and then the woman came out. She walked past without seeing me. When she had a good enough lead, I followed her. I was wearing shorts, and an untucked guayabera shirt. The gun was in my waistband, at the small of my back. It'd be easy to grab it and bring it to bear.

She didn't stay on the streets for long. She was drawing stares, and low catcalls. After two blocks, I wasn't the only man following her. She hailed a taxi, whistling with two fingers in her mouth. She stepped in, and I watched the red and blue station wagon limp off. I caught the next one and asked the driver to follow hers.

"Disculpe?"

"Sigue ese auto," I said.

The driver looked at me like I was crazy.

"Mi novia," I said.

Now he nodded. That was a perfectly legitimate reason to follow another car. We went along the waterfront. The sea was calm enough that I could spot coral heads half a mile offshore, dark shadows over patches of white sand. By then I'd had time to think. I hadn't really seen her face, but I'd followed her from behind for nearly a minute. So I knew how she moved, and I knew the shape of her body beneath her clothes. I would have bet all the money in my bank account that I knew who she was.

She was two cars ahead of us.

The driver kept pace without being obvious. There was plenty of traffic. Cars and microbuses, and men on three-wheeled bikes hawking hats and ice cream. Her cab took a right, into a marina. The sun was bright enough to blister new paint. I held my hand over my eyebrows to block the glare. There was a pink hotel down where the marina's breakwater began. My driver looked at me. To turn, or not to turn?

I nodded.

He veered in, but before we reached the hotel's roundabout, I tapped his shoulder, handed him a bill, and got out. I caught up to the woman as the doorman was letting her into the lobby. I came in right behind her and put my hand on her shoulder.

"You were looking for me?"

She turned. Her mouth tightened in anger before relaxing in recognition. She took off her hat and shook out her light brown hair. Then she took off her sunglasses. I'd had my right hand close to the gun's taped-up handle, but I relaxed it.

"Lee Crowe," she said.

"Last time, you said we wouldn't see each other again."

"So I was wrong," she said. She glanced toward the lobby bar. "Can I buy you a drink?"

I didn't move.

"How'd you find me?"

"Our mutual friend."

"Olivia?"

"Jim," she said. "He sends his regards."

"What's this about?"

"First, to say thanks. You saved me ten million dollars. And possibly my soul."

"You talked to Olivia, then."

"I did," she said. "Forget the bar. We can go upstairs."

She took my arm, the way she had when she'd caught me trespassing on her porch. This time, she led me across the lobby. She pushed the elevator button, and when the car came, we got in. She had a suite on the fifth floor, maybe the best room in La Paz, but compared to her perch above L.A., everything here looked like it had been plucked from a roadside fire sale.

She pointed me to a rattan chair on the balcony, took two bottles of beer from the refrigerator, and handed them both to me. They were warm, but cooler than I was.

"You didn't come all the way to La Paz to say thanks."

"I didn't," she said. "I came to hire you — I told Jim I needed the best. He said that would be you. If you're taking cases."

"It depends."

"On what?"

"Does it have anything to do with Stefan Larsen?"

"Not at all."

"What do you want me to do?"

"It's complicated."

"I can sometimes figure things out."

"And it's delicate. It might not be exactly legal."

"Then I guess I'm your man," I said.

"I guess you are."

I pried open the beers with my thumb and handed her one of the bottles. We touched their necks together, then looked out over the rail. The sea was turquoise near the shore, and a deep blue farther off, where the depths stole all the sunlight. It was nothing like San Francisco, and I liked that just fine. But I supposed I'd go wherever my client needed me. That was okay with me, which was a new feeling. I'd known who I was for a long time, but I'd only just learned to live with it.

Acknowledgments

Taking a trip through Lee Crowe's world was fun, and I'd love to go back there someday. Especially if I could do it with all the people who helped me write this first book. My wife, Maria Wang, has supported my writing from the very beginning and has helped me in more ways than I could ever enumerate. My children, Bruce and Sally, inspire me. I work a little harder every day because they're here. Nathaniel Boyer, M.D., is still my go-to guy for crazy medical questions. He's better than Google, because the NSA can't keep a file on all the things I've asked him over the years. My editor Naomi Gibbs helped me fine tune this manuscript. She was ideally matched for the project and came into it knowing more about genetic engineering than I did. The people at Houghton Mifflin Harcourt — including, but by no means limited to Laura Brady, Michelle Triant, and Alison Kerr Miller — have been beyond amazing, are wonderful to work with, and have never lost faith. And finally there's Alice Martell, my agent. She's the agent every writer deserves and few get; if you could have one person in your corner in the publishing world, you'd want Alice.